WINDSWEPT

Pamela Ann Cleverly

CLEVER INK, LLC,
Mentor, OH

ISBN-13: 978-0-9970522-7-5

DEDICATION

This book is dedicated to my brother, Doug Jones, who left his beloved Key West too soon. Doug and his partner, Diana lived in the historic district for many years. He embraced the city and all it had to offer. He would get up early in the morning to watch the sun rise on the White Street Pier and watch the sun set from Mallory Square. Every stranger he met became a friend and every friend became family.

Rest in peace, my dear brother.

ALSO BY PAMELA ANN CLEVERLY

The Tanner's Series
In The Shadow of The Lighthouse, Book 1
A Beacon In The Dark, Book 2
It Started With Besse, Book 3
Bent Tree Cottage, Book 4

Standalone Titles
Windswept

ACKNOWLEDGEMENTS

First and foremost, I want to thank my daughter, Marianne Blystone, for her unending support, her encouragement and for believing in me and the stories I have to tell. Secondly, I must thank Polly Sue Poppy who works tirelessly to clean up my drafts and pushes me to expand myself as a writer.

Portions of my first four books had been written while sitting on the porch, overlooking the canal, in our house in Eden Pines Colony on Big Pine Key. We were snowbirds. During those winter months my intention was to begin a novel set in the Keys. With every trip to Key West and every trip across the Seven Mile Bridge I searched for the inspiration for the perfect mystery, but my head always seemed to be stuck in the current manuscript. It wasn't until after twenty-six years of loving life in the Lower Keys did a story finally begin to percolate––the year I was saying goodbye.

I'd been taking a different route home from Winn Dixie due to road construction on Key Deer Boulevard. One of the dead-end streets to my right seemed to pull at my SUV. Without a thought as to why, I turned right and followed it to the end. Before me sat a large, beautiful gate with groupings of tropical trees beyond. A For Sale sign hung to one side. I could have turned around and left and taken my groceries home--but no-- I'm a writer! So, I parked and pulled the listing up on the internet. The sprawling, ground-level house overlooking the Gulf was built in 1962 and priced over four million. The grounds were fabulous; the house was fabulous and there was a canal next to it that went nowhere. Hmmmm--interesting--why? The early sixties were a time of crime bosses, Cuban unrest, Hollywood and Las Vegas. As I sat there bits and pieces of a new plot began tumbling around in my head. Finally, fearing that my frozen food would begin to melt, I slipped my SUV into drive and headed back to the stop sign. I looked up at the street name--it was Winifred. By the time I had the groceries put away the story was racing through my brain. I sat down at the dining room table, opened my laptop and began writing.

You quickly learn that living in the Lower Keys, even part-time, is a way of life--a mindset. One that I would fall into every time I crossed the Seven Mile Bridge. You slip into Key Time, where the days move slower and everything can be put off until tomorrow if the weather is perfect for fishing or the beach or just hanging out. There was never a need to pack before heading south from my "official residence" in Northeastern Ohio. The conservative wardrobe wasn't welcome down there. Waiting for me was a closet full of bright colors, tropical prints, dresses, skirts, big jewelry and hats. And I had the best of both worlds. Life on Big Pine is quieter, more laid back than the high-energy festivities of Key West which I enjoyed while staying at my brother's place on weekends.

I tried to bring the dichotomy of that world into the story. I changed the names of well-known establishments, but many of you who have been to the Keys will recognize them. Any mistakes or altering of facts that I've made are strictly my own as I created a new, more colorful, history for Big Pine Key dating back to the 1560s. Actually, the first recorded settler didn't appear until 1870.

I hope you enjoy untangling the mystery.

CHAPTER ONE

January 1, 1960
Las Vegas, Nevada
Lorenzo Barilli, Detroit's most notorious crime lord, reads the faces of his fellow players. The Godfather's connection to most of the Las Vegas casino owners and the various celebrities who came with the package garnered him acceptance at the highest stakes poker games. Tonight was the night of all nights—the game of all games—the *killer* table. Every player was packing, and every player had his own bodyguard at his back.

This was the day the head of the nations' crime families met in secret at the luxurious Tropicana to discuss the current uncertainty in the political world, the future of the industry, and the directions needed to maintain control of their lucrative business ventures. And this could be the biggest pot ever—there was more on the table besides money—there was power. Chicago's Sam Giancana was now out. It was down to two of them. Lorenzo and the little Italian from Key West, Salvatore Giordano they'd nicknamed Havana, who tossed a deed on the pile of chips in the center of the table.

Lorenzo slowly fanned his cards on the table with the flare of a man who was accustomed to winning—a man who liked to put on a show of his own. He stretched his arms out in a calculated movement that would impress the current magician gracing the stage at the Tropicana or Caesars Palace. As his hands locked around the pile, pulling it toward him, large gold cuff links sparkled with the initials LB set with only the finest diamonds. The Cheshire cat grin spread across his handsome, clean-shaven face, then faded quickly as he unfolded the so-called deed.

Lorenzo scanned the ornate, and very old, document filled with gold lettering, all of which was in Spanish. The only thing he could recognize was a date of 1560. "What the hell is this?" Lorenzo flicked the document with his fingers and tossed it back into the center of the table. "Some worthless piece of land and I have no idea where the hell it is." His voice raised enough octaves to be heard through the bulletproof walls. "I want money—cash, or at least a chest full of Spanish doubloons. Don't they believe in honor down where you come from?" Lorenzo fought to regain control of his emotions. People in his league didn't lose control. If it were anyone else, he'd be lying on the floor with dark-red blood oozing from the hole in the center of his forehead.

A cloud of cigar, cigarette, and testosterone hovered above. The other players at the table scooted their chairs back. The bartender crouched down behind the ornate mahogany structure, hoping it would shield him from the bullets that were sure to fly any moment. The waitress, decked out in black-and-white satin, looking like a feathered Playboy Bunny, scurried to join him on the floor. The bodyguards shoved their right hands into their suit jackets like a well-rehearsed chorus line—waiting.

Havana stood pressing both hands against the edge of the table. "That land is not *worthless!* It was granted to my family in 1560 by King Philip II of Spain for our loyal service—on my mother's side—the island has history." He swallowed hard. "It is a big island. Ten square miles. It is worth more than all the money on this table."

In Barilli's world, money talks, and this money had history. "It's a big island? Where is it? Key West?" he asked, beginning to sound interested. Key West had been a hot spot for corruption since the days of the pirates and was getting even hotter with the Cuban situation.

"Well . . . not exactly. You see, back in 1819, Spain ceded all of Florida and the Keys to the United States."

Lorenzo knew a thing or two about business, and this was sounding like a really bad deal. Like owning a chain of liquor stores during Prohibition. "So, I'm right. You're paying a gambling debt with a worthless piece of paper. Worthless for the last two hundred *years!*" He hastily folded the document and hurled it at Havana.

"My family now owns a thousand acres on Big Pine Key." The little man's chest puffed up. He lovingly smoothed out the deed in front of him, caressing it like a long-lost lover. Then he pushed it back toward Detroit's king of crime as tears welled in his charcoal-dark eyes. "It is better than Key West—it has history."

"Never heard of it." Lorenzo scooped up the document. Studied the fancy lettering and all that gold. If nothing else, it would look impressive framed and hanging on his office wall back in Grosse Pointe. He'd built an empire in Michigan; maybe this was the road to expansion. Much of the morning's meeting revolved around how for the last decade Cuba's dictator, Fulgencio Batista, and Key West's Mafia had a well-organized partnership. Heroin, marijuana, and other illicit drugs were flown and shipped into Havana from Columbia and Turkey and then sent by speedboat to Key West. It was the perfect setup—until now. One year ago, today, Batista fled Cuba, and Fidel

Castro took over effectively, shutting down the Mafia operations. Cuba was now in bed with the Soviet Union, and the Key West pipeline terminated.

"Are these thousand acres on the ocean?" Lorenzo asked.

"Yes. On the Gulf of Mexico, with easy access to the Atlantic."

The inkling of a plan was beginning to form in the Don's head. "How far away is the closest airport?"

"There is one located on Marathon Key." Havana was beginning to see a glimmer of interest in Barilli's eyes. So, he continued. "Marathon is the next largest island and is in direct line with my property. About eighteen miles away."

Lorenzo Barilli, Detroit's Godfather, could now have his own heroin pipeline. "You better be right, Havana." He paused a beat. "History, huh?"

Lorenzo relaxed in his chair. The room filled with the sigh of relief from a dozen organized killers, just as the outer door burst open with hotel security—guns drawn.

CHAPTER TWO

Present day
Chicago

Winifred O'Reilly Forrester stood, glaring at her therapist from across the antique, highly stylized black-lacquer desk from Chicago's art deco period. Dr. Shannon Mulaney embraced the Windy City's colorful history and its many buildings that were built during the height of the art deco period. She prided herself in always being impeccably dressed in what she considered to be understated elegance, which was somewhat at odds with her rather flamboyant personality. And as such made her a therapist for those who were *not* true introverts or faint of heart. Her patients tended to fall into the category of Chicago's upper crust. Today, she took on the day wearing a black cashmere pantsuit, a Christmas-red silk blouse opened dangerously low, three strands of pearls, and shiny-black stilettos with red soles—Christian Louboutin, of course. You would think that all that bright red would clash with her carrot-red hair—but it didn't. It only made the short curls framing a heart-shaped face look sassy.

"Look, Shannon, you've been my therapist for almost three years now. You know more about me than I know about me, and one thing I know for sure is that I'm as Irish as mulligan stew, the Blarney Stone, leprechauns, and Guinness—there isn't one drop of Italian blood in my veins." She felt her body shiver with anger and leaned over, splaying her hands against the desktop to steady her wobbly knees. Her tan, floral embroidered suede vest trimmed in faux fur fell open, revealing a white turtleneck. Tight tan pants, tucked into knee-high brown leather boots, completed the look. Her long ginger-colored hair was pulled back in a pony-tail with bangs that barely covered her eyebrows. She looked like she'd just jumped off the back of a Thoroughbred and landed in Shannon's den of opulence. "Please. Just read the report and tell me this is one huge mistake." Winifred stood straight, reaching out in a helpless gesture. "I have no one else to turn to," she pleaded.

Doctor Mulaney opened the navy-blue folder containing a mere three pages from the private eye firm of Harry Lincoln Investigations. She looked up into the emerald-green eyes of her patient. "Okay. I'll take a look. But while I read, you need to sit down and breathe deeply before you have a panic attack."

Winifred nodded her agreement and then walked slowly over to the two club chairs in front of the windows overlooking the Chicago River. She chose the chair to the left so she could easily watch the expression on Shannon's face as she read without obviously watching. She rearranged several soft, colorful throw pillows and scooted back, nestling into the corner of the tufted black leather. She'd performed this routine for what seemed to be a hundred times before—only the color of the pillows changed with the seasons. The first year had been the worst. Digging deep within her heart and mind for scraps of feelings and thoughts, which she'd served to her therapist on a platter of tears. It was easier now, but the pain was still real, and the tears crouched, ready to spring forward without warning.

She'd let a few moments go by in silence thinking about how her life could easily turn upside down yet again. She felt ready to explode with anxiety. "I closed on the house yesterday."

Shannon glanced up. She hadn't gotten further than studying the name and Detroit address on the letterhead and then began to read: Dear Mrs. Forrester. This is what Winifred did. Interjected a safe subject into a difficult session. One that she didn't want to face head-on. One that meant making or thinking about making life-altering decisions. "How do you feel about that?" she asked in her best soft, even-toned therapist voice that evoked a well-thought-out response from her patients.

"Good—I think. Relieved that I won't feel the pain every time I walk through the front door. Glad that the memories that are held so tightly in every room won't be rushing at me. Their voices filling my head—my heart breaking." She paused a beat to redirect her thoughts away from feelings. "I'm driving out there after I leave here. My in-laws have been on a fourteen-day Mediterranean cruise with friends. They're returning tomorrow. I need to check their house, turn the heat up, and pick up a few things at the store for them. Milk, eggs, bread—you know."

"Would you like me to come along? I don't have another appointment until three-thirty," offered Shannon. She hoped her patient would say no. Winifred had been making excellent progress in handling her grief and taking baby steps toward an independent life. But her friend might need the company. Someone to talk to and break the stillness. Someone to keep her focused on the task at hand and not the finality of no longer owning the home where she'd raised her children. "We could stop somewhere for lunch and a glass of wine."

Winifred took a moment to consider the offer. It might be a nice break, and one of her favorite restaurants was on the way. But chances were that she'd end up a tearful mess, and she didn't want her therapist witnessing her breakdown. "Thank you, but I think it best that I do this alone."

Shannon nodded her agreement, then focused on the letter.

Less than ten minutes went by when Doctor Mulaney's voice broke the silence. "Sorry, Freddie, but this report says you are part Italian. The DNA report says you are part Italian. Are you telling me you never met with Harry Lincoln and didn't give him a specimen for the test?"

"I met with him about a month ago. I thought he had the wrong Winifred Forrester, so I let him swab my mouth for the sample just to prove that I'm not the woman he was looking for. I still don't believe it's me."

"What do you think the chances are of another Winifred O'Reilly Forrester whose family lived in Detroit, Michigan? One in a million or two?" Shannon stood, waving the report in front of her. "Look at the facts, Freddie."

"Well—there could be."

Winifred watched as her friend walked around her desk and over to the chairs. She handed the report to her patient, then sat down in the opposite chair. "I very much doubt it."

Freddie focused on the letterhead of Harry Lincoln Investigations. "What do you think?"

"As your therapist or your friend?"

"Both." She sounded as if she'd just climbed the first leg of Mount Everest and was faced with the challenge to the summit.

Shannon crossed her legs and inhaled. "Your therapist has read the facts and recommends accepting the findings and follow through with the stipulations. You call Lincoln and agree to the inheritance, then contact the lawyer in Key Largo on or before December thirty-first and go from there."

"And . . .?"

"And your friend wonders what you know about your great-grandfather. Maybe he was somehow adopted as a baby from this Italian mob family, and it was kept a secret. Maybe the mothers knew each other and the swap was prearranged and the families didn't know. Maybe the mob mother claimed the baby died and the secret was kept until the detective found said mob mother's dear friend and she spilled the beans. Maybe—"

"Maybe you've read too many romance novels."

"Okay. So, what *do* you know about your great-great-grandfather?"

Winifred had wished countless times over the last year that while growing up she had asked more questions about her grandparents and great-grandparents. She knew she had strong Irish roots, and that had been enough. "Not much really. I know more about my great-great-grandfather. His story has been told so many times over the years that I could recite it in my sleep."

"Don't keep me waiting. Tell me."

Freddie took a deep breath and began. "Colin O'Reilly was born in Ireland in 1899 at his ancestral home, Dunmont Hall. He'd been a captain in the Fifth Royal Irish Lancers during World War I, which was part of the British Army. He was severely wounded while fighting in the Battle of Mons, in Belgium, on November 11, 1918. The war ended the next day during the battle." She paused a beat. "Bad luck seems to run in the family even in his time. Well, back to the story." She inhaled and continued. "He would have died there on the battlefield had it not been for a Canadian soldier who carried him to safety. Several days later, he was flown to a hospital outside of Paris. That's where he met my great-great-grandmother, Chivonne. She was working in the hospital where he spent many months recovering. They fell in love and married. After she got pregnant, he took her home to his family in County Cavan, Ireland. He was the fifth and youngest son of the Earl of Dunmont. No chance of inheriting the title, but it was said that he and his wife returned to Ireland with more cash than the earl had in the impoverished estate. Five years later, he died of complications stemming from his war injuries. Chivonne returned to Detroit with her son, Colin O'Reilly the second."

"Wow! Talk about the makings of a romance novel," Shannon exclaimed. "Then what happened?"

"Nothing much. She helped out at the family's hardware store, Harrigan's, for a year, then married again and had two more children. She was married a total of four times. She moved back to Paris with her fourth husband where she eventually died. My father claimed she was the wild one of the family."

"Anything else?"

"That's all I know. Or at least all I remember from the stories I was told as a child. It sure doesn't add any light to a mob boss connection."

"I must agree. It looks like the only person with any facts that can be woven together into a plausible answer is your Harry Lincoln." Shannon looked into emerald-green eyes that showed more defeat than fight. "Freddie, I know you've suffered more in the last two years than anyone should have to endure, and all you want is a quiet life. But I don't believe you will find peace until you put this problem to rest." She stood and reached out her hand for Winifred's. "I don't have any answers for you, but I believe Mr. Harry Lincoln does."

CHAPTER THREE

The Palos Heights trip following her meeting with Shannon had been a tearful disaster. It was hard pulling into her in-law's driveway knowing that her former driveway was off-limits. She'd been pregnant with Bridget when Danny's parents announced that the house next door would be going on the market soon. It would be perfect for the young couple and with the added benefit of having grandparents living next door for babysitting. The young couple had scraped together enough for a down payment, and by the time Sean came along eighteen months later, Danny had his fledgling company living in the basement. He'd taken his hobby of designing apps for friends to a successful enterprise that kept them in a comfortable lifestyle. Sixteen years later, they had moved the company to loft space in an old warehouse building in the Fulton Market District near the Loop. Winifred had taken on a major role in Forrester & Forrester, and together they had big dreams for the future. Once Sean and Bridget finished college and were on their own, she and Danny would sell the Palos Heights house and buy a condo overlooking Lake Michigan. They had visions of spoiling their grandkids with many trips to Chicago's Field Museum of Natural History, Griffin Museum of Science and Industry, the Art Institute, and Lincoln Park. But now, it was only her—their dreams had died with Danny.

Winifred stepped down from the driver's seat of her Cadillac Escalade and grabbed the three shopping bags from the back seat. She avoided looking to the left at the house that was no longer hers and proceeded up the front walk to the other Forrester house. After putting away the groceries, turning up the heat, and making a quick run-through, she was back in the Escalade and pulling out of the driveway. She kept her eyes focused on the street and the pavement stretching before her until the houses were no longer peeking at her from the rearview mirror.

Back in the city, she stopped by the office to check on the progress her staff had been making on their latest project. It would be a short week with the Thanksgiving holiday in three days. The office would be closed until the following Monday. She felt bad turning down the dinner invitations from members of her staff, but socializing with families was not something she could handle now—especially after having to walk away from the home that held the memories of so many holidays with Danny and the kids. Now, home was a condo on the upper floor of a new high-rise that had been built within walking distance of Forrester & Forrester. It wasn't the same as the dream life she and Danny had envisioned, but she did have a panoramic view of the city and lake. Before leaving, she called the number for Harry Lincoln's office. He didn't sound surprised to hear from her and scheduled a meeting for Wednesday morning at eleven. Her next call was to Shannon, inviting her for Thanksgiving in Traverse City.

Two days later, Winifred finished packing the SUV with enough clothes to last five or six days, a cooler, and two tote bags with her favorite comfort foods; the rest she could pick up in town as needed. The decision to turn the Wednesday meeting in Detroit with Harry Lincoln into another five days at the cabin in Traverse City came after her mother-in-law chided her for not including a turkey with the grocery items. Another Forrester Thanksgiving dinner was too much for Winifred to even consider. Not only didn't she want to be at the family dinner table in Palos Heights, but also she didn't want to be in Chicago—period.

The GPS instructions took her to one of the newer office buildings in downtown Detroit. After finding an open parking spot in the adjacent garage, Winifred walked the short distance to the front of the high-rise and entered through the heavy glass doors to the lobby beyond. The young woman at the desk was on the phone. Perhaps in her late twenties. Her blond hair was neatly pulled back and secured at the nape of her neck. A dark navy suit and white blouse finished the look. She could easily have been serving drinks to first-class passengers on a UNITED flight. Winifred glanced around at her surroundings. What wasn't covered in gray-and-white marble was trimmed out in glass and chrome. This wasn't even close to what she imagined would house the office of a Detroit private investigator. More like an old, rehabbed factory building in the older part of town.

"I'm sorry to make you wait," said the woman in a pleasant voice. "How may I help you?"

"Harry Lincoln Investigations."

"Twenty-ninth floor. Take the high-speed elevators to your right," the woman said as she grabbed for the ringing phone.

Winifred walked over to the doors and pressed the button. She hadn't been told the office number, but before she had time to ask, the doors opened. She stepped on thinking she would walk the hall on the twenty-ninth floor until she found his name.

It was totally absurd that she was even forced into this position of defending her Irish heritage when the elevator stopped, and she was faced with the scene before her. This was no dingy gumshoe, Dick Tracy operation. If it wasn't for the name Harry Lincoln Investigations in bold letters on the opposite wall, she would have thought she'd gotten off on the floor of a high-end attorney's office or corporate accounting firm for the auto industry giants. She hastily stepped into the room as the elevator doors began to close. The walls were lined with cherry paneling dotted here and there, with paintings by Robert Bateman. She knew them well. The famous naturalist artist was one of her favorites, and she had several of his works—only hers were prints. Elegant Queen Ann furniture rested on a large oriental rug.

"Good morning. You must be Mrs. Forrester," said a middle-aged woman of Asian descent dressed in a dark-gray suit. Her short, bobbed hairstyle and low-heeled, black pumps portrayed an efficient, no-nonsense authoritative figure. "I'm Maxine Liu, Mr. Lincoln's assistant. He's expecting you."

Winifred followed her through a door leading into a large open area with hallways extending in either direction. Maxine ushered her through the doorway at the end of the hall to the left.

"Mrs. Forrester, please come in," Harry Lincoln said. "Does this visit mean you are accepting your inheritance?"

She couldn't be any more surprised at the decor in this corner office as she had been at the Hunt Club look of the reception room. Scandinavian wouldn't have even been on her list of options for a guess. Chocolate walls were the perfect backdrop for light-colored woods with lots of rounded edges. Floor-to-ceiling windows added drama and gave the impression that Harry Lincoln's world went on forever. His black turtleneck under a tan V-necked sweater and crisp jeans didn't fit either. Winifred's gaze swept the interior settling on a bookcase. She walked over to examine shelves full of model cars. "Are all of them Lincolns?"

"Yep. From the very first, made in 1920 to the present. Of course, there were none made during the war years. Collecting is a fun hobby. People have given me everything from cigarette lighters to the front end of a 1961 Continental. It hangs over the side door of my garage. People come by to take selfies of them standing under a car."

"Wow. That must make you the coolest person in the neighborhood. Any relation to the president?"

Harry chuckled. "I wish, but no. My ancestors came here in 1887 from Sweden. It was during a time of great poverty, and my family scraped together every cent they had to make the ocean voyage. The name was Lindholm. But between their heavy accent and being rushed through the line, Lindholm became Lincoln."

She hadn't put it together during their previous meeting in Chicago, but now his tall, athletic build, blond hair, and blue eyes screamed Nordic. "I must admit that you and your office don't fit the profile I had worked out in my mind. You are definitely not Dick Tracy. And whoever your clients are, they have very deep pockets."

Harry motioned her to one of the two saddle-brown leather side chairs that sat in front of his desk. "I do have a rather diverse group of clients," he said as he walked to his high-backed chair, upholstered in the same leather, and sat down. "And speaking of clients, I'm sure you have a million questions, or you wouldn't be here."

There was only one folder on the top of his desk, and it was a thick one. "As I mentioned during our last meeting, except for a bit of German and English tossed in, I'm Irish—no Italian. So, based on that, how or why did you ever start sniffing around my family tree?"

He looked into Winifred's green eyes and inhaled deeply, seeming to debate his next move. Harry opened the folder and removed a rather small photograph, which he then pushed across the desk. "I found this among a stack of old photos and letters that Lorenzo Barilli had kept in his private safe located in his bedroom. Up until that moment, I was convinced that there was no direct heir still alive and was ready to close the case. Something about that photo kept me awake at night. It was as if it spoke to me, and I had to figure out why."

Winifred picked up the tattered photograph and studied the content. A small boy of perhaps five or six sat on a tricycle in front of a storefront. She checked the back for a date, but it was blank. "It's old, worn like someone kept it close or often looked at it. What does this have to do with me?" she asked while setting it back on the desk.

"Look closer," Harry said as he nodded toward the photo.

After picking it up, Winifred studied the details. "The boy is wearing a tweed jacket and matching cap. His shoes look new. He's smiling at the camera as if he's proud of his new bike."

"What else? Where is he?"

Winifred's expression became confused. "Harrigan's. He's on the sidewalk in front of my family's old store. The building burned down back in 1930 along with the other stores on the block. The family pooled their money and bought out the other store owners and increased the size of the new building, plus added apartments above. It was just after the big stock market crash, and they got the other properties for a steal."

Harry checked his notes. "My records show that your great-great-grandmother Chivonne O'Reilly returned to the United States with her five-year-old son Colin II in 1924. That time frame works with the photo. I believe Lorenzo Barilli carried that photograph and often looked at the image of your great-grandfather. Why? I asked myself."

"First off, I'm not convinced that the boy is Colin. Perhaps Barilli bought his son the tricycle at my family's hardware store and took the photo after presenting his son with the bike." Winifred tossed the photo back on the desk. "If you're basing this whole investigation on an unidentified boy in a hundred-year-old photograph, then this meeting is over. You'd better find another lab to do your DNA testing, because the one you're using has nonexistent quality control. I'm *not* Lorenzo Barilli's long-lost heir!" Winifred grabbed her purse and headed for the door.

"What do you know about Chivonne Harrigan?"

CHAPTER FOUR

Winifred crept along I-75 north out of Detroit toward Traverse City. It was a well-known fact, anywhere in the country, that the day before Thanksgiving was the busiest travel day of the year. It didn't matter if you were on the ground or in the air. And here she was, at noon, crawling along with the rest of the travelers. She would lose a lot of the other vehicles once she passed the Route 69 exit to Flint and Lansing, and traffic would lighten even more once she got north of Saginaw and Bay City. The normal four-hour trip was going to take her closer to five, which would leave Shannon waiting at the Traverse City airport for an hour. Inviting her friend to join her at the cabin was a last-minute impulse offer that she didn't expect her to take—but she did. Now, Winifred had an added commitment and responsibility as host that she'd been trying to avoid by skipping town. She needed the four days alone in seclusion to sort out her thoughts and feelings about losing her father, Danny, Bridget, and Sean in such a short time. She needed time to mourn. She needed time to come to terms with the possibility that she could be a crime lord's great-granddaughter. Maybe she needed her therapist more than her friend.

After passing signs for Houghton Lake, Winifred called Shannon on her cell phone. "Hey, I know I promised that I could meet you at the airport for your four o'clock arrival, but I totally forgot about holiday traffic. My GPS is putting me there closer to five twenty."

"No problem." Shannon sounded relieved. "My flight was delayed for over an hour at O'Hare. Looks like our timing is perfect. How was your meeting? Did you get your mystery inheritance put to bed?"

"Unfortunately, no," Winifred said with a sigh. "I'll tell you everything after we get to the cabin." She pressed disconnect on the Escalade's info panel, ending the call. She didn't want to rehash the meeting with Harry Lincoln while driving. And she certainly wasn't ready to think about his last question to her as she stormed out of his office: "What do you know about Chivonne Harrigan?"

Winifred stopped the vehicle at the entrance to the long driveway that would take her and Shannon to the cabin. She hadn't been back since Danny passed—she couldn't. This is where special family memories had been made, now locked away as precious parts of her past. She was here now. She couldn't turn back. Whatever her first feelings would be upon seeing the house again would be the ones she would deal with—good or bad.

Shannon sensed her patient's, Winifred's, anxiety. But why at this moment? "Are you okay? What are you feeling?"

Winifred jerked her head as if she were coming out of a trance. "Yeah. I'm fine," she said, without an explanation for her odd behavior. Then she pressed her foot against the gas pedal and proceeded up the long lane, with the vehicle's high beam giving an eerie glow to the old-growth trees and underbrush. Minutes later, they broke free of the forest, and the house was before them, sparkling in the night sky like a newly lit Christmas tree. She was suddenly filled with almost chokingly feelings of comfort, calm, welcoming security—and love. "We're home," Winifred said in a tone of reverence.

"Wow! This is what you call a *cabin*?" Shannon exclaimed in disbelief. She took in the huge, three-story facade of part log cabin and part stone manor. It had two-story wings at each end that curved toward the driveway; the one to the right had a covered walkway that led to a three-car garage. "I would expect to see this on the side of a mountain overlooking Lake Tahoe."

Winifred stopped in front of the front steps leading to a wide front porch. "This is the original porch of the cabin from 1885. It started out as a small hunting and fishing retreat for the early Harrigans, then began to grow with each generation." She opened her door and hopped down from the Escalade. "Come on, help me carry all this stuff inside."

Winifred unloaded the cooler and put away the groceries, while Shannon brought in their luggage. "I can give you a tour later, but I think we should dig into all this Chinese takeout before it gets cold."

"Sounds good to me. Can we eat in front of that big fireplace? I haven't been able to enjoy a real roaring fire close-up in years. Not counting ski lodges and rustic restaurants," begged Shannon.

"Do you have any idea how long it takes to produce a roaring fire? Of course, you don't, *city woman*."

"Well, you should have thought ahead and asked whoever came by and turned on the heat and all the lights," Shannon teased.

"How about you set out the food, open the bottle of wine I left on the counter, and get the table ready while I build the fire?" She looked over her shoulder as she walked out of the kitchen. "As for the lights and heat," Winifred said as she held her cell phone over her head for her friend to see, "Danny and I created an app for that."

For the next two hours, Shannon was pleased to witness the change that came over her patient. The stress that had been apparent in Winifred began melting away between mouthfuls of her favorite Chinese dishes. Shannon listened as her friend told stories of life at the cabin since she was old enough to have memories and tossed logs on the fire while sipping glasses of wine from a local vineyard. She snuggled against pillows of fall colors in the large Mission style chair and laughed through memories of the past. Shannon hated to destroy the mood, but she knew it was time to bring her patient back to the present. "How was your meeting with Harry Lincoln? Did you convince him that you are not the person he's looking for?"

Winifred was jolted back to the troubling present. But she was thankful for at least a couple hours of happiness while living in the past. "No. It's not over. It won't be over until I do my own investigating." With that, said she stood and began scooping up the empty food containers, wine bottle, and her glass and headed for the kitchen. "How about I show you to your room and I'll come back down and clean up?"

An hour later, the dishes were washed and put away. The counters had been wiped down, yet Winifred wasn't ready to face what came next. She went over to the fireplace and sat on the wide stone hearth, letting the warmth from the glowing embers warm her heart. The room upstairs was waiting for her—their room. The room she'd shared with Danny for so many years, yet not enough. They were supposed to grow old together spoiling their grandkids with life at the cabin as all the grandkids had been spoiled by their grandparents for generations. And there were the memories—the private memories she hadn't shared with Shannon. Would she be able to fall asleep in their bed without his warm body next to her? Would she be able to open their closet filled with his clothes? Perhaps she should keep that door and memories closed and move into her parents' room. But in the end, it was as she raised the handle of her carry-on that she felt Danny draw her into their room.

The next morning Winifred followed the aroma of freshly brewed coffee and bacon downstairs to the kitchen. Shannon was in the midst of cracking eggs into a bowl. "Good morning and Happy Thanksgiving."

"It's a wonderful morning, and don't you look festive in your red-and-green plaid flannel pajamas? I've already fallen in love with your cabin, and it's not even eight o'clock." Shannon added a splash of cream and began whisking. "I found the makings for an omelet. How did you sleep?" She'd been concerned when she heard Freddie in the next room well after midnight. That would have been her first night in the house without Danny.

Winifred tucked her hands into the pockets of her pants and walked over to the counter. "I was half expecting to end up in my parents' room, but I actually slept like a baby. I'm glad you decided to come. I'm not sure how I would have handled being alone here for the first time since . . . well, since Danny . . . since the accident."

Shannon went over to the stove and poured the egg mixture into a hot frying pan. "I haven't slept this soundly in years. I woke up at my usual five with the energy of a twenty-year-old. I saw a green light on the security panel by the front door, so I went for a run. I followed the drive down to the road and back and then couldn't resist the charm of the moonlight on the water. I ended up on the dock, but I wasn't dressed for the cold, so I came back, made a pot of coffee, then grabbed a blanket off the couch, and spent the next hour on the back porch watching the rising sun paint the water in all shades of pink, like a giant abstract. The back of the house is even more beautiful than the front."

Winifred poured herself a mug of coffee, set it on the table, and then went over to the warming oven for the plate of bacon, while Shannon dished up the eggs. "After breakfast, I'll give you a tour."

"Already done that. At least, I've checked out the first floor. I was afraid I'd disturb you if I started opening doors upstairs." Shannon took a sip of orange juice. "Who's responsible for creating the kitchen any professional chef would die for? Commercial-grade appliances and granite countertops do not fit the cabin vibe."

Winifred swallowed a mouthful of omelet, then chuckled. "That would be Mom. She loved cooking, and with a house overrun with kids for the summer months, she was always experimenting with new recipes. She would like to hear you say that. She was very proud of how it turned out. Dad thought the stove was overkill, but the regional manager for the brand was a friend of theirs, and Mom convinced him to get her a scratch-and-dent."

"Wow. That baby would have cost thousands—many thousands," Shannon acknowledged while helping herself to another slice of bacon.

"Not for Mom. She can always get what she wants and makes you think it was your idea." Winifred pushed her plate aside and took the last sip of coffee. "I'm stuffed. Thank you for a delicious breakfast. And speaking of food, I've made a reservation at The Lodge for a proper Thanksgiving meal. I took the last available slot; unfortunately, it's at four o'clock. But that will give us the whole evening to enjoy another fire and wine. Now, if you wouldn't mind cleaning up while I run upstairs and change, I'll show you *my* favorite room in the house."

"Deal" was all Shannon said as she stood and began clearing the table.

⇥⊢⊣⇤

"Your favorite room in the house is the attic?" Shannon belted out in something between a laugh and a snort. She nearly choked.

"You'll see. This is where the cast-off Harrigans live. Everything they no longer wanted or perhaps wanted to hide. I would come up here when my noisy cousins played hide-and-seek or board games or chased each other through the house." Winifred walked past threadbare chairs, furniture, and lamps that no longer fit in with the current generation's taste. She skirted the large chimney that rose through the center of the large space to the far wall. There she removed a stack of bedding from the top of an old trunk and tossed them on the cushion of a wingback chair. "Now, if you sit there, you won't feel the spring that pops through."

"This looks like a cross between an antique shop and neighborhood flea market."

"Wait; it gets better," Winifred said as she pulled the trunk out from the wall and pointed to a small brass nameplate on the front—CHIVONNE HARRIGAN. "My favorite ancestor. Everyone called her the Wild One." She lifted the lid to reveal a tray of beaded headpieces with large ostrich feathers and strings of crystals, beautiful handbags, and gloves. Winifred removed the heavy tray and set it on a battered dresser. She then pulled out a heavily beaded dress and handed it to Shannon. "I taught myself the Charleston wearing that." She then pointed to an old Victrola and a stack of thick records. "That steamer trunk has the O'Reilly family crest on the top. She brought it with her when she

24

returned to Detroit from Ireland with her son after her husband died. It's full of clothes too. I think some of her son's clothes are in there as well."

"This is amazing! Can I try the dress on?"

"Sure, and there are plenty more in here. A few of them are trimmed in fur. These are her things before she moved to Paris." Winifred reached down to the bottom and pulled out two shoeboxes. "This is what I need. As a child, I was more interested in the beautiful clothes than I was in the letters and photos in these boxes."

Shannon stepped out of her jeans, then pulled the black turtleneck over her head. "So why the interest now?"

"Because the last thing Harry Lincoln said to me as I stormed out of his office was 'What do you know about Chivonne Harrigan?' His words have haunted me. I think somehow, she may be the key to his investigation. I need to find out why."

"So, while you look for answers up here, I can play dress-up. I can't think of a better way to spend the day."

There were more photos than Winifred remembered, and at a glance, nothing clicked. She then searched the steamer trunk. Chivonne's clothes were now truer to the postwar era, yet her sense of style was still present. There was a box of photographs and another box of letters. Winifred set those next to the boxes. There was just one more drawer in the trunk to check, and she pulled it out. "It can't be the same one!" she exclaimed as she removed the contents from the drawer. "What are the odds?"

"What did you say?" Shannon shouted above the scratchy music coming from the Victrola. She was now attired in a calf-length brown lace dress with black trim and some long black fur thing draped around her neck.

Between the modeling and the music, Winifred's investigative skills just weren't happening. "I'll show you later," she shouted back. Half an hour later, she was sure that she had gone through every drawer, box, and trunk in the attic to find anything that had to do with Chivonne Harrigan O'Reilly. It took two trips to carry everything downstairs and set it on the floor next to the large square coffee table in front of the fireplace.

"Ready to dig in and sort photos?" Shannon asked.

Winifred looked up at the clock on the wall. "It's nearly three, and I'm covered in dust. Our dinner reservations are at four, and I need a shower. It will take fifteen minutes to get there. I suggest we leave this for our evening activity."

"I need to shower as well. How about we give the evening some ambience with wine and a fire?" Shannon added.

"Deal," Winifred answered as she headed for the staircase.

CHAPTER FIVE

Winifred drove up the curved, brick-lined drive to the covered entrance and parked in front of the valet stand. She opened her door and had one knee-high black leather boot on the ground, when a middle-aged man approached, then took her hand as she exited the Escalade.

"Well, well, look who the wind blew in and driving a beautiful new ride," the man said in a teasing voice. "It's good to see you again, Freddie. I'm so sorry to hear about Danny. He was a really good guy," he said while watching her smooth the front of her mid-thigh-length, black turtlenecked dress. The wide black leather belt cinched her tiny waist.

"Jimmy? Looks like you've been a bad boy. Demoted from general manager to valet."

"You wish!" They stepped away from the vehicle. "Between the COVID-19 years and the flu, we're running on a skeleton crew. I figured my talents would be best served out here and not waiting on tables."

Shannon joined them and was happy to see the happy bantering. She reached out her hand to Jimmy. "Hello! I'm Shannon Mulaney. Freddie's . . . ther . . . ah, her . . . friend."

"Sorry for the lapse in manners. Shannon also lives in Chicago, and this is her first time in Traverse City. I hope she joins me for many more visits in the future."

"So do I," Jimmy said as he admired the tall, beautiful woman with short, curly, carrot-red hair. Her conservative black pantsuit, ivory-colored silk tank top with a plunging neckline, and a single strand of pearls shouted self-confidence and something else—but what? Freddie didn't have friends that looked like her.

"Nice to see you too, Jimmy, but we have a four o'clock. We'll be here till Monday or Tuesday. Maybe we can catch up later."

"I'll get the gang together. Do a wine crawl." Jimmy watched as she began to walk away. "Hey! We installed a new wash station out by the maintenance area. I'll have one of the guys run this baby through. Get all the road grime off her. Can't have you driving around in a dirty Cadillac."

"Thanks, Jimmy. You're the best," Winifred said over her shoulder.

"Two foxy redheads dressed in black. Double trouble. I'll warn the staff—Freddie's back!" They quickly walked toward the entrance doors, their heels clicking on the brick pavers. Freddie's long leopard print overwrap fluttered behind her. "Yep. Wonder what mischief she'll get into next without Danny to rein her in," Jimmy said under his breath.

Once inside, Winifred led the way across the lobby to the restaurant's entrance. "I think even your Chicago standards will be impressed," Winifred said as they entered and walked over to the maître d'.

"Freddie! Happy Thanksgiving. I was told you would be here. I'm so sorry to hear about Danny. We're all going to miss him."

Winifred's chest tightened. She wiped the one tear that had escaped from her cheek. The heartfelt condolences shouldn't have taken her by surprise—but they had. Perhaps it was because she hadn't been back since the accident, and raw emotions that she had learned to control were suddenly clawing their way to the surface. "Thank you, Edwin. This is my friend Shannon. She's staying with me at the cabin."

"It is a pleasure to meet you, Shannon," Edwin said while holding her hand and giving a light kiss to the back. Then he turned to Winifred. "I have two table choices for you. Next to the fireplace or a lake view."

She turned to Shannon. "Well?"

Shannon looked into the dark-brown eyes of one of the most handsome men she'd ever met. His longish black hair was pulled back from a face with high chiseled cheekbones and closely trimmed beard. She could almost see his well-built, athletic body under the tuxedo. She envisioned him on the deck of a pirate ship. "The fireplace would be lovely."

After reaching the designated table, Edwin pulled out Winifred's chair and got her settled, then did the same for Shannon. "I hope this meets with your approval," he said to Shannon as their eyes locked with some primal message.

"Perfect," Shannon answered. "Just perfect."

"Heather will be your server. She's new but knows the menu well." He pointed to a beautifully printed card resting at each place. "Today we have the special Thanksgiving dinner featured, or you may order off our usual menu."

"Thank you, Eddie."

Shannon watched him walk away. "Eddie? Don't tell me he's one of *the gang*."

"Yep. And one of the owners of this fine establishment."

"Well, now. Isn't that interesting?" Shannon said softly as Heather walked over to their table.

Winifred ordered a bottle of wine for a specific year and from a local vineyard. Then she told Heather that they would both be having the special but adding a side of Mom's Cherry Sauce.

"Mom's Cherry Sauce?" asked Shannon, rather skeptically. "That sounds pretty sweet. Who's Mom?"

"Mine."

"Yours?" Shannon asked with raised eyebrows.

"Yep. She won first prize for the best cherry sauce at the Blessing of the Blossoms Festival in 1990—and every year since. The Lodge is the only establishment in the region to have her recipe."

"Why here? What's so special about The Lodge?"

"Dad was one of the initial investors. He and a few of his buddies believed the world-class tourists that were arriving by increasing numbers each year, primarily for the vineyards and outdoor sports, deserved world-class accommodations and dining." She paused a beat. "So, The Lodge was born."

At that moment, the sommelier arrived with the wine. "Freddie! I should have known this bottle was for you. I think you are the only one who orders it now."

"Still my favorite, Maxie. And I'd like you to meet my good friend from Chicago, Shannon Mulaney." The two women shook hands. "Maxine and I have known each other since—well—since forever. Our fathers were friends, and their farm is just down the road from us."

"I'm so sorry to hear about Danny. We all miss him and often reminisce about his practical joking," Maxine said while pouring the wine into the two glasses.

Winifred took a sip. "Wonderful, as always. We will be here until Monday or Tuesday."

"I'm off on Sunday, and I know Eddie can be available. I'll get the gang together. Maybe do the winery crawl."

Winifred laughed. "Jimmy's already on it."

"Sounds like the wine industry is the biggest thing around up here."

"Not really. It's a young industry. Started about fifty years ago. One of Granddad Harrigan's buddies thought we had the perfect climate for grapes, because we're on the forty-fifth parallel, the same as Bordeaux in France. Bernie Rink wanted to take a chance, so he plowed up his kid's baseball field and planted the first grapes. The venture began to look promising, so the guys all invested in the first vineyard. The so-called experts of the day said it wouldn't last—the winters were too cold. But here we are today with fifty different wineries and growing."

"So, the whole family has been instrumental in the progress of the region."

"We've been here for about one hundred forty years. It makes sense that every generation dabbled in something."

They had nearly finished eating when Jimmy appeared at their table. "Sorry to interrupt, Freddie, but this fell out from your car while Mark was spray-washing the underside." He placed a small black plastic part on the table. "Neither of us knows what it might be, but considering all the electronics on these new models, it could be important."

"Thanks, Jimmy, for bringing this to my attention. I'll run it into my dealership when I get back home."

"This tiny thing could be important. I'd hate for you to break down somewhere along the interstate and be stranded. Maybe stop by the Cadillac dealer over on Garfield tomorrow."

"You're probably right," Winifred said as she dropped the part into her purse. "I'll give them a call first thing tomorrow."

⚒

Back at the cabin, Winifred got a fire going, while Shannon stacked the photos of Chivonne on the coffee table. "If you keep insisting on roaring fires every day, then you'll need to help me bring in another load of wood tomorrow."

"Will I need to go out and chop it at dawn first?" Shannon teased.

Winifred laughed at the mental image of Shannon in her designer workout clothes, four-hundred-dollar running shoes, and acrylic nails slinging an axe and then sobered. "Danny did that."

"Sorry, Freddie. Should we sort these pictures by time frame or something?"

Winifred took the photo of the little boy on the tricycle and handed it to Shannon along with a magnifying glass. "According to Harry Lincoln, that is what set him off in my direction, or should I say Colin O'Reilly's direction? A copy of this picture, only worn and tattered, was found in Lorenzo Barilli's safe—the one in his bedroom."

"Huh." Shannon studied it for a minute. "What was his explanation? I don't see how this connects. Looks to me like Barilli bought his son a bike for his birthday or something. Yeah, and the little boy is wearing a new coat and hat. Even his shoes look new—not dirty or scuffed."

"Exactly what I thought. And at the time, Harrigan's Hardware sold tricycles. So, Barilli presents his son with a fabulous present and takes the photo to catch the moment."

"Exactly! Lincoln's wrong."

Winifred picked up the articles of clothing from the drawer she'd pulled from the steamer trunk that morning. "Then I found this." She spread it out on the table, then added the small cap. "Look closely at what the boy is wearing."

Shannon studied the image through the magnifying glass. "Nice tweed. Matching cap with a little button on top. Very fashionable for the time." She glanced at the suit on the table. "Perhaps Harrigan's sold children's clothes."

"I'll ask my uncle, but I think the store only carried work clothes." Winifred scooped up the coat and hat and set them back in the drawer. "The answer lies with Chivonne. We need to look at every photo on this table. Hopefully, it will tell us who she was before she went to Paris."

"That's going to take a while. How about I open a bottle of wine and find some snacks?"

For the next two hours, Winifred kept the fire fed, while Shannon kept the wineglasses filled. She made a plate of crackers and cheese and then the ladies finished off the slices of cherry pie they'd brought back after dinner.

Winifred stood and stretched tight muscles. "What we know so far is that Chivonne loved beautiful clothes and loved being photographed wearing them. She frequently went clubbing and attended parties with Grosse Pointe society. She had a large circle of friends who also liked being photographed." Winifred slowly walked around the room as she recounted what they had discovered through the photos. "Apparently, she had her own car—a very flashy, expensive one at that. The name Pierce can be seen across the radiator grill in one of the photos. They had a very distinctive hood ornament. Having grown up in Detroit, I know my cars, even the old ones. Pierce-Arrow was the American version of the Rolls-Royce. I know my family had money back then, but I never heard of them having that much."

"Maybe the family didn't pay for it. Maybe one of her Grosse Pointe *friends* bought it for her. If you know what I mean. After all, you did say your family called her the *Wild One*," Shannon added.

"But then there is the other side of her. She served on the line at a soup kitchen. Collected and delivered clothing for the poor. There's one that shows a young man of about her age leaning up against her car with his foot firmly planted on the running board and a cigarette hanging out of his mouth. And he definitely isn't dressed like one of her society guys."

Shannon stood and leaned down to pick up her empty wine-glass and bottle. "Sorry, Freddie, but I've hit a wall. My brain is fried, and I'm done for the night. I'm sure you are too. How about we call it a day and pick up in the morning?"

"You're right. The pieces just aren't coming together. Yet, I know the answer is here. But I'm too tired to dig any deeper. You go on upstairs, and I'll finish cleaning up."

It was after midnight when Winifred finally crawled into bed mentally exhausted. She couldn't break free of Harry Lincoln's last words. *"What do you know about Chivonne Harrigan?"*

CHAPTER SIX

Friday morning had Winifred once again waking to the aroma of coffee and bacon. After slipping on her robe and slippers, she headed down to the kitchen. "Good morning. I could easily get used to this," she said, while pouring coffee into the mug that Shannon had sitting on the counter next to the pot.

"Good morning. I've already had my early run, showered, dressed, and had my first coffee while wrapped in a blanket on the porch watching the rising sun dance across the water. I do have a question, though. I've seen you set the alarm in the evening, yet the light on the panel turns green when I open the front door for my run. How come the alarm doesn't sound when I return, or I need to turn it off before I leave?"

"The system is intuitive."

"I don't understand."

"Danny designed the app that runs the security system. Each member of the family who use the house has their own code that they punch in when they arrive. The system works off their habits or can also be turned to a default setting."

"So, my leaving the house early each morning means what?"

"It thinks you're Danny. He pretty much had the same morning routine as you. Even to sitting on the back porch with coffee."

"Huh." Shannon turned back to the stove. "I found the loaf of Italian bread you brought and a bottle of maple syrup in the fridge. Hope you're hungry. We're having French toast with lots of cinnamon and sprinkled with powdered sugar. I'll let you set out glasses of OJ."

"Right, chef. I'm on it," Winifred teased.

Neither of them seemed ready to discuss the life of Chivonne Harrigan. They kept the conversation centered around the history of the Traverse City region, and Shannon managed to dig as much information as she could about the *gang*, especially Edwin.

"Eddie is single, not gay, not weird, a super nice guy, and I have no idea about his current love life," Winifred offered before Shannon could ask.

"Thanks for the info, but I'm not the least bit interested in Edwin." She stood and began clearing the table. "It's a beautiful morning. Do you mind if I explore the property while you shower and get dressed?"

"Not at all, but the property is one hundred acres. I suggest you stay within sight of the buildings. I'll unlock the garage, barn, and boathouse."

"I don't want you running around outside in your pajamas." She watched Winifred hold up her cell phone and begin punching in numbers. "The app! Of course!"

An hour later, dressed in well-worn jeans and a kelly-green sweatshirt from a local winery that showed a half-full glass of wine on the front, Winifred found Shannon on the porch with another cup of coffee. "I called the Cadillac dealer. We can swing by today around noon. They'll have time to run a diagnostic test if needed."

"Great. You know, I could get used to this. What a wonderful way to get away from the stresses of the city. If it were about ten degrees warmer, I'd take one of those kayaks I found in the barn and explore the shoreline."

"I'll bring you up in the summer. The place is alive with activity during the day and tranquil at night. There are panels of screens that are inserted in tracks around the porch to keep the mosquitoes and bugs out." Winifred pointed to the ceiling. "The porch and grounds become a fairyland with lights at night."

"I'm going to hold you to that," Shannon said with a warm smile.

"Stay out here as long as you want. I'm giving you the day off," Winifred teased. "We didn't find the connection to Lorenzo Barilli last night, so I'll pack up what we've already looked at and begin today with Chivonne's life in Europe."

The side tables in the great room were stacked with photos, when the sound of stiletto heels could be heard against the wood floor. "Hey, Freddie. I thought I would save you the trouble and take the Escalade to get checked out."

Winifred turned and looked up to see Shannon dressed in tight black jeans, black turtleneck, and a waist-high white faux jacket open at the front. Her short carrot-red curls fell impishly around her face. "Wow! You are wearing *that* to the dealership? More like a session with Vogue."

"Afterward, I thought I might stop by The Lodge for a quick lunch—if you don't mind."

Winifred thought about Eddie. Poor guy didn't have a clue what he was in for. "Sure. Thanks. I appreciate you taking care of that for me." She nodded toward the console table next to the front door. "The mystery part is in my purse."

She had been sorting and studying old photographs for hours and was now fighting to squelch sick feelings churning in her stomach. The evidence was now turning against her. Winifred looked up as the front door opened. It was a little after three.

"Hey, Freddie! Good news. The car is fine. The parts guy doesn't know what it is but thinks it might be some piece of road debris you picked up on the highway." Shannon carried a grocery bag into the kitchen. "I noticed a market on my way home. Tonight, we dine on fresh salmon, tossed salad, and garlic bread." She paused long enough to put the items in the fridge. "There was an amazing bakery next door. We have cherry crisp for dessert and cherry strudel for breakfast. The merchants here really know how to take advantage of this 'Cherry Capital of the World' designation." She wondered why there was no response from Freddie but continued. "Eddie was at the front desk when I entered the lobby and joined me for lunch. Jimmy was in his office but came out to say hello, and Maxi stopped by our table. They are looking forward to Sunday. So far, there will be six, maybe seven, of us for the wine crawl."

"Good" was all Winifred said.

Concerned about the lack of emotion in her friend's voice caused Shannon to rush to her side. Her ashen skin tone and the dead look in Freddie's eyes sent Shannon into her therapist mode. "Freddie? What happened?" She took her patient's hand. "Can you tell me about it?"

"Don't worry. I'm okay." She scooted to the side and motioned for Shannon to sit next to her. "These appear to be early after her arrival in Paris." She handed Shannon a stack of photos. "Note that she is wearing beautiful dresses and coats, many trimmed in fur, taken in front of the usual tourist spots. Several are near the Eifel Tower."

Shannon glanced at the first dozen or so and set them on the table. "Whoa! I didn't see this coming! She's naked!"

"If you look, each pose and background is different. In the last one, she is wearing a long wig and reclining outside under a large tree."

"She's an artist's model!" Shannon flipped them over. "Each one is dated 1919. Nothing else." She looked at the next one in the stack. "Wow! This one she is on some kind of theater stage and naked—except for a couple of fans."

"And the next two show her in a dressing room. In one, she is wearing an evening gown and the other a fur-trimmed negligee. In both, she is wearing heavy makeup, especially blush. I think it was called rouge back then."

"What on earth was she doing? This was your great-great-grandmother?"

"It gets more confusing. Go to the next one."

"Wow! Chivonne does a three-sixty. Now she's wearing a very plain high-necked dress with what looks like a white apron over it. The background looks like a hospital ward."

"The next few she is with a patient who appears to be in bad shape. His head is wrapped, his leg in some kind of sling, and his left arm is tightly wrapped. Probably Captain Colin O'Reilly. We know they fell in love while he was a patient in a hospital in Paris. They got married after he was released. But look closer."

"Awwww. She has a baby bump."

"Yep. And it's pretty obvious to me that he didn't make that baby."

"Maybe he isn't Colin O'Reilly," Shannon stated firmly.

"It is. There are plenty of him in later pics, taken at Dunmont Hall." Winifred reached to the bottom of the stack and handed a photo to Shannon.

"Well. Well. This answers one of our questions." She turned the card over. "1925. It's Chivonne and Colin, with little Colin standing between them—and he is wearing the same tweed jacket and hat."

Both women turned and looked at each other. "Who's the father?" they said in unison.

Moments went by, with each deep in her own thoughts. Finally, Shannon stood and shrugged out of her jacket and draped it over a chair. She then went to a chair opposite Winifred and sat down. "With Colin eliminated as the father, who do we have in the daddy pool?"

"Well . . . Chivonne was naked a lot. Maybe the artist she posed for? What are the chances we can find out who that was?" Winifred asked sarcastically. "And then there is the theater—probably dancing for a primarily male audience." She looked at the dressing room pictures. "There is a vase of roses reflected in the mirror in both. She's giving a very sexual look to whoever is taking the photo in the negligee scene. A lover?" She paused a moment. "The evening gown one leads me to believe their relationship is more than sex. He's taking her out in public."

"Good point. But I have another angle," Shannon offered. "Of all the places in the world to move—why Paris? Unless it was a favorite of someone she knew well in Detroit. Like the guy with deep pockets who bought her the expensive car. I bet her Grosse Pointe crowd knew Paris well."

Winifred considered the scenario. "Maybe." She stood and began pacing. "Maybe he's married so he takes their affair to a different level and continent, but she quickly gets pregnant. He can't marry her and heads back home. She's left alone, makes money as a model and an aid in a hospital. Colin falls in love with the beautiful woman who is caring for him and agrees to raise her child as his own."

"Sounds plausible to me." Shannon stood and headed toward the kitchen. "How about you take a break from all this while I throw together a fabulous dinner?"

"Great idea. Every inch of my body is sore from sitting for so many hours, and I'm hungry. I'll set the table after I put this mess away."

"And get another fire going?" Shannon asked.

Winifred chuckled. "Looks like you're in danger of becoming a pyromaniac."

"I admit to enjoying the dancing flames, the glowing embers beneath, and the soft smoky scent."

"Maybe you could get one of those fake, electric fireplaces installed in your condo."

"Naw. It just wouldn't be the same. Besides, it gives me a reason to come back."

"Any time." Winifred thought about how nice it was to have her there. "You are welcome anytime."

An hour later, Shannon announced that dinner was ready. Winifred sat down to a beautifully presented salad with multicolored tiny tomatoes, sliced egg, roasted pecans, and freshly grated Parmesan, accompanied by garlic bread and another blended local wine that Shannon had found in the wine cooler.

"You may want to come back for my roaring fires, but I want you to come back so I can enjoy your culinary skills."

"If you think this is good, wait till you taste the entrée," Shannon said as she collected the salad plates. "I'll be back in a minute." It was a little more than a minute when Shannon returned with plates of rice and asparagus artfully arranged to one side.

Winifred admired the presentation but wondered what happened to the promised salmon. "Looks yummy."

"But wait. There's more." Shannon went back to the stove. Suddenly the lights went out and she returned to the table with a flaming skillet. "I present you with my very own version of salmon jubilee." The flames died down, and Shannon carefully lifted the fish onto Winifred's plate. "I found a jar of your mom's cherry sauce in the pantry—and a bottle of brandy in the liquor cabinet."

"Shannon, you are amazing! And yes—you are absolutely welcome to join me here anytime—as long as you do the cooking!"

"Deal."

They finished off the evening in front of the fireplace sipping wine and indulging in the cherry crisp that Shannon had brought back from the bakery. Winifred offered to clean up while Shannon enjoyed the last of the dying embers.

After putting the last pan away and wiping down the counter, Winifred wrapped herself in the blanket she pulled off the couch and went out to the back porch. Leaning against the railing, she watched the moonlight shimmer across the blackness of the lake. Two days of searching through stacks of photographs and she was no closer to finding the dots that connected her to Lorenzo Barilli. Maybe she had misunderstood the meaning of Harry's last words. Maybe this was just one big wild-goose chase. Regardless, there was one good thing that had come out of her search so far—she was certainly getting to know Chivonne Harrigan.

"Freddie, I'm heading up to bed. See you in the morning. Sleep well."

Deep in thought, Winifred was startled by the voice—she hadn't even heard the door to the porch open. "I'm right behind you. Good night. And thanks again for a fabulous meal."

The weather had been unusually warm for the end of November, but the evening temperature was now dropping, and Winifred decided to call it a night. Headlights caught her eye as she turned to go in. The vehicle appeared to be stopped at the mouth of the driveway. Perhaps they had parked to check their location. With few homes along that stretch of road, people often used their driveway to turn around. The lights went out, and she headed back into the house.

Once in bed, Winifred couldn't shake the feeling that she had missed something. Something important. Something that hovered over her like a dark, menacing cloud.

CHAPTER SEVEN

Winifred was jarred awake by the ringing of the door-bell and someone shouting. She glanced at the clock on her nightstand—two o'clock. Wondering what could possibly be happening at such a late hour, she reached for her phone while trying to shove her feet into the slippers at the side of the bed. She couldn't find the phone and gave up trying as the ringing bell and shouting became more important. She ran into Shannon in the hallway in the process of pulling up a pair of sweatpants.

"What the hell is going on?"

"I have no idea," Winifred said as she ran for the stairs, turning on lights along the way. She got to the door first and pulled it open. "Jason? What the hell is going on?"

"You're asking me? What happened? Are you okay?" he asked in a panicked voice as he pushed past her. "Where's the break-in?"

"What break-in?"

At that moment, they were interrupted by a police car racing up the driveway with lights flashing and siren blaring. It came to a screeching stop at the base of the steps. "Freddie, what are you doing here?"

"More like what are *you* doing here in the middle of the night making enough noise to wake the dead?"

"Your alarm. The night operator called me about your alarm system going off. He knows we're friends and that I keep an eye on the property, so he called me first."

Winifred watched as a young officer hurried up the front steps. "Then he called the police."

"Standard procedure," Jason said as he stepped to the side, away from the doorway.

"Evening, Jason. I got here as soon as I could. Looks like everything is under control."

"Who are you?" Winifred asked, sounding confused.

"I'm Officer Sherman. Are you ladies all right? Where did the break-in occur?"

"You must be new. Sherman? Any relation to Sam Sherman?"

"Yeah, I'm his son. Been with the department for thirteen months."

"Nice to meet you, Officer Sherman."

"Did someone break in?" Shannon asked Winifred.

"Hell, if I know!" she said while throwing her arms up. "Jason? Do you want to tell us why we're having this little get-together?"

"Freddie, your security system sent the code for a break-in—one of the outbuildings. Didn't you get a message on your phone?"

Winifred remembered then that she had given up looking for it upstairs. Where was her phone? She motioned for everyone to be quiet. "Shush." A faint alarm could be heard off in the distance. Winifred followed it to the couch she had been sitting in the night before. She reached down and pulled it out from between the cushions. Suddenly, the room was filled with the shrill ringing of the app alarm. She turned it off and returned to the others. "Sorry, I usually keep my phone with me."

"So, we did have a burglar! Does this kind of thing happen often up here?" Shannon asked to no one in particular.

"We're safe," Winifred answered while punching in digits. "Follow me. It's the garage."

The security light was on over the side door when they arrived. Jason checked the lock. "Whoever it was didn't try very hard to get in. I don't see any marks or damage to the wood."

Officer Sherman looked up at the corner of the building. "There's a security camera at the corner. Looks like it covers both the front and side."

Winifred opened the security app on her phone. "Got it!" She and Jason studied the screen. "The guy was startled by the sudden spotlight coming on. Shown right in his eyes. I don't recognize him," Winifred commented.

"Me neither," Jason said as he handed the phone to Officer Sherman. "Ever see this guy around town?"

"No. But he looks like a pro. That's no kid wearing a hoodie."

Jason took the phone back. "You're right. He's dressed in black and holding something." He enlarged the photo. "I'll be damned. He's about to use a lock-picking set. Freddie, send me that photo and to the police."

"Excuse me, but where are the lights?" Sherman asked. "Dad mentioned when I joined the force that if anything ever happened on the Harrigan property, the place would light up like Yankee Stadium."

"He's right. There are spotlights mounted to the corners of all the buildings, and several on the trees. The problem this time is that I turned them off, since we're only here for a few days."

"Like you didn't bother to inform me that you were coming!"

"Sorry; it won't happen again."

"Jason, if you don't need me for anything else, I'll head back to the station. I want to check the security cameras in town. At this time of the year, we don't get much traffic after midnight. Too late for the summer crowd and too early for the skiers. Maybe we'll get lucky with a vehicle that doesn't belong."

"Good idea. Give me a call if you get something."

The three walked back into the house. "There is no way that I'll be able to go back to bed. I think a pot of coffee is in order," Shannon said.

Jason and Winifred followed her to the kitchen. They sat on the stools that lined the front side of the island and watched as Shannon made coffee and then placed the cherry strudel on a platter. "I think sleep is out of the question for me too. What about you, Jason? You gonna head out too or hang out with us?"

"No way I'm walking away from fresh coffee and pastry."

For the next two hours, Jason listened as Freddie and Shannon filled him in on why they were in town. Getting a male's point of view, and especially one in the security business, added a new perspective. By the time he was ready to leave, Winifred found herself newly energized and ready to take on the day.

The coffeepot was empty and the strudel gone when Jason eased off the stool. "Thank you, Freddie, for sharing everything you are going through. Please call me and let me know what you find out and decide to do. I'll help any way I can." He slipped into his coat. "Shannon, it was a pleasure. I have a feeling we'll see a lot of you in the future. I'll call if we have anything on your intruder." As he opened the front door to leave, he looked down at the table and stopped. He picked up the car part. "What are you doing with this?" he asked while walking back toward Freddie.

"Nothing. It fell out from under my car when Jimmy had one of his guys wash it on Thursday. Do you know what it is?"

"A tracking device." Jason set it on the counter. "Freddie, this is a long-range, very sophisticated, tracking device."

CHAPTER EIGHT

"I don't understand. Why would someone want to track me? Who?"

"I'm ninety-nine-point-nine percent sure that the *who* is the person paying the guy who tried to break into your garage. But why was he trying to gain access to your car if he already had it bugged. Unless he was about to *add* something. Something like a listening device. As for *why*? After what you've just told me about Harry Lincoln believing you are the long-lost relative of Lorenzo Barilli—he's your reason."

"I'm still not understanding. I don't inherit anything until I sign the document as the legal heir—and I'm not convinced."

"But maybe he, whoever *he* is, doesn't know that. You did meet with Lincoln before you came up here. He—let's call him Mr. X—assumes you signed."

"So, Mr. X believes I signed Harry's document, agreeing to inherit a thousand acres in the lower Florida Keys, but instead of heading south, I immediately drive north. What kind of sense does that make?"

Jason thought about that for a moment. "Yeah. You heading north throws Mr. X off. He wants to know exactly what you're doing. He needs you bugged."

"Since his guy failed, is he going to try again? Do you think Shannon and I are safe here?"

"This is the best place for you. You have a state-of-the-art security system—providing you turn it on." Jason gave her the raised-eyebrows look. "And you know practically everyone in town. We look out for each other."

"And I'm here," Shannon added. "Freddie won't be alone."

Jason's cell phone rang. He looked at the caller ID. "It's Sherman," he said and walked into the kitchen. A minute later, he returned. "He wants me to come and look at some footage he found."

"Should I come with you?"

"No. You and Shannon stay here. I'll call you after I see what he's got. And, Freddie, set the alarm!"

"Right," she said as he opened the door and walked out. Freddie then locked the door and turned on the security system.

"Well, I guess I'll skip my morning run," Shannon joked, trying to lighten the moment.

Freddie didn't respond. She always had a quick comeback to Shannon's jokes and teasing. Instead, Freddie stood still, head bent staring at the floor.

Shannon moved to her patient's side. Then she put her arm around her shoulder, pulling her close. "Freddie?"

"Why is this happening to me?" Freddie finally looked up. "Someone bugged my car. He tried to break into my garage." She broke free of Shannon's arm and took a step back. "This only happens in movies—on TV—not to people like me." She looked pleadingly into her therapist's eyes. "Why me? Why me?"

"How about we go upstairs, shower, get into comfortable clothes, and find out why?"

An hour later, Freddie entered the great room dressed in gray sweats, with her hair pulled back in a ponytail. Shannon was busy arranging stacks of the photos they had already gone through on side tables. The large coffee table contained an amazing number of letters. It appeared she was back in her friend role. She looked up as Freddie walked in. "You're looking much better. You even have makeup on."

"My war paint. I'm ready to go into battle and get to the bottom of this nightmare." Winifred surveyed the room. "I see you've been busy."

"Working on your battle plan." Shannon pointed to the table in the corner. "All the photos from Chivonne's life up until she left." Next, she pointed to another table along the wall. "Paris photos. And on that side chair is everything in Ireland."

"I'm impressed. How did you have time for all this?"

Shannon flipped a few damp curls. "Didn't take time for makeup or the hairdryer. Fortunately, we won't be having guests for a while."

Winifred walked over to the table. "What's this?"

"These, my friend, are the letters. They are all addressed to Chivonne's mother, Coleen, and bundled by year. They range from 1915 to 1925. If Chivonne was born in 1899, that would make her age sixteen in 1925."

Why would she be writing letters to her mother if she were living at home? Winifred wondered. She picked up the 1915 stack, untied the pink ribbon, and fanned through them. "Huh. Shannon? Are any of the others postmarked?"

She checked the top letter in each ribboned bundle. "That's odd. No. It appears that none of them are postmarked."

Winifred removed the letter from the first blue-tinted envelope and handed the second one to Shannon. Both women sat down in chairs on opposite sides of the table. "How about we read these in order? Hopefully, she clues her mom into what's happening during her teenage years." Less than a minute went by when she looked up and set the letter in her lap. "Shannon! Are you seeing what I'm seeing?" Winifred exclaimed with excitement. "There's no postmark because these are diaries!"

<hr />

It was nearly noon when Shannon stood. "I'm getting hungry. I think I can find enough ingredients for chicken noodle soup and tuna salad sandwiches. We still have half a loaf of Italian bread."

Winifred followed her to the kitchen and climbed onto one of the stools lining the counter. "We've got a good picture of Chivonne's life so far. I wonder why she chose to write letters instead of the traditional book journals?"

Shannon opened a can of tuna and scooped the contents into a bowl. "The first letter that I read mentions how she had found her grandmother's journal and read about her life in Ireland and the difficult ocean voyage to America. Maybe she didn't want someone in the future to come across typical journals and read about her private life. Perhaps she figured that no one would be interested in reading uninteresting letters to her mother."

"Seems plausible. I wish she had spelled out people's names instead of just using initials. I'm not even sure if I'm looking at first or last names, except for the rare instances where she uses both initials. She gives such detailed accounts of what she is wearing and events, yet keeps people private."

"So much for our 'married man' affair. This new information was *never* on my radar," Shannon acknowledged.

"Yeah. I'm happy, and it gives new light on the Harrigans." Winifred paused as Shannon set a mug of coffee on the counter. "I know my father was a member of the Masonic order, but I didn't know it went all the way back to the original Harrigans from Ireland."

"How nice that your"—Shannon paused to calculate the date in her head—"your great-great-great-grandfather was able to hook up with the Detroit Lodge of the Freemasons shortly after the family arrived. That would have helped them get established quickly."

"It must have been the luck of the Irish that the man who became his best friend was also a Lodge brother from the Grosse Pointe elite. Who then became Chivonne's godfather and gave her the Pierce-Arrow for her sixteenth birthday."

"But why, during the summer of 1917, did he send her off to France with a boatload of money to live with friends in Paris?"

Winifred wondered the same thing as Shannon placed a bowl of steaming chicken noodle soup and a tuna salad sandwich in front of her. "We need to go back and reread the 1917 letters and match those up with the photos. There were references to a newly arrived immigrant that she befriended."

"Yeah, I remember but discounted him because he's only mentioned for a month or two. My focus was on her Grosse Pointe friends and parties." Shannon set her food on the counter and climbed onto the stool.

"Chivonne picked up a hitchhiker on her way back from Grosse Pointe. She had a hard time understanding him because his English was so bad. He was impressed with her car, so they drove around for a while. She felt sorry for him and offered to show him places around town. They would meet on a corner, somewhere along Gratiot Avenue, and spend the day together."

"I don't know Detroit. Was that street near her home?"

"At that time, the Harrigans lived in the Cork Town area, where early Irish immigrants tended to settle. It's a little pocket bordered by Interstate 75, where it makes a loop to skirt downtown. Gratiot is on the other side of the downtown area. A lot of Italians would have been living in that area. Grosse Pointe is further up along the Detroit River."

"What you're telling me is Chivonne could have met a newly arrived Italian."

Winifred tried to reconstruct Detroit during that period. "There were no highways back then, so she would have taken streets through downtown to Jefferson and on up to Grosse Pointe. I guess it is possible that the hitchhiker could have been Lorenzo Barilli. I wish we knew what he looked like back then."

Shannon pulled her cell phone from her pocket. "That's what Google is for." A few seconds later, she turned the screen toward Winifred. "Got it! Lots of pictures of him but only in later years. Wow! It says here that Lorenzo Barilli arrived at Ellis Island on February 2, 1917, from Palermo, Sicily. He then traveled by train to Detroit, Michigan, to live with his uncle Luigi Barilli. The timing is right." She continued reading. "This is interesting. He married at twenty-five and had a son, Anthony. Lorenzo Barilli passed away alone at his winter home on Big Pine Key, Florida, on December 31, 1979." Shannon scrolled through the photos. "I found an early picture."

"I'll get the one of the guy leaning against the Pierce-Arrow." Freddie headed to the great room and the stack of photos from the early years. "Got it," she said as she climbed onto the stool.

They matched Chivonne's hitchhiker with the picture on Shannon's cell.

Winifred's stomach churned. "Looks like I could be related to a mob boss." She looked pleadingly into her friend's eyes to say it wasn't so. She had made a mistake and was looking at a different Lorenzo Barilli. At that moment, her cell phone rang. "It's Jason."

Winifred put the call on speaker. "Hello, Jason. Did you find something?"

"Yeah. I'm turning into your drive now."

"I'll turn off the alarm," Winifred answered, then ended the call. "Wonder what he's got!" she said as she jumped down from the stool and headed to the alarm panel next to the door.

"Couldn't you just do that from the app on your phone?" Shannon asked.

"Oh, yeah. I guess I'm not thinking straight after our bombshell news." She opened the door as Jason parked and took the stairs two at a time. He was carrying a large manila envelope.

"Good afternoon," he said as he walked into the room and tossed his jacket on a chair. Then they both joined Shannon at the kitchen counter.

"Freddie and I just finished lunch. I have enough tuna salad to make another sandwich if you'd like one."

"That would be great. I wanted to get you these camera shots as soon as I could." Jason spread half-a-dozen letter-size photos on the counter, while Shannon made his sandwich. "Have you seen this van?"

Winifred studied each one before answering. "This one." She pointed to a silver cargo van with a large lightning-bolt logo and Zappy Electric on the driver's door panel. "It was parked across the street from the entrance to the Lodge. The sign caught my attention as we left after dinner." She thought back to the moment. "It seemed out of place. The driver was just sitting there like he was waiting for someone."

Shannon set a plate with the sandwich and a handful of potato chips in front of Jason. She then bent over and scanned the images on each page. She pointed to one. "While I was waiting for the diagnostic test at the Cadillac dealer, I noticed that van. Only the sign on the door was for Detroit Auto Parts. I wondered if he were really delivering parts this far north or was only visiting. Odd color for a commercial van—like it was custom-ordered."

"Good point. I didn't catch that. Here's another one that shows him sitting in a lot across from the bakery. There are multiple street cams that picked him up. Sherman and I are positive that this is your burglar."

"I've never seen that guy before. But Shannon and I just figured out why he's tracking me." She glanced at her friend with a look asking whether she should spill the beans or not. Shannon nodded her agreement. "Turns out I could very well be the great-granddaughter of Lorenzo Barilli."

"Holy crap, Freddie. Are you sure?"

"Ninety-nine percent. This afternoon Shannon and I are going to read the letters from the period after Chivonne arrives in Paris looking for that last one percent."

Jason finished his sandwich in silence while sorting out in his head everything he now knew. He pushed the plate to the side. "This guy seems to show up everywhere you have been, or should I say everywhere your car has been. But is he also *listening*? Perhaps he was breaking into the garage to place a bug."

"If he was attempting to place one on the car, did he place one—or more—around the outside of the cabin?" Winifred asked.

"If so, he now knows that you've stumbled onto the critical bit of information."

"Can you search the outside of the house for the bug?" Shannon asked.

"Not worth the time to search. This place is way too big, and it—or they—could be around windows, doors, and on the porches."

Winifred felt a massive headache coming on; she hadn't felt this out-of-control since she had gotten the news about Danny's death. "So, what do we do? Pack up and leave?"

"Don't do anything until you hear back from me. But for now, I would look for any additional proof in the letters. You're safe here until Monday when you can hook up with Harry Lincoln and sign the documents."

"Okay. Shannon and I will plan on leaving Monday."

Jason put his finger to his lips, then began a text message.

I'm going to put out a statewide search for stolen vans fitting that description. I did a local search earlier and came up with nothing. Read the letters as you mentioned, then pack everything up and put it in a safe place. Keep talking as usual, but remember that someone is probably listening. If you decide to go through with the inheritance, call Lincoln's office and leave a voicemail that you will see him on Monday. That will let our bad guy know of the time frame and give the police department time to drop a net over the city and track him down. I will only text with important information—do the same.

"Okay, that wraps it up for me. Give me a call if you find out any new information in the letters. Otherwise, I'll talk to you tomorrow." Jason grabbed his coat and headed toward the front door.

"Jason, I almost forgot. Jimmy is getting the gang together tomorrow for a wine crawl. Should I call and have him cancel it?" Freddie asked.

Jason nodded his head to cancel and motioned with his finger that he would make the call, then spoke in a slightly raised tone. "No, I think it would be great for the two of you to get out and have a fun afternoon. Safety in numbers as they say. And I'll be joining you." He then opened the door and stepped onto the porch. He ran his hand along the outer edge of the doorframe and gave Freddie a thumbs-up sign before heading down the steps.

After locking the door and turning on the security system, Winifred stood, as if nailed to the spot, wondering what to do next, and wondered how they were going to continue with any scrap of normalcy knowing they would have to monitor every word. They needed to assume the cabin was bugged even though they didn't know for sure. "This is going to be a long, difficult afternoon."

"No doubt," Shannon confirmed. "I guess we begin where we left off with the Paris letters."

Winifred shrugged her shoulders in agreement, and they both headed into the great room and their usual chairs around the large square coffee table. "Want me to build a fire?"

Shannon glanced at the pile of cold, gray ashes. They pretty much depicted the feeling in the room. "No. I don't believe even a warm fire is going to help my mood."

"I must agree, and not worth the trouble. Maybe tonight," Winifred added in a somber tone.

Twenty minutes later, Shannon tossed the letter she had been reading onto the table. "I don't know about you, but this isn't working. I can't concentrate, and after what we found yesterday, I don't know if this even matters."

"I agree. This whole project for the last two days was to determine, once and for all, whether Lincoln's DNA report could be correct. Turns out it is, and I *am* directly related to Barilli. Unfortunately, we've connected the dots." Winifred surveyed the many stacks of letters and photos strewn around the room. "No point in continuing. All we're going to get out of another day of reading is eyestrain."

Shannon stood. "I suggest we return everything to the attic. Come back down and choose a movie from your vast collection, then spend the rest of the afternoon in front of that giant screen TV." She paused a beat. "And we have steak and baked potatoes for dinner."

"Sounds like a plan to me. I'll even get a roaring fire going." *And we won't have to think before we speak.*

CHAPTER NINE

"Fire!" Winifred shouted as she was awoken by the smell of smoke and flames dancing across her bedroom windows. "Shannon! Fire!" she screamed while grabbing her cell phone and ran for the door, then out into the hallway.

Shannon opened her bedroom door and ran out into the arms of Freddie. "I heard you scream, then saw the flames."

"We need to run for the front door! The back of the house is on fire!" Winifred shouted.

They ran down the stairs and through the great room. So far, the rooms were free of smoke, and both women made it easily to the front entrance. Winifred pulled open the door to a cloud of smoke and a spray of water. "Run!" she shouted.

After racing across the smoke-filled porch and down the slippery steps, Winifred and Shannon reached the water-soaked lawn with the sprinklers going. At that moment, the driveway filled with flashing red lights and the sound of blaring sirens. Two fire trucks, the fire chief's car, police car, and Jason all came to a stop before them.

Winifred stood, glued to the spot, dazed. She felt the spray of water smacking against her ankles as she watched vehicle doors open and men scramble out.

Standing in the midst of the spray, Shannon bent slightly, knees together as she tugged at the front and back edge of the oversize T-shirt that she had grabbed from a dresser drawer after being awoken from a sound sleep by the word "fire." The white shirt with the images of grapes, surrounded by the words "Be Happy Drink More Wine," barely covered her butt cheeks.

Winifred easily read the thoughts in the grin on each man's face. *She's naked!*

The chief quickly took off his coat and ran over to wrap it around Shannon's shoulders.

"Well, I'll be dammed," Jason said as he looked up at the cabin. He sounded amazed. "It works!"

Winifred walked to his side. The cabin sat under a spray of water. Jets drenched the shingles on the roof as additional ones on the ground covered the sidewalls. The lawn sprinklers had the grass and shrubs and trees well doused.

"What the hell is going on?" demanded the fire chief. "Can someone shut this thing off?"

Winifred scrolled through the apps on her phone. Within seconds, all was quiet, except for the soft hiss of steam coming from under the porch.

The chief turned toward the truck. Two firemen stood holding a limp hose. "Put that thing down and check the perimeter of the house." He turned back to Jason. "Sounds like you know what the hell happened out here."

"Danny Forrester was designing a new app for a group of residents in LA. He used the cabin as a test site. I helped him with it. Unfortunately, he was killed in the accident before he could do the final test."

"Interesting." The chief turned toward Freddie. "How come I wasn't told about this little detail?"

"I wasn't directly involved. What I know is that a group of three homeowners who live in the hills outside of Los Angeles had asked Danny if he could design an app and system to help protect their homes from the wildfires that were becoming more frequent. He'd been working on it for over a year. After his death, a few things fell through the cracks. I totally forgot about this one."

"Danny's biggest problem was how to store enough water on the three adjoining properties to last for hours of operation. He ended up building three huge tanks or reservoirs along the back walls of the properties. Each tank, made of concrete block, was lined with stainless steel. A lid could be taken off during the rainy season to help keep the tanks filled and covered during dry times."

"Amazing. This application could be adapted to many types of fire-prone areas."

"Also, Chief—it's intuitive. If the sensors detect the threat as mild, then the yard is saturated. If actual fire is detected, then the roof and wall sprays kick on."

The two firemen returned. "The fire's out, Chief. But you'd better have a look."

"Okay. Pack up the truck and head back to the station. I'll check the perimeter. Jason, you and Officer Sherman come with me." He looked over at Freddie and Shannon. "You ladies are soaked and must be freezing. Go back inside. I'll stop in before I leave."

⚎

It was nearly an hour before Jason, Officer Sherman, and the fire chief entered the kitchen. Shannon set three mugs of steaming coffee on the counter.

"Thank you. I think all three of us could use this right about now," Jason said. "I'm sorry, Freddie. Both porches will have to be rebuilt. We found a considerable amount of accelerant that was used. If it hadn't been for Danny's new sprinkler system, this house would have gone up like a box of matches."

"This is now an official arson investigation," said the chief. "I'll have a crew out here this morning to do a thorough search and take photos. You can stay here, Freddie, but use the side door near the garage."

"I'll be putting out an APB for the guy we caught in your security cam," Officer Sherman added.

The rising sun was breaking through the night sky with streaks of pink and gold as Freddie, Shannon, and Jason watched the last of the vehicles exiting down the driveway.

Shannon wrapped her arms around Freddie as she began to shake.

"Freddie, are you okay?" Jason asked.

Winifred looked up with anger in her eyes.

"Someone wants me dead."

CHAPTER TEN

Winifred broke free of Shannon's arm. "We're leaving, *now!*" she shouted.

"Freddie, relax, deep breaths. Let's walk through what you are feeling." Shannon snapped into her therapist mode. "It's Sunday morning. Think about stepping back a moment, and let the professionals do their jobs." There was no response from her patient. "Freddie, you're safe. We can leave first thing in the morning and be in Lincoln's office, sign the documents, and be on our way back to Chicago by noon."

"That fucking bastard tried to burn down my family's cabin—and *kill* me—*kill* us!" Winifred angrily waved her arm at Shannon. "Don't give me your therapist shit—this is war!"

Jason stood silently, feeling Freddie's pain. This house had withstood every type of storm Mother Nature could throw at it, and it only became stronger, but even more, it had survived 140 years of feisty, Irish Harrigans. Despite that strength, it was nearly brought down by an arson's match. There was nothing he could say to ease the hurt, the injustice, or the plain meanness of the act. He felt the same.

Shannon moved to hug Freddie, then thought better of it. She squeezed her hand instead. "I need to go upstairs and put some clothes on. Maybe even a quick shower. I smell like smoke and gasoline." She gave Jason a nod before heading for the staircase. "I won't be long."

Jason followed Freddie into the kitchen and watched as she eased onto a stool. She rested her head on bent arms—her shoulders went limp. He climbed onto the next stool and waited. Her breathing slowed. "I'm listening," he quietly offered.

"I didn't say anything," Winifred answered, without moving her head.

"I know. Just wanted to let you know I'm here for you."

She lifted her head and looked deep into his eyes.

"Why is this inheritance such a big deal? Why is it worth killing over?"

"I don't have a clue. What I do know is this guy isn't going to get far. The police will find his van, and he'll be in custody by the end of the day."

"What if he ditches the van, steals a car, and comes back to finish the job?"

"He's good. He won't risk getting caught. My guess is that he's already on the way out of town."

"I don't know, Jason."

"If you'll feel safer, I'll stay here with you today. The fire investigators will be arriving soon, and I can help coordinate."

Shannon arrived wearing tight-fitting jeans and a black cable-knit sweater and smelling of lavender-scented soap and shampoo. "I agree. I'd feel better if Jason were here."

"Jason, you're not getting it. I don't want to be here! Someone nearly killed me!"

"And I was supposed to be *collateral damage!*" Shannon added.

Winifred picked up her phone from the counter and punched in a number from her contacts. "Hello, Harry, this is Winifred Forrester. I've decided to accept. I'll be at your office later this afternoon around three to sign the documents." She set her phone on the counter. "It went to voicemail." She drummed her fingers on the granite. "He'll call."

"Freddie, are you sure about this? You and Shannon are safe here. Give it the day. The guy won't come back."

"Take a whiff, Jason. The place reeks. I've found what I was looking for." Her phone buzzed. "Why prolong this nightmare?"

Shannon went to the sink and filled the coffeepot with water. "I don't know about you two, but I need caffeine."

Freddie answered the call. "Hello, Harry. I see you got my message."

"Winifred, I'm glad that you've made a decision. But it's Sunday. It is *very* early on Sunday—the sun isn't even up yet. Can't this wait until tomorrow?"

"Things have heated up a bit here, Harry. I need to sign whatever documents you have while I still can."

"But, Winifred—"

"This is not up for negotiation. Your office, Harry—three o'clock!" Freddie ended the call.

"Wow. I do believe a few of those Barilli genes are surfacing," Jason teased.

"I knew there was another side of you lurking below the surface," Shannon said as she surveyed the contents of the refrigerator. "Okay, we have six eggs, half a pound of bacon, two strip steaks, enough leftover potatoes for hash browns, cheddar cheese, and a handful of strawberries—I hope you're hungry."

CHAPTER ELEVEN

Winifred parked in front of the high-rise office building at two forty-five. No need to use the adjacent garage—it was the Sunday afternoon following the Thanksgiving holiday. The downtown streets were deserted. She was about to shut down the engine when an incoming call registered on the Escalade's info screen. "It's Jason." She pressed accept. "Hello, good timing; we just arrived."

"Looks like you made pretty good time. Hey, I've got news for you." Jason paused a beat. "The silver van was found at the airport. This guy is a pro. The inside was wiped clean—not a print anywhere. That caused us to think FBI, so we sent them the photos. Within minutes, we got quite an impressive dossier on Aleksy Petrowski."

"So, what you're telling me is whoever wants me out of the way is paying big bucks for the job."

"Yeah, but you can relax. He took the first plane out of Traverse City—he's in Cleveland at the moment. I'm sending you the dossier now."

"And the cabin?"

"The two porches will have to be rebuilt. I'll get a cleaning crew in tomorrow. Don't worry about anything here—I've got it."

"Thanks Jason; you're the best. I'll touch base after our meeting with Harry."

⚒

The elevator doors closed behind Winifred and Shannon. "Wow! I wasn't expecting to walk into the Metamora Hunt Club. I'm betting Harry Lincoln paid big bucks for this. I'm wondering which clientele demographics he's trying to impress."

The room was void of any human activity. The wildlife lurking down from the Robert Bateman paintings challenged the women's right to break the silence of a Sunday afternoon. The large oriental rug silenced the sounds of their heels.

Harry Lincoln walked into the room. "Mrs. Forrester, I'm hoping this visit turns out to be as important as you implied. I left out-of-town family to fend for themselves," he voiced while directing the ladies down the hall to his office.

Upon entering his domain, Shannon leaned over Freddie's shoulder and whispered, "I wasn't expecting this either."

"Mr. Lincoln, I would like you to meet my friend, Shannon." Harry seemed to take a few seconds before shaking her hand.

"It's a pleasure to meet you, Doctor Mulaney. You have a very impressive practice and reputation."

As she walked to the desk, Winifred wondered how he knew about Shannon. His thorough investigation of her was now made very clear. Perhaps he was using this little bit of unsolicited knowledge of Shannon to prove just how good he really is. She pulled several sheets from a manila envelope and set them on the desk in front of Harry. "Do you know this guy?"

He fanned the letter-size photos in front of him. "No. I don't."

Winifred then set a small black plastic device on the desk. "That little thing fell out from under my engine while Shannon and I were having dinner on Thursday."

Harry picked it up. "It's a high-tech tracking device. Very expensive. I have several."

"His name is Aleksy Petrowski. He was found an hour ago in an FBI database. He gets around—international. A type of mercenary who will do anything for the right fee." Winifred paused for a reaction. "He, too, is very expensive for those who know how to find him. I'll send you his dossier."

All three had remained standing while Harry studied the photos. "Please sit," he said and did the same. "Are you sure this guy was tracking you because of the Barilli deal?"

"Look, as you well know from your investigation of me, I own a company that develops apps. If a competitor wants to get some kind of inside information, he or they are going to bug our offices, not me during a holiday. I come up with the applications. I know nothing about the tech side—and anyone in the industry knows that."

"By the way, I assume since you are here to sign the inheritance documents, you've gotten to know Chivonne Harrigan-O'Reilly?"

Winifred inhaled deeply. "Yes. Shannon and I spent days looking at photos and reading letters. It was young, teenage hormones that briefly took control of my great-great-grandmother's emotions. It didn't last long."

"Long enough," Harry said as he opened the center desk drawer and pulled out a folder.

"What happens if something were to happen to Winifred? Who would then gain possession of the thousand acres in the Florida Keys?" Shannon asked.

"Monroe County. I don't have the details. But it's been in the works for years. Something about increasing the Key Deer habitat."

"Are you saying a wildlife preserve?" Shannon asked incredulously.

"From what I know, the whole island is."

Shannon looked over at Freddie with raised eyebrows. "So, all this cloak-and-dagger stuff is to keep land in its current state—for deer?"

Winifred scooted closer to the desk. "Okay, I give up. Where do I sign?"

After receiving her copy of the document, Freddie pulled the rest of the photos from the envelope and pushed them toward Harry. "These were taken by the Traverse City Fire Department. As you can see, the front and back porches are damaged to the point of needing to be replaced. There are also signs of blackened stone and logs around the perimeter of my family's cabin. That man, Aleksy Petrowski, tried to murder Shannon and me last night. The only thing that saved us was an app that my husband had designed to save homes in Southern California from wildfires. He was using the cabin as a test site—fortunately, the app worked."

Lincoln studied the photos. "I'm sorry. That had to be frightening. I understand now why you didn't want to stay there until tomorrow."

"I want to hire Harry Lincoln Investigations."

"To do what?" Harry asked, as if he weren't hearing her correctly.

"I want you to find out who wants me dead."

<hr />

Winifred pressed the start button on the dashboard. The Cadillac Escalade's powerful engine roared to life. She pulled away from the curb. "What do you think?"

"I like Harry Lincoln. His office space threw me, but he does a thorough investigation for his clients without giving everything he's uncovered. He proved that when you introduced me as your friend—first name only. Then he acknowledges me as Doctor Mulaney."

"I don't believe he knew Petrowski. Which tells me there is an unknown player out there. Lincoln was hired to find a possible heir. He found me—as unlikely as that may be. The case should be closed."

"But it isn't. And I don't believe for a moment that Monroe County is hiring the likes of Petrowski to stop you." Shannon reached into the back seat and grabbed her briefcase. "I was surprised when you hired him."

"When I realized that Lincoln was genuinely surprised by what he was looking at in those photos and he didn't have a clue who Petrowski was . . . well, killing me was about something else. Or at least another aspect that Harry isn't a part of."

"I get it. But if I understand the process, you've only accepted Harry Lincoln's findings. Nothing is final and legal until you meet with the attorney in Key Largo."

"Right. Tomorrow, I spend the day at Forrester & Forrester and make sure everything is in place so I can be away for a month or so. Danny made sure we had the best, most talented staff. The company can get along just fine without me—we can still have our weekly meeting through Zoom."

"And you and I can have Zoom meetings," Shannon added as she began typing on her laptop.

Winifred glanced over at her passenger. "What are you doing?"

"Checking out the National Key Deer Refuge." Shannon turned the screen so Freddie could see the images. "Awwwww! The little deer are so cute. It's not a confined refuge area. It's basically all of Big Pine Key. You need to see these photos, Freddie. The little guys are so tiny and walk around the island. Imagine them on your land." She turned the screen back and continued typing. "Maybe I should go with you and help. This map shows an airport on Marathon—it's close to Big Pine Key."

"Maybe you should stay in Chicago and help your patients."

CHAPTER TWELVE

Winifred spent Monday morning at Forrester & Forrester conducting her usual weekly staff meeting, at which time she informed them of her trip to Florida. She then stopped by the post office to have her mail forwarded to her secretary, Caroline Stevens, nicknamed Caro. Freddie's last stop was the local AAA to pick up maps and travel information for the route. Sure, as someone deeply buried in the tech industry, she relied on the Escalade's GPS and Waze that was installed on her phone, but Winifred also had a healthy appreciation for old school. What she didn't want to hear was about severe weather moving across the region. If she left early enough, she might be able to miss the worst of the snowstorm due to hit Indianapolis late Tuesday morning.

The gate to the underground parking garage opened at exactly five fifteen the following morning. Winifred wanted to get far enough away from Chicago before the six o'clock rush hour traffic began. The agent at the AAA office recommended taking three days to make the trip, but that was too long on the road, especially if someone didn't want her to reach Key Largo.

Perhaps she should have flown and rented a car. But it was a little late for those thoughts. Google had calculated the drive time at twenty hours—an easy two-day trip for someone who enjoyed driving. Danny was the nervous one behind the wheel, which put Winifred in the driver's seat for family road trips. She'd made a reservation at a Marriott south of Atlanta for the night, which would give her eleven hours to Key Largo, including meal and potty breaks. She'd called the attorney's office to say she would be there between four and five on Wednesday. The plan was perfect.

The first of the snow began on I-65 an hour out of Gary, Indiana. She'd been in and out of snow squalls by the time she passed the Lafayette exits. It was eleven o'clock when she eased the Escalade onto an exit ramp of what looked like a heavy commercial district with several gas stations and a Cracker Barrel outside of Indianapolis. After topping off the tank, the next stop was the restaurant across the street. With all Cracker Barrels, you have to weave your way through a plethora of enticing merchandise before reaching the hostess stand in the far corner. This time of the year it was stocked to the hilt with Christmas items. A bright-red knit vest trimmed in white faux fur caught her eye. Winifred stopped to see if they had her size. Then common sense took over—she was on her way to the Florida Keys—no need for anything fancy and warm. She continued past all the other glittery things that called out to her.

Winifred surveyed the half-full dining room. She needed comfort food and the warm fire blazing in the fireplace. After being seated, she ordered coffee and a chicken potpie with southern biscuits and jam. While waiting for her food to arrive, she pulled up the weather map on her phone. Nothing on the screen looked good, at least nothing north of Cincinnati where she would catch I-75 and continue south. An hour later, Winifred stood, slipped into her long white puffy coat, and pointed her key fob toward the Escalade and pressed auto start.

Standing on the long porch lined with rocking chairs, Winifred's heart sank at the sight of her SUV now covered in an inch of snow. She pulled the hood up over her head and headed to the rear door and the snow brush. Five minutes later, she climbed onto the warm driver's seat, unzipped her coat, and restarted the engine, then glanced at the clock—noon. The GPS screen gave her ETA in Atlanta at eight o'clock. She could still make it even with the storm.

Giant flakes of snow were coming down with a vengeance, causing near whiteout conditions. Winifred crept along in the right-hand lane following in the tracks of a tractor trailer. Not a snowplow in sight. Traffic slowed to a crawl as she passed cars that had slid off the road landing in all directions. Jackknifed semis blocked the left two lanes. One o'clock—if she hadn't stopped for an early lunch break, she could have been one of those poor stranded motorists. Then, not more than half an hour later, she drove out of it. She was down to wet pavement, and the sky began to clear. She was making good time until the I-75 split north of Cincinnati. Between road construction and heavy traffic crossing over the Ohio River, she'd lost an hour. GPS was now getting her into Atlanta at nine thirty.

Light rain began south of Lexington and then turned heavy as she approached the mountains of Tennessee. During her lunch break back in Indianapolis, she'd calculated a five-hour drive to Knoxville, where she found an exit with gas stations and an Applebee's. But it had taken more than six hours, and she had been on the road for over thirteen. Winifred zipped her coat and pulled up the hood as she stood at the pump stiff from sitting behind the wheel for so many hours and mentally drained. Her body needed comfort food, and her brain needed to look at something other than traffic. The wind had picked up, and the temperature was dropping. She'd give herself an hour to rest and arrive in Atlanta around ten thirty. Not ideal but doable.

For mile after mile, the Escalade's headlights illuminated signs for the Great Smoky Mountains National Park, warning signs for possible fog and ice. Winifred rounded a bend to a sea of red brake lights for as far as she could see. Traffic slowed to a crawl while giant signs to her right proclaimed a Pilot Flying J truck stop at the next exit. Whatever was ahead wasn't good, and she had already spent hours sitting in stopped traffic. Getting off what had turned into a parking lot could be possible if she used the berm. The heavy vehicle slid to the right as the front tires hit the icy pavement. Winifred let up on the gas and let the SUV right itself. She then crept along until she reached the exit and then fought to keep control on the icy surface until she reached the safety of Pilot's parking lot. Minutes went by as she sat under the bright overhead lights, her hands tightly gripping the steering wheel as her heart began to slow. *Thank you, God, for keeping me safe on my journey and putting this island of warmth and food in my path.*

Nearly every seat was taken in the food area of the truck stop. She ordered a large coffee at the counter, then glanced around the room. Mostly men of all ages and appearances huddled around tables. If not in heated discussions about the weather, then they were on their phones. She spied an open seat opposite a middle-aged fellow with a full salt-and-pepper beard and long hair. There were only two options for her at that point—either take her coffee and go back to the car or ask if she could join him. He looked harmless enough, so she walked over to his table.

"Excuse me. Do you mind if I join you? I really could use a break from what looks like a parking lot out there," Winifred said with a smile that she hoped would win him over.

The rather grizzly man stood and offered his hand. "Please sit. Name's Charlie. You look a little frayed around the edges. Been on the road long?"

"Winifred," she said while shaking his hand. "I started out this morning at six. Do you know what happened?" she asked while unzipping her coat and pulling out the chair to sit.

"This sudden ice storm caused a fifteen-car-truck pileup at the bottom of the mountain. I've been here two hours and likely to be here another two hours while they clear the mess."

"That's not good."

"Where you headin'?"

"Atlanta for the night, then on to Key Largo in the morning."

Charlie laughed. His blue eyes twinkled. "Bet you wish you were there now."

"You have no idea," Winifred said, as if she had the weight of the world on her shoulders.

"Where ya comin' from?"

"Chicago." She took a sip of hot coffee.

"Oh. Well then, a bit of ice doesn't freak you out like a lot of these idiots who shouldn't be on the road."

"No, but these mountains add a new dimension."

"Be glad you ain't drivin' in West Virginia. Now there's a challenge for ya. Folks in those fancy RVs take this route instead of Route Seventy-Seven so they don't have to negotiate those conditions. This is a piece of cake."

"I know what that stretch of highway is like, but only in the summer. Even then, you need to stay alert."

Charlie nodded toward the road. "It's gonna be bad from here to Chattanooga. I'm running empty, so I'll spend the night here and head out in the mornin'."

"Hopefully, they will clear the accidents and open up soon, and I can be on my way to Atlanta."

"Is your vehicle comfortable?" Charlie asked.

"Very. Why?"

"You might want to spend the night here. The food isn't bad, and they have showers. This rain is due to stop in a few hours, and tomorrow is looking clear and dry."

Winifred considered the option. "I think I'll take my chances."

"Unless you're talkin' life and death, you might want to stay," Charlie said as he stood to leave.

"It might just be," Winifred answered as she took another long sip.

She ordered a bowl of nachos and a Coke, then called the hotel to inform them that she would be very late and not to give up her room. The only option available at that moment was to settle back and watch the traffic sitting idle on the highway. As Charlie predicted, nearly two hours later, vehicles began to move.

The large Marriott sign shined its welcoming glow as she pulled into the parking lot at midnight.

CHAPTER THIRTEEN

Late the next afternoon, Winifred followed the Overseas Highway after leaving the Florida Turnpike in Florida City. For the next forty-five minutes, she drove through what appeared to be desolate swampland before entering the first sign of a town and signs that she had finally arrived in Key Largo. The pleasant-sounding female voice that had kept Winifred company for the past two days through the Cadillac Escalade's GPS system told her that she had reached her destination on the left. The clock on the info screen showed 4:50 p.m. She pulled into a spot in front of a single-story stucco building, painted a seafoam green with a bright yellow door and shutters. A vine of bright pink flowers climbed haphazardly over the left side of the doorway. Every muscle in Winifred's body seemed to stiffen as she removed herself from the SUV. She had changed out of sweats and boots and into tan cotton slacks, a short-sleeved turquoise top, and sandals at the Florida Welcome Center. She closed the passenger door and shook her head in dismay—her beautiful black Escalade looked like she'd driven through the apocalypse.

Winifred entered the front door and was immediately greeted by a very attractive, middle-aged Latina woman. "You must be Mrs. Forrester. Thank you for calling ahead and letting us know when you would be arriving. Mr. Gonzales is finishing a phone call; he shouldn't be long. Please have a seat."

Winifred laughed. "I've been sitting for over eleven hours; what I'd really like is a quick jog around the block."

"You must be exhausted. How was the trip?"

"We don't have enough time for me to discuss yesterday, but I made great time today—except for the wildfires. At times, I wasn't sure if I was driving through smoke or clouds of bugs!"

"It's been unusually dry this season, and fires do happen. I remember one year when we had fires on both coasts at the same time. Sections of I-75 on the west and I-95 on the east were closed."

"I detect a slight accent. You weren't born here?"

"No. My family immigrated to Miami from Cuba when I was five. I've worked for Mr. Gonzales for the past fifteen years."

Winifred glanced around the waiting room. Whitewashed paneled walls met sand-colored ceramic tile. Several hefty rattan chairs, covered in cushions with large palm fronds over a black background, were arranged in small seating groups. Lamps in the shape of dolphins hovered over side tables. Prints of the colorful Florida foliage and landscape dotted the walls, giving the comfortable space a welcoming vibe.

"Can I get you some coffee or tea while you wait?" Rosa asked with a smile. "It's no trouble."

"No. Thank you. I've been mainlining caffeine since five this morning," joked Winifred. "What I really want is to finally get to the house, get out of these clothes, and jump in the shower. I smell like a chimney."

Rosa's smile faded. "You don't know, do you?"

"Know what?" Winifred asked as the inner door opened.

"Mrs. Forrester, I'm so happy to meet you."

The man approaching was probably in his middle seventies. He was a bit on the short side, with only a slight pouch. His thick, wavy gray hair was cropped rather short. Charcoal-colored eyes hovered beneath dark bushy eyebrows. He strode forward with an air of confidence and perhaps a man who was accustomed to respect—or was it power?

"I'm Edwardo Gonzales. Your attorney." After shaking hands, she followed him into his office. Winifred immediately noticed the print of a large fishing boat on the wall behind his desk.

"Ah! You like her?" he exclaimed as he sat behind the heavily carved mahogany desk. "My pride and joy. She's docked at the yacht club before you get into Key Largo."

Winifred remembered seeing the signs and the road that branched off to the side. A boat that big would account for keeping in good shape, as well as his dark tan and heavily wrinkled skin. "Yes. I did notice it. Having the boat so close must be nice."

"During high traffic times, it might as well be in Miami." He must have noticed her puzzled expression and continued. "I'm sure you noticed that there is only one road into the Keys once you leave Florida City. That means bumper-to-bumper traffic during peak times. It can take nearly an hour to drive those few miles to the club."

"It didn't seem that bad. Mostly one lane except for the few passing sections."

"You are here on a Wednesday. Middle of the week. Try to get here on Friday afternoons or leave on Sundays—that is something for you to remember."

"Hopefully, I won't have to consider high traffic times on Big Pine Key."

"You will," Edwardo said bluntly as he placed a manila envelope and a heavily carved box on the desk. It looked like a cheap reproduction of a pirate's chest with an ornate rounded lid and lots of nailheads. "We've been holding this until Lorenzo Barilli's rightful heir could be substantiated and the estate finally closed before the county takes possession of the lands." His warm, charming demeanor seemed to chill.

"Up until this past weekend, I wasn't convinced that I *was* the heir. I figured Harry Lincoln, the private detective you hired, could have been lying just to close the case before the deadline." Winifred's voice filled with defeat and bone-chilling weariness. "But I left his office a week ago today, with him asking how much I knew about my great-great-grandmother. I spent the next three days studying photos and reading her letters. I was ninety-nine percent convinced that it was possible when a high-tech tracking device was found under my car and then Saturday night an arsonist tried to burn down my cabin—with me in it." Winifred paused to collect herself. "So, yes. Now I'm one hundred percent sure. As sure as I can be without a birth certificate."

Gonzales removed several light-blue folders and turned to pages in each. "I'll need your signatures on these documents, which I will file with the county tomorrow." He pressed a button on an intercom unit and Rosa entered a moment later.

After notarizing each signature, Rosa left the office with the blue folders, officially making Winifred the owner of a thousand acres of property on Big Pine Key, Florida.

"Well, Mrs. Forrester, this completes our part of the transaction." He placed his hands on the edge of the desk and pushed off to stand. "He reached into his pocket and pulled out a pair of keys and handed them to her. If that's all, you can be on your way. It's about an hour and a half's drive if you don't run into heavy traffic or an accident on the Seven Mile Bridge."

Wow, this was it, Winifred thought. Sign some papers, take your keys, and go? Never mind that someone out there wants her dead, and he may be the key that unlocks the mystery. Not a chance. She wasn't leaving without answers.

"No. This is not everything, Mr. Gonzales." Winifred inhaled deeply to steady her frayed nerves. "Not by a long shot." She felt her control slipping away. She didn't want to be seen as a hysterical female, but she could feel the fury roiling up inside her. "I've just spent two days driving for nearly thirty hours on a trip that should have taken twenty-two. I've driven through snowstorms in Illinois, ice storms in Tennessee, and wildfires in central Florida." Winifred took another deep breath and let it out slowly. "Do you really think for even a second that another hour or two is going to concern me?" She stood, palms resting on the edge of the desk, and held his gaze. "I want to know exactly what I am going to find when I get to this inheritance that I don't want. And I want the details now!"

Winifred watched as Mr. Gonzales crumbled in around himself. All signs of bravado melted as he folded back into his chair. "I thought you knew. I thought Harry Lincoln and your lawyers explained everything to you. The place is closed up—has been for decades. You know against hurricanes. Everyone down here has their shutters at the ready during the season. Not to worry, we have someone on the island who checks on it periodically and after storms. Hector Morales. Sort of a caretaker." Gonzales gave Winifred a challenging look. "Mrs. Forrester, how could you come here not knowing what your inheritance entailed?"

"Harry Lincoln Investigations were hired to find a possible direct descendent of Lorenzo Barilli—he found *me*. And *you* are my attorney!"

"I'm truly sorry. This must come as quite a shock."

"You have no idea! Harry tried hard to convince me of the fact that I am a direct descendant of one of Detroit's most notorious crime lords." Winifred winced at the thought. "He explained that due to some convoluted agreement made with the county at the time Lorenzo Barilli tried to build on his land in 1961, he basically had signed over a sixty-two-year lease. If at the end of the term there were no direct heirs to inherit the property, the land and all buildings on it would pass to Monroe County."

Gonzales threw up his hands. "There you have it. You *do* understand."

"I understand how I got saddled with an estate that's been closed up for decades. Now what, exactly, is on that land . . . tell me now!"

"Well, now. Let me see." He rubbed his forehead. "There's a large house, a guest cottage—I think it's still there—and a long dock or canal big enough for a ferry. And it all sits on fifteen beautiful oceanfront acres. Oh, I almost forgot about the groundskeeper's house across the road."

A deep frown drew Winifred's brows together. "I thought there were a thousand acres. What happened to the other nine hundred eighty-five?"

"Oh, the property runs across the width of the island. The caretaker lives in a house on the other side—a carryover from the old days."

This was beginning to sound worth the trip, if nothing more. She could certainly use some hours under the sun and sand between her toes on her own beach. She'd left a lot of cold behind in Chicago. "Oceanfront? A beach? A big house? So, I can just stop at a grocery store along the way for supplies and move in?" She waited for a response that didn't come. "I take it the caretaker has taken the storm shutters down."

Gonzales's sheepish look said it all. "Well, not exactly. You'll want to call Hector before you arrive. I notified him yesterday of you coming and asked him to remove the plywood covering the windows. Not sure if it's done yet." He shrugged his shoulders. "Things move a little slower down here." He nodded toward the key, which rested firmly between Winifred's fingers. "That key will unlock the back door just off the driveway. The other doors are all sealed shut—hurricanes—you know."

"If I'm reading this right, the house is boarded up and the doors are sealed?" That creepy, sinking feeling began churning in her stomach. "Is there any furniture? I can't just move in, can I?"

Winifred watched as Gonzales struggled to find the right words. Since when did an attorney find himself at a loss for words? Her fun in the sun had just turned stormy.

"Perhaps, you should give it a day or two before you arrive. Give Hector more time to get the place ready for you." Gonzales sparked a bit of energy, as if he'd just gotten a game-winning thought. He pressed the intercom. "Rosa, please call the Island Beach Resort on Marathon. Book a suite for the week for Mrs. Forrester."

"This isn't necessary. I'm sure I'll be fine. My husband and I used to take the kids camping when they were young—and before life got crazy—and apps took over our lives. I'm okay with ruffing it, shouldn't take more than a day or two."

The horrors of camping were etched across his eyes. "I insist. Enjoy the luxury. The Island Beach Resort is new, post–Hurricane Irma. Study the documents I've given you and the contents of the box. The key to the padlock is in the envelope."

"What's inside the box?" Winifred asked.

"I don't know. The instructions were to keep it in the safe until it could be given to the rightful heir." Gonzales stood and quickly moved to her side. His energy seemingly restored. With his hand on her back, he carefully nudged her across the room. "You'll love Marathon. There is a lot to do and an endless variety of dining experiences. Big Pine Key isn't far after you cross the Seven Mile Bridge. Bahia Honda State Park is on the way if you're in the mood for a day at the beach."

Gonzales couldn't close the door fast enough behind her, but Rosa was all smiles. "I've booked your suite. They're all ready for you." Her cheerful voice and doe-like eyes that said she understood helped settle Winifred's frayed nerves. "I'm sorry about that," she said while nodding toward the office door. "He isn't usually like this. But I think this case is way more than he's ever handled. There is something much bigger going on here, and he's not willing to talk about it." Rosa leaned in over her desk, then lowered her voice to that just above a whisper. "It's like a big secret that he's kept locked up in the safe all these years. I think you were a surprise. Whatever this whole inheritance thing is about, you weren't supposed to be part of it."

Winifred nodded slowly in agreement. Yep, something else was definitely going on—but what? "Look, I appreciate your input. But I've been on the road nearly all day and missed lunch. I just want to forget all this and head down to Marathon, check into the resort, take a shower, and put my feet up."

"I hear you. There's a great place to stop for dinner. Mile Marker 88 and ask for a table outside next to the water. That will relax you like nothing else could." Rosa's warmth lit up her whole face. "Good luck. Call if you need anything—just between us."

"Thanks. I'll take you up on that. I feel like I already have a friend in the enemy camp. From now on, you'll know me as Freddie. A name only family and friends dare to use. Call me if you hear anything important." She gave Rosa a wink before walking through the door with her briefcase slung over her shoulder and the wooden box tucked under her arm.

———

Dusk had settled in when Winifred pulled out onto US-1 and headed toward Islamorada and Mile Marker 88. The setting sun shined directly into her eyes. So, she was heading west, not south as she assumed. The restaurant's large sign caught her attention, and she easily found a parking spot. Winifred mentioned to the young hostess that this was her first time in the Keys. That bit of information seemed to get her special attention, as she was taken to a small table next to the water. Winifred learned that they had been a popular dining destination since 1967. She ordered the Lobster Linguine and a salad. Fish swimming just beyond her chair kept her entertained along with the setting sun. A warm breeze off the Gulf reminded her how lucky she was to have left all the nasty weather behind. The food was delicious, and her waiter brought her a slice of key lime pie—on the house. The word must have gotten around the kitchen that this was her first time to the Keys, because everyone made a point of stopping by to welcome her.

An hour later, Winifred climbed into her massively dirty SUV. She could very easily get used to this life.

The hour's drive to Marathon seemed extra-long, since the only lights to illuminate her surroundings came from the various islands she passed over or the oncoming headlights. The shimmer of the moon and the signs naming the bridges and channels were her only indication that she was following a narrow strip of land with the Atlantic Ocean on her left and the Gulf on her right.

After traveling mile after mile of tiny islands over a two-lane road, the city of Marathon was a surprise. Commercial buildings of all kinds lined both sides of US-1, including an airport. There were traffic lights and gas stations and a Home Depot. Her trusty GPS lady dropped her off at the front entrance of the Island Beach Resort. She let out a long sigh of relief—this was going to be pure luxury.

CHAPTER FOURTEEN

Thursday morning, Winifred woke at six feeling totally refreshed after the stressful two days on the road. After making a cup of coffee in the tiny kitchen, she went out onto her third-floor balcony. She was too warm in her red-and-green flannel pajamas. The moonlight danced across the water for as far as she could see until it met the slightest glow from the rising sun—her room faced east. She noticed a pedestrian pier jutting out only steps from the small pool below. It was all too inviting to remain indoors.

An hour later, she returned to her suite at seven fifteen. After ordering breakfast from room service, Winifred made another cup of coffee and went out onto her balcony and dialed Shannon's number. She answered on the third ring. "Hello, Shannon. Is this a convenient time to talk?"

"Yes. I was about to call you. I was concerned when you didn't call last night. Did you make it to the hotel all right?"

"Sorry. I stayed longer than I expected at Mile Marker 88 enjoying the sunset and all the lovely lights that came on, turning the outdoor patio area into a fairyland. My GPS showed an hour and forty-five minutes to the resort, which didn't seem that far. But driving for that long over small islands, with few lights and stretches over water, was mentally fatiguing. I wish my first trip down could have been during the day, so at least I would have known where I was. By the time I checked in and got to my room, all I wanted was a shower and a bed."

"How do you feel now? Is the hotel nice?"

"The woman at the front desk knew that this was my first time in the Keys and that I was traveling alone. I explained that I would be driving back and forth from Big Pine Key each day. She was very sweet and put me in a third-floor suite at the quietest part of the resort, away from the majority of the outdoor family activities."

"What are your plans for the day? How's the weather?"

"After getting up at six and realizing how warm it was outside, I filled my travel mug with coffee and went outside to explore the grounds. This place has five pools, beach volleyball and bocce ball courts, beach bar and sushi cabana, a marina with water sports, and that's just what I saw on my walk. I ended up at the Sunrise Pier that juts out into the Atlantic. It wasn't long before I was joined by a dozen other guests to welcome the sun." Winifred paused to watch a young couple walking hand in hand from the pier. "I could get used to this." There was a knock on the door. "Sorry, Shannon. It sounds like my breakfast is here."

"Dining alfresco sounds heavenly. I'll be wading through three inches of the white stuff. Talk to you later."

After two days of grabbing breakfast sandwiches and coffee at whatever fast-food drive-through was open at six, she'd opted for a hearty meal of scrambled eggs, bacon, hash browns, toast, and OJ. Shannon had been right—Winifred carried the tray to the balcony and set it on the large coffee table. She watched as several boats headed out to sea and listened to the sounds of a city waking up.

An hour later, she had showered and changed into white shorts, a bright yellow tank top, and sandals. With the help of the hairdryer and round brush, her hair fell in soft waves over her shoulders. Sitting at the desk with a notepad, she punched in the number she'd been given for Hector Morales. She almost had given up when he answered. "Hello, Mr. Morales?"

"Yes. Yes, this is Hector Morales." He sounded out of breath.

"This is Winifred Forrester. I'm staying on Marathon and can be there later this morning if that is convenient for you."

"Yes, Mr. Gonzales, the attorney, said you would be here today. I have a crew helping me, but it would be better if you waited until this afternoon. The house has been boarded up for a long time." Winifred could hear shouting in the background. "Maybe come around two o'clock. That would be better." His voice was a bit gravely with an accent. She got the impression he was an older man.

"That will be fine. I'd like to find a car wash. Get rid of all the road salt."

"You should wear long pants and shirt with sleeves—rubber boots would be good."

Winifred checked the weather icon on her phone. It would be around seventy-seven and sunny at two o'clock. *Why the clothes for cooler temperatures?* she wondered before continuing. "Fine. I'll have time to do some shopping." That was an odd request, and she was mulling over the possible reasons for wearing long pants and shirtsleeves when his voice interrupted her thoughts.

"Are you still there?" Hector asked.

"Yes. I'll see you at two."

"I'll have the gates open," he added, then ended the call.

With a list of things she needed to do and no idea of how to go about the morning, Winifred grabbed her purse and headed for the lobby and the concierge's desk.

"Good morning! My name is Jeffrey; how may I help you?" He was somewhere in his late twenties, blond, blue eyed with an athletic build, and looked like the tour director on a cruise ship. "We have several great activities scheduled. Our daily snorkel group leaves in an hour."

"That sounds great, and maybe I'll think about it for later in the week, but right now I need more along the lines of local directions."

"Of course. Where are you from?" the young man asked.

"Chicago. I drove through snowstorms, ice storms, and wild-fires, and it all shows on my SUV. I'm in desperate need of a car wash. Also, a store that would have rubber boots and women's clothing."

"I imagine that besides the road salt, you have a gazillion bugs plastered like wallpaper to your vehicle—I hope it isn't black."

Winifred grinned sheepishly. "It is."

"There is one car wash that also does detailing. Marathon has a dozen places to buy sandals, but I'm not sure about rub-ber boots. Home Depot has a garden center as you drive into their parking lot. They might have waterproof gardening shoes or boots. Bealls is up past the airport on the same side of the road. They have clothes and some shoes. There's a Ross store in Key West."

"How about a Walmart or Kmart?" Winifred asked.

"We had a Kmart here, but it closed in 2021. The closest Walmart is in Florida City."

"That has to be an hour and a half away. Where do you buy household stuff like a toaster or coffee maker?"

"Amazon."

Winifred thought about how inconvenient it would be for residents to drive so far for common everyday items. "Prime same-day delivery might be easier than searching for stores down here."

He laughed. "Maybe in Key Largo, but same day is more like three days in the Lower Keys. If you want major beach time, Bahia Honda State Park is just over the bridge, and there is a Bealls on Big Pine Key, just a few miles down the road." He wrote down the name and address of the car wash and handed it to her.

"Thanks, Jeffrey," Winifred said as she turned and walked toward the door.

"Home Depot is less than a mile on your right," Jeffrey shouted.

━┿┿━

The garden center was indeed at the entrance to the Home Depot parking lot, which was filled with trucks, trucks pulling boats, trailers, and RVs. Winifred was amazed at the number of beautiful floral trees and bushes that lined the walkway. She recognized the hibiscus in all shades of pink, red, and yellow, but the shrubs in powder blue and the thorny ones with masses of pink flowers were unknown to here. Once inside the store, she was surprised at the number of plants ready for outdoor planting that she only knew as houseplants up north.

A salesperson approached. "Where are you from?" she asked.

Winifred was startled by the question. "How do you know I'm from out of town?"

"Your amazed expression at the variety of plants ready to be planted in the yard."

"Garden centers in Chicago aren't this colorful."

"I know what you mean. My husband and I came down here on vacation twenty years ago and never left."

"Where are you from?" Winifred asked.

"Wisconsin—Green Bay. Are you looking for anything in particular?"

"Rubber garden boots. I have a pair at home that was purchased at Tractor Supply." Winifred bent down and motioned to her midcalf. "I inherited a place on Big Pine Key. I imagine you will be seeing a lot of me. I want to fill the yard with these beautiful bushes and plants."

"I have the same boots, but we don't sell them here."

"Where did you get yours, if I may ask?"

"Amazon."

"Thanks; I'll try Bealls." Winifred turned to leave.

"Big Pine? Mind the deer—they love flowers—so do the iguana."

Winifred passed a dozen or more touristy type shops and liquor stores before spotting the car wash sign. She pulled into the small lot and was greeted by a man in his midfifties with a deep tan and a bright smile.

"Hello, you must be Mrs. Forrester. Jeffrey called and said you would be by." He surveyed the outside of the Escalade. "Looks like you drove through a war zone." He opened her door and helped her down. "I'm Joe. Come on into the office, and we'll get your vehicle's makeover underway."

"I detect a Boston accent. I had a college roommate from somewhere around Wellesley. How long have you lived here?"

"Ten years. My wife and I used to rent a house down on Cudjoe for the months of January and February. My wife was an accountant, and I owned a couple car washes and detail shops in Bedford and Newton. One winter we got home the first of March to a foot of snow and decided we'd had enough of Massachusetts weather. Two months later, we were down here looking for a house."

"Wow. That sounds risky. What about your business?"

"Sold them. If you have strong northern work ethics, you can make a good living down here. You'll find a lot of snowbirds that end up with a permanent roost in the Keys."

Joe gave Winifred directions for Bealls, several tropical gift shops, and a small restaurant that specialized in local fish, all within walking distance. He explained that he would only have time to do the outside of the SUV if she wanted to make Big Pine by two o'clock.

The seafood bar and grill was housed in a colorfully painted, freestanding cement block building of an indiscriminate age. The interior of seafoam green and flamingo pink was all things maritime. She settled into a corner booth and placed her three large shopping tote bags along the opposite seat. Rubber boots were not to be found, but Bealls did have a pair of brightly colored waterproof shoes, lightweight slacks, long-sleeved shirts found in the men's department, sundresses, and a cute wide-brimmed hat. Several gift shops added a knee-length T-shirt that read I LOVE MARATHON to replace the flannel pajamas she'd brought, scented candles, and two wineglasses with dolphin stems. After being told that grouper was a delicious fish best caught in the winter months, she ordered a sandwich with fries, coleslaw, and a large, iced tea. She then pulled up her Amazon account searching for garden boots.

After finding the perfect ones in a bright floral pattern, she hit the Place Order button after adding the new shipping address for the Island Beach Resort. Winifred let out a sigh of relief that at least one problem had been solved and settled back to skim through a book she'd found on the history of the overseas railroad.

⚓

After stopping by her suite to drop off the bags and change, she arrived at the concierge's desk wearing navy cotton slacks, an oversize coral-colored shirt, tropical print shiny plastic shoes, and floppy hat. A new beach tote bag was slung over her shoulder.

"Well, hello there, Mrs. Forrester! It looks like you had a successful shopping spree."

"I did, and thank you for setting me up with Joe. My black SUV is black again and looking fabulous."

"Speaking of appearances—not sure what I call yours. Maybe gardening in paradise?"

"Close. I'm on my way to Big Pine—check out a property that I'm sure is overgrown."

"Good luck. You shouldn't run into much traffic on the bridge at this time of day."

Turning left onto US-1, Winifred approached the beginning of the seven-mile-long span that would take her into the Lower Keys. Her only reference to the historic bridge was what she had seen in movies, TV shows, or commercials; none of those prepared her for what was ahead. She quickly left any trace of land behind and was now barreling along at fifty-five miles an hour with the cerulean waters of the Atlantic to her left and the seafoam waters of the Gulf on her right—with only the guardrails between. Intimidated drivers might find the journey traumatic, but Winifred found it exhilarating. She lowered all four windows, filling the cabin with the wonderful fresh scent of the sea. Fishing boats dotted the horizon on both sides, while large pelicans perched on telephone poles waiting for their next catch. She felt alive and free of the horrors of the past week. She tossed her hat on the passenger seat and let the warm breeze pull through her hair. Big Pine Key was ahead, and she imagined an island filled with palm trees and the beautiful flowering plants she had seen at the Home Depot.

CHAPTER FIFTEEN

The Seven Mile Bridge ended, and signs for Bahia State Park appeared on her left. She crossed over Spanish Harbor Channel, and the terrain on either side of US-1 began to look more like crushed stone than soil. She had arrived on Big Pine Key with signs declaring that she had entered the National Key Deer Refuge, and the speed limit dropped to forty-five, with the nighttime speed of thirty-five. Tall fencing lined both sides of the road, and dense shrubs grew at the water's edge. Land expanded out on both sides with little in the form of buildings until she made the curve. Commercial buildings lined the road. She passed a hardware store, small restaurants, boat storage, and even a Goodwill. At the traffic light was Coconuts, a cute little bar and drive-through liquor store surrounded by lush trees and shrubs and colorful plants. Also, at the intersection, she noticed two banks and two drugstores, CVS, and Walgreens. Her GPS lady said to turn right onto Key Deer Boulevard and travel for three miles and her destination would be on the right. After making the turn, she passed the Winn Dixie shopping plaza, and the speed limit dropped to thirty miles an hour. A group of tiny deer grazed on the grass along the road. As she continued, it became obvious that Big Pine Key was nothing like the highly commercial and populated Marathon. She passed the fire department, with a big Smokey the Bear sign out front, a radio station, churches, and a few small businesses and a ballpark, all with expanses of open land between and more deer. She also noticed several long, unpaved roads that seemed to lead nowhere, or at least she couldn't see a house or building. After passing Watson Boulevard, there was nothing on either side of the road but dense trees and underbrush and then ahead was open land dotted with tall scrawny trees with little foliage. She began to wonder if she'd entered the wrong address in the navigation system. Then the soft-spoken voice came on to say that her destination was ahead on the right. The landscape suddenly became filled with more lower-growing trees and bushes on both sides of the road. Winifred stopped at the mailbox at the entrance to a long, unpaved road like the ones she had seen earlier. The address on the box was correct; so was the name WINDSWEPT.

Winifred's heart took a dive to her stomach. What happened to her lush tropical inheritance? She'd driven through hell for this wasteland? She held tightly to the steering wheel as the Escalade bounced along the dirt road. After driving for what seemed like a quarter of a mile, Winifred came to a large metal paneled gate, its design preventing any glimpse of what may lay beyond. The high stucco walls on either side were softened by the dense shrubs that lined the front facade. Tall trees and flowering shrubs gave the impression of a jungle beyond. The gates were open as Hector had promised. She drove over iron grating and followed a narrow curving driveway that appeared to be nothing but cleared bedrock, palm fronds scraped against the sides of the Escalade. She passed a cannel with a fairly large fishing boat that hung from a lift and continued to a single-story, stucco house painted what must have at one time been pink. She was sure there must be a front door, but thick palms and shrubs blocked the entrance. She continued around the side and found the double doors of the garage. After jumping down from the vehicle, she found herself wondering what to do next. Should she stumble through the foliage, some of which looked a bit ominous, or should she call for Hector?

Thankfully, he came around the corner of the house, his shoes crunching on the gravel. "Mrs. Forrester, your timing is perfect. My men left not five minutes ago." He reached out his hand. "I'm Hector Morales." He nodded toward the garage. "We put all the plywood panels in there." He glanced at her attire. "You'll do, but tall boots would be better. You'll see why. Follow me."

Hector appeared to be in his late sixties with a full head of hair that was more gray than black, with bushy eyebrows arched over dark-brown eyes. His complexion had seen way too much sun and she guessed had never been good. He looked to be shorter than her by a good four inches, with a no-nonsense attitude.

The path around the side of the house was barely discernable. "Watch the yucca," Hector said as he stood to the side of the daggerlike points of a large plant. "These have always been part of the original landscape. You'll find groupings of the yucca at each corner of the property where the walls meet the water."

"They look lethal," Winifred acknowledged as she carefully stepped clear.

"Exactly. Anyone trying to illegally gain access to the property could be impaled if they ran into or dropped down on one."

Winifred shuddered at the mental image. "What about the shrubs I noticed running along the outside walls?"

"Oleander. They have beautiful flowers that bloom from April through the fall. Every part of the plant is poisonous, so the deer and iguanas leave them alone."

"What is this horrible smell? Like rotten eggs."

"Seaweed. Sargassum to be exact. You'll smell it at times, especially in the Lower Keys. When washed ashore, it decomposes and gives off hydrogen sulfide gas. We never bothered to clean it up, since the place has been closed up for so many years. I'll have it raked and disposed of. You'll get used to it."

A huge tree caught her attention. Although planted inside the wall, half of the huge canopy hung over the side. "Huh." She studied the leaves. "This tree looks a lot like the umbrella plant in my office."

"Schefflera. Same thing. It just grows bigger down here. That one is close to thirty feet. During late summer, it gets long, red pointed spikes that shoot upward." He pushed many verities of palm fronds aside for her to walk by.

They rounded the corner of the house, and there it was—the beautiful blue ocean lapping against the shoreline—her shoreline. "Wow!" The yard was much more open. She dodged a few palm trees and hopped over exposed roots on her run to the beach—or what could be a beach. "Wow!" Winifred turned back to look at Hector. "I don't understand. How can this be so tropical and outside the walls it's scruffy and barren? Except the areas along the drive or road or lane or whatever you call it."

Hector's eyes lit up with the wide toothy smile. "I take care of this," he said with pride as he stretched out his arms to include all there was to see.

Sand, little stones, and dead seagrass found their way into her waterproof shoes, along with what felt like mosquitoes only worse. She limped back toward the house, then stopped. "Is that—or was that—a heart-shaped swimming pool?" Winifred asked in disbelief.

"Yep. It was built for Lacy Lorin, Lorenzo Barilli's fiancée. I don't know how much serious swimming one does in a pool that shape. Between the cracks and decades of filth, it might be better to take it out and start over."

"Huh. It is still cool." Winifred seemed to be collecting stones by the minute, so she headed toward the patio at the back of the house and knocked the sand out. She began itching at her ankles.

"The no-see-ums got you. That is why I told you to wear boots. You don't see or hear them."

"What is a no-see-um?"

"Sand flies. They love it down here." He helped her over a row of sandbags. "We didn't have time to remove the bags. The windows took longer than I expected—the screws were rusty. The sandbags help keep the storm surges from reaching the house."

"Huh. In that case, don't move them. I can manage just fine with them in place."

"That works for me. Now let me show you the house." They had reached the back doors when he stopped. "Now you need to remember that it's not been lived in for forty years or more. And she's seen a lot of bad storms."

"I understand. How bad can it be?" Winifred said optimistically.

It was bad. The rooms were empty of any furnishings. Water stains marked the walls up over four or five feet. The kitchen appliances were 1960s vintage, kinda cool but rusty. The bathrooms were decorated in pink tile with black trim and still had the original sink, tub, and toilet.

Twenty minutes later, Winifred was ready to exit out the back doors. "Well, Hector, the good news is that the utilities are in working order and the view is fabulous. The bad news is that the house isn't livable. I guess I have some major decisions to make."

"Before you leave, there is one more room you need to see—it might make a difference." She followed him back in the direction of the garage.

Hector stopped before a heavy-looking steel door. Very industrial, yet it seemed to fit in with the decor of midcentury modern. "This was the original viewing room, complete with projection room and raised flooring for theater seating." Hector pulled a door handle similar to those on refrigerators of the time. The door swung out instead of in.

"Don't most doors open inward?" Winifred asked.

"Yes, they do," he said as he motioned for her to enter the room. "However, if you're worried about outside pressures, whether from hurricanes or bombs, you want the forces to help keep the door from opening."

"I remember reading something last night about the plans for this room—very cloak-and-dagger." Winifred searched her memory for the references. "If I recall correctly, Lorenzo Barilli"—she still couldn't think of him as her great-grandfather—"had quite the interest in what was happening with the Cuban Missile Crisis during that same year of 1962. The whole atmosphere was fired up with Fidel Castro and Nikita Khrushchev. Lorenzo and his Key West crime buddy, Salvatore Giordano, made sure they were one step ahead of what could surely come down. Through their mutual connections, Lorenzo was able to hire the navy department's engineers to design a bomb shelter in the guise of a Hollywood viewing room."

"Yep. That's correct." He walked over to a corner and pulled back a tattered curtain. "Take a peek." Hector raised what looked like a telescope, or the periscope on a submarine.

Winifred put her chin against the tube and looked into what could only be compared to binoculars. "I can see outside."

"Now turn," Hector said.

"This is incredible. I can see in a complete circle around the property, and rather far out into the ocean."

"I waited out Irma in here. I've been in here for every hurricane and tropical storm since Georges in 1998. That was a bad one, with winds reaching one hundred ten miles per hour. We had a storm surge of six feet. I opened the door too soon and water flooded the room. Now I keep the doors sealed and the sandbags outside. I don't leave until I see that the water has receded."

"So that's why the doors and windows are calked—to keep the high water out."

"I haven't taken the seal out for years now. Never thought anyone would ever live here again."

It was close to five o'clock when Winifred followed Hector out of the safe room. "It's going to be getting dark soon. I should probably be getting back to Marathon, have dinner, and continue reading the information I received from the attorney."

"I would like to show you the rest of the property if you can come again tomorrow. It only gets better—I promise."

"Don't worry, Hector. I don't scare easily. The view alone is worth my time."

"My crew will be here in the morning at seven to begin clearing out the dead stuff in the landscape."

"How about I get here around ten and bring lunch? I have a cooler."

"That is very generous of you, Mrs. Forrester, and there is a fridge in the guest cottage." He motioned for her leave by the garage.

"Great. I'll see you tomorrow," Winifred said as she walked toward the Escalade.

"One more thing. You might want to stop at one of the drugstores at the light and pick up bug spray. Make sure it says no-see-ums on the label. And sunscreen."

"Thanks, Hector. I'll do that. My Irish complexion doesn't do well in the sun."

Winifred jumped into the SUV and turned over the engine. She turned around and headed back down the winding drive to the gate—her gate.

CHAPTER SIXTEEN

O n Friday morning, Winifred began the ten-minute drive across the Seven Mile Bridge with all four windows down. She wished for a convertible. The weather was predicted to be sunny with a high of seventy-eight, and there she was dressed in the long navy pants, coral shirt, plastic garden shoes, and the long, men's cotton tube socks she'd picked up at Walgreens the evening before to ward off the no-see-ums.

Traffic came to an abrupt stop due to what looked like a disabled van ahead. Her thoughts returned to last night. Once back in her suite, Winifred had made a reservation at the resort's restaurant for seven, jumped in the shower, then called Shannon for her daily update. She'd arrived on time for her reservation wearing an off-the-shoulder floral print dress, in a pattern of red, orange, and yellow hibiscus that complemented her ginger-colored hair, now flowing in soft waves. Glitzy sandals and large hoop earrings finished off the *I'm in the tropics and loving it* look— all purchased at Bealls. After being seated at a table overlooking the water, she ordered the mahi-mahi, garlic potatoes, broccoli with key lime butter, and paired with a sauvignon blanc. And although declining dessert, she was eventually talked into the house-made key lime pie.

Afterward, Winifred decided she needed to work off the meal with a stroll around the large pool and outdoor bar. While sipping a recommended cocktail with the name Tropical Sunset, Winifred met a young couple from Sioux City, Iowa, on their honeymoon and an older couple from New Jersey celebrating their retirement. Winifred wondered if they too would catch the Key fever and return with house-hunting in mind. After a highly competitive game of miniature golf with her new friends, she finally returned to her room around ten.

Those thoughts kept Winifred company until the flow of traffic resumed. Running twenty minutes late, she finally turned onto Key Deer Boulevard and noticed banners for hurricane sales. There had been a similar sign posted on an easel outside the market where she had picked up the box lunches and bottled drinks. Perhaps she needed to start tuning into the Weather Channel.

Winifred's focus was on the poisonous oleander that grew along the high walls as she bumped along the long roadway to the house. She imagined a sea of pink to break the drab gray of the surrounding landscape. She pulled up to the security box in front of the gates and punched in the code that Hector had given her. Sounds of metal grinding against metal were heard as the motor struggled to open the thick heavy panels. The jungle had been cut back allowing space for two vehicles to pass side by side. She arrived at the back of the house to see six or seven men off in the distance cutting and raking the underbrush along a part of the driveway that the day before had appeared to be not much more than a path leading to another part of the property. Now and then, a chainsaw broke the murmur of voices speaking in Spanish.

After exiting the Escalade, Winifred waved to Hector as he walked toward her with a big grin. "Good morning,

Mrs. Forrester. My men have made great progress. They will have the road to the guest cottage cleared today."

"I'm amazed at how much they have accomplished already."

"They are good workers. Today, they will work until three and then go home to their families."

"Hector, should I be worried about a hurricane?"

He looked confused. "Hurricane?"

"I've been seeing signs for hurricane sales, but it sure doesn't look like a storm is coming."

Hector laughed. "No no! Today is December first, the official end to our hurricane season. There will be celebrations in Key West." He nodded toward the back seat. "Did you bring the cooler and food? We need to get it out before the inside of your vehicle becomes an oven."

Winifred walked around to the back of the SUV and opened the liftgate. Hector grabbed the cooler while she took a canvas tote bag with a change of clothes—just in case she had an opportunity for shorts and a tank top.

"I opened up the guest cottage for you. The men are clearing the way."

Winifred followed Hector to where the workers were tossing long palm fronds onto an already overfilled trailer hooked to the back of a pickup truck.

"Good morning," Winifred said as she approached.

The men stopped what they were doing. "Good morning," said one man. "Buenos días," others said while removing their large straw hats.

Ahead, the roadway became a narrow path through the dense foliage until they reached a clearing. The charming little house sat on stilts. Its seafoam green siding and pink shutters gave it the look of a dollhouse. A white staircase led to a small porch with a door that was painted the color of a brilliant Florida sunset. The steeply pitched roof framed a round window.

Winifred followed Hector up the stairs and through the door. They entered a small kitchen with a counter that divided it from a two-story living room. A bathroom took up space on the opposite wall, next to the kitchen. "This is so cute," she said while tossing the tote bag on a chair and walking to the large windows overlooking the ocean. "This view is amazing. And I can also see the property beyond the walls." She turned to face Hector and noticed the sleeping loft over the kitchen and bathroom. "I love it!" She glanced around the small space. "The furniture looks old and worn but in good shape. You said the appliances work?"

"There's been some . . . some . . . some unusual activity in the area the last couple of years. I stay here at times to watch over this side of the property."

Hector had hesitated a little too much while searching for his words. A chill ran up Winifred's spine. "What kind of activity? Can you explain?"

"We'll talk about it later. Right now, I need to get back to my men. If you'd like to stay here instead of the hotel, I can have it ready on Sunday."

Winifred took a quick walk around to survey what might be needed beyond a good scrubbing. "How about I do the cleaning and let you know if I find anything broken?"

Hector scratched his head. "Well, if you want to. There really isn't anything else for you to do," he said while taking the items from the cooler and putting them in the fridge.

"How about cleaning supplies? Where can I find those?"

"There is Bealls up at the Winn Dixie Plaza. And the Ace hardware will have cleaning stuff—turn right at the light and down a bit."

He reached into his pants pocket and pulled out a ring of keys and handed Winifred several. "You'd better have a set made." He gave her a warm smile. "Welcome home, Mrs. Forrester."

Welcome home. Hearing that and seeing the twinkle in his dark chocolate eyes made her feel like she belonged. "You'd better start calling me Winifred."

"Right. And I'll be back in an hour for one of those lunches, Mrs . . . Winifred."

During that hour, she did a thorough inspection of the cottage while making a list of what she needed—she filled two pages of a legal pad.

⚬

After lunch, Winifred changed into shorts, a tank top, and sandals; grabbed her tote bag and keys; and headed to the car. She decided to hit the hardware store first. Traffic on US-1 was bumper-to-bumper for as far as she could see. After the light turned green, she was able to make the short distance to the store. There she found the buckets, rubber gloves, cleaning products, mops, broom, dustpan, window cleaner, garbage bags, and a large package of paper towels. A store employee even found her a Mr. Coffee tucked away on a top shelf and made a duplicate set of the keys that Hector had given her.

"You look like there is a major cleaning job in your future," the cashier commented as she scanned the items while another person bagged them.

"Yeah, I'm moving into a cottage here on Big Pine for the next month or so. It hasn't been lived in for a while."

"Really? Whereabouts?" asked the cashier.

"Oh, it's way up at the end of the island; you can't see it from the road—Windswept."

"Windswept?" Both cashier and helper looked at each other with shocked expressions.

The cashier studied the name on the credit card she was handed. "Winifred Forrester." Then she returned it. "Nice to meet you," the cashier said, but not in a particularly friendly manner.

After loading the car and climbing onto the driver's seat, she wondered why the sudden cold shoulder after they had been so friendly and helpful.

Making a left-hand turn and crossing traffic was proving to be a problem with the steady stream of cars, trucks pulling trailers, motor homes, and RVs of all sizes heading toward Key West. Back on US-1, she made the left-hand turn onto Key Deer Boulevard. She passed the First State Bank of the Florida Keys—maybe she should open a checking account. She pulled into the Winn Dixie parking lot and nearly ran over a chicken—they seemed to be everywhere. She found a parking spot halfway between Bealls and the grocery store. There she found a few beach towels that she could throw over the two upholstered chairs and a bedspread in a tropical print for the threadbare couch. She loaded her cart with towels and a shower curtain for the bathroom, a set of silverware, glassware, and an assortment of coffee mugs, and she also found a set of sheets and pillows for the mattress on the loft floor—that would have to go—soon. After loading the Escalade, she popped into Winn Dixie for coffee and toilet paper.

Winifred arrived back at Windswept after three. The men had finished clearing the road to the cottage. She parked at the base of the staircase. The workers had gone, leaving only the sounds of palms rustling in the breeze.

The last bag had been added to the pile in the living room when Hector arrived. "Looks like my timing is perfect. You have already unloaded," Hector teased. "How did you make out? Did you find everything?"

"Not everything, but I have a long list. I've got enough to get me started." She set the Mr. Coffee box on the counter. "The people at the hardware were very helpful and friendly until I mentioned that I was getting the place ready to move in. Then they looked horrified and turned as cold as an Alaskan iceberg."

"You don't say." A deep frown creased Hector's brow. He seemed lost in thought.

"Is there a problem with me mentioning that I'm living here? I didn't think before I spoke." Winifred had become so comfortable and happy with the cottage that she had momentarily forgotten about its connection to the Barillis. "I'm sorry, Hector."

"Look, it's going to start getting dark in an hour or so. Maybe you should wait until tomorrow and get an early start on the cleaning. I'll bring over a ladder and connect a hose outside."

Something had suddenly changed with Hector—something that sent Winifred's nerves on edge. "Sure. I'll close the windows and lock the door. See you downstairs."

Less than ten minutes later, she found Hector at the water's edge looking out toward the small islands beyond, a troubled look on his face.

Winifred wondered what he was seeing that troubled him. Several fishing boats were heading in a line to somewhere off to the left. A small boat was heading toward shore down a way to her right. "Hector, is something wrong? What are you looking at?"

"No. Nothing wrong."

It didn't go unnoticed that he hadn't told her what had caught his attention. "I'm ready to leave. What time should I arrive tomorrow?"

"The weekend traffic will be especially heavy with the pirate festival in Key West. Best if you get over the bridge before eight. Maybe leave your hotel around seven. There's a little place on your right before you get to the light that serves a good breakfast—Eggs In Paradise. That way you'll be going with the flow of traffic."

"Thanks. See you in the morning." Winifred handed him his set of keys, then walked back to the Escalade. Something was troubling Hector, and she didn't believe it had anything to do with her.

CHAPTER SEVENTEEN

Hector dumped the mountain of yard debris in the area on the property that he had designated for that purpose. Waste Management had a specific day of the week when they picked up the local residents' yard waste. But with a thousand acres, Windswept could handle its own. Several deer wandered over to inspect what he'd left—it amounted to enough to keep the whole herd munching for the rest of the day.

The drive to his house in the Rockland hammock on the opposite side of the island took only a few minutes. He still expected Perro to come running out to greet him from the front porch. His loyal beagle of twelve years had died two years before from old age. It had been a good life of nearly constant companionship. Perro means "dog" in Spanish, and Perro had been the best dog. Two years ago, Hector had begun noticing things—odd comings and goings around the property. Then last year he began seeing lights where there should be nothing but total darkness. The sound of boat motors broke the nighttime silence. He went to the pound and got a dog—a dog much bigger than Perro. He got an older German shepherd, one with experience, one that knew the ropes, one that no one else wanted—his name was Sam. He thought it a wimpy name for a dog that looked more like a Bullet or Rambo, but a name was just a name; it was appearances that counted, and his growl was terrifying. Although friendly enough, his look was menacing. Not knowing how Mrs. Forrester felt about dogs and not knowing how Sam would take to her, he'd left the dog at home for the day.

Hector let Sam out of the house and watched as he raced off in the yard to do his business, then retrieved his Frisbee from under a stand of sea grape trees. The two then walked the few hundred feet through the pine forest to the seawall and dock. He stood looking across Pine Channel to Middle Torch Key and Big Torch Key, while Sam went off in search of any new scents.

He'd stood in that very spot for the past thirty years, watching over and caring for Tony Barilli's land. Sure, he had known who the Detroit, Barilli family was and how Tony's father, Lorenzo, came by the thousand acres in a poker game at the Tropicana back in 1960—everyone knew. By the age of thirty-five, Hector had worked hard, backbreaking jobs with various landscaping companies. He had endured the unforgiving heat and humidity of the Lower Keys since his first part-time job in high school. So, being the property manager of Windswept seemed like a dream job. Along with a generous salary came the house nestled in the hammock and a credit card with no limit. He just needed to remember that the Keys had been the site of nefarious activities since the days when pirates roamed these waters in the 1500s, and the wreckers in Key West made it the wealthiest city in Florida in the 1800s. Smuggling had been a part of the Keys history—and still was.

After Tony Barilli's death in 2000, Windswept had become quiet. Sure, the main house had been closed up since Lorenzo Barilli's death in 1979, but the waterfront areas and canal had often been used by Tony's family. But for the last twenty years or so, Hector saw nothing on Windswept except deer and iguana—until two years ago.

Sam returned from his adventure with a piece of driftwood. He dropped it at his master's feet and picked up the Frisbee. Together, they walked back to the house.

Hector had finished turning on lights and was putting Sam's bowls of fresh water and food on the floor when his cell phone rang. His sister's name appeared on the screen.

"Sophia, is everything okay?"

"Yes. I have a few minutes before the dinner rush and wondered how it was going with Mrs. Forrester."

"She's not at all the cold, all businesswoman that I expected. I figured the condition of the house would send her racing back to Chicago, but she took it all in stride along with the jungle that threatened the paintjob on her fancy Cadillac. In fact, she's decided to move into the cottage—spent two hours shopping for supplies. From the amount of stuff piled in the living room, it looks like she's bought everything but a vacuum cleaner and microwave."

"Wow. And she plans to do all the work herself? I would have expected her to have you bring in a crew for the dirty stuff."

"Not at all. I like her. I hope she stays. But she's going to need a friend. Someone to help her navigate life down here, even if it's just for a month or two."

"And then there's the Barilli land trust," Sophie added.

"Yeah. I don't know what nationality Forrester is, but she's all Irish with red hair and green eyes. As nice as she seems, I've heard from Gonzales that she won't back down from a fight."

"What fight?"

"That investigator in Detroit told Gonzales that last Saturday night someone set fire to her cabin—with her in it. Mrs. Forrester was madder than a hive of hornets. Demanded that Lincoln be in his office the next day, Sunday, to sign the inheritance papers. Then she hightailed it down here."

"You sound worried, Hector."

"I am—I'm real worried."

"Sorry, brother, gotta go. Half a dozen pirates and wenches just arrived. The dinner rush begins. Maybe Mrs. Forrester would like to come down and become a Key West wench for a day."

"Maybe. I'll mention it to her."

"Talk soon," Sophia said and ended the call.

Hector set his phone on the kitchen table. He thought about the large fishing boat that was anchored off Porpoise Key. It wasn't the first time he'd seen that particular boat, but it was a boat that didn't belong here—its home port was Miami.

"What's it doing here, Sam?" Hector asked his dog.

CHAPTER EIGHTEEN

Saturday morning, Winifred pulled up to the Eggs In Paradise and parked at the base of the steps. She had left the hotel at six thirty and made it across the Seven Mile Bridge before the heavy weekend traffic began. The small building painted in bright yellow with lime-green shutters and trim was easy to find. A purple bench sat next to the door surrounded by plants with yellow and blue flowers. She was surprised to see that the restaurant was already half-full at seven. After seeing several orders of French toast, generously sprinkled with powdered sugar and plump strawberries being taken to tables, she ordered the same with bacon. Winifred people-watched while sipping a full-bodied coffee. It was a male crowd with the exception of one older woman, whom everyone addressed as Captain Sally.

The waitress arrived with her meal. "Heading to Key West for a fun day with the pirates?" Her name tag read Katie. "The weather will be perfect."

After the response she'd gotten yesterday after mentioning that she was moving to Windswept, Winifred decided to keep that bit of information to herself. "No. I'm here on Big Pine for a while."

"Have you been to the Blue Hole yet?"

"No. But I've passed the sign."

"It's a nice place for a hike around the nature trail. Lots of wildlife, including alligators."

"Thanks. I'll be sure to check it out."

The regulars had cleared out by the time Winifred finished her meal. She checked her watch. Eight o'clock. She'd better move on.

Katie appeared with the check. "Can I get you more coffee?"

"No, thank you, Katie. The French toast was delicious; I'll definitely be back."

"We have a nice lunch menu, if you're interested. We close at three."

"I noticed several of the men leaving with containers of food."

"Charter fishermen. They provide food and beverages for their guests. If you're interested, I would highly recommend Captain Sally Rogers. You can pull one of her cards off the message board by the door."

Winifred paid the bill and left a generous tip. "Thanks, Katie. I'm Winifred. See you tomorrow."

Winifred noticed Hector standing at the water's edge looking out over the horizon when she pulled up to the cottage and parked. She got out of the car and began walking toward him, then stopped abruptly—a large dark-colored dog sat at his side.

"You missed a beautiful sunrise," Hector shouted. He held onto the dog's collar. "It's okay; just walk slowly."

"Good morning. You were right about Eggs In Paradise. The food was great, and Katie seems very nice." Winifred made a point of keeping eye contact with Hector and not the dog. The fact that he was keeping a tight hold on the collar didn't go unnoticed. "Who's your buddy?"

Hector held out his hand for Winifred to shake. "Buenos días, amiga."

Winifred remembered enough from her high school Spanish class that he had called her friend. She would need to brush up on the language.

The dog's tail began wagging so hard that it sent tiny pebbles flying in all directions.

"Well, aren't you a handsome devil," Winifred said to the dog.

"This is Sam. I didn't know if you liked dogs or not, and this guy intimidates a lot of folks. He understands a little English. The amiga was for his benefit."

"I don't have a dog now, but we had one when the kids were little. A golden retriever."

Hector let go of the collar and Sam nuzzled Winifred's hand to be petted. "He likes you," Hector said, as if that was unusual. "Do you have anything to unload?"

They began walking back toward the Escalade. "A vacuum cleaner and microwave. I stopped at Home Depot on my way to the hotel last night."

Hector's only response was a laugh that could have been heard over the entire thousand acres.

≈⊰⊱≈

Winifred had wholeheartedly accepted Hector's offer to help with the cleaning. He had explained that being the weekend, his crew was off until Monday, and he and Sam had no plans. By noon, Hector had the dark-paneled walls in the loft and kitchen scrubbed and had started on the bathroom. Winifred had the cabinets and counter finished and was about to start on the stove when Hector got down off the ladder.

"My stomach is telling me it's time for lunch, and we need a lot more bleach and rags. How about I pick those up and bring back lunch? Do you like Cuban?"

"I'll also need a gallon of cleaning vinegar; I bought a bottle, but I've already used that, and the lady at the hardware store said it's the best for windows. And I don't think I've ever had Cuban food." Hector began walking toward the door. "These appliances have had very little use. They are almost like new."

"The old ones were rusted out. I didn't want to take a chance and cause a fire. I had my sister pick these out at Home Depot two years ago."

A lot of things seemed to happen around that time. Winifred wondered if they could all be connected. "Hector—?

"Great. Cuban it is. Sam will stay here with you." The dog watched his master leave and close the door behind him. He tilted his head and looked up at Winifred, as if confused.

"Seemed rather abrupt to me too, fella. I guess it's just you and me. I'll have to pick up a bag of treats for you, if we're going to be hanging out together." Sam suddenly moved to her side, sat at attention, and raised his paw. "Sorry, boy. I don't have anything." Then she spied a bag of pretzels. "I guess this will have to do for now." Sam gently took the snack from her hand and headed over to the open slider that led to the wide porch and curled up to catch the breeze.

An hour later, Hector returned with more supplies and lunch. They stood at the kitchen counter and ate the Cubanos. The soft bread with a flaky crust was filled with a generous amount of sliced roasted pork that had a citrus flavor, honey-glazed ham, Swiss cheese, and pickles. It had been toasted in a press until crispy and a golden brown.

"This is delicious. I can't believe I've never had one, although there is a Cuban restaurant in Chicago's Fulton Market District where I live. I'll check it out when I get back home." Home. Winifred realized that except for her daily calls to Shannon, she hadn't thought about her life up north, as the locals called anyplace above Jacksonville. After tossing the wrappers in the black garbage bag, Winifred walked out onto the porch and leaned on the railing.

A minute later, Hector joined her. "You look deep in thought. Something bothering you?"

"I don't know what's happening to me. My whole adult life has been building and growing Forrester & Forrester with my husband, Danny. Then I get sucked into this whole Barilli nightmare. I still can't believe it's true." Winifred waved her arm out in an arc to emphasize the huge expanse of the sea before them. "Yet here I am buying stuff and cleaning a cottage. Thinking about furniture and moving in—I haven't thought about home since I left Key Largo."

"You don't have to stay. Once the paperwork is filed with the county, you will be the legal owner and can do with it what you want. You have time to decide. The house will be a total gut job, and getting permits down here will take months. Then there are the various contractors and their time frame." He turned to look into her troubled eyes. "Winifred," he said softly, "it could take a year or more before the house is finished if you decide to leave it as is."

"What do you mean?"

"Old ground-level houses like this one are grandfathered in. You can make upgrades to the structure but not alter them. The building code requires homes to be built on stilts with materials that are hurricane proof. You either restore the house or tear it down and build a new one on stilts." Hector paused a beat. "And you can't get insurance on these ground-level homes."

More problems, more decisions. Winifred just wanted to sit back and enjoy the view. She glanced down at the empty space below. Yes, she wanted to sit. She wanted to sit right there and watch the sunrise in the mornings. "I saw a small table and chairs at Home Depot. I think I'll stop after I leave here and pick them up—and a case of no-see-um spray."

"I think we both have breathed in enough bleach fumes for the day. How about we continue this in the morning? I need to pull my tall ladder out of storage to reach the higher part of the walls."

"Sounds like a plan to me. I'll put everything away and meet you and Sam outside."

Fifteen minutes later, Winifred joined the two as they came along a path from the direction of the house. Suddenly, Sam stopped and began sniffing around a large yucca plant.

Winifred bent down to get a closer look. "Hector—is that blood?"

CHAPTER NINETEEN

Winifred arrived at the Eggs In Paradise a little before seven. She waved at Katie as she found her way to the same table. The waitress immediately came over with a menu and coffee. "It's Winifred, right?"

"You remembered."

"You are one of those women who will always stand out with all that red hair, startling green eyes, and a complexion that shouldn't see the southern sun."

Winifred chuckled as she pulled out the SPF-50 tube of sunscreen from her tote bag. "I never leave home without it—along with the no-see-um spray."

"I bet you'll go back home with at least a little tan. Where ya from?"

"Chicago." Winifred decided chitchat might not be a good idea considering the whole Barilli thing. "I'll have the French toast again with bacon."

An hour later, Winifred drove around the potholes and bounced over the ruts on the dry, dusty road to the gate. She punched in the code for the gate and waited while it slowly opened with a good amount of grinding.

Hector was sweeping off the concrete floor under the cottage when she parked in front of the steps and pushed the button to raise the rear liftgate. She jumped down as Sam came running toward her. "Good morning, Hector. Good morning, Sam." Winifred walked over to Hector with Sam at her side.

"Good morning. I see you bought the table and chairs. I'll take them upstairs as soon as I finish." He made a motion with the broom to show the cleaned-out area. "You can park under the cottage now. It will keep that fancy car of yours cooler and dry."

"Thank you. I can carry the two chairs up. They are plastic and lightweight, but the table will need to be assembled."

"I'll get my tools out of the truck. You might want to open all the windows and doors and turn on the ceiling fan."

"Sure." Winifred looked over at the beach. "Hector, what do you think about the blood on the yucca?"

"Probably a deer or iguana rubbed against it. You really need to be careful when walking around the property. Many of these trees and large shrubs have roots that are above ground—you can trip."

She remembered the grating buried in the ground at the gate to keep the deer from crossing into the yard. Would they swim around the two ends of the walls to gain access? She needed to be more observant.

An hour later, the Escalade was tucked under the cottage, the small table and two chairs were placed on the wide balcony, and Hector was on the tall ladder washing the wall. Winifred was about to start on the windows when Hector's phone, that was sitting on the counter, rang.

"Can you please see who that is?" he asked.

"Someone named Sophia."

"Ah. My sister. Can you please tell her I'm busy and will call her back in a few minutes?"

"Hello, this is Winifred Forrester. I'm afraid Hector is on a ladder at the moment. Can he call you back?"

"Mrs. Forrester, I was actually calling to see how you are. Hector has been filling me in on your progress with the cottage. He said that this is your first time in the Keys."

"You're on speaker, so Hector can hear. I have two aunts who live in the Villages. My husband and I would visit them each year and take the kids to Disney World. I'm used to manicured lawns and lots of palm trees. This is like a different world down here."

"I know Windswept is a jungle now. But his men will have it looking beautiful again—if that is what you decide—once the paperwork has been filed."

"The attorney said it could take a couple of weeks. So, for now, I'm enjoying my time in paradise."

"If you want to experience all that the Keys has to offer, then you should come down here, to Key West."

"I'm sure I'll get around to it in the next week or so."

"We're having our annual Pirates in Paradise festival. It's a week-long event. You should come."

"I've been hearing people mention the pirates and how I have to adjust my drive times from Marathon because of the increased traffic."

Sophia chuckled. "The festival is held in the first week in December. We have parades, historical reenactments at encampments, a pirate's ball, and you can watch schooners fight battles in the harbor. Maybe you could take a break from cleaning and come down for the day."

"Sounds like a lot of fun. But I'm checking out of the hotel tomorrow, and I want to get the cottage ready. You wouldn't believe how dirty a place this small can get."

"It's our weather. The rainy season brings mold, and the dry season brings dust, and during it all are the bugs."

"I get it. How about Tuesday? I don't have much besides my clothes to unpack tomorrow. I can have the day to sit back and relax and then jump into the festivities."

"I manage Chico's, a restaurant across from Schooner Wharf. My thirty-year-old daughter, Maria, grew up pirating with the crowd. I'm sure she would love to show you our town."

"I'm looking forward to it. But I don't want to be a bother."

"Are you kidding? Maria works at the Key West Historical Society over at the old Custom House. You can't get a better tour guide. Get here early before traffic. Hector will give you the address and directions on getting here without having to deal with the encampments."

"Should I wear anything special?" Winifred asked, hoping she wouldn't have to add a major shopping trip on Marathon.

"No. Maria will take care of that. See you Tuesday, and good luck with your move-in."

Winifred ended the call. "I like your sister already."

"I think the two of you will get along fine," Hector said while handing her his bucket and rags. "Give me the spray bottle and I'll do these high windows while I'm up here. You will have a beautiful view from bed, up in the loft."

Winifred gave the last corner of the glass door a wipe, then handed the bottle and roll of paper towels to Hector. "I love how these door panels slide back into the wall. It opens the room up to the outside. But I've noticed that it also lets in the bugs and little geckos."

"Once upon a time, like twenty some years ago, the porch was screened in. Between the tropical storms and hurricanes taking them out, I decided not to bother replacing them, since no one lived on the property. There is a newer, dense screening that even keeps the no-see-ums out."

"That would be wonderful. I might even look for a comfortable lounge chair."

"I would suggest checking out the Goodwill store every week or so. They sometimes get some very nice furniture from folks who are selling and moving out."

Winifred leaned against the doorframe. "Looking out over the water is so beautiful. I would expect to see more boat traffic, like I did up on Marathon."

"You were looking at the open water of the Atlantic and all the boats that pass under the Seven Mile Bridge. It's a whole lot different here."

"How so?"

"Big Spanish Channel is out beyond those small islands that you can see. It's part of the Intercoastal Waterway." Hector pointed to the land that was barely visible to her left. "That is Annette Key, and straight out is Mayo Key; they are tiny islands mostly made up of mangrove trees and shrubs. Those are the trees you see growing along the Overseas Highway or US-1. They are salt-tolerant and protect the shorelines from waves and storms. They are vital to the ecosystem in the Keys."

"But it looks like miles between us and those Keys. Why aren't boats fishing or waterskiing?"

"It's too shallow. Although there is a channel out a way between here and the grasses—about five to ten feet or more deep—it follows the shoreline all the way through Spanish Harbor to the Atlantic. Our own canal and dock, here on the property, connects to it, as do all the canals along this side of Big Pine. I'll show you that part of the property tomorrow if you'd like."

Living close to a body of water wasn't anything new to Winifred. The family cabin in Traverse City was on the water, and she had been driving speedboats and sailing for as far back as she could remember, but these waters looked nothing like the cold, deep waters of upper Michigan. She was already calculating how easy it would be to gain access to Windswept from the water. There was a bait and tackle shop next to the hardware store; perhaps it would be wise to purchase a set of charts. Understanding what lay below those beautiful cerulean waters might be more important than what lay within Windswept's high walls.

Winifred wondered about whose blood had been left on the daggerlike finger of the yucca plant—and how long ago.

CHAPTER TWENTY

Monday morning, Winifred stood on the balcony sipping her first coffee of the day. It was the day to say goodbye to the Island Beach Resort. Except for the few evenings spent at the beach bar sipping tropical-named cocktails and games of miniature golf with the various couples she had met, there hadn't been time for the many outdoor activities. As for the beautiful oceanfront view off her balcony . . . well, she had her own waterfront view. And if she really wanted to partake in deep-sea fishing, snorkeling, diving shipwrecks, or parasailing, they were all readily available.

With the few items she still had in her room tucked into a gym bag that she had purchased at Bealls, Winifred made her way down to the front desk. She was happy to see that her Amazon order had arrived early that morning. Dressed in jeans and the oversize coral shirt, she paid the bill, tucked the box under her arm, and headed for the Escalade. Next stop, Eggs In Paradise.

⇒╬⇐

Instead of the jovial 'Good morning, Winifred. Take a seat anywhere,' she was greeted at the door with a stern-looking Katie. A menu held tightly against her chest.

"Winifred. Winifred Forrester?" Katie asked in an accusatory tone.

Totally thrown off guard by the sudden change in the greeting, Winifred only nodded her confirmation.

"Please come with me," Katie said as she crossed the nearly full dining room to a small private alcove and set the menu on the table.

"Did I do something wrong? I don't think I mentioned my last name on my previous visits."

"You didn't. Elenor over at the hardware store did."

"Okay. I'm confused. Does my name matter? You have been so nice to me. Why the change?"

"It's not the name, Forrester. It's the fact that Elenor said you moved into Windswept. All of us old-timers know what that means—you're a Barilli!"

Winifred gave a deep frustrated sigh. *Was this the way it was going to be?* "Katie, how about I order my usual and then you join me while I explain?"

Fifteen minutes later, her breakfast arrived, along with Captain Sally. Katie and the captain pulled out the two chairs on the opposite side of the table and sat down.

"I liked you on your first visit, but I don't like anyone connected to the Barilli business, and neither does Sally." Katie looked over at the captain and nodded for her to talk.

"Twenty years ago, I was young and stupid. I bought a used boat big enough for doing charters to help make ends meet. All the locals knew to stay clear of that stretch of Big Pine if there was unusual activity, especially around the canal." Captain Sally removed her windbreaker. "Like I said, I was young and stupid. I decided to follow a speedboat heading out toward the Gulf. They got into deep water and began firing." She pulled her shirt away from her right shoulder, exposing a large ugly scar. "I limped back to my dock, the hull riddled with holes—I learned a very expensive lesson."

Winifred nearly choked on a sip of coffee. She saw the pain the old memories brought forward on Sally's face and the concern on Katie's. For no good reason except a gut feeling, Winifred decided to spill all. "I'm so sorry. This is all new to me, and I, too, have a story." An hour later, Winifred sat back in her chair. "Well, that's it."

Katie and Captain Sally looked at each other with a silent nod. "Crap! Honey, you have no idea the hellfire you're in for, if this is a Barilli fight," Sally said.

"So, the only person watching over you is old Hector?" Katie asked in disbelief.

"There is Hector's sister, Sophia, in Key West. I'm going down there tomorrow for the pirate festival. She is aware of the situation."

"I know Sophia's daughter, Maria. She sends me charter gigs if the folks are staying up on Marathon. You can trust her." Sally chuckled. "Get into costume tomorrow and have fun. Be a wench for the day!"

"It will be a nice break from continually watching over my shoulder or wondering if my car is bugged."

"So, it sounds like no one knew about you until recently. But there has been at least some activity on both sides of the property in the last two years, yet the last Barilli died in 2000," Katie said.

"That leaves Monroe County. But from what I can see except for the fifteen walled acres, the Key deer have free roam of the property. Why would the county go to these extremes to control the land? Do either of you know what the plans are if I end up dead?"

"The staff at the National Key Deer Refuge office are regulars here. I know they have talked about using the house as a new learning center. They rent the space they're in now so it would be nice to have a location that they own outright," Katie explained.

"That still doesn't make sense to me. The house is ground level. Every year it would be in danger of being washed out by a storm surge. I have watermarks up to six feet on the interior walls. They would have to bulldoze the house and rebuild on stilts." Winifred inhaled deeply. "No, I don't believe the county is responsible. Besides, even if the title to the property holds and I am the owner—what am I going to do with a thousand acres? I'd probably end up donating much of the unused land to the refuge anyway."

"So, that leaves us with the Barilli family who have all died out—except for you. What we need to know is: If you are out of the picture, who wins the pot?" Sally asks.

"That is what I have hired Harry Lincoln to find out. Lorenzo Barilli had a couple of sisters. Perhaps one or more of their descendants are vying for control. Although Harry tells me it's unlikely."

"So, we need to help Hector keep you safe until Lincoln comes up with an answer or Monroe County files the paperwork," Katie said as she got up and cleared the table. "What are you doing today?"

"My garden boots arrived, so Hector will be taking me on a tour of the property."

"I don't have a charter today, so how about I swing by in the boat—say, an hour or so? I'll text you when I'm close."

"Only if you're sure about this. I don't want to drag the two of you into my mess."

"Look, honey, I've got skin in this game as well." Captain Sally rubbed her right shoulder. "I'm reminded every time it's about to rain, or I'm reeling in a big one."

Winifred pushed her chair back and got up from the table. "Thank you, Katie. And I'll see you later, Captain. I think it is time the two of you call me Freddie." She walked toward the door and turned back to look at her two new friends. They were still sitting at the table, heads together.

⊰⊱

Winifred pulled onto the concrete slab under the cottage and parked. Hector's crew was clearing the area down to the water's edge. The smell wasn't as bad this morning. "Buenos días," she shouted to the men as she headed up the steps with the gym bag slung over her shoulder.

"Buenos días, señora," shouted the men while waving their hats.

At the sound of her voice, Sam came running toward her from the opposite direction and charged up the stairs. "Well, buenos días to you too!" Winifred said while rubbing his head. Hector soon followed from the direction of the canal. "Checking on your boat?" she asked while tossing her gym bag on the couch.

"Hmm. It is fine."

"I had breakfast with Katie and Captain Sally. I told them my story. They are both concerned. Sally is going to swing by on her boat in an hour or so."

"Good" was all he said as he watched Winifred put on her new rubber boots and spray herself with the bug spray. "Follow me to the canal."

The foliage was dense as they made their way along a narrow path. Winifred was glad for her long sleeves. Hector grabbed a couple of blue fenders and dock line from a storage shed near the boat ramp, then crossed the yard at an angle ending up at a clearing that ran alongside the widest and longest section. He tossed one of the fenders to Winifred and motioned for her to tie it to the cleat nearest her. "I don't want to encourage folks to tie up here, so I keep the dock wall clear."

Winifred felt her phone vibrate. "Sally is coming up from Bogie Channel; she's passing Doctor's Arm now." She and Hector walked out to the end of the concrete wall. He pointed to his right, and they both looked out toward the sound of a large boat motor. They watched as she passed Porpoise Key and continued the short distance and made the turn into the canal. Hector caught her stern line and tied it to the cleat while Winifred took the bowline.

Captain Sally shut down the motors. "These waters up here are really tricky, especially with that grassy bank over there." She then nodded toward Hector's boat. "As you well know." Sally grabbed something off the boat's console before jumping onto the dock. She handed a folder to Winifred. "This is an extra set of charts I keep on board. Study them, Freddie. Especially the waters around Big Pine. You told me that you grew up around boats. Now you need to memorize where you can and can't drive them." She looked at Hector for confirmation.

"Yep. You can run aground in a heartbeat. And in some cases, a reef can rip the bottom out of a boat."

Winifred understood Sally's unspoken meaning. *Your life may depend on it.*

"Come on, ladies, let me give you the grand tour."

It turned out that Captain Sally was also an army vet during Vietnam. During the next two hours, she and Hector planned the clearing of the underbrush like a general strategizing for the next battle. Instead of trenches, she directed Hector to clear enough foliage along the high walls to allow enough space to walk or crouch down and avoid being seen from the yard. Tall palmetto palms, fan palms, and areca palms were to be left in place to give coverage. Small breaks next to the softer palm fronds and the tall Norfolk Island pines were to be cleared to give safe access to the wall. "Stay clear of the Bougainvillea; they have thorns," Sally said as she pointed to a large shrub with vines running along the top of the wall.

After the fifteen acres were mapped out, Sally and Winifred walked over to the cottage, and Hector went to give his crew the new directions. Once upstairs, Winifred pulled two beers from the fridge, and the ladies went out onto the balcony.

"This is impressive. You have a great view from here," Sally said while pointing out various landmarks. "Freddie, you need to study what you see out there, not just look at the beauty. Compare what you see, like the landmarks, with the readings on the chart." She pointed to Annette Key. "The water between the island and the grassy bank is only a foot deep; it drops to six inches between the key and the tip of Big Pine. Much of what you see close in is only two to three feet. A flat-bottom skiff can skim over the shallows where a hulled boat will get trapped."

"I understand. You've given me quite a lot of homework."

Sally put her arm around Winifred's shoulders "Look, I don't want you to become paranoid, but considering what you told Katie and me, and what I know about the Barilli family and Windswept's history . . . well, best be prepared." She walked back inside. "I'd like to stay and join you and Hector on the rest of your property tour this afternoon. But I need to leave and pick up supplies. I have a charter in Key West tomorrow. Taking a group of *pirates* out to the Dry Tortugas National Park. It will be an all-day event with a ringside seat to watch the tall ships do a mock battle."

"Now, that *does* sound like a lot of fun. Wish I was going."

"Another time," Sally said as she descended the stairs.

Winifred and Hector, along with Sam, walked Sally back to her boat. The landscape crew was already working along the wall.

Sally looked over at Hector's skiff sitting on a trailer at the top of the ramp. "Perhaps you should put that in the water." She paused a beat. "Just in case Freddie should need it." She stepped aboard and reached for the dock line. "Why is there pink chalk on the cleat?"

Hector chuckled. "You noticed. I cover the cleats each day. That way I can see if anyone has tied up overnight or when I'm not here."

"Good idea," Captain Sally said as she started the outboard motors. She pushed the throttles forward and turned the *Sally Anne* and headed out to sea.

"She is already a good friend. You can trust her. She will fight for you," Hector said as he removed the blue fenders from the dock. She followed him and Sam to the storage shed where Hector showed her where everything pertaining to the boats and dock was stored.

The alarm signaled on Winifred's phone. She reached into her pocket and turned it off. "Do you mind if we put off the rest of my tour this afternoon? That was my reminder that I must prepare for a Zoom meeting with my staff at home. I'll be holding my meetings in the Escalade since it has Wi-Fi, and the cottage doesn't. Which reminds me that I need to call the attorney and find out when I need to transfer the utilities into my name."

"That is better for me. I should spend today working with my crew. I need to look at the property as a place to keep you safe."

Winifred felt a tingle run through her body at the thought.

CHAPTER TWENTY-ONE

The sun hadn't yet begun to show its brilliant face when Winifred pushed back the slider and stepped onto the balcony. The decking was cool beneath her bare feet. Her back was sore from attempting sleep on the lumpy mattress. She set the mug of coffee on the small bistro table and joined the gecko that was sitting on the railing to do some stretching exercises. Captain Sally had told her about a place on US-1 just before entering Key West that sold mattresses and furniture. They usually delivered within a few days. She made a mental note to leave a bit early and stop on her way down. She didn't know how many more nights she could fight with the mattress before she ditched it for the couch.

Winifred and the gecko were the only occupants of the balcony to enjoy the sunrise. Apparently, the mosquitoes, iguanas, raccoons, and large birds decided to sleep in. Hector had said that the geckos eat no-see-ums and mosquitoes. Winifred was happy to share her space with the little guys with the beady eyes.

Cereal and milk were Winifred's only option for breakfast, and while eating, she put in an Amazon order for a toaster and a twelve-piece cookware set in teal. Tomorrow she would make time for a trip to Winn Dixie.

⇐╫⇒

Winifred made the turn onto North Roosevelt Boulevard at ten thirty, much later than she had planned, but at least she now had a mattress and bed frame that would be delivered to the cottage Friday afternoon. It wasn't long before she passed shopping plazas on her left—the right side of the road was the Gulf of Mexico. She made note of the stores she would need, TJ Maxx, a large furniture store, Ross, Office Max, and, of course, Home Depot. She followed Hector's directions to his sister's house to avoid the pirate encampments and extra traffic. She turned right at the light onto Palm Avenue, then left on Eaton Street and snaked her way through a maze of one-way streets to Chico's on Caroline Street. He explained that his sister lived in the house directly behind the restaurant and she could park in the driveway—parking in Key West was a nightmare. Winifred also realized that driving a Cadillac Escalade in streets built for Ford Model Ts was also a problem. A little Fiat convertible might be a better choice of transportation.

Sophia met Winifred in the driveway. "Mrs. Forrester, it is so nice to meet you. Hector has been keeping me informed. I feel as if I already know you."

"Please call me Winifred or Freddie."

"Thank you for texting that you were close. I had my car parked at the street so no one would decide that they could use my driveway. We are close to Schooner Wharf." She motioned across the way to where a line of masts could be seen over a row of single-story buildings. "It gets crazy during special events like our pirate festival, which lasts for ten days, Then there is bike week. The offshore world championship powerboat races in November. Fantasy Fest is in October—that's a big one. We basically have a major event each month and the smaller ones in between."

"Wow! I had no idea. It must make everyday routines difficult, especially with all these one-way streets."

"You get used to it. It's great for Chico's. Which reminds me that I need to get back to work and prepare for the lunch crowd. They will be lining up on the street by noon. You can wait at the bar until Maria gets here."

Winifred followed Sophia across the narrow patch of lawn to the back door of Chico's and through the kitchen to the bar. "What can I get you to drink?"

"Iced tea if you have it, or Coke, Pepsi, it doesn't matter."

Sophia poured a tall, frosted glass of tea and added a mint leaf. After placing it on a coaster in front of Winifred, she grabbed a few menus from a rack and greeted several customers. They were all dressed in costumes for a day of pirating. Only one other person sat at the bar. The middle-aged man was dressed in jeans and a lightweight denim shirt with the sleeves pushed up. His light-brown hair was tucked under a black ball cap. He glanced over at her and gave a quick nod. He had one of those unremarkable faces that showed a hard life lived in the south. He hunched over the edge of the bar, with his left arm tucked under his right. His fingers wrapped around a half-filled tumbler of some dark-colored liquor. He had a deep, guttural smoker's cough. This was not a tourist out for a fun day in the sun. Winifred watched as Sophia stood talking to the group that she had seated. She was probably a good ten years younger than Hector, maybe five foot one or two and a little on the heavy side. Her salt-and-pepper hair was cut in a riot of short layers that framed a round face with chubby cheeks. But it was her eyes the color of milk chocolate and an electric smile that made her stand out above a crowd.

Winifred checked her watch—eleven thirty. She wondered where Maria was coming from when the door opened, and a young woman walked in dressed as a wench. Her white cotton, ankle-length dress had a low-cut off-the-shoulder bodice with puffy elbow-length sleeves. A shorter overskirt of burgundy brocade was cut up the middle, giving a touch of elegance to the tight-fitting black corset. Her long mahogany-colored hair was pulled to one side, falling over her left shoulder. She walked up to the bar with the confidence of someone who did it every day and needn't consider anyone around her.

"Winifred Forrester?"

"Yes."

"I'm Maria. I'm so happy to meet you."

Winifred looked into the most beautiful hazel eyes surrounded by thick lashes. "It's Freddie, and I'm pleased to meet you as well. Your costume is magnificent. If I didn't know better, I would think you had just stepped off a movie set."

"I'm the director for the Key West Historical Society. Occasionally, I need to step back in time for events and speaking engagements—the right costume helps. You should see what I'm wearing for the Pirates Ball tonight!"

"Sounds like a fun time."

"Are you ready for *your* adventure to begin?"

"Not so fast, ladies," Sophia said. "I have Cubanos coming off the grill. You eat first, then you play."

Maria rolled her eyes. "Yes, MaMa."

⚔

Half an hour later, Maria guided Winifred into a large tent in a courtyard near the wharf. "Now we get *you* into costume."

"This is amazing," Winifred said as she looked at racks of pirate and wench costumes in every size and color imaginable.

There were shelves of hats and boots and every accessory a well-heeled pirate could ask for.

Maria told the attendant she was looking for one of the better wench outfits. Something special. But after each one was brought forth, Winifred kept looking back at the pirate costume on a mannequin in the corner of the tent.

"Why do I have to be a wench? Why can't I be a fancy Jack Sparrow like that one?" Winifred pointed to the corner.

"I'm sorry, but I don't carry any of the pirates in sizes small enough to fit you, and the children's wouldn't be large enough," said the salesperson.

Winifred walked over to the elaborately dressed pirate. Black tight-fitting pants were tucked into tall brown suede boots with laces up the front. A white deep-V open-necked shirt with long sleeves and lace cuffs was held in place under a brown leather vest. A bright red sash accented with gold fringe was tied off to the side. A knee-length dark-brown brocade coat with large pockets and wide black cuffs completed the look. A black tricorn hat with two black and one white ostrich feathers sat on top of a black wig with dreadlocks. "This looks like my size," Winifred said.

"That is for display only. I don't even carry that brand anymore. It's too expensive."

"Then why do you have it out in plain sight if you don't have them in stock?"

"It gets people's attention," said the clerk.

"That is called a loss leader in marketing. I'm sure you know that. But in your case, you can't even sell it at any price," Winifred explained.

"Are you a lawyer?"

"I'm better than a lawyer. My company, Forrester & Forrester, designs and produces apps, so the buying public doesn't fall for scams like this."

The attendant looked around the empty tent. "Okay. But it is expensive. Those sold for over a thousand dollars. That doesn't include the boots and sword."

"I'll try it on. If it fits, you have a deal."

Twenty minutes later, Winifred exited the changing room looking like a fancy Jack Sparrow. "I'll take it and the sword. Do you have boots in a size seven?"

A pair of boots were found that fit, and Winifred slipped off her sandals and pulled on the boots.

"Jack Sparrow always carried two pistols. How about these?" Maria asked while holding them up above her head.

"Sure. Add them as well."

Winifred tucked them into the red sash and handed the woman her credit card.

"Winifred Forrester," the clerk said out loud. "And you really do own an app company?"

"Yep." After signing the receipt, Winifred tucked the credit card into a case along with her driver's license. She waved her sword in the air. "Now I leave this tent as Captain Jack Sparrow." The two stepped to the side as four new customers entered. Winifred stepped outside, while Maria stayed behind to give directions to one of the newcomers. She glanced around reveling in her new attire, a shopping bag in her hand containing her street clothes. Off in the distance, someone coughed—she recognized the irritating sound. She scanned the immediate area and stopped when she spotted the man standing against a parked car smoking a cigarette. The same man who had been sitting at the bar in Chico's. She turned and caught Maria's arm and steered her back inside the tent.

"Maria, do you remember the man who was sitting at the end of the bar?"

"Kinda."

"I think he's watching the tent."

"Why would he be watching the tent?"

"I don't know. Maybe he isn't. But I had this creepy feeling about him. Like he was watching me and listening to our conversations during lunch."

"I think you're being overly sensitive. Maybe it isn't even the same guy."

"I got a good look at him just now. It's him."

"Did he put out his cigarette or walk this way when he saw you?"

"No. But he wouldn't have recognized me dressed like this. But I'm sure it's the same guy."

"Okay. He knows what I look like, but not you."

"So, we just walk out of here together and hope he doesn't put two and two together and realize I'm dressed as a man! This black wig doesn't cover my face, which is definitely female."

"Okay. Put the case with your credit cards and ID in one of those giant pockets in your coat." Maria glanced around the tent and spied a stack of hand baskets on the floor. She grabbed one. "Give me the bag with your street clothes."

Winifred handed her the bag and watched as she stuffed it into the basket and then reached over and took one of the white cotton maid's hats from a shelf. She pulled her long hair back from her face, tied it in a knot, and tucked it under the cap. "Hopefully this will make me look a little different." Then she grabbed an eye patch off the counter and tossed it to Winifred. "That should help."

By now the other customers in the tent had changed into their new costumes and were talking in raised pirate-sounding voices.

"Okay. You leave and blend in with those guys when they leave. Stay with them and fall into the role—you're Jack Sparrow now—act like it. Get the Sparrow swagger on."

"What about you?"

"The back corner of the tent is open. Her trailer or motor home is probably parked there. I'm going to sneak out that way and wind my way through Schooner Wharf and down Lazy Way Lane to Front Street. That will take me to my office, in the old Custom House." Maria paused. "No. Give me your keys. I'll hang out by the docks until he leaves, then wind my way back to your car. I'll drive it to my parking space at work. If the guy goes back to the house to check, your car will be gone, and he'll figure you left."

"If the Escalade is bugged like it was in Michigan, then he will be able to track it. It won't matter where you park it."

Maria considered that for a moment, then nodded. "Don't worry; I've got it covered."

"But he's watching the tent. Won't he expect us to leave as a couple of wenches out for a good time?"

Two rather inebriated women entered the tent demanding to become fancy wenches.

"There's your answer. I'm going to help one of them find the perfect costume. Hopefully one with a long and colorful skirt— he's going to follow them all over town."

"But won't he notice the difference?" Winifred asked.

"He's a man. They never see the details. There are hundreds of pirate wenches walking around. After a while, they will all blend in together, and he will give up, see your car gone, and leave."

The first group was getting ready to leave. "I heard one of them mention looking at the tall ships. That's good. Schooner Wharf will be packed with revelers. Hopefully they will end up somewhere around Mallory Square. If not, then find your way to the Custom House. It's at the end of Greene and next to Mallory Square. My office is on the second floor. I'll leave the door unlocked in the event I have to leave."

Winifred patted one of her large pockets. "Cell phone," she mouthed, then followed the group out of the tent.

She blended in, perfected her swagger and sword swishing. What she couldn't get right was her voice. No matter how hard she tried, she sounded like a woman trying to sound like a man. So, she made do with the occasional guttural groan. The wharf was close by, and her group did spend a good amount of time admiring the tall ships and stopped at a kiosk to buy tickets for a sunset sail and followed the sound of live music to the bar. Winifred then blended in with a group who was leaving the bar and thankfully followed them past the trolley stands. She was nearly to Mallory Square when she heard his distinctive cough behind her. The Sponge Market gift shop was just ahead. She ducked in and began browsing the shelves. A scented candle caught her eye. She picked it up and sniffed. *A guy wouldn't be smelling candles,* she thought and put it back. She wondered, *What a tourist dressed like Jack Sparrow would be looking at?* She picked up a beer cozy and a map and got in line at the register. There was definitely no question in Winifred's mind that the man was searching for her. She waited until he left by the back entrance, then set her items down and strolled out the front of the building. The Custom House was the largest building around, and Winifred easily found Maria's office on the second floor.

The door was unlocked, and she entered to find Maria sitting behind her desk. Winifred removed her tricorn hat and gave a sweeping bow. "I have returned from my long journey through your fine city, my lady."

"Freddie, you made it!" Maria pushed her chair back and stood. "Do you think you were followed?" she said as she rushed to Winifred's side.

"Yes! He was looking for us. At one point, he was right behind me. I lost him in the Sponge Market. I was careful about blending in yet kept watch for any signs of him." Winifred removed her wig and ran her fingers through her hair. "You people sure know how to throw a party. The last time I saw this much revelry was New Orleans during Mardi Gras."

Maria chuckled. "Wait till I take you down to Mallory Square for our sunset celebration."

"I would have enjoyed the area more if I wasn't constantly looking over my shoulder."

"Speaking of that, I have an old friend whose father owns a bicycle-and-scooter-repair shop. With all the tourists who leave the Wreckers' Museum and feel the need to search for treasure, he also rents metal-detecting equipment. I took your car over to him, and he has a gadget that can find bugs and tracking devices—you're clean."

"Huh. So, I'm not being tracked."

"No device. But that guy was definitely watching you. And he *did* follow the tipsy wenches. They appeared to be drinking more of the Grog than serving it!"

"If he followed me into Key West, then how did he know where I was going? Because he was already sipping a drink when I arrived with your mother."

"I stopped in the kitchen when I picked up your car and asked her about the guy. She said he arrived a few minutes before you texted her. After serving him, she went outside to move her car so you could park behind her. She'd never seen him before."

Winifred didn't need to answer. They both knew what she was thinking. *He knew beforehand where she was going that day.*

"What should I do now?" Winifred asked.

Maria was suddenly looking older than her thirty years. Her festive demeanor was gone. "We need to leave. He knows we're together. But does he know where I work?"

"You mentioned when you introduced yourself at Chico's that you worked for the Historical Society. But he was sitting at the end of the bar. He might not have heard. We both were speaking softly."

"I admit I wasn't looking for him when I moved your car. But if he had overheard me mention the Historical Society, and then finally figured out that he was following the wrong ladies, he probably would have come here."

"And he was. After not finding me in the Sponge Market, his next stop would have been Mallory Square and then here at the Custom House—and your office."

"We need to get you out of here."

"Captain Sally mentioned that she has a charter today to the Dry Tortugas and then they are going to watch one of the pirate ship battles. She told me to call if I needed her. Maybe I should see if they are anywhere near and can pick me up."

"Let's not put you out in the open if we don't need to. Even if our guy doesn't know what you look like."

"Good point."

"There's a private sunset party that will begin in about an hour in the building on the other side of the courtyard. There will be plenty of food, prepared by an outstanding chef. You'll experience one of our fabulous sunsets and best of all its costume only."

"I don't know what I should do."

"Look, it will put you in a safe place until the wee hours. Your guy will be long gone by the time you leave."

"What if he's camped out watching my car?"

Maria snorted. "Not a chance. I parked it over on a wooded lot that few people even know about near the Truman Annex. Be my plus one—you'll have a great time. The couple hosting the party are tech giants from Chicago, Mira and Peter Chen." Maria pointed to a dock. "That boat down there belongs to them too."

Winifred saw two boats. "The boat or the ship?"

Maria tilted her head and raised her eyebrows.

"The ship." Winifred took in a deep breath and let it out slowly. "Okay. I'll go. But what do we do now?"

"I use part of the attic space here for storage. There are windows that look out over the harbor. We can watch the Mallory Square festivities while we wait for the party to begin."

Maria had just unlocked the door that led to the attic stairs when Winifred heard the loud raspy cough from someone coming up the staircase from the floor below. "That's him!"

Maria quickly closed the door behind them and turned the lock.

Winifred wanted nothing more than to enjoy all that Key West had to offer, but the ugly side of her world was raising its ugly head—again.

CHAPTER TWENTY-TWO

Sounds of truck engines and men talking loudly in Spanish jarred Winifred awake the next morning. It seemed like only minutes since she had crawled into bed, but the cottage was now filled with bright sunlight. She made her way down the steep loft steps and into the kitchen, where she got a pot of coffee going before moving on to the bathroom.

The coffee was still dripping into the carafe when she returned. She grabbed the largest mug, the yellow one with a palm tree design; did the quick pot-and-mug switcheroo; and headed for the slider with a full dose of caffeine. To her surprise, she stepped onto a fully screened porch. Two men were working at the water's edge raking what looked like dead seaweed. The others were off to the side clearing dense underbrush between the cottage and the house.

"Buenos días," Winifred shouted down to the men. They all turned and waved. She really needed to get proper pajamas or at least a long swim cover-up if she was going to have these early-morning encounters with a crew of men. She pulled up one of the plastic chairs and sat with her long T-shirt barely protecting her butt from the damp seat.

Within a few minutes, her brain kicked in. Memories of yesterday's events and the lonely drive home made it clear how vulnerable she had become. She and Maria had left the Chens' party at one o'clock, and after collecting Maria's car from the parking garage next to the Custom House, Maria drove the short distance to where the Escalade was tucked safely in a stand of tropical foliage. Only a few die-hard pirates were left walking the streets as she followed the GPS directions through town. Once leaving the last traffic light of Stock Island, it became clear how isolated the Lower Keys were. Except for the occasional bar or gas stations, US-1 was devoid of lights. There were no other vehicles on the road, no taillights to follow, just the white lines in the pavement. The only indication of approaching habited Keys were lights from homes, and at one thirty in the morning, there weren't many of those. The first signs of any real civilization were the radio tower's blinking lights and the signs warning that one was approaching the National Key Deer Refuge, and the speed limit dropped from fifty-five to thirty-five. She stopped at the first traffic light since leaving Stock Island and turned left onto Key Deer Boulevard. Winifred thought about how easily someone could have run her off the road and dumped her body into either the Atlantic or the Gulf—they had a choice—either was only a few feet from the road. A shiver raced through her body. She needed to put those thoughts aside and get on with her day. But she had no idea what that day would bring.

After a quick shower, Winifred changed into a pair of yellow cotton slacks and a multicolored short-sleeved shirt. She pulled her hair back in a ponytail and brushed her bangs. She had already succumbed to the fact that her Irish hair frizzed at the least sign of humidity. Her stomach let her know that it needed more than coffee for breakfast, so she pulled an egg, sausage, and cheese sandwich from the freezer and popped it into the microwave.

Juggling a paper plate with her breakfast, a mug of steaming coffee, and a legal pad and pencil, Winifred headed back to the bistro table on the porch. She reviewed her list of supplies that she still needed including a set of queen-size sheets for the bed that would be delivered on Friday—it was now Wednesday. She wanted to eat off real plates, not paper. She needed more than one sharp knife. She needed more than one dish towel—she needed house stuff. She needed more clothes. Key West had TJ Maxx, but she wanted Walmart, Kmart, Best Buy—a TV would be nice—once she got cable. She wanted Macy's and HomeGoods. What she needed was a real shopping event and knew that could only happen in Florida City or Miami. Looked like a road trip was in store for Thursday.

Hector's crew had moved to another part of the property, breakfast was over, and Winifred needed a session with her therapist. She texted an SOS.

———❋———

"Shannon, that was quick. You don't have a client?"

"You sent an SOS, Freddie. That means emergency. I cut the session short. What's happened?"

"Sorry. It isn't life and death—at least, I don't think it is." Winifred wondered why she had sent their code for drop-everything-I'm-in-trouble. "Something happened in Key West yesterday, and now I don't have *anyone* to talk to. I don't know who I can trust."

"So, you need an emergency therapy session?" Shannon asked in a bewildered tone.

"I need the friend who nearly died in an arson attempt in my cabin."

"Oh. That friend. What's going on? Yesterday morning you were excited about making friends. Captain Sally helped Hector lay out a safe landscape plan. What's changed?"

"It changed only minutes after I arrived at Chico's, Sophia's restaurant. There was only one man sitting at the bar when I sat down to wait for her daughter, Maria. He looked like a local. He was having a drink and never even looked my way. I didn't think twice about him until Maria and I were about to leave the costume tent, and I noticed him leaning up against a car in the parking lot—he was watching the tent."

"What did he do when he saw you leave the tent?"

"Nothing, because I was dressed as Jack Sparrow. Maria came up with a plan to . . ." Winifred didn't stop talking until she had given Shannon the details of the whole day.

"You chose to dress as Jack Sparrow—a man?"

"Brilliant, right? It was the perfect cover. The guy never found me."

"So, now you're wondering how a total stranger, the guy who was to follow you, got to Chico's first?"

"Someone sent him there. Someone who knew my schedule."

"That should narrow your list of suspects. Who had you told?"

"Everyone!" Winifred took a deep breath and continued. "Hector knows everything I do. I trust him."

"Hector has been employed by the Barilli Trust for twenty years or more. Maybe his loyalty is still to them," Shannon added.

"Katie only figured out who I was after being told by the hardware store lady. She introduced me to Captain Sally. And she has a long-standing hate for the Barillis."

"Did both of them know you would be meeting at Chico's?"

"Yes."

"And because of her brother's connection to the Barilli family, you can't actually rule Sophia out either," Shannon surmised.

"Now you understand!" Winifred shouted. "I can't trust anyone down here. What can I do?"

"I'm thinking that number one: you keep to your normal routines. You can't tip any of them off that you've made the connection. Number two: watch and listen for any slipup that they might make. Number three: maybe get a gun."

"This morning, I need to make a trip to Winn Dixie and stock up on frozen food. All I have to cook with is the microwave until my Amazon order arrives. And down here, that could take a week."

"What happened to the grilling queen of Palos Heights? You never let a little thing like a bit of snow stop you from burger night."

"Huh. Thank you for reminding me. I'll add steaks and ground meat and even chicken to my grocery list." She would need a grill. "Home Depot is just across the bridge. You've given me today's project."

"Glad I could help."

"Tomorrow, I'm doing a road trip to Florida City for a major shopping spree. The closest Walmart is two hours away, without traffic."

"Sorry, Freddie, but you won't get any sympathy from me on that score—it's nineteen degrees and blowing up here."

"I remember Chicago winters all too clearly. I've been here a week, and it still hasn't rained. I'll be shopping for more summer clothes," Winifred teased.

"Sorry to run, but my next client arrived. Call me tonight."

"I will. Now for my day in paradise." Winifred was smiling as the call ended.

A moment later, she heard Hector coming up the steps. Was he her Judas?

CHAPTER TWENTY-THREE

Hector had gotten a call from his sister with the story she had gotten from Maria about the events of the previous day. Winifred confirmed what Sophia had told him but didn't give any additional details. He seemed genuinely concerned, but at this point, she couldn't trust anyone. Hector explained how he would have his men clear much of the area between the cottage and the house so she wouldn't be so isolated from the rest of the property. He would follow the original landscape layout from the 1960s, giving a lush tropical feel without the dense lower, wilder foliage.

After he left, Winifred reviewed her Winn Dixie list and then called her office to check in. Everything was going as planned with their new client in California. This was Winifred's first time running Forrester & Forrester without having hands-on. So far, it was going well—but she'd only been gone a week.

Before leaving the cottage, Winifred began to close the slider. That's when she saw Hector standing at the water's edge with

Sam at his side. He had both elbows raised as if shielding his eyes from the sun and was looking toward where a large fishing boat was anchored. She was about to yell down to him and ask if anything was wrong when he turned slightly. He was looking through binoculars.

Winifred pulled the slider closed, although she no longer needed to since the porch was now completely screened in. She was high up on stilts. No one could get in. Yet she closed it anyway—and flipped the lock.

Hector was heading in the direction of his crew by the time Winifred reached the ground. She decided to put off questioning him about the boat until she got back from shopping.

On her way to the Seven Mile Bridge to check out the grills at Home Depot on Marathon, Winifred noticed the sign for Goodwill and pulled in. Hector had mentioned that she should make it a weekly stop even though she only ever dropped off, never bought. She took the last available space out of four in front of the store. Parking seemed to be at a premium even for the Goodwill. Upon entering, the women's clothing was on her right. A mannequin stood before her wearing the most beautiful oriental-style dress she had ever seen. The tangerine-colored fabric had a dragon of blues and greens clawing its way up from the ankle-length hem. The high-neck collar held a sleeveless bodice cut deeply into each shoulder. A long slit up the side finished off the dramatic look. A large-brimmed floppy hat adorned the mannequin's head. "Wow!" Winifred said as she took a closer look.

"Beautiful, isn't it? I just put that out this morning. Although the label has been cut out, I believe it might be vintage couture. That dress would be set off beautifully with your hair color."

Winifred checked the back for a size. Yep, it could work. And the price was right. "I'll take it. And the hat too," she said to the salesclerk. "If it doesn't fit, I'll donate it back."

"Are you looking for anything in particular?"

"Not really. I'll walk around while you get that ready." She entered the room beyond and was amazed. Everything from furniture and lamps to comic books. She laughed under her breath—there were even several toasters. She noticed a set of colorful Fiesta Ware in good condition. She went back to the front of the store and got a cart. She walked past a shelf full of board games and picture puzzles. The top one caught her attention. It showed all the famous landmarks in Key West, including the Custom House.

"Souvenirs like that are purchased by our snowbirds or vacationers to while away rainy days, then drop them off on their way out of town."

Winifred added it to her cart. "All I need now is a card table."

"Follow me," said the clerk.

Sure enough, there were three stacked against a dark-wood early American dresser. She chose the best one. "I'll take this up to the register for you. Is there anything else?"

"Well, I'm on my way to Home Depot for a grill," Winifred answered, knowing the store wouldn't have one.

"Gas or charcoal?"

"I guess charcoal. Nothing adds flavor like good old charcoal."

"Follow me." Winifred maneuvered her cart through the narrow aisles to a private back room. "This is our delivery room, where we sort the items and store any that we don't have room for up front." She pointed to the far corner.

"No way! You have a Big Green Egg?"

"It's been here for a while. I'm trying to give it to my son, but he won't use anything but his fancy gas monster. It's in good condition, just needs a good cleaning."

"I'll take it."

"Don't you want to know how much?"

"It has to be less than a new one."

The clerk chuckled. "It sure is. I'll have one of the guys put it outside. Back around to the side of the building and he'll get you loaded. He can grab your card table as well."

"This has to be it for the day, or I won't have room in my SUV for groceries!" Winifred teased. She then wheeled her cart through the store to the register. While waiting for the clerk to add up everything, Winifred noticed a pair of binoculars on the top of the display case behind the counter. "Can I see those?"

"The binoculars?" She pulled them down and handed them to Winifred. "They are really good. Sorry, but I can't come down on that price."

"Wow! These *are* good. I know the Steiner brand. My husband had a similar pair. I'll take them as well."

After giving her the amount of the bill, Winifred handed her the credit card.

The clerk looked at the name. "Well, Winifred Forrester, I hope to see you again. Are you staying somewhere close by?"

Not knowing how much information to give, she decided to keep it simple. "Yes, I am. And you will *definitely* see me again."

Everything was unloaded from the Escalade, except for the Big Green Egg, and put away. Winifred set the card table up next to the 1960s floor lamp with the bullet-shaped globes that could be turned in all directions. She still wasn't sure if the midcentury-modern furniture was going to stay or find its way to the Goodwill store—she was leaning to the latter.

Winifred pushed the sliders back into the wall and stepped onto the porch. A gentle breeze sent small waves washing on shore, an egret fished undisturbed by any boat traffic. The only sounds were the rustling of the palmetto fronds. She could almost make out the pink house in the distance. Since she had a major shopping trip to Florida City planned for the next day, Winifred decided to make the most of the afternoon she had left. After pulling on her new garden boots, she headed down the steps and across the yard to find Hector.

The crew was carefully cleaning out from around a clump of yuccas and pine trees. "Hector?" she asked one of the guys. He pointed toward the house. "Gracias," she said and walked on. "Hector?" Winifred yelled as she continued to walk toward the house. "Hector?"

"Here!" he shouted as he stepped out from behind a beautiful bush with large reddish-orange flowers. It covered the whole corner of the house that faced the water. Hector was holding pruning shears and loppers. "Come. Look what I've done."

He motioned for her to duck down and squeeze between the bush and the wall of the house. "See, I've made a little room behind."

Winifred did indeed find herself in a tiny space big enough for her to squat down. She could see his boots between the lower branches but nothing more.

"I made a good hiding place for you. Come out and see."

Winifred shimmied out on her haunches. She stood and joined Hector. The large bush reached nearly to the roof and was at least ten feet wide. "This is magnificent. The clusters of star-shaped flowers are so big that it helps act as a shield. You really can't see behind the foliage."

"I take good care of my Ixoras. They are common in South Florida and come in many colors."

"How come I haven't noticed them before this?"

"They need direct sun to grow big. Most of the property inside the wall has become overgrown. But the ones along the walls and this side of the house are doing well. The crew is finding some that are still alive as they clear. Now that they have sun, they will grow big. I will fertilize."

"So, in time, this *will* become my tropical paradise," Winifred said proudly.

"But we must keep you safe first."

"Yes. You are right about that. Perhaps, I'll feel better if I understand my surroundings from the water. All I've seen of Big Pine is from driving back and forth on Key Deer Boulevard. Can you take me out on your boat and show me the shoreline?"

"Of course. I should have thought of that sooner. And you haven't seen the other side of the property yet. The Rockland hammock." He checked his watch. "My men will be leaving in an hour. We can go then."

He looked down at her boots. "Why don't you spend some time here, around the house, and down by the pool?"

"That's a great idea. I've only been here that one time. Maybe I'll get a feel of what I want to do with the house."

"Remember, nothing can happen until the paperwork is filed with the county."

"What about doing something about that poor motor that struggles to open the gates?"

"Sorry, no. The motor is old. It needs to be replaced with a larger one that can handle that thick steel. I've asked for years. The trust won't approve the expense."

"I see. I'll call Mr. Gonzales. Maybe he can check it out. I know he said it would take at least a couple of weeks, but it's already been a week."

At three ten, Winifred, still wearing her garden boots, stepped onto the concrete dock. A large green iguana darted past her and into the thick foliage. Startled, she screamed and nearly fell into the canal.

Hector looked up from tying the dock lines for his boat. He then ran to her side. "What happened?" he asked while glancing around the area.

"A giant green animal nearly ran me over." She pointed to the thicket.

Hector let out a hearty laugh. "That was Pappa Grande. He likes this spot to catch the afternoon sun."

Winifred searched for the English words. "Big Daddy?"

"Yep. He's at least five feet long. He lives here with his whole family. Mama and the little ones." Hector went back to the boat and jumped down. He then held up one hand to help Winifred step on board. "I prepared the boat while the men worked. It saved time, since it is getting dark earlier now."

Hector turned over the large outboard motor while Winifred released the dock lines. They left the Windswept canal and continued straight out a way until they got into deeper water, then made a right turn passing Porpoise Key. The fishing boat that had been anchored there earlier was gone. Hector pointed to a finger of land that jutted out.

Winifred paid special attention to the shoreline as they passed the walled-in area. Except for short expanses that were open to the water, most of the property consisted of mangroves and what she had been told were sea grape bushes and trees. The tall narrow-trunked pines dotted the landscape beyond. With a depth of only one to three feet, anyone could either walk ashore or beach a small boat. She understood now why this had been such a lucrative spot for smugglers for perhaps hundreds of years. Definitely valuable for the Barilli family business.

"That's the tip of Doctor's Arm. It's over by the No Name Grill. Best place around for pizza."

"Where is that?"

"Remember passing the intersection of Watson Boulevard?"

"Sure."

"Take that to the left, same side as Windswept, and it will take you right past it. Funky-looking place, can't miss it. Tell them Hector sent you." He pointed to a landmass ahead on the left. "That is No Name Key." He slowed at the entrance to a canal. "See all those houses? They all back up to canals that were put in back in the 1950s and '60s."

"So, Windswept's canal could be older than the house?"

"Sure, but my guess is that it was dug at the same time or after—for the ferry to dock." He then turned back out into Bogie Channel and continued past No Name Key. He pointed to his depth gauge. "You must keep an eye on your instruments at all times."

Winifred noted that they were in eight feet of water; then it dropped to five, then four as he swung in closer to more canals. "Wow. Some of the homes along here are beautiful. So is the landscaping with lots of tall palm trees."

"Windswept was once the showplace of Big Pine. Filled with coconut palms, foxtail palms, and a riot of color. It could be again."

"That would be wonderful."

"We are now not too far from the Winn Dixie Plaza. If we continue, Bogie Channel would take us out into the Atlantic. I'll leave that for another day."

Winifred watched the depth gauge as Hector wove his way past No Name Key and out into Big Spanish Channel. "There are even more housing developments and canals on the other side of Big Pine, along Pine Channel. Take some time and drive around. I'll get you a street map and highlight some of the neighborhoods."

They were in thirteen to fifteen feet when Hector made a turn to the left and headed between No Name Key and Porpoise

Key. The depth dropped to five feet until he was back in Bogie Channel passing a long desolate stretch of land, then approached Windswept's canal entrance.

"Do you know why we have our own canal and all the other ones I saw led to housing developments?"

"I asked that when I first started working here and was told that what Lorenzo Barilli wanted Lorenzo Barilli got. His movie star fiancée was flying her California friends into the airport on Marathon. Then the ferry that took passengers to Key West would make a special stop at Windswept. A ferry boat would need a large canal to dock at."

"Hmmm." Winifred wondered what came first, the canal or Lacy Lorin.

CHAPTER TWENTY-FOUR

A thunderstorm jarred Winifred awake from a sound sleep around 1:00 a.m. She rolled over to look out of the large triangular-shaped windows that sat below the peaked roof. Hector had been right about it being the best view from the cottage. She remembered that she had left the sliders open. She carefully went down the steep loft steps to close the door. The storm was coming from the other direction and wasn't raining in. For the next hour, Winifred sat in the plastic chair and watched Mother Nature's brilliant light show dance through the rain clouds.

The coffee was still dripping into the pot when Winifred walked out of the bathroom. The rain had long stopped, and she wanted to be sitting on the porch with her first cup of caffeine for the sunrise a few minutes after seven.

She pushed back the sliders and walked onto the porch, but it wasn't the glow on the horizon that she saw first—it was the vultures circling beyond the wall.

Winifred felt sorry for the deer that must have died, hopefully a natural death. Suddenly the sound of Sam's frantic barking broke the silence of the morning. Then Hector's raised voice as he tried to quiet the dog.

Winifred went inside to the kitchen counter, where she had left her phone, and called Hector's number.

She was about to hang up, when he answered. "Hello, Winifred. Sorry, I was on the phone with the Sheriff's Office—we have a body."

"A dead body? Where are you?"

"At the first open stretch of land from the canal wall. About five hundred feet. The place where you said it could be a good place to launch boats."

"Oh. Should I come over? I could put on my tall boots and walk in the water. It would get me there faster."

"No. You stay where you are. I'm waiting for the deputy to arrive. He lives close by, so it won't be long." Winifred heard the crunching of stone beneath tires. *It must be the Sheriff's car,* she thought. "Winifred, lock the door."

"I live in Chicago—my doors are always locked!"

"I'll call you when I know something."

Not more than five minutes had gone by when Hector called. "We are waiting for the coroner to come down from Marathon. I'm sending you a picture. Tell me if it's the guy who was following you in Key West."

The photo came through. Even dead, it didn't look anything like the guy. "No. It isn't him. My guy had longish light-brown hair and almost no eyebrows. No beard either."

"Okay. Thanks. I'll see you when we are done here."

Two hours later, there was a knock on the door. Hector entered, followed by an officer of the Monroe County Sheriff's Department. "Winifred, this is Lieutenant Michael Connor. He would like to ask you a few questions."

"Of course. Why don't we talk out on the porch?"

The men followed her with Lieutenant Connor going to the wall overlooking the canal side of the property. "You can't see much of anything from here. Hector told me on the way that he has a crew clearing out much of the underbrush. It's looking good. The last time I was inside the walls, it was a danger zone with all the mature yuccas."

"You've been here before?"

"Oh yeah. Not often. Only when Hector would see signs that someone had been inside the walls. Never been up here, though. I've often wondered what it was like. Very cute—old-school Florida."

"Lieutenant Connor knows about you. His brother Michael is with the Key Deer Refuge."

Great! Winifred thought. *Now I've become the enemy who is preventing the refuge from getting their precious thousand acres.*

"What time did you get up this morning, Mrs. Forrester?"

"About six thirty. I like to make coffee and be out here, on the porch, to watch the sun rise. I noticed the birds circling and thought it might have been a dead deer. Then I heard Sam barking."

"Did you hear anything suspicious, say, around three or so?"

"The storm woke me around one. I came down here to watch. I stayed for about an hour, then went back to bed. I was probably sleeping when it happened."

"Hector filled me in on what happed in Key West Tuesday. He also mentioned the threat on your life back in Traverse City. Do you think this could have anything to do with you?"

"All I know is it wasn't the guy who was following me. Aleksy Petrowski is Eastern European. And the man who was watching me in Key West was light-skinned. Your guy is Hispanic. What happened out there?"

"Initially I thought that he had washed up on shore during the storm last night. But the coroner doesn't think he drowned. And his clothes aren't wet. He has a nasty gash on the right side of his head."

"I noticed tracks that look like someone had pulled a boat onshore. A boat with a bright green bottom," Hector added.

"That would tell me that a boat was there *after* the rain stopped or the green paint would have been washed away. The storm had moved out around three thirty," said Lieutenant Connor.

Winifred thought back to her early days at the cabin. Her dad had painted the hulls of his old wooden dingy and aluminum skiff with green paint. Anyone who was responsible for scraping the bottom got hell, then had to sand out the bottom and touch up the paint.

"The boat would most likely have been a small fiberglass or aluminum skiff," Winifred said. "No one would take a wooden boat out in these shallows in the dark. And an inflatable wouldn't be painted." She then remembered Captain Sally's warnings about the low water levels and how easily a vee-hulled boat can get trapped. "The driver of the boat is familiar with these waters. He or she maneuvered in and out of here at low tide."

"Very good, Nancy Drew," Lieutenant Connor teased. "Any other ideas you would like to share?"

Winifred chuckled. "Not at the moment. But give me a day or two."

Lieutenant Connor reached into his breast pocket and pulled out a business card. "Here's the number for the office." He pulled out a pen and added another number to the back. "My cell, in case you need it, Mrs. Forrester. I live over off Watson."

"Thank you. I hope I don't need it." She shook his hand. "Call me Winifred."

Winifred stood with Hector and Sam as they watched Lieutenant Connor drive toward the gate. "I think this would be a good day to show me the property outside the walls. You could start with where the body was found."

"I sent the workers home. We can start now if you like."

⊱──⊰

Hector's truck bounced along the lane toward the street. After a distance of a few hundred feet, he made a sharp left turn through a break in the dense foliage that grew along the lane. He snaked his way through until they came to an opening, and the landscape thinned out. He parked near the water, and all three got out of the truck, including Sam.

Winifred scanned the area. The ground was completely clear of any of the small palmetto and fan palms that she was now familiar with or the ground cover that seemed to thrive under the low-growing shrubs. Someone could easily park several trucks with access to Key Deer Boulevard and yet be shielded from the street by large sections of dense underbrush that grew under the tall scrawny trees. "Looks like a good place for smuggling. Access to the water yet shielded from the street."

"Yep. Been doing it since the early Barilli days. Once law enforcement started using drones, activity on the property dropped off. But it started up again about two years ago. I try to keep an eye out. I call Lieutenant Connor when I see something odd going on, but he's usually too late."

They joined Sam, who was already sniffing and pawing at the waterline. Winifred noticed the green scuff marks. "Those were certainly made by a boat. You have been taking care of this property for over twenty years. What do you think happened? What are they smuggling?"

"Drugs. This property is perfect. The thousand acres includes waterfront access on both sides of the island. You have Pine Channel giving easy access from the Atlantic over in the Rockland hammock, and here you have the Intercoastal Waterway out there with quick access to the Gulf. And a thousand acres in between for cover. In the early days, there were a bunch of sheds and cabins that were used by Lorenzo Barilli for stashing stuff. In those days, they smuggled anything that made money."

"Are any of them still standing?"

"Hurricanes wiped them out. I know of only one." Hector turned and walked back to the truck. "Time to head out. I have a lot more to show you." He whistled and Sam came running.

They drove down narrow roads that snaked through the portion of the property outside the Windswept walls. Off in the distance, Winifred saw a large stand of trees surrounded by dense underbrush. Hector drove toward what looked like an oasis in the middle of a desert. He slowed the truck, then stopped in front of a small pathway. They got out, and Sam took off running as if exploring a place he hadn't been for a while. Winifred followed Hector into a clearing containing three large ponds. A family of deer continued nibbling on leaves completely unaffected by the human presence. Hector called Sam back to his side. Apparently, the dog understood that he wasn't to chase the animals that were only slightly taller than him.

"These are fresh water. You will find them scattered all over Big Pine."

"Like the Blue Hole? I've noticed the sign as I pass."

"That was formed from an old rock quarry that was used by Henry Flagler to build the Overseas Railroad. Big Pine is made of oolitic limestone. It can hold fresh water. I don't know how or when these smaller ones were made. There are two inside the walls of Windswept."

"Where? I haven't seen them."

"They are at the far end—past the cottage. You won't be able to find your way through until the crew begins clearing."

"Don't you ever go there?" Winifred asked, amazed that there was any part of the estate that he didn't monitor.

"I walk along the water. It's only a foot deep."

"Huh." Winifred thought about that. Inside the walls she should be safe. And she did have her high waterproof boots.

Hector then made his way back to Windswept's lane and out toward Key Deer Boulevard. There he crossed the road and followed another lane, which led into an area of dense trees and underbrush. He stopped in front of a rustic, dark-stained single-story house with a wide front porch. It sat a few feet above ground, not like the cottage which rose eight feet on stilts. "This is where Sam and I live. The forest keeps the house cooler in the summer months."

They got out of the truck. Sam ran off, while Winifred followed Hector down a path toward the water. "This is a Rockland hammock. Rich tropical forests of hardwoods that grow on higher ground where limestone is near the surface. You will find this type of hammock throughout the Keys. It is very important for the island's ecosystem. The Blue Hole trail and wildlife center is a part of the Key Deer Refuge and borders your property. There are a few alligators that call it home."

Winifred noticed how a thick blanket of dried leaves covered the floor beneath the canopy. The large tree roots snaked above ground. Sam came trotting back with a green Frisbee in his mouth.

"These trees are different from the other tall skinny ones I see all over."

"You are seeing slash pine. A type of yellow pine that can grow up to one hundred feet. Hurricane Irma took out thirty percent of the trees, which is why there are so few now. There are many different trees here in the hammock."

Winifred walked over to one with a mottled trunk in shades from orange to black with leaves that were long and shiny.

"Don't touch that! It's poisonwood. It can cause rashes and sometimes severe blistering of the skin. I'm having all the poisonwood removed from inside the walls."

"I'm well aware of what poison ivy looks like, so I'll add this nasty tree to my memory bank as well."

"You will also need to add our common varieties of snakes to your memory bank. This hammock is home to the peninsular ribbon snake. The largest that can be over three feet long. The red rat snake is midsize but can reach four feet in length—they are great climbers. The Florida brown snakes are the smallest at only twelve inches and are only found on the islands surrounding Big Pine."

"I'm not afraid of snakes—they just startle me. Of course, we don't have poisonous ones in Michigan, except for the eastern massasauga rattlesnake, which is rarely seen anymore."

"Just put snakes on your radar. Since I've left Windswept go wild, it has become the perfect habitat. Now that we are clearing the underbrush and undesirable trees and shrubs within the walls, they should move on. I have a field guide to Florida snakes. Remind me to give it to you before we leave."

Winifred followed Hector to a long dock that jutted out into the water. A small double-hull, center-cockpit boat was tied at the end. Winifred could see other long docks off in the distance.

"Where there are no canals, folks need to have docks that extend into the deeper depths. This type of boat lets me move around in the shallower waters."

Winifred followed Hector through the trees to where the terrain was more barren like the rest of the area. "This is where I see most of the activity on this side of the property."

"What can you do about this? This smuggling."

"Winifred, I am employed by the Barilli Family Trust. Everyone knows what business the family is in. I'm paid well to watch over and take care of the land—period."

"But *I* own the land now."

"Not until the papers are filed with the county."

CHAPTER TWENTY-FIVE

Frustrated beyond belief as Hector's truck bounced along the rutted lane from his house in the hammock, Winifred pulled her cell phone from her pocket and punched in the number for her attorney in Key Largo. It went to voicemail. She debated whether to leave a message or hang up and call when she got back to the cottage. The beep sounded, she decided on now. "Hello, this is Winifred Forrester. I know it has only been a little more than a week since the paperwork was filed with the county. But we've had a situation here and I'd like to get the status on where we stand with the paperwork. Please call me as soon as you can. Thank you. Goodbye."

Hector glanced over at Winifred. "Don't get your hopes up. Things move slower down here."

They waited at the gate as the motor struggled to open the heavy steel panels. The loud sound of grinding gears set Winifred's already stretched nerves to snap. "Can't you shoot that poor thing and put it out of its misery?" Winifred shouted in anger.

"A new one is very expensive. This afternoon, I'll give it some oil and grease," Hector said calmly.

The metal grid rattled as they drove over it. That, too, escalated Winifred's heightened anxiety.

"I'm not ready to be locked up in the confines of the cottage. Can you take me over to the house? I think I need to relax in a world when life was easier—Lacy Lorin's world of fun in the sun and Hollywood stars lounging around the pool."

With the underbrush cleared away from the front of the house, sunlight was once again finding its way to the dramatic front entrance. And with the large flower heads of the reddish-pink Ixora at the corners, the house was taking on a welcoming, tropical feel. Winifred could imagine the tall double front doors painted in the same color as the Ixora with large pots of colorful blue and yellow flowers. Hector pulled around the corner and parked in front of the garage. The bright pink bougainvillea growing against the wall was filling out. Winifred smiled for the first time all day.

The three jumped down from the truck and walked around to the back of the house. Winifred walked down to the water's edge. Several boats were seen off in the distance, in what she now knew was the Intercoastal Waterway. She turned back and looked at Hector, who was standing on the patio. Now that much of the low-growing brush was removed, she got a better view of the house. "I see now that the house is built in the shape of an *H*. All those big windows and sliders would give a constant changing view of the ocean."

She walked up to the patio. "The rain last night washed the last of the debris off the terra-cotta tiles," Hector said as he pointed to the entire expanse of the space.

"I guess, between the low walls and sandbags, this area was covered in leaves and branches. I didn't notice how beautiful it is. I can imagine it with umbrella tables and comfortable chairs.

Lacy Lorin's friends sitting here with drinks, smoking cigarettes and cigars."

"Yep, right out of a 1960s movie. Old Florida. There aren't many estates like this left."

"I'm beginning to see remnants of walkways that snake through the property between here and the cottage. Many of the trees and flowering shrubs are ringed in large stones."

"Lorenzo Barilli had a professional landscaper lay out the fifteen acres inside the walls. The stones kept the soil that was brought in for the various beds from washing out. Over the last forty years, Mother Nature has made her own soil with the leaves and twigs."

"I see. Do you know if those plans still exist somewhere?"

"Inside the safe room is a waterproof tube that has the house and landscape plans. I'll get them if you like." Hector walked over to one of the rocks at the base of the tall tree with the wide canopy that shaded the patio. She now could recognize the royal poincianas by the long brown seed pods. He picked up the stone and reached under pulling out a small black metal box. "I keep a spare key for the house out here. You should know where it is in case you don't have your keys on you."

"Great. And leave the door to the garage unlocked. I'd like to take another look at the inside. I'll lock up when I leave."

Hector returned about ten minutes later with an aluminum tube. "Here you go." He handed it to her and replaced the key under the rock. Winifred made note of which stone it was.

"I have a few errands to run. I'm leaving Sam with you. I'll be back this evening for him."

Winifred watched Sam follow his master around the side of the house to his truck. A few minutes later, she heard Hector start the engine and drive away. Sam returned as if to make sure she was still there, then he ran off to do whatever dogs did. She sat on the low wall that bordered the patio and looked out over the yard past the pool to the water. Geckos scurried everywhere in search of bugs. Palmetto and fan palms rustled in the gentle breeze. It was quiet, serene, and peaceful. Yet that morning, a body had been found on the property—not far from the wall. Winifred thought about Lacy Lorin's friends. Would it have been too quiet for the Hollywood set who were used to clubs and parties? Or perhaps it was a temporary escape from the scandals and paparazzi. Did they know what business was being conducted beyond the flower-covered walls? Did they care?

Sam returned carrying a small coconut in his mouth. He dropped it at her feet, then ran back several feet waiting for her to throw it. Not wanting to hit him in the head with the rather heavy fruit of the palm, she threw it to the side. After a while, Winifred tired of the game before Sam. "Enough. I need to get you a proper ball. I remember our golden retriever's favorite toy was a tennis ball." Dusk was settling in. Winifred thought about the long walk to the cottage through the uncleared areas. She was alone, and it got dark fast. "Come on, Sam, let's lock up the house and head back."

Hector called while Winifred and Sam were halfway back to the cottage to say he would be later than he originally thought. His errands had taken him to Key West and he was having dinner with his sister. He should be back around nine.

"Well, Sam, it looks like you will be joining me for burgers and hot dogs."

Sam's ears perked up at the word "dogs."

"Hot dogs it is for you."

On Tuesday, while Winifred had been in Key West, Hector raided his storage building and dropped off several things to make her outdoor time more enjoyable. She now had a picnic table that sat under the porch, an old folding lawn chair, and a dock box for her to store charcoal and grilling supplies—and extra bottles of no-see-um spray and sunscreen.

Winifred got the Big Green Egg going, then grabbed the aluminum tube and went upstairs. She laid out the house blueprints and landscape plans on the card table, then weighted down the four corners so they wouldn't curl back up. After arranging the package of hotdogs, buns, condiments, paper plates, silverware, and the tub of macaroni salad on a tray, she headed back downstairs. The coals still had a way to go before they were hot enough to grill. She went back upstairs for a can of Coke and a large bowl for Sam's water. It was dark when Winifred returned to the picnic table, so she lit several citronella pots to ward off the mosquitoes, filled the bowl with water from the garden hose, and put the hot dogs on the grill. The grill marks were looking good when Sam's ears suddenly perked up and he took off running. Ferocious barking ensued, followed by a large splash in the canal. Winifred wondered if she should check out what all the fuss was about, but that would mean leaving the meat on the grill unattended to burn to a crisp or take them off and have to start over. Suddenly all went quiet, and the decision was made—she grabbed the tongs and began turning.

A few minutes later, Winifred pulled the well-charred hot dogs from the Big Green Egg and Sam came running back from wherever he'd been carrying a stick in his mouth. "Just like a man! Show up to eat after all the work has been done!" She placed two hot dogs in buns for herself and cut up six for Sam, waiting for them to cool before placing the paper plate on the ground. "Sam! You're all wet! What were you doing out there?" He put his front paws on the edge of the table and sniffed at the plate. "Okay. Here's your dinner, but keep your distance—you stink!"

They dined by the light of the citronella candles and the one overhead light bulb.

Two hours later—after clearing the table and taking everything back upstairs—Winifred sat in the lawn chair near the water's edge sipping a glass of wine. She checked her phone's weather app for Chicago—nineteen degrees and snowing. "It doesn't get much better than this. Well, it would if someone out there wasn't trying to kill me." Sam looked at her as if waiting for a command, then put his head back down on his paw.

Their peaceful time together ended a few minutes later when Sam jumped up and began a low growl that became more aggressive. Fear set in as Winifred realized how vulnerable she was even behind high stucco walls. Sam stayed at her side as his growl became vicious. Then he immediately quieted seconds before the loud engine of Hector's truck could be heard in the distance. "Good boy," Winifred said as she patted the dog's head before he took off to greet his master.

Hector and Sam walked down to where Winifred was standing next to the chair. "Wow! I must say that you nearly sent me into a panic attack for the second time tonight. Sam and I were sitting here enjoying this beautiful night when suddenly he let out a terrifying growl that sent my heart racing. He must have heard the gate opening," Winifred said while Sam trotted back to her side. "He was a good boy and stayed right with me this time. He didn't run off until he recognized the sound of your truck."

"Is that so?" Hector glanced at Sam with raised eyebrows. "He was protecting you. Looks like he still is. Why is he wet?"

"Oh, a couple of hours ago, he heard something over by the canal. He took off doing his terrifying bark. I heard a loud splash. He probably chased Big Daddy into the water."

"Hmmm." Hector smacked his thigh twice and Sam ran to his side and sat at attention. "We will leave now. I'll swing by and check the canal and outside the walls—where the body was found."

CHAPTER TWENTY-SIX

Hector's last words sent a chill racing through Winifred. She blew out the candles and headed upstairs, making a point of locking the door behind her. After refilling her glass of Chardonnay, she made her way out to the porch and pressed Shannon's number from her contact list.

She answered on the first ring. "Hello, Freddie. I was hoping you'd call. How was your day?"

"Memorable. It began early in the morning with Hector finding a body on the beach outside the wall. I use the term 'beach' loosely."

"Body? Who? Are you okay?"

"I'm fine. I don't know who he was. Hector sent me a photo while he and Lieutenant Connor were at the scene. He's Hispanic. I've never seen him before."

"Do you think the guy is part of the Barilli family business—smuggling?"

"He had no ID, so I won't know anything for a few days. The coroner has the body, and the DEA office in Miami is checking for possible identification."

"You're sure you are okay there by yourself?"

"Shannon, I'm fine. Hector took me on a tour of the whole thousand acres today. The only time Hector isn't close by is when I leave the property. Even Sam is watching over me now. Did you get the photos I sent you?"

"Yes, I did. I can't tell you how much I appreciate you sending them to me each day. It's like I'm there with you. Is the place where the body was found one of them?"

"Yeah. The first one by the water. The next one shows Hector and Lieutenant Connor looking at the green paint marks on the stones."

"He's cute. Married?"

"Honestly, Shannon!" Winifred huffed. "I have no idea and don't care. He's with the Monroe County Sheriff's Office here on Big Pine. Anyway, whoever the dead guy is, he hasn't been following me. If he was, he would have been *inside* the walls, not *outside*."

"True. So maybe whoever is still running the Barilli operation is trying to make one last big haul before you take ownership of the land."

"Maybe. All I know is that there has been no attempt on my life while I'm inside the walls—or since I've been in Florida."

"So, our arsonist needed to kill you before you arrived at Windswept. And before the title to the property was filed with the county?" Shannon asked.

"Maybe. I've left a voicemail message with Gonzales asking for an update on the filing. If I don't hear back by noon tomorrow, I'll call again."

"Sounds good. Let me know what you find out. Have a good night. Talk to you tomorrow."

"Yeah. You too," Winifred said, then ended the call.

She then went inside and pulled the bottle of Chardonnay from the fridge. After refilling her glass, she stopped by the card table and glanced down at the landscape print. Something about the layout seemed wrong—out of proportion. She took a sip and continued to study. The house and the cottage were surrounded by generously sized beds and pathways that wound throughout. It was the canal that seemed to take up too much space. The longest part came in from the Gulf with a shorter leg off to the right. The outer walls were actually in a sort of serpentine design, but with very long stretches between curves that she hadn't noticed before. Why wasn't the canal on the *outside* of the walls with perhaps a second gate leading to the house? The heart-shaped pool was surrounded by a wide expanse of tile that went all the way to a beach. A tennis court was tucked in between the house and cottage. "Huh. So, Barilli had sand brought in. Lacy Lorin had a beach," Winifred said out loud. She would study the prints in the morning. Right now, there was something troubling her thoughts—something that Hector had said.

Winifred went back to the porch. She wished she had a comfortable lounge chair where she could put her feet up. Maybe she would stop in at the Goodwill store tomorrow. She needed to reschedule the shopping trip to Florida City that she had missed because of a dead body. The gentle breeze was beginning to strengthen. Rumbles of thunder could be heard in the distance. She searched her brain for the problem. It was somehow related to the canal, but her mind, after a little too much wine, couldn't find what was eluding her. She decided to start fresh in the morning.

Which came first, the chicken or the egg? That was the thought in Winifred's mind when a loud clap of thunder woke her in the middle of the night. She sat up in bed. What was bothering her and why had she been dreaming of chickens? Unrelated thoughts about their boat trip had her piecing them together. Hector had stopped the boat and commented on the various canals that created waterfront property for the houses in Doctor's Arm and all the other developments around Big Pine during the '50s and '60s. "That's it!" Winifred said out loud, then got out of bed and headed down the steps to the card table.

She turned on the floor lamp and studied the landscape print. Why was the canal so large? Why was it needed at all? Other properties had long docks that went out into deeper water.

Which came first, the house or the canal? Winifred didn't have an answer, and nothing in the journal labeled WINDSWEPT that she had found in the wooden box Gonzales had given her addressed the canal. It was an accounting of the construction of the estate from the time it was built until Lorenzo Barilli's death. Mostly financial accounts, relative purchases, and services.

She went back upstairs and pulled the box down from the shelf in the closet. She dumped the contents on the bed. There was a stack of letters addressed to Lorenzo Barilli at his Grosse Pointe residence. She figured they were from Lacy Lorin and set them aside. A ring of keys. A document showing the ownership of a 1955 nineteen-foot Chris-Craft Capri runabout. "Nice. Wish that was still here," Winifred said out loud. There was another boat registration for a sixty-two-foot yacht. An envelope stuffed with old photos. She fanned them and decided they could wait for another time, as they were mostly of Lacy and her friends. The last item was a small notebook titled Casa Santiago. It had lists of various companies with names, addresses, and costs. It appeared to be the contractors Barilli was working with to build the estate. Tucked in the back was a folded sheet of paper. Winifred carefully unfolded it and put it in her lap. It was a hand-drawn sketch of two housing developments containing canals. But there were no names or identification of where the developments were.

"Huh. Well, this is something worth digging into," Winifred said as she set the box and its contents on the dresser. The storm seemed to have moved on, giving her at least a couple hours of uninterrupted sleep.

CHAPTER TWENTY-SEVEN

Trucks and many men talking in raised voices jarred Winifred from a sound sleep. She reached for her cell phone on the nightstand. "No way!" she shouted. How could it be eight o'clock? She never slept past seven. She needed to get back into her morning routine of up by six, a morning jog or workout, shower, breakfast, and to the office at nine. Not having the office part was nice.

After getting the coffee started and a trip to the bathroom, Winifred was ready for her first dose of caffeine on the porch. Except everything out there was wet from the storm that seemed to have lasted half the night. She noticed that the large fishing boat was anchored off Porpoise Key. Her phone buzzed. It was a text message from the store where she had bought the mattress saying they would deliver the three pieces late that afternoon.

"Great. That changes my day," Winifred said. She had decided while at the store to buy a king-size bed instead of a queen. The space in the loft was large enough, and she missed her big bed. The lumpy single was definitely not cutting it. Problem now was that she didn't have the sheets, since yesterday's shopping trip didn't happen. Bealls would have sheets—maybe not a good selection—but at this point, she couldn't be picky. She would also need to find a Laundromat to wash the items before the delivery.

It was close to ten when Winifred, dressed in bright yellow shorts, a colorful, tropical-print sleeveless top, and sandals opened the door to leave. Hector was halfway up the stairs. "Good morning. I see your men are back at work." She glanced around. "Where's Sam?"

"Oh, he is over by the house with the crew. It looks like you are heading out."

"The new bed is being delivered late this afternoon, and I need to buy sheets and stuff. Is there a Laundromat nearby?"

"Yes. Over by Winn Dixie. Next to the pizza place."

"Thanks. I still haven't gotten my Amazon delivery. Back on Tuesday I ordered a toaster and a set of cookware. Normally I would have something like that the next day or two. I'm not even sure where the driver would leave it."

"Not down here; it takes longer. It might come today. From now on, use my address. The drivers know to put deliveries on the front porch."

Winifred pulled her phone from her tote bag. "What's your address? I'll change the shipping instructions now." She entered the information. "Oh, by the way, it was really dark last night when I was cooking. The one light bulb under the house isn't enough. Do you think you could install a couple of floodlights? Maybe one pointing toward the driveway and the other toward the water?"

"I should have thought of that when you first moved in. I'll take care of it in the next day or two." Hector glanced back toward the main house. "Did you remember to lock the door to the garage yesterday when you left?"

"Of course. I checked the front door and sliders to the patio before I left. Why?"

"No reason. It just came to mind as I stand here. I better get back to my men." He turned and walked back down the steps.

"I'll see you when I get back," Winifred said as she pulled the door closed behind her, checking to make sure it locked.

Bealls had three choices of king-size sheets—white, dark-blue, and brown. She chose the white. Winifred loved pillows and bought two more plus extra cases. A lightweight blanket was also added to the cart. Not having a washer and dryer in the cottage, Winifred decided she'd be wise to check out the selection of underwear. Next, she went to housewares and found a large mixing bowl, a laundry basket, and a casserole dish that was added along with a giant dog bed for Sam and a can of tennis balls. She walked out of the store juggling three large shopping bags and the dog bed tucked under her arm. She had to shoo three chickens away before opening the Escalade's liftgate.

She then drove to the other side of the plaza and pulled the sheets and pillowcases out of the SUV along with her bag of dirty clothes. After filling the machines, Winifred noticed the Monroe County Library in the next strip of stores and decided to check it out. She found books on local history and spent her laundry time reading.

An hour and a half later with clean clothes and bedding folded and placed in the back seats, Winifred's stomach told her it was time for lunch. She headed out onto US-1 to Eggs In Paradise.

"Well, hello, stranger," Katie said as she greeted Winifred. "You caught us during our busiest time. All the tables are full at the moment."

"I see you've put up a Christmas tree since I was here last."

"Yep. My husband strung lights around the outside windows and framed the building. I have two giant candy canes for either side of the door that he will get to later today."

Captain Sally was sitting at her usual table in the corner and waved Winifred over.

Katie handed Winifred a menu as another customer walked in.

Winifred admired all the interior holiday decorations as she wound her way among the tables to the corner.

"Freddie, please join me. I've been wondering how you are. Mike Connor was in earlier for breakfast." Sally glanced at the people sitting at the nearest table. She whispered, "He told me about the body."

Winifred pulled out the chair opposite and sat down.

"Yeah, that was bad. Hector sent me a photo. I've never seen the guy before. It will probably be next week before we get any information from the coroner or DEA."

"Have you settled in at the cottage?"

"Slowly. I have a new bed being delivered later this afternoon. I spent this morning shopping at Bealls for bedding, then at the Laundromat washing the bedding."

"I know how inconvenient it is not to have your own washer and dryer."

"One good thing came out of it—I found the library. I'm now quite knowledgeable on the early indigenous Calusa people. By this time next week, I should be an authority on the Spanish explorations of the 1500s."

"Ah, yes. And our very own pirate, Captain Diego Alverez."

"Pirate? Here? I look forward to researching him," Winifred added.

"I doubt very much if you'll find anything in print. He's mostly part of our local folklore."

"Speaking of the Spanish, do you know if there is a place called Casa Santiago?"

Sally thought for a moment. "No. Doesn't ring a bell. But the name Santiago was a rather common name. Why?"

"It came up in a journal I'm reading."

"Journal? Whose?"

"Lorenzo Barilli. My attorney in Key Largo gave me an old wooden box once I signed the inheritance documents."

"An old wooden box? That sounds mysterious. Sorry to interrupt, but do you know what you want?" Katie asked. "It's fish fry Friday. I'm getting a lot of good comments on the grouper sandwich."

"Great. I'll have that with pepper jack cheese, extra tartar sauce, and an iced tea,"

Katie wrote down the order and looked over her shoulder at a customer who was waving at her. "Gotta go," she said and walked away.

"So, what was in the box?"

"A couple of small notebooks, letters, photos, and a journal. Mostly financial expenses during the building of the estate. I haven't gone through everything, but I did find a pencil sketch of what looks like a couple of housing developments. One of them was marked Casa Santiago."

"You should take a drive around Big Pine and see if any of the neighborhoods match the drawing. Maybe the name was changed. Maybe it was a drawing of a place that Barilli had visited somewhere else. Those canals were being dug for housing developments all over Florida during the '50s and '60s."

"Interesting. I didn't know that."

"Yep. I was born in 1968, so the construction was winding down by then, but my father had operated a steam shovel and helped dig the canals. Mom knows all the stories, and there are lots of photos."

"I would love to talk to her," Winifred said as her phone rang. She looked at the name. "My attorney. I need to take this." She got up and walked to the front door and went outside. "Hello, Mr. Gonzales?"

"No, it's Rosa. Mr. Gonzales is in Miami for a meeting. I got your message this morning when I came in." She hesitated before continuing. "I called the clerk's office to check on the status of your filing." Rosa paused again. "I don't know how this could happen, because I know that Mr. Gonzales took your paperwork to the county office himself."

"What happened, Rosa?"

"They don't have anything. There is nothing with your name. I just don't understand. I've called Mr. Gonzales several times today, but he hasn't gotten back to me."

Winifred's heart raced double-time. Her chest tightened. She wondered how much more could go wrong. "Okay, Rosa, don't panic. Perhaps the documents were directed to the wrong department, since Mr. Gonzales dropped them off personally. I'm sure they are floating around somewhere, and now that you have alerted them to the problem, someone will find them."

"I'm sure you're right. I'll check back with you before I leave the office around five."

Katie was placing the food order on the table as Winifred returned.

"Thank you. That looks yummy," Winifred said as she sat down.

"What happened?" Sally asked. "And don't say nothing. A new problem is written all over your face."

Winifred placed the napkin in her lap. "The Monroe County Clerk's Office has lost my paperwork."

Captain Sally leaned forward placing her elbows on the table. "How is that possible?"

Winifred swallowed her first bite of the sandwich. "I have no idea, since my attorney hand-delivered them on Thursday, November thirtieth. That was ten days ago."

"What does that mean?"

"It means my official ownership of Windswept is in limbo."

CHAPTER TWENTY-EIGHT

Hector was working at the front gate. He had removed the casing from the motor. The gears and chain were rusty, as was everything made with steel in the keys. He greased and oiled the moving parts, but it did need replacing. His phone rang as he was wiping the lubricants off his hands. He pulled it out of his pocket and checked the screen—Sophia. "Hello."

"The last of my lunch crowd left. I thought I would check in and see how Winifred is doing. Any news on the body?"

"Mike Connor called not five minutes ago. Miami DEA identified his photo right away. His name is Enrique Flores. He has a rap sheet a mile long, but not for smuggling—burglary. Mostly on the east coast and Miami. Coroner's examination showed blunt force trauma to the head. The wound was clean, so not a rock or anything on the beach. But get this—he had infected puncture wounds to his thigh and right hand."

"What are you thinking?"

"The first day I took Winifred on a tour of the property, she noticed blood on one of the yucca plants down by the water. I told her it was probably a deer so she wouldn't worry. A few days ago, I found a piece of torn black material on a yucca that is close to the house. And this morning I found the side door to the garage unlocked."

"Maybe Winifred was looking around and forgot to lock up."

"I thought that too. I talked to her this morning before she went shopping and she said she checked all the doors when she left."

"She went shopping?" Sophia asked.

"Yeah. A new bed is being delivered later today, and she needed to buy sheets and stuff. I think she was going to Bealls and then the Laundromat. She texted me after to say that she was going to the Egg for lunch."

"You let her go to the Laundromat *alone*!" Sophia shouted.

"Well, yeah."

"Hector! Someone was following her on Tuesday! Someone tried to kill her up north!"

"So, you are thinking that our dead guy was really after her? Even though all activity outside the walls has been for smuggling?" Hector considered what his sister was saying. "I don't think so. I think he was trying to get into the house. And he wasn't alone. Someone with him got away in a boat with a green-painted bottom." Hector paused to think. "I don't know what to do. Should I tell her about the trespassers? That maybe the dead guy was after her?"

"What the hell is going on? The house is empty. There is nothing to steal."

"Sophia, I don't know how to handle this. I want to protect her. I'm making the property as safe as I can. I'm even making hiding places for her."

"Well, for one thing, if she were my daughter, I wouldn't want her hanging around a shopping plaza doing laundry. Is there any way you can hook up a washer and dryer in the cottage? They have those single stacked units that don't take up much space."

"Hmmm. Maybe."

"I'll go online and check Home Depot and text you the measurements."

"Sophia, Winifred is a grown woman. I can't keep her a prisoner. I've given her maps so she can drive around, and I know she wants to explore the Keys."

"Unless she hires a bodyguard, I don't know what else can be done. Do you know if Winifred wears a smartwatch?"

"I don't know. Why?"

"Maria got one for work. Her activity and location can be tracked by her office if necessary. It's an extension of her phone. Plus, it has safety features like fall detection and emergency SOS. They are also waterproof."

"Really? I guess I'm not up on all this newfangled stuff. I'll ask her when she gets back."

"Okay. You work on that. I have a customer to take care of. Call me tonight," Sophia said, then ended the call.

"Bodyguard?" Hector thought about that for a moment. "I may have an idea," he said as he got in his truck and drove to where his men were working.

CHAPTER TWENTY-NINE

Winifred arrived back at the cottage around two and had everything unloaded and taken upstairs except for the dog stuff, when Sam came running along the driveway and nuzzled her hand. "Hello, boy. I bought you a big bed, so you don't have to lie on the hard concrete floor." He followed her over to where she had arranged it next to the picnic table. Sam immediately stepped in.

"Well now, don't you look important sitting in your own bed," Hector said as he approached. "Somebody is spoiling you."

"I bought him a water and food bowl as well. He had a problem with the paper plate last night. I thought he should have his own, since it looks like he'll be hanging out here from time to time."

"How did it go at the Laundromat? I caught hell from Sophia for letting you spend so much time alone at the plaza. I promised to install a washer and dryer before you have to wash clothes again."

"Thank you. That would be a great help, although I did spend some quality time at the library brushing up on local history." Winifred then remembered the phone call from Rosa.

"What's wrong? Your face is telling me something bad happened," Hector said in a concerned voice.

"Rosa, from my attorney's office called me while I was having lunch at the Egg. She was following up on my voicemail message." Winifred took a deep breath to calm the anger that was suddenly causing her blood to boil. "The Monroe County Clerk's Office doesn't have or can't find my paperwork!"

"No! How can that be?" Hector sounded furious. "You said Mr. Gonzales took the papers himself."

"That is what Rosa believed and why she never followed up with the office."

"What did Mr. Gonzales say?"

"Rosa couldn't reach him. He's in Miami." Winifred took another deep breath. "She will call me as soon as she talks to him."

Hector didn't respond but looked over in the direction of the main house. His silence was becoming uncomfortable for Winifred, and she was about to ask what he was thinking when he turned his attention back to her.

"Someone broke into the house during the night. The side door was unlocked." Hector paused a beat. "I found scratch marks on the safe room door."

Winifred went cold. A flashback of the burglar trying to break into the garage in Traverse City and then the fire sent her into a dizzy spell. She reached out for Hector's arm.

"Here. Let's sit down at the table," he said as he guided her over to the picnic table. "I'll run upstairs and get you water."

"No, I'm okay. It was only a memory of Aleksy Petrowski breaking into my garage, then setting fire to the cabin."

"You think it was him? This Aleksy is here?"

"I don't know. I don't think so. If he is still after me, then he would have set fire to the cottage." Winifred's heart rate was returning to normal, and the dizziness was gone. "I'll call Harry

Lincoln and see what he has found. He is trying to find the person who hired Petrowski. Maybe there is a connection."

"There is more." Hector hesitated before continuing. "Mike Connor called a little while ago. The dead man is Enrique Flores. The FBI has him on a list for burglary, not smuggling. And the coroner found infected puncture wounds. That means to me that he was *inside* the walls before he was killed."

"Burglary?" Winifred was dumbfounded. "Why would anyone want to break into an empty house?" She thought about that for a moment. "Hector, could Barilli's people have been storing drugs in the house over the years? Maybe that's what they are after."

"No way. The house has been sealed up tight against storms since Irma. My men took down the boards, and I opened the doors for you. No one has tried to get in before—I check."

"Irma was in 2017. And you sealed the house after that?"

"Well, not *right* after. There was some furniture and stuff that was thrown out from water damage. Big fans were brought in to dry the place out. It was about a year later that I was ordered to have the place sealed up."

"Who gave you the orders? Did someone from the Barilli Trust come here?"

"Mr. Gonzales came here while we cleaned it out and gave the orders to have it sealed."

"Do you report to anyone besides Edwardo Gonzales?"

"No. Only him. I give him a report on the property the last day of each month."

Winifred found this bit of information extremely interesting, especially after Rosa's call earlier. "What do you include in the reports?"

"Everything. The money I spend. What needs to be fixed. Who I see on the property and what I see at night. Lights and stuff."

"When was the last report that you gave him?"

"November thirtieth."

"Did he tell you to stop reporting since I signed the documents in his office the day before?"

"No." Hector shook his head. "I still write everything down. I guess I give it to you now."

Winifred was thinking that Gonzales appeared to be at the center of everything relative to the Barilli family and her missing inheritance paperwork. What she now wondered was how involved was Hector. Her phone buzzed before she could ask him. She pulled it out of her pocket and checked the screen. "It's a text message from the store. The delivery truck will be here in twenty minutes."

Hector stood. "I will go and bring my truck. It is best if Sam stays locked in there while the delivery men are here. He doesn't like strangers."

⊨+⊨

Winifred stood at the bottom of the steps as two men got out of the large delivery truck. The driver approached her with a clipboard in hand, while the passenger went to the rear of the vehicle and raised the door. Sam let out a vicious bark with teeth bared. The man stepped away from the pickup truck as Hector walked over to the aggressive dog and said, "Amigos! Amigos!" At once Sam sat quietly and watched the activity beyond the truck's windows. At the same time, her phone rang. She pulled it from her pocket and checked the screen. "I'm sorry, but I must take this. It's Rosa," Winifred said to Hector.

"No problem. I will take care of the delivery," Hector said, then began directing the two men to the stairs.

Winifred walked over to the picnic table. "Hello, Rosa?"

"Yes, Freddie, I have news. I talked to Mr. Gonzales, and he swears that he took the paperwork to the Monroe County Clerk's Office, and it was date and time stamped."

"So, why don't they have it now if someone in the office logged it in?"

"I asked him that. He said that he is on his way back from Miami now and will go directly to the clerk's office in the morning when they open. I'm sure he will sort this whole mess out. Mr. Gonzales is a very important attorney. He will make it right."

"Okay. I hope he does find that it was simply misplaced, and I haven't lost a week in the process."

"He will call you tomorrow to explain what happened," Rosa said, in a voice that was meant to sound encouraging.

"Thank you, Rosa, for getting back to me so quickly. I hope you are right." Winifred ended the call. Except she wasn't feeling encouraged at all. Her gut was telling her something altogether different. She wondered just how important Mr. Edwardo Gonzales really was—and with whom.

Hector seemed to have the delivery under control, as the two men were now struggling to get the king-size mattress up the narrow stairway.

They didn't need her, so she scrolled her contact list for Harry Lincoln's personal number. He took a while to answer. "Hello, Mrs. Forrester. Everything okay?"

"Hello, Harry. I'm still here, so I guess that's good. How is everything going on your end? Any news on Aleksy Petrowski?"

"No. He's still in the wind. I'm following the money that has led me to several offshore accounts. But I *can* tell you that they all lead back to Detroit and Miami."

"Okay. Keep on it. I want to know who wants me dead. And *why* seems to be the biggest question at the moment. I emphasize the why because I don't think it is only drug smuggling going on down here."

"Then what? The Barilli family wasn't into anything else in the Keys that I am aware of. And since the death of Tony Barilli, the family's power has all but dried up."

"Maybe they are no longer a major player in Detroit, but who is the head of the family now?"

"That would be Bianca Barilli Morano. She's the grandniece of Lorenzo Barilli. She lives in Las Vegas and runs the hotel and casino side of the business. Her younger sister, Katerina, was also part of the Vegas operations."

"Where is she?"

"Katerina died in 1980."

"So, why didn't Bianca inherit?"

"She's a descendant of Isabella, Lorenzo's sister. To inherit the trust, you must be a direct descendant of Lorenzo."

"Well, something is going on. A body was found on the beach yesterday morning. Name is Enrique Flores, and his rap sheet is full of burglary arrests, not smuggling."

"Got it. I'll check it out and let you know what I find."

"One more thing. I want you to do a deep dig on Edwardo Gonzales."

"The attorney? But he was the one who hired me in the first place—to find you."

"I know. That's a priority, Harry," Winifred said, then ended the call.

CHAPTER THIRTY

Five o'clock rolled around by the time Winifred had her new king-size bed made. Hector and Sam followed the delivery truck out the front gates and headed home. She felt mentally and physically exhausted and was sweating like a prizefighter in the afternoon's heat. A window air conditioner would help control the humidity—one more thing to add to Hector's list along with the washer and dryer. She didn't want to bother with grilling, and a microwave frozen dinner didn't sound appetizing. A pizza and beer sounded much better, and Hector had said that the best pizza around could be found at the No Name Grill. She figured that had to be almost around the corner—pizza it was.

After a long cool shower, Winifred spent extra time with the hairdryer and round brush. Between the humidity and warm breezes, that sent her red hair into the frizzies, Winifred hadn't bothered to do more than ponytails. Now, with a few sundresses in her closet, she wanted to feel feminine and free of problems— at least for a couple hours. Fifteen minutes later, she checked what she could see from the bathroom mirror above the sink.

Her hair fell in soft waves around her shoulders, bangs neatly brushed in a straight line above her eyebrows. She had chosen a dress with a low-scooped neckline and spaghetti straps. Its seafoam background was sprinkled with large white flowers, with accents of purple and dark-green palm fronds. A pair of strappy low-heeled gold sandals finished the look. Her limited view in the bathroom mirror didn't match her tropical mood—it was too Chicago. Instead, she plugged in her curling iron. Twenty minutes later, she was ready to leave with her hair in a sassy, messy look.

The No Name Grill wasn't hard to find. As the crow flies, it was practically around the corner. Darkness had fallen when Winifred saw the brightly painted building ahead with its many outdoor lights and quirky look. It brought an instant smile to her lips, and a throaty chuckle broke the silence. A car was just backing out from a parking space under the huge tree that grew in front of the building. Luck was finally with her as she eased her way into the spot. Winifred exited the Escalade and carefully walked across the uneven terrain and entered through the front door. She glanced around the dimly lit room decorated in festive strings of colored lights—and money. Every table was full, and a line had formed at the far side of the room of guests waiting to be seated.

On her way to join the others waiting, she heard the woman behind the bar. "Miss, are you alone?"

Winifred looked over at her. "Yes. I am."

"There is one open seat here at the bar, if you don't mind sitting in front of the door. If you want a table, it could be a thirty-minute wait."

"I'll sit here," Winifred said as she climbed onto the really high barstool.

The barmaid put a coaster and menu down. "First timer. What can I get for you?" Her name tag read Anneliese. She had happy eyes that crinkled at the corners.

"I'll have a Guinness on tap if you have it. How do you know this is my first time here?"

"I pegged you not ten steps inside the door. You were gawking at all the dollar bills stapled to the ceiling, walls, and posts. First timers always look like they just fell through the rabbit hole."

Winifred laughed. "Hector did warn me," she said to herself.

"Hector? Not Hector Morales?" The woman sounded surprised.

"Yes. I take it you know him."

"Hector? All the locals know Hector." The woman took a hard look at Winifred. "I'm surprised *you* know him." She turned at the sound of another customer calling to her. "I'll be back with your drink in a minute."

Winifred had a moment to think, and getting too chummy with the locals too quickly could be a problem. Her name was already a source of local gossip, thanks to the ladies at the hardware store. She needed to keep conversations with strangers generic.

The barmaid brought the tall glass of Guinness and set it on the coaster. "Will you be ordering food?"

"Thank you, Anneliese. That's a beautiful name. I don't believe I've ever heard it before."

"My family is Italian. The name was from my mother's side."

"Lovely." Winifred glanced at the menu again. "I'll have a deluxe pizza."

"Good choice. But I need to warn you that it could take longer tonight. We are always busy on Fridays, but this time of the year, our snowbirds begin arriving, and this seems to be the first place they come."

"Not a problem. I don't have plans for the evening."

"You look lovely. I figured you were waiting for a date to arrive." She picked up the menu. "I'll put your order in," she said and walked toward the kitchen.

Winifred took a sip of Guinness. If she was going to be out in public, then she needed to come up with a plausible story without mentioning Windswept. And she was certain the chatty barmaid was going to ask how she knew Hector. Fortunately, the bar was so busy that Anneliese didn't have time for small talk.

Winifred was in the midst of developing a story of why she was staying in the Keys when she noticed a man sitting in the last seat on the far side of the bar. That type of guy could only happen in a gushy romance novel. His eyes were too blue to be believable, the color of the water on a bright sunny day. His full, nearly black beard and mustache were trimmed to perfection. Winifred had never been drawn to men with facial hair; she liked clean-shaven with a hint of expensive cologne. He wore a black T-shirt that said, "Fish Me." Her men wore Armani suits with shirts unbuttoned just a bit to say, 'I'm wealthy but casual' and anchored by solid gold cuff links—so why was she looking? This disturbed her more than the five-foot-long iguana that nearly scarred ten years off her life on the boat dock. She mentally slapped herself for the brief attention she had given him and focused on the many dollar bills stapled to the supporting post next to her. Emily & Fred, Newark, NJ 2020 was printed in red marker across the face of the dollar bill. Her gaze found its way back to the drifter. Her heart skipped a beat, then several more, as their eyes locked for just a second. The atmosphere was getting uncomfortable when Anneliese returned with her pizza and another Guinness.

"Thank you. This looks great."

"Can I get you anything else?" Anneliese asked.

"No. I think this will be more than enough for me." *Except tell that drop-dead gorgeous man at the end of the bar not to watch me while I try to eat pizza without dropping it down the front of me,* Winifred thought as she pulled apart the first piece.

The line at the door had long ago ended, and several of the tables were opening up as she started on the second slice. Her thoughts went back to Mr. Handsome. Why was he watching her? She'd spent an unusual amount of time on her makeup and hair before leaving the cottage. Winifred knew she looked good—hot even. So, why hadn't he come over and started a conversation? The people next to her had left before the pizza arrived. She was 99 percent sure he wasn't gay. Not that she wanted him to come over—she hadn't had a date since Danny passed, and she wasn't ready to start now.

Winifred had finished half the pie and pushed her plate to the side when Anneliese returned. "Finished?"

"Yes. And looks like I will need a box. This will be tomorrow's lunch."

"How about coffee and a piece of key lime pie?"

"No, thank you. I think I'm finished," Winifred said while patting her stomach.

"It's our own recipe; we make it here. How about a piece to take home?"

"Okay. You sold me. And the coffee sounds good."

Mr. Handsome stood and reached in his pants pocket. He pulled out a couple of bills and set them on the bar. He gave a slight nod to Winifred, then walked to the front door. That's when she noticed that he was wearing cutoff khakis and a pair of sandals. Old scruffy ones that looked about to break loose at the briefest of assaults. He definitely wasn't her type.

There were only two other customers at the bar when Anneliese returned with the pie and coffee. "So how do you know Hector?" she asked as she set the bill on the bar.

Winifred knew the question had to come. "A friend of a friend. I live in Chicago, and he helped me find a place at the last minute. So, I guess I fall into your snowbird category." She then cut into her first bite of pie.

"Hector's a great guy and knows everyone. I'm sure he will be very helpful while you are here."

"Yes. I couldn't have done it without him." That at least was the truth.

"Are you here on Big Pine?"

"Yes. Not far from here," Winifred said as she forked another piece.

"I work part-time here to help out during busy times. I own a property management company, so I know a lot of people in the area."

"That sounds interesting, because I know practically no one. I'll be sure and stop by again. I've become quite the connoisseur of key lime pie, and yours is at the top of the list." Winifred pulled her credit card from her purse and looked at it before handing it over along with the bill. She suddenly realized that she didn't want Anneliese to know her by her real name, at least not yet. She put it back in her wallet. "I'll pay in cash."

Anneliese counted the bills that Winifred had given her to cover the amount, plus a generous tip. "Thank you very much . . . I guess you never gave me your name."

"It's Freddie," she said as she jumped down from the high barstool. "By the way, do you happen to know who the man was who was sitting in the last seat near the wall?"

"Ah, yes. I saw that he was taking a particular interest in you." She thought for a moment. "I only know him as Hunter. He's not what you would call a local, but he comes in quite a lot for a time. Then I don't see him again for months. Then he's back. Kind of a loner. I believe he stays somewhere in Doctor's Arm or No Name Key when in the area."

"Interesting" was all Winifred said as she grabbed the pizza box, then turned to leave. "See you soon," she said as she walked toward the front door.

After leaving the restaurant, Winifred noticed the large sign for Doctor's Arm. She wondered how it got its name as she made a right-hand turn and drove into the housing development.

Besides the amazing number of Christmas decorations that rivaled any neighborhood in Chicago, it became obvious that the handsome Hunter could have walked to any of the houses from the No Name Grill. Once back on Watson, she headed for Windswept admiring the many holiday decorations along the way. Windswept was very dark—she had left the holiday lights behind.

Once upstairs at the cottage, Winifred put the pizza box in the fridge, kicked off her sandals, turned on the ceiling fan, and went out onto the porch and stood at the railing looking out over the water. She had a million questions bouncing around in her head and not a single answer. She entered Shannon's number in her phone. She answered on the second ring.

"Hello, Freddie, I was hoping you would call. How was your day? Did your new bed arrive?"

"It arrived, and I can't wait to snuggle into all of my new pillows. Just getting that awful old mattress out of here has the place smelling better."

"I got the selfies you took of your night out. You looked fab, and I love the one of you sitting at the bar with all the dollar bills."

Winifred had forgotten about that particular photo. "Hold on a minute. I want to check something." She pulled up the photos on her phone. "There he is."

"There's who?" Shannon asked.

"Look at the one of the bar. Do you see the guy in the last seat?"

"Kinda. It's pretty dark in there, and he's in the far corner. Why?"

"He seemed to be watching me. I thought he was going to hit on me but then left with only a brief nod. Even Anneliese the barmaid noticed."

"Pretty name. Odd. Are you going back?"

"Yeah. They have great pizza, and the burgers that I noticed looked amazing. And it's practically around the corner from here. I drove around the neighborhood on my way home. You wouldn't believe how beautiful palm trees can be if you throw some lights on them. I think these people plan for Christmas all year long."

"Speaking of Christmas, are you going to put up a tree? Put some lights up?"

"No. I'll enjoy everyone else's. Christmas is the last thing on my mind."

"I know that tone. What's happened? Did you talk to the attorney?"

"Rosa called. Gonzales swears he delivered the paperwork. He will go to the county office in the morning and call me with the results. I also talked to Harry Lincoln. Nothing is adding up."

"Like what?" Shannon asked.

"The head of the Barilli family business is a grandniece of Lorenzo's named Bianca Morano. She lives in Las Vegas and runs the hotels and casinos. She has nothing to do with the trust, and she may have no connection to whatever is left of the Detroit business. Hector had said that the operation down here all but dried up after Lorenzo's son Tony died in 2000. But he began seeing activity about two years ago. So, what was the dead guy, Enrique Flores, into? Maybe he was part of a team that tried to break into the safe room at the main house. And who killed him? And what is so important in the house?"

"Freddie, are you sure you are okay alone down there?"

"I wish I could give you a positive yes. But truth is I really don't know."

CHAPTER THIRTY-ONE

The new mattress should have had Winifred enjoying the first good sleep she'd had in weeks. Instead, she tossed and turned trying to get the myriads of troubling questions out of her mind so sleep could come. Finally, around three o'clock, she got up and padded down the steps to the porch. A warm breeze off the Gulf combined with the gentle lap of waves made for the perfect night for a walk under a thick blanket of stars. Thoughts that perhaps one day it would be safe enough for her to fully enjoy her tropical paradise were interrupted by a foreign sound—a metal-hitting-metal sound. She grabbed the binoculars off the table and walked to the far side of the porch that faced the main house. A light moved inside. Someone was in the house.

Winifred ran inside for her cell phone and pressed the number for Hector. It took him too long to answer. She was about to hang up.

"Hello?" He cleared his throat. "Winifred, what's wrong?"

"Someone is in the house!" Winifred shouted. "They are moving around with a flashlight."

"Make sure your door is locked, then go out to the porch and watch, but keep quiet. I'm on my way and calling the police!" She could hear him moving around. "Don't leave the cottage!"

Winifred checked the front door to make sure it was locked, then pulled an iron skillet out of the stove drawer that she had bought at the hardware store and set it next to the door—just in case. Back on the porch, she picked up the binoculars and focused on the house. The beam of light was stationary, not moving as it had been before. Winifred wondered what they were doing and what was taking Hector so long. And why wasn't she hearing a police siren? Another minute went by before she heard the sound of the gate opening, then Hector's truck approaching. The reflection of red-and-blue lights followed behind. At that moment, a boat motor started, and two men ran from the house toward the canal. Winifred also heard Sam's ferocious barking. Then a man screamed. By then, the area in front of the house was filled with red-and-blue flashing lights, along with a bright beam focused on the canal and moving in a searching pattern. Winifred waited for what seemed like an eternity before she got the call from Hector that it was safe for her to come out.

After changing into slacks, a shirt, and her gardening boots, Winifred ran down the driveway to the main house. Sam greeted her as she approached Hector. "They got away. Three men dressed in black."

"I heard one of them scream," Winifred said as she petted Sam's head. "Was that your doing, boy?"

A police officer who had been standing at the end of the canal walked back toward them while focusing a flashlight beam on the dock. He stopped at one point and bent down to look at something.

Hector and Winifred headed over to check it out. "Got something?" Hector asked.

"A bit of blood. They left in a hurry leaving a dock line behind." He stood and shook Winifred's hand. "I'm Officer Mathews. Sorry, ma'am, but they got away in a flat-bottom skiff. By the sound of the motor, I'd say they were expecting trouble."

"You mean they had a powerful motor on a lightweight boat. The driver knows these waters. A foot either way and they would be stuck out there where you could just wade out and get them," Winifred added.

"You're right, He or she knew exactly how to get in and out of this canal at low tide. Looks like Sam might have gotten one of them. I'll take a scraping and send it to the lab. We might get lucky."

"Yeah, I heard one of them scream a moment after Sam started barking."

Officer Mathews nodded. "I would like the two of you to check inside the house while I finish out here."

The side door was wide open. Sam was the first one in with his nose to the ground. He gave a little yip and seemed to follow a scent that he recognized. He led them to the steel door of the safe room. A canvas bag containing a power drill, tools, and a pry bar sat on the floor. "Officer Mathews is gonna want to see this," Hector said as he ran his hand along the edge of the door. "Barilli sure knew what he was doing when he had this installed. Nothing short of explosives is going to open this baby."

"Yeah, and I'm afraid these guys may have just figured that out. I think we should do a thorough search of the room in the morning. There is something important in there, and I think we should be the ones to find it," Winifred said. "We should also check the rest of the house while we're at it."

"Hello?" Officer Mathews said as he came into the hallway.

"We're around the corner," Hector shouted.

He joined them a moment later. "Wow!" he said as he walked up to the door. "I'd heard stories about Barilli having a safe room in the house, but this *really* is a safe."

"It was originally designed as a viewing room for Lacy Lorin and her guests. Gave the Hollywood crowd a place to watch movies. I used it to wait out Irma," Hector explained. "I guess you're going to want the stuff these guys left behind. I didn't touch anything."

Officer Mathews pulled a pair of gloves out of his pocket and put them on. "I take it nothing has been damaged or taken." He picked up the bag by the handles. "I'll leave now. The captain will probably be calling you later today to follow up."

Winifred and Hector walked the officer out to his car. Sam went trotting off in the direction of the canal.

Officer Mathews opened the rear door of the patrol car and tossed the canvas bag onto the back seat. "I don't have a clue as to what this break-in is about. I thought the Barilli business was finished, then that body the other day." He closed the rear door and turned to Winifred. "Mrs. Forrester, I know what the deal is with you and the Barilli Trust, the whole department knows what's at stake here. I don't believe anyone from the Refuge is responsible for this. But something new is going on, and you need to be extra careful." He looked at Hector. "You understand."

"Yes. I'll be installing additional security in the next several days."

"Good," Officer Mathews said as he got into his car, then drove away.

"Give me a minute to lock up, and I'll drive you over to the cottage," Hector said.

"No, I think I need to walk to clear my head. This has been a lot to deal with."

Winifred then headed for the shoreline and the stars.

CHAPTER THIRTY-TWO

The next morning, Winifred was in the process of filling a large travel mug with coffee when she heard the sound of Hector's truck in the distance. They had agreed to meet at the house around nine o'clock after he got an electrician friend of his started on a project. Being Saturday, his usual landscape crew was off until Monday. It was now a few minutes after nine. Dressed in her usual shorts and T-shirt, she slipped on a pair of running shoes, grabbed her coffee, and headed down the steps. Geckos were out in full force darting in and out of fallen leaves and perched on nearby trees. Palm fronds rustled in the cool morning breeze off the Gulf. Winifred couldn't think of a place she'd rather be as she followed the driveway to the main house—and it was all hers—almost.

She reached the house as Hector was unlocking the side door.

"I have new hardware that I will install today along with a ring doorbell. That way, when someone tries to break in, we will get a clear picture of their face."

"Good idea. Can you please put one on the cottage as well?"

"Yes. I bought two."

"Thank you. We had one on our house in Palos Heights. And we have plenty of security cameras at the business in downtown Chicago. I'm surprised someone from the trust didn't have them installed."

Hector looked at her with raised eyebrows.

"Oh yeah, I guess a crime family wouldn't want cameras." She followed him to the safe room and waited while he entered a code in the keypad and pulled the lever. The door opened out into the hallway.

After flipping on the lights, they both entered what was left of the viewing room. It was approximately the size of a two-car garage with a small stage at the far end. Winifred could imagine comfortable seating with luxurious drapes at the raised platform. She wondered which Hollywood stars had graced those boards with their friends clapping at the antics being performed or watching a movie while sitting in comfortable chairs. Now there were only a few pieces of old patio furniture.

"I know practically everything in here and can't imagine what our thieves are after, but maybe a fresh set of eyes will find it," Hector said as he opened a closet at the opposite end from the stage and wheeled out a metal cart with what looked like odd-shaped luggage.

Winifred walked over and stood next to him. "Are these movie projectors? My grandparents had cases that looked just like those. I grew up watching old family movies."

"Yep. Like I said before, I hunkered down in here during Irma. I spent hours watching movies while the winds roared outside."

"You had power during the storm?"

"There is a gasoline-powered generator. It's old, but it still works. I keep it filled—just in case," Hector said while pointing to an electrical box on the wall. He then went to a closet and opened the door. He stepped inside and pulled the chain of an overhead light. The naked bulb lit rows and rows of round metal cans, along with metal file boxes. "Whatever these guys are after, it's probably in here. But I suggest we start with a close look at the room first."

Winifred walked over to what must have been a bar in Lacy Lorin's time. It was now serving as a tiny kitchen. A hot plate sat on the top with a mini fridge underneath. A clear plastic tote bin contained paper plates, cutlery, paper towels, and a few other essentials. Next to it was a first aid kit and a small skillet and saucepan.

"Once we get word that a storm is coming, I stock up with canned goods and lots of peanut butter and bread," Hector said as he joined Winifred at the bar.

"I'm impressed. I see you have a card table, chairs, and even a folding camping cot."

"Yep. All the comforts of home!"

They both looked up at the sound of footsteps. "Hector, I've got a few questions," said a middle-aged man dressed in jeans and a denim shirt. He was holding a clipboard and large tape measure.

"Winifred, this is Larry Reynolds. He is going to help me install the security cameras and lighting around the property."

She walked over to the door and shook his hand. "It's a pleasure to meet you. I'm sure I'll feel a lot safer. Hector can text me if either of you need me for anything."

"It's nice to meet you. Hector has told me about what's been going on around here since you arrived. I have a lot of ideas already." Larry glanced around the room from the doorway. "So, this is the safe room. I'd like to snoop around sometime."

"Sure," Hector said to Larry, then turned to Winifred. "Okay, you work in here while I go with Larry. How about starting in the closet? I'll be back as soon as I can."

"No problem. I'll use the bar top and card table to sort stuff."

Winifred walked over to the closet. She glanced at the shelves wondering where to start. Probably not the film cans. A couple of the larger boxes on the top shelf would need a ladder and strong arms. She decided on the smaller ones that were about the size of your average shoebox. She carried two of the boxes over to the bar and opened the lid of the first one. It was filled with black-and-white and some color photos. After fanning through them, she put them back and opened the second box. It contained photos as well. Winifred stacked them on the floor and went back into the closet. She pulled out a row of old film cans and recognized *The Sound of Music, The Birds, From Russia with Love, West Side Story, Psycho.* The next row had movies from the '50s. Two small suitcases were filled with home movies with dates from 1962 to 1966. Winifred was wondering if watching some of those would give her an idea of what it was like living at Windswept back then with Lacy Lorin and her friends, when Hector walked in.

"Find anything interesting?"

Winifred nodded toward the bar. "Those two boxes are filled with old photos. I think I'll take them to the cottage and look through them." She removed a home movie from the box labeled Windswept Christmas 1964. "These look like they might be fun to watch."

"Yeah. I watched one and got bored. So, I stuck with the regular movies. There's a lot of them in here."

"Do you know if the projector still works? I'd like to spend the afternoon watching these home movies. I know it's a long shot, but maybe there's something here that will tell us what these guys are after."

"There's another machine that runs these smaller films. I'll get it down and see if I can get it working."

"You have spent many hours in here. Do you have any clue as to what these guys are after?"

"No," Hector said as he pulled the case, which was about the size of a large electric kitchen mixer, down off the shelf.

Winifred considered everything she knew about the early 1960s. "Maybe something illicit or illegal was going on and it was caught on film."

"The Cuban revolutionaries used No Name Key to plan the Cuban Revolution of 1895 that started the Spanish American War."

"Interesting. But I don't think the dates match."

"Well, around 1963, Cuban freedom fighters used No Name Key as a training camp for their guerrillas. It was used for all kinds of illegal operations from the time of the pirates till 1967 when the concrete bridge was put in. That's when the building of home sites started."

Winifred watched as Hector carried the heavy machine over to the card table and took the cover off. He then went over to the stage and pulled back the curtain, revealing a large movie screen. "And I suppose everyone here on Big Pine knew what was going on."

"Yep."

"Okay. So, Lorenzo Barilli took possession of the thousand acres in 1960. He started building Windswept in 1962. Maybe Barilli had some top-secret documents about the Cold War, President Kennedy or the Cuban Missile Crisis and someone believes they are hidden in here."

"Where?" He gestured with his arms to encompass the room. "There's nothing else here. No hidden safe, no secret panel. The room is made of concrete!"

"It just doesn't make sense."

Hector grabbed an extension cord and plugged in the projector. "Give me one of the home movies and I'll get this started for you." After adding a drop of oil to a few holes in the machine, he showed Winifred how to thread the film through the sprockets.

"Larry gave me a list of supplies he wants me to pick up. I need to head over to Marathon and Home Depot. Do you need anything?"

"No, but I'll buy lunch if you stop at the Egg and pick it up."

"Deal. I'll have the Cuban sandwich and fries," Hector said as he headed out the door.

Winifred thought about everything that Hector had told her about what had been going on just a short distance from them on No Name Key and how it tied into the political events of the early 1960s. *Could the answer be something as unlikely as proof of who really killed JFK?*

CHAPTER THIRTY-THREE

Winifred was about to turn on the projector when her phone rang—she checked the screen—the attorney. "Hello, Mr. Gonzales." She waited for a response. "Hello? Mr. Gonzales, can you hear me?"

"Hello? Are you there?"

Winifred decided the reception probably was bad in the room, so she walked out into the hallway. "Hello, Mr. Gonzales, can you hear me?"

"Yes. Yes, now I can. Hello, Mrs. Forrester. I am at the County Clerk's office. They are open today until noon."

"Okay. Do they have my paperwork?" she asked while walking into the living room.

"Yes. The documents are here."

"What happened? Rosa said that the office didn't have them. Apparently, the documents were misplaced or lost."

"No worries. Everything is in order. I will follow up next week."

His answer wasn't good enough and his tone condescending. "But what happened? How long before the filing is complete?"

"Please, Mrs. Forrester. Be patient. I have everything under control. Sit back and enjoy our beautiful weather. Have Hector take you on a boat ride. Be thankful you are not in Chicago; I hear it is very cold up there."

"Mr. Gonzales, my patience is running out! I signed those papers on the twenty-ninth! You were going to hand-deliver them the next day and have them expedited. It is now December tenth! How long before I legally own this land?" Winifred was getting angrier by the minute. "Hector is, as we speak, installing security equipment just to keep me safe! How long before this nightmare ends?"

"Mrs. Forrester, please calm down. You are getting yourself worked up over a simple clerical error. Hector's men are making the property beautiful again. Relax and enjoy. Maybe put up a hammock."

"I can't re—"

He cut her off. "Goodbye, Mrs. Forrester. I'll be in touch." Then the call ended.

Winifred was furious. She was on the way to hyperventilating when she opened the living room slider and walked outside onto the patio. A warm breeze was blowing in off the Gulf. She followed what looked like an old pathway down to the water. The rhythmic sound of waves washing onto the shore eased her frayed nerves. The fishing boat was once again anchored off Porpoise Key.

"Decided against watching movies?" Larry asked as Winifred inhaled sharply. "Sorry if I startled you." She wrapped her arms around herself. "Lost in thought? Is anything wrong?"

"Yeah. I'm frustrated and angry."

"Anything I can do to help?" Larry asked, seeming to be genuinely concerned.

"Know anyone in the County Clerk's office who can push paperwork through?"

"You wouldn't ask that if you knew how long it takes me to get permits for simple jobs."

"That bad?"

"You'll find that the world moves slower down here. Is it bad? You learn to live with it," Larry said in a philosophical manner.

"My attorney just told me a hammock would solve my problems."

"Huh. Yeah. Hammocks are good." He glanced around. "The place could use some chairs and benches. I just came from making notes in the yard around your cottage. A hammock would hang nicely between the pilings."

"Do you know who owns that boat out there?" Winifred asked as she nodded toward Porpoise Key.

"*Gemini?* No, I don't know her captain, but I've seen the boat everywhere from Key West to Key Largo."

"Interesting" was all Winifred said as she turned and headed back toward the house.

<hr/>

An hour later, Winifred was in the process of loading the third 8mm film dated July 1963, when her phone rang. Knowing that reception was poor to nothing in the safe room, Winifred walked into the living room before answering. "Hello?"

"Freddie, it's Maria."

"Hello. This is a surprise. How are you? Have you recovered from Key West's pirate invasion?"

"Yes, and busy preparing for all the Christmas festivities. Uncle Hector has kept Mom and me up on everything that is happening up there. I know he's really concerned about keeping you safe."

"Yeah, he has an electrician here working on security lights and stuff."

"Larry. You can depend on him." Maria paused. "Hey, I just got a call from the Chens. You know the Chicago family whose pirate party you went to."

"Sure do. Why?"

"Monday morning, they are traveling to Cancún for a week. They invited you and me to go along as their guests on that fabulous yacht. I can't get away, but I said that I would check with you. Considering everything that is going on up there, I think it would be a great idea. You would be totally safe while Uncle Hector has the week to install all the security. Have you been there?"

"No, I haven't. Danny and I wanted to take a quick trip with friends a few years ago, but I came down with the flu. I know it would be a once-in-a-lifetime experience, especially on that floating palace."

"Then go!"

"I don't know. Let me sleep on it. I'll call you first thing in the morning."

"Okay. Talk to you then," Maria said, then hung up.

Winifred was walking back to the safe room, when Hector and Sam entered with lunch. He handed her one of the two bags. "Where do you want to eat?"

"I think outside. Maybe it will help clear my head. I just got off the phone with your niece, Maria."

"How about I join you? We can sit on the wall by the patio."

"Works for me." Winifred took the bag and followed him out the living room doors to the patio.

"Did Maria have anything interesting to say?"

"The Chens invited us on their yacht for a week in Cancún. Maria can't get away, but she thought it would be good for me to go." Winifred sat down and pulled the club sandwich and Coke from the bag.

"That is a great idea!" Hector spread his food out on the ledge and gave Sam a French fry, then motioned with his hand for the dog to leave. "You will be safe and not have to worry about burglars, or dead bodies, or trespassers. And when you get back, I will have all the security stuff done."

"I don't know. I hate to leave." She flipped the tab on the Coke can and watched as Sam trotted off toward the canal probably hoping to find an iguana to chase. "Gonzales called. He said my paperwork was found and everything is in process. But my gut isn't buying it. What if there is another glitch and I get put off for an additional week or more? I can't do anything if I'm out of the country for a week. Hector, it could easily be the end of December before I can legally take control of Windswept."

"I understand. But you would be safe. Sophia says that the Chens' staff travel with them on the boat and at least two bodyguards."

"Wow! That's impressive. I told Maria that I would let her know in the morning."

"I still think you should go. Did you find anything interesting in the movies?"

"I've only watched two so far—the building of this house. I guess Lacy Lorin comes later. I'm ready to load number three. I'll give it another couple of hours and see where I am. I want to be back at the cottage before dark."

"Text me when you are done for the day, and I'll help you put things away."

"Gonzales says I shouldn't worry. Instead, I should spend my days lounging in a hammock. Larry says I should hang one from the pilings at the cottage."

"He is right."

"Who? Larry or Gonzales?" Winifred asked.

"Both."

Winifred and Hector finished their lunch in silence—each in their own private thoughts. Afterward, she went back to the safe room to watch movie number three, and Hector unloaded the supplies he had purchased into the garage.

It was a few minutes after four when Hector entered the safe room. The movie Winifred was watching was of landscaping being done between the house and where the cottage now sits. The images ended and the film began whipping around the spool. Winifred turned off the machine and prepared to rewind. "I'm finding these fascinating."

"How so? I would think you would skip these and start with Lacy Lorin."

"No, this is far more interesting to me. I know we are basically living on limestone, but how they originally prepared for landscaping is amazing. They didn't waste anything that was already on the site. The underbrush that wasn't going to be kept was ground up and mixed in with the soil for the beds that were dished out with sledgehammers and pickaxes. Wide holes were dug for the coconut palms and other large trees. Soil that had naturally been created over hundreds of years was scrapped up into large piles to be used for planting."

Hector chuckled. "That is exactly what my crew is doing now. Inside these walls, the plants have been left to become overgrown over the last forty years creating compost. We have cleared the underbrush and undesirable trees and taken them to a landscape dumpsite elsewhere on the property where it is composting. The pathways you are seeing now were created by pulling back the soil down to the caprock. You will have beautiful fertile planting beds again."

After putting the rewound film back in its box, Winifred put the cover on the projector. "I think I'd like to come back here tomorrow and look at more movies. It's interesting to see how the site is progressing, and the walls haven't been built yet."

"Okay. Larry and I will be back around eight thirty. So, any time after that will be fine. You have the keys if you want to get here earlier."

They left the safe room door ajar in case they had any late-night visitors.

Better to leave the door open than have them blow it open.

Hector locked the side door and whistled for Sam. Winifred followed the driveway to the cottage.

⊱✦⊰

Winifred reheated the leftover pizza, made a tossed salad, and took both out to the porch, along with a glass of Merlot, to watch the setting sun turn the sky gold. After finishing, she took her plates to the kitchen, then returned to the porch to light candles and call Shannon.

"Hello, Freddie. Tell me how your day went. Did you watch the home movies? Were there ones with Elvis and Marilyn Monroe? Did you find out what those burglars were after?"

"I did watch a few of the eight-millimeter films made while the house was being built in 1962. So, there was no Elvis, and I think Marilyn would have already been dead when Lacy Lorin was living there. The weird thing is that there just isn't anything in that room that is worth taking. Mostly a lot of old movies and the stuff that Hector has in there for when he rides out tropical storms and hurricanes."

"Huh. Well, *someone* thinks it contains *something* worth a breaking-and-entering charge. Do you think the dead guy was after that mysterious something, or the smuggling activities?"

"That's the problem. Hector thought the drug activity was over years ago, and there isn't anything here worth stealing."

"But, apparently, there is. And you are in the way."

"Yeah. That's why Hector and Maria think I should leave for a week." Winifred debated whether she should tell Shannon about the trip. Her therapist would convince her to go, and that get-away was still up in the air. But she knew she would slip up at some point and her friend would be furious that something that important had been kept from her. Better tell all. "Remember me telling you about the Chens and the pirate party Maria and I attended?"

"Yes. Of course. Super-rich Chicago tech giants."

"Well, they are traveling to Cancún on their yacht for a week and invited me to join them."

"What? You are kidding, right?"

"No. I really am invited. But I'm not sure I want to go."

"Freddie! It's one of my favorite places! The beaches are fabulous! The food is amazing! You can visit beautiful ancient Mayan temples. And the shopping—you can return with a whole new summer wardrobe!" Shannon stopped talking long enough to take a breath. "You can't say no! I'm sure they have staff on board. Freddie, this is a once-in-a-lifetime adventure. You must go!" She paused long enough to come up with another reason. "Besides, I know the Chens will travel with security. You'll be safe. Safe for a whole week!"

"I know. But there is the whole issue about the documents being misplaced at the county office. That puts the time frame off a week or more for me taking official ownership of Windswept. And, think about it, Shannon; this whole nightmare revolves around the trust. Someone wants control or access to this property before December thirty-first. There is something important here that must be retrieved before the end of the month."

"All the more reason to leave and let them find it—and you are in the way."

That statement alone should have convinced Winifred to start packing her swimsuit and sundresses. "I told Maria that I would give her my answer first thing in the morning." Winifred gave a fake yawn. "I'll sleep on it and let you know tomorrow."

CHAPTER THIRTY-FOUR

Winifred wore a white swimsuit. Her hair loose, uncombed, and falling across her eyes as she ran toward the beautiful white yacht glistening in the afternoon sun. It seemed to be drifting further and further away. She struggled to keep her flip-flops on as she ran through the deep sand. "Wait! Wait!" she screamed, but the wind grabbed her desperate words and took them away. She was out of breath. Her lungs burned as she abandoned the useless footwear and dug her toes into the sand with each step. She could feel him getting closer. Hear him struggle for breath as he reached out to grab her and pull her back. "Help! Help me!" she screamed.

Winifred's flailing arms hit the pillow next to her. She woke dripping in sweat, her heart pounding in her chest, gasping for breath. Her mind began to clear—it was just a dream—a horrible dream so real she could taste the salt air in her throat. She sat up and glanced at the clock on the bedside table. Two o'clock. Still early. If she lay back down, would the dream come again? She could feel the damp sheet beneath her. The whirling blades of the large ceiling fan above did little to cool her heated skin. She got up and went downstairs to the bathroom and looked at herself in the mirror. She looked like hell. She turned on the shower.

Twenty minutes later, she walked into the living room wrapped in the white oversize bath towel. She loved the luxurious feel of thick, expensive cotton against her skin. It was one of the things she wouldn't skimp on. She glanced up at the loft. Would the dream come back? Would she reach the boat in time to escape the person trying to hold her back? Why was the yacht leaving without her? Winifred wondered as she stepped out onto the porch. Her body chilled, but from the cool night air—or the dream. A flash of lightning and soft rumble of thunder caught her attention. A storm was moving up the Gulf, sending bursts of light dancing within the clouds. Winifred went into the living room and pulled the couch through the glass slider and positioned it against the wall. She then went upstairs and grabbed a couple pillows from the bed. After making a comfy little nest, she curled up to watch Mother Nature's nighttime show.

The raucous cry of birds and palm fronds rustling in the morning breeze woke Winifred at dawn. She didn't remember dozing off, only the dream that prevented her from going back up to the loft. The storm had moved north, leaving the Keys with a cloudless blue sky. She got up feeling stiff from sleeping on the old couch but eager for a new day in paradise. Even if paradise was filled with certain danger. She got a pot of coffee started on her way to the bathroom and traded the bath towel for the large T-shirt that hung on the back of the door. Back in the kitchen, she leaned against the counter thinking about the dream, while the coffee continued to brew. Was her subconscious trying to send her a message about the decision she needed to make regarding the Chens' trip? The yacht was drifting away from her, and someone was trying to catch her to pull her back. She shook her head to clear her mind and filled her favorite mug with a strong dose of caffeine.

Back on the porch, she curled up on the couch to enjoy the intense gold and pink colors to welcome in the day. A gecko had found its way inside and was perched on the railing looking at her with its tiny round eye. "Well, good morning to you too," she said, then took a sip and nestled against a pillow. Despite the dangers and the fact that less than a month ago, she'd never heard of Windswept and living in the Florida Keys was *never* on her radar, she was falling in love with this new life. A life without shopping malls, movie theaters, fast food on every corner and highways. A life living on a coral reef only five feet above sea level, isolated, with only one narrow road in and out for 130 miles. A life with the uncertainty each year of whether a tropical storm or hurricane will change the landscape. Windswept belonged to her, and she was willing to fight to keep it—the yacht would be leaving without her.

An hour later, dressed in yellow shorts, a brightly colored T-shirt, and running shoes, Winifred jogged down the lane toward the main house. She carried a large, insulated container of coffee in one hand and a can of pepper spray attached to a stretchy band on her other wrist. It wasn't much of a weapon against an intruder, but it was all she had. She was thankful to see that the side door was still locked, and the safe room door was in the same position as it had been the evening before. She flipped on the lights and set her coffee on the counter. Hector and Sam wouldn't arrive until after church let out and he had time to go home and change. She estimated he would show up around eleven, and that would give her enough time to watch several of the early home movies. The first reel was loaded and ready to start, when Sam came charging into the room followed by Hector, who was dressed in black slacks and a white shirt and tie.

"Wow! You clean up well!" Winifred teased. "I thought you were going to catch the early service."

"I am. I'm leaving Sam with you." He said something to the dog in Spanish and Sam curled up on the floor. "See you later." Hector then left the room.

After watching two movies of the house being built and painted pink and the heart-shaped pool being dug, Winifred and Sam went outside for a walk around the grounds. She called Maria to let her know that she would not be joining the Chens. The conversation didn't go well. She knew it wouldn't be the last time she would be called crazy for staying at Windswept and putting herself in danger. Winifred wished she had something stronger than coffee waiting for her in the safe room.

She had finished two more movies and was threading the third, when Sam's ears suddenly perked up and he stood listening to a sound outside. A second later, he was racing out the door. Winifred followed him to the side door as Hector walked in dressed in work clothes.

"Winifred! Are you crazy?" He closed the door behind him. "What are you thinking? The Chens are offering you *safety*! For a whole week! You can't stay—"

Winifred cut him off. "So, you have heard from Maria." It wasn't a question.

"And my sister—she was yelling in Spanish!" He paused. "Sophia says we are both loco. You for not going and me for not making you go." He gave her a sly grin. "I suggested she look up the temperament of the Irish."

"Good! Because I am going to make my ancestors proud and fight for what is mine!" She pursed her lips. "Even if it isn't official yet."

"Well then, we'd better get to work on a plan of how to keep you safe until that day," Hector said in his best Irish accent.

⟞⟊ ⟊⟝

It was close to four when Hector entered the safe room to find Winifred at the bar sorting the remaining boxes of home movies. "You couldn't have watched all those by now," he said as he walked over to see what Winifred was doing.

"I'm putting these in order by date. I must have missed the earliest ones because I'm now at the point where the house is furnished and decorated. But I missed the very beginning."

"I don't understand. You must have a dozen more to go."

"That's just it. All of these that I haven't seen yet are after Lacy Lorin moves in. The first ones were of the concrete pad being poured for the house and the landscaping being started. The canal is already in, and the location for the house had been determined."

"Okay? So, what are you looking for?"

"Hector, Lorenzo Barilli documented *everything*! After watching these, I think I could operate a jackhammer! I watched the coconut palms being planted—which *was* interesting. I watched how difficult it was to dig a heart shape in the limestone for the pool. Rectangular would have taken half the time. I even watched the interior decorator place the furniture. But not one of these shows *why* he chose this location for the house. Did Lacy Lorin choose it? Why was the canal put in first? Perhaps Barilli used it to bring materials to the site?" Winifred shook her head. "It doesn't make sense."

"I see your point. But does it matter?"

"After two years of therapy? Yes, it does!" She took a deep breath and modulated her voice as if she were speaking to a child. "When faced with a problem, you need to dig for the root. What is the source? Why did it happen?"

"Okay?" Hector still sounded confused.

"Barilli seems to have fit the ESTJ personality. Extroverted-Sensing-Thinking-Judging. They have a detail-oriented approach to life and always need to be in control. He would have documented his thousand acres and chose the site for his house carefully. It would be on film just like digging a hole for a tree or a heart-shaped pool."

"Now I get it. But these are all the films."

"Hector, think about the whole of the property. Is this where you would build the house?"

He thought for a few moments. "The canal—yes. Because the mouth is closest to the deeper water, but the house—no. I would place the house closer to where the cottage is. The land is higher there and juts out further, giving a better view."

"Is there an advantage for having the canal closer to the house?"

"When you drive around Big Pine, you will see that houses and canals are close together. But that is because the lots are small, and they were designed that way. But here it doesn't matter." He scratched his head and scrunched his face as if making calculations. "In fact." He paused again. "I would put the house further away since much of the storm surge comes up from the canal and floods the yard. I would have put the house on higher ground and put the cottage here since it is on stilts."

"Interesting. I wish I knew why Barilli did it this way."

Hector's phone buzzed. He looked at the text message. "Sorry, but I have Larry working on the security, and he needs me." He checked his watch. "It's getting on four o'clock. He'll want to finish up before it gets dark."

"I think I'll clean up here and call it a day."

"How about we meet back here tomorrow? My crew will start around eight, and I will get them started. Then I'd like to work with you on another project," Hector said as he headed for the door.

"Sure. How about nine?"

"Okay. Wear comfortable clothes—long pants and a shirt with sleeves." He stopped and looked down at her shoes. "Those will do. We'll be working outside."

Winifred watched him disappear around the corner. She wondered what project he had in mind that required her to be covered up and wear running shoes.

CHAPTER THIRTY-FIVE

W inifred arrived at the main house a little before eight. She'd had a rough night trying to get some sleep when her mind wouldn't let go of the images of Lacy Lorin looking like a movie star and the interior decorator directing her crew in placing furniture in the various rooms. The empty rooms with their water-stained walls were coming alive as they had once been back in 1963. She could visualize Lacy in the center of the high vaulted-ceiling living room wearing the beautiful large-print floral sundress. It's fitted, strapless bodice ended at a full skirt that reached below her knees. The many layers of tulle swished from side to side as she seemed to float across the floor in pink low-heeled pumps. Her platinum-blond hair styled in a bouffant flip that was so popular at the time. Winifred studied the large free-standing stone fireplace that acted as a room divider between the living room and dining room. It seemed out of place. Perhaps because of all that rough, heavy stone in the middle of a room that otherwise appeared light and airy with its tall windows overlooking the Gulf. The room belonged on a mountainside out west somewhere, not in the tropical Keys. A sudden chill caused Winifred to wrap her arms around herself as she glanced around the room. *What are you hiding that is so precious?*

"Good morning. Are you ready for a challenge?" Hector asked while lifting the two black garbage bags that he carried in each hand. He saw Winifred gasp at the sudden interruption. "Oh. I didn't mean to startle you. Were you lost in thoughts about what you had seen in the movies yesterday?"

"More like still wondering what I didn't see."

"Right. Well, I need to head to the bathroom and—"

"Hector, you started working for Tony Barilli in 1993. Did he spend much time here or talk about his dad?"

"It was in old man Barilli's will that the place be boarded up after his death. But Tony liked coming down here during the winter months. Not often but just to keep an eye on things. He would let me know when he was coming, and I'd have the plywood taken down and put back up when he left."

"Do you know if Lorenzo spent much time here after Lacy left?"

"According to what Tony told me—no. He never came back until the last few months of his life."

"So, he died here?"

"Yes. It was in the summer. The person who watched over the place before me said that all he talked about was the past. The day he won the property in a Las Vegas poker game. It was horrible hot that year, and there were no air conditioners in the house. But he wouldn't go back to Detroit and be with his family. Just stayed here alone."

Alone with his memories. Or was he protecting something? "Do you know if this person is still alive?"

"Last I heard, he was. Living in an old folk's home in Miami. I think his daughter lives up that way. Look, I really need to change so we can get on with your training," Hector said as he turned and headed toward the bedroom wing of the house.

Winifred sat down on the hearth. *I wonder what he died of. Was he in pain? Did he have a nurse? The answers are out there; I just need to find them.* She was struggling with these thoughts while she pulled her cell phone from her pants pocket and pulled up the private number of someone who might be able to find the answers.

"Mrs. Forrester. How's everything in sunny Florida?"

"Beautiful. How's everything in gloomy Detroit?"

"Do you ever watch the Weather Channel? I could tell you what; it's cold enough to freeze, but it's too early in the day for that kind of profanity."

"No cable or Wi-Fi service. I sit in the Escalade to get and send my emails."

"Lucky you! What can I do for you?" Harry Lincoln asked.

"I need to know who the caretaker for Windswept was before Hector Morales took over in '93."

"Wouldn't it be easier if you asked the attorney, Gonzales? I'm sure you could get an immediate answer and probably his address."

"I'd rather not tip my hand on this one."

"Could it be why you have me doing a deep dig on the guy?"

"Harry, you are just too smart," she teased. "But, yeah. I'll give you the details when I have them, but he's lying about filing my paperwork. I have a horrible feeling he's knee-deep in whatever is going on down here." She was about to hang up when another thought came to her. "Harry, one more thing. Find out as much as you can about what Tony Barilli was into both in Detroit and anything down here. Just a hunch, but I'm betting that he was using Windswept for an operation in Florida."

"You got it," Harry said while Winifred could hear the keys on a computer or laptop clicking away. She wondered when private investigators had traded in their notebooks and pencils for a keyboard!

She looked up at the sight of Hector who had entered the living room. "What the hell?"

"Winifred? Is everything okay?" Harry asked in a concerned voice.

"Yeah. A Hispanic version of the Pillsbury Dough Boy just walked in. Talk to you later," she said, then ended the call.

⫘⊹⊹⫘

"Your training begins. Follow me," Hector said as he literally waddled down the hall and out the side door.

Once out in the driveway, he gave a loud whistle, and Sam came running and stood in the heel position. If it was possible for a dog to look confused, then Sam was definitely wondering what was to come next.

"So, are you going to explain to Sam and me what is going on, or do we just jump into the game?"

"You need a bodyguard." Hector nodded toward Sam. "*He* is your new bodyguard!"

"Oh no!" Winifred turned toward the house. "This is ridiculous. I—"

"Winifred! Wait! I've been training Sam to patrol the grounds, here and in the hammock. He is learning. He knows the commands. Now you will learn too."

"He's a dog!"

"Yes, and dogs go everywhere down here. Haven't you noticed?"

He had a point. She had noticed people with their dogs, of all sizes, in the grocery store, Home Depot, and even some restaurants.

"Give it until noon, and if you want to quit after that, then I won't say another word about it. Except maybe get a gun and take shooting lessons."

Winifred had a fear of guns. "Okay. You're on."

227

"First thing is to know the commands for Sam, and then the boundaries of the property. Remember the safe hiding places I have been making for you? Well, you need to know how to find them in the dark. And treat the yuccas like land mines—IEDs."

Three hours later, both Winifred and Sam were catching on as to what their roles in this new game were—and why Hector was covered from head to toe in protective wear. Winifred ran back and forth across the property with Hector in an angry pursuit, at which time Sam grabbed him and often knocked Hector to the ground. At other times, Sam would run interference and hold Hector back while Winifred ducked into one of her hiding places. She had difficulty with some of the Spanish commands like the word "stay," which is *quédarse*, and to hold or guard, which is *guardar*. Sam seemed to understand the English versions, so it was decided that Winifred would work with him on the language part as well as the hand gestures.

By the noon hour, everyone was out of breath and Winifred welcomed Sam as her new roommate and bodyguard. She took a minute to order seat covers for the Escalade on Amazon.

⚒

An hour later, Winifred was pulling burgers and hot dogs off the grill. She nodded toward the water. "Hector, is that *Gemini* out there anchored off Annette Key?"

"Looks like her. She's been there all morning. Not a good place for fishing and dangerous for a boat of that size."

"Yeah, but good for watching us," Winifred said as she set the food on the picnic table and filled Sam's bowl.

They ate in silence. Each in their own private thoughts.

Hector finished first. "I should go and check on the crew. This is the last day for them. After you decide what you want to do with the place, we can finish the landscape any way you want."

"That will be down the road. I don't even have legal possession yet." She was silent as Hector rose from his seat. "Do you think Tony Barilli was using Windswept as a stash house? Maybe there are drugs or something hidden here."

Hector sat back down. "I don't see how. Government agencies have been watching this place since the old man's days. There have been weird things going on the last couple of years—but drugs? It is too risky. But maybe." He thought for a moment. "Tony was more concerned about trespassers and vagrants. We have a big homeless population in the Keys. He had me checking the house and grounds every day while he was alive. After his death, Mr. Gonzales and the trust took over. He didn't seem to care all that much. Made a yearly visit or two. I checked in once a month with a report and expenses."

"Huh. My gut still says something important is here—but what and where?" Her phone buzzed for an incoming text message. "We can touch base before you leave later," Winifred said.

Hector stood. "I'll bring Sam's food and some of his toys by after the crew leaves."

She looked at the screen. "I need to call Rosa; maybe she has heard something about the filing."

"Hope its good news." Hector then walked away.

Winifred pressed the contact list for Rosa's number. She answered immediately. "Freddie, I just got off the phone with a friend of mine at the clerk's office. She's the one who actually does the filings. Get this! Your documents are date and time stamped for this past Saturday at eleven a.m. Edwardo didn't take your papers to the office on November thirtieth, the day after you signed them here. I thought it was strange at the time when he insisted on doing it himself, because I'm the one who always hand-delivers to the county office."

"So, he's been lying. I wonder what else he's lied about!"

"I'm sending you the address for the website. All you have to do is enter your address and follow the prompts. Right now, it is showing as *pending.* Any outstanding permits or liens will also show up there. Keep your fingers crossed—I asked her to rush it through."

"Thank you, Rosa. You are a true friend. Let me know if you see anything else odd." Winifred ended the call. She glanced at *Gemini* still anchored off Annette Key. Then she closed her eyes and rested her forehead against folded arms on the table.

What the hell is going on?

CHAPTER THIRTY-SIX

It was well past midnight and Sam continued to pace back and forth around the cottage. An hour earlier, she had opened the glass slider so he could go out onto the porch. She went downstairs and moved his bed from the middle of the room to the porch, thinking that perhaps he often slept outdoors. But that didn't work. By two o'clock, she'd given up any chance of sleep. Hector had said that she needed to become so familiar with the property that she could outrun or outsmart an attacker. This was the night to begin her training. After putting the same clothes back on that she had worn during the day, Winifred grabbed her phone, a penlight, and the small can of mace and started for the front door. "Come on, boy. We start our night training." Sam was waiting at the foot of the stairs, appearing to wait for a command. She looked at her surroundings as her eyes adjusted to the dark. A full moon gave light but also created shadows on the ground. Sam looked up at her expectantly—waiting.

"Patrol!" It was the command for Sam to begin a systematic search of the property within the walls. He took off at a full-blown run, heading along the driveway toward the gate. She followed at a slower pace but tripped on an exposed tree root not more than a hundred feet into the run. Maybe it was too soon for all-out running, and besides, she wasn't going to escape her attacker by running down the open driveway. Perhaps she should work on the outsmarting part first.

She could hear leaves crunching and palm fronds rustling as Sam continued his search. The moonlight reflected off the white caprock on a path to her left. She carefully followed it until new sounds of water washing over stones, the faint smell of salt, and the decaying seagrass along the shore alerted her that she was getting closer to the water. Once at the shoreline, she looked out in the direction of Annette Key—*Gemini* had left. She turned right and followed the shoreline to the grounds around the main house. The smooth concrete dock that edged the canal shown against the dark water, and the smells were more pungent. The way to the patio was clear, and she was careful to stay clear of the empty pool. She had almost reached the house, when the floodlight came on illuminating the yard. Wondering if her hiding place would still work with the bright light, she ran to the large Ixora shrub at the back corner of the house. Getting behind it was easy, and she crouched down with no trouble. She decided to put the dog's training to the test and gave a loud whistle and waited. Moments later, she heard Sam running across the yard. He was getting closer, but would he find her? It seemed like only seconds before he came around the corner and was licking her face.

"Good boy, Sam," she said while rubbing his head. She was impressed at how well he had searched the property, then raced to her side when she needed him. He would do just fine; she was the one who needed a lot more work.

Winifred stood, and together they left her hiding place. Another floodlight came on as they approached the garage. She was happy with what Hector and Larry had done so far with the lighting. They walked along the driveway to the cottage. "Well, Sam, I hope you are ready for bed, because I sure am."

⌗

Winifred woke at seven and peeked over the loft's railing. Sam was sound asleep in his bed. After changing into shorts and a T-shirt, she headed downstairs. "Hey, fella. How about a morning run before breakfast?"

He must have picked up on what she meant, because he beat her to the door.

She did an easy jog down the driveway to the gate and then along the canal to the main house. Throughout the entire distance, she took note of the terrain on either side and decided she would need to create a relatively smooth path that would make a large loop. With daily runs, she would not only become familiar with the area but also create safer footing should she need to escape an attacker at night. And after talking to Rosa and Harry, she realized that she was still a threat or obstacle to someone. The *someone* was still a mystery.

To complete the loop to the cottage would require clearing a path along the shoreline above where the seaweed collected. The smell wasn't as bad as it had been when she first arrived at Windswept, twelve days ago. Probably a combination of Hector's crew routinely raking up the decaying debris, and she was slowly getting used to it. From the entrance of the canal, the two of them walked the distance back home, which, for the most part, was free of plantings.

Half an hour later, Sam was finishing the last of his kibble, when his ears perked up and he ran for the front door.

"Has Hector arrived, boy?"

In answer, Sam whined and pawed the door.

"Okay. Off you go," Winifred said as she watched him race down the steps and charge down the driveway toward the gate.

After washing her breakfast dishes and giving herself a good dousing of bug spray, she left the cottage and jogged along the drive to the main house, where she found Hector and Larry laying out supplies on several folding tables in the garage.

"Morning," they said in unison. Hector motioned for her to join them. "Some of the security equipment arrived yesterday. Larry is going to run the added electrical connections today."

"Sam and I couldn't sleep, so we did a little night training. I was impressed with the motion floods on the house. It lit up the yard almost to the water."

"There is also one at the entrance to the canal, one at my fish-cleaning stand, and one at the main door at the front gates," Hector said.

Larry pointed to two large boxes. "These two devices will take pictures of anyone approaching and entering the property at the front gate and canal. It's the same technology that the Florida Turnpike Authority uses to read license plates at the toll sites."

Winifred looked at the front label. "Wow! That is amazing. How will it work?"

"It will be triggered by an electronic sensing unit placed at the entrance to each site. Once activated, you will get a message on your phone and a photo. Like ring doorbells, only more sophisticated. It also lets you lock the gates and prevents someone from using the keypad to enter or in the case that someone is trying to leave the property. And unlike the turnpike models, these also have voice capabilities. If you will be off property for extended periods, like vacations or up north for the summer, it will alert the police."

Hector pulled out his phone and pulled up an app. "You and Sam were out roaming around the property around two and three this morning."

"Yes, but how do you know that?"

He turned the phone so she could see the screen. "Wow! I never noticed them!"

"Larry installed several solar-powered wildlife cameras with Wi-Fi. I'll add the app to your phone when we are done today. Each one has a memory card, which you can remove and plug into your laptop."

For the next hour, Hector took Winifred on a tour showing her where the wildlife cameras were strapped to palm trees and the royal poincianas. She showed him where she would like the new running path to go and keep it above the high tide mark, and he explained how she could lay it out with little more than a push broom.

By four o'clock, Winifred's muscles in her arms and back were screaming, and she'd only gotten halfway from the main house to the cottage. It wasn't hard brushing off the light coating of stone to get down to caprock, but the distance was long and the stress hard on muscles that were unaccustomed to the movement. Hector and Larry had spent the day working on the new wiring for the gates, so it wasn't until after everything was cleaned up and put away that Hector and Sam caught up with her at the cottage.

Winifred felt a certain dog's cold nose nudge her hand for some attention as she slumped against the picnic table. "You look bushed," Hector said as he sat on the opposite bench.

She held up a glass of iced tea. "I've been upstairs, and I feel worse than I look. Let's just say that I won't be lifting anything heavier than this glass."

"You worked hard today."

"Yeah. And I'm only halfway done. I hope I'm up to finishing tomorrow."

"Well, if you don't, it will still be waiting for you when you're ready. The good news is that Larry and I are almost finished with the gate cameras. We only need to set the censoring units, which are hidden in new light posts. The one at the canal will be tricky, since the location for the devices will be out in the open. Larry needs to come up with something creative."

"Maybe I can help him with that. I'll think about it tonight." She took a sip. "I took a class in college that explored the creation of Venice and the workings of their canal system. The moorings got rather elaborate. Maybe I'll create my own Venetian canal."

"Think about it *inside* the cottage. I might come by after dark and test the system."

"The heaviest thing I'm going to lift is a pizza from No Name."

"Be sure and take Sam with you," Hector said as he got up and walked to his truck.

CHAPTER THIRTY-SEVEN

At six o'clock, Winifred climbed up on a high barstool, near the side door at the No Name Grill. She was feeling better after a long hot shower and happy to be wearing one of the three dresses she'd bought on her first day on Marathon. She glanced around the dimly lit room. Only four tables had customers, with only a handful at the bar.

Anneliese saw her and smiled as she walked over with a coaster. "Freddie, right?"

"Yes. I'm just ordering a pizza to go."

"How about a Guinness while you wait?"

"Okay. I'm surprised you remembered my name and the brand of beer."

"Not many women drink Guinness. And you have an unusual shade of ginger-red hair. You're all Irish. And I see you spent the day outside—that sunburn is going to hurt."

"Yeah, I was working in the yard. I was so busy spraying myself to keep the no-see-ums away that I forgot to reapply sunscreen."

"I'll get your beer and a menu. Be right back."

Winifred noticed that the last stool, in the corner, was empty, then chided herself for looking. What did she care if she never saw that perfect specimen of a man again?

"Here you go," Anneliese said as she set the beer and a menu on the bar. "How about moving to a stool away from the door?"

"No. This is fine. I can't stay. I have Hector's dog in the car. I left the engine running and the air on."

"Sam? Why do *you* have him? Sam doesn't like anyone but Hector."

Winifred was at a loss for words. She'd spoken again without thinking first. Her brain was searching for a plausible answer when Anneliese cut into her thoughts.

"Mondays are always slow, and the end of the bar is open. Just bring him in. He can curl up on the floor next to you."

"Okay. I'll have the deluxe pizza," Winifred said as she jumped down from the stool and went out to the Escalade. She opened the rear door. "You're coming inside, boy, but you better behave, or it will be your last." She clipped the leash to his collar, and they walked back into the restaurant.

Anneliese was moving the one stool to the side when Winifred and Sam approached. The other diners watched with interest. He sat at attention at her side, looking up with a questioning look. Poor guy. This was obviously his first time in a restaurant and not sure what he was to do. She stroked his neck. "Lie down," she said and pointed to the cleared space. "It's okay. Down." He curled up on the floor but kept an eye on Winifred as she climbed up onto the high stool. "I'm surprised that these seats aren't taken."

"It's usually regulars who sit down at this end. And I haven't seen Hunter since you were in here last."

Winifred took a deep breath. *What was I thinking? I should have called in my order, walked in and out with the pizza, and driven back home. Now I'm in an uncomfortable situation with a dog, who doesn't get along with strange people in a restaurant that I've only been in once before.*

"So how come you have Sam?" Anneliese was back behind the bar.

"Oh—well—well, Hector is working on a big project with an electrician, and they—"

Anneliese cut her off. "Larry Reynolds. He's a friend of my parents and my next-door neighbor. He's a regular. Larry's been working over at Windswept putting in a new security system. I'm sure you'll hear about the place from Hector. Its history goes all the way back to the sixties when the land was won in a Las Vegas poker game by a mob boss. There's a big dispute over who will own the place at the end of this month. The Key Deer Refuge was supposed to take over the thousand acres of land. Then some last-minute heir from up north was found." A bell sounded from the kitchen. "I need to grab that order. I'll be right back."

Winifred's heart raced. She wanted the earth to open and swallow her. But that wasn't going to happen. How many people were going to learn who she was? Katie and Captain Sally and those gossipy clerks at the hardware store. She'd been careful on her last visit to pay in cash so Anneliese wouldn't see the name on her credit card.

"Your pizza still has a way to go. Can I get you a refill?"

"Sure," Winifred said, but it didn't come out as a positive statement.

"Freddie? Is everything okay? You sound like something happened."

"It's been a grueling day, and I'm tired. You have other customers who need your attention."

Anneliese left to take care of several customers at the bar and two walk-in orders for takeout. Winifred picked at a paper napkin. She liked the barmaid's bubbly personality and seemed to genuinely care about people. They were about the same age, and Winifred could see them becoming friends. What would happen when she found out her real name and that she was the great-granddaughter of Lorenzo Barilli? She would remain Freddie—the regular customer with the red hair—the woman who stole a thousand acres from the Key Deer Refuge.

Anneliese returned and set the fresh beer on the bar. "Hey, I've taken care of everyone else in here, and you haven't even finished the first beer. Freddie, what's wrong? You look like you've lost your best friend." She rested her hand on Winifred's. "Did something happen? I know you're new to Big Pine. Freddie, can I help?"

Winifred inhaled deeply. "I'm Winifred Forrester, the unexpected heir to Windswept."

CHAPTER THIRTY-EIGHT

Anneliese set the pizza in front of Winifred. Her face went ashen. "Larry said your life is in danger. That's why he's installing security lights and cameras around the property."

Winifred nodded as she broke apart the first slice of pizza.

"That's why you have Sam with you." She seemed to be choosing her next words carefully. "Please don't say anything to Larry or think badly of him for talking. He and my parents were in here yesterday evening for dinner. I took a break and joined them while he was telling them about you. He's very impressed with you and how well you are handling the situation. He mentioned the break-ins and the body that was found outside the wall. Larry is doing everything he can to keep you safe. He said he has even installed wildlife cameras to the palm trees!"

Winifred chuckled. "Yeah. Hector is going to test the lights and cameras tonight."

"I should tell you that Lieutenant Michael Connor and I have been dating, so I hear things from him as well."

"Wow! It sounds to me like if I get in a jam—I call you first!"

For the next two hours, Winifred finished half of the pizza, two beers, a piece of key lime pie, and a cup of coffee between stories of her life at the cabin in Traverse City, the apps that Forrester & Forrester had designed, and her daughter and son. Anneliese talked about life on Big Pine and stories about her various clients and their properties that she manages along with their many quirks. It was Sam that finally stood, signaling that it was time to go, or at least *he* had to go.

Winifred promised to stay in touch and paid the bill, this time with her credit card. She juggled the pizza box and Sam's leash through the bar to the side door. Once outside, he lifted his leg and peed against the rear tire while she unlocked the doors. She had truly enjoyed the conversations with Anneliese and was already looking forward to getting to know her better. Winifred glanced at the clock. It was nearly nine—later than she'd thought. She lowered the windows and cranked up the radio for the short drive home.

As she pulled up to the gate, Winifred noticed that the floodlights that Hector and Larry had installed that day hadn't come on. Perhaps the glitch was the highly technical license plate reader that had somehow cut off the power to the lights. But it still surprised her because when she last talked to Hector, he said he would come back after dark to test everything. But those thoughts were put out of her mind as the gates opened and she drove through. The wind had picked up while she was gone, and now, as she drove along the dark lane to the cottage, the sound of waves hitting the shoreline filled the car. She looked in the rearview mirror. Sam was sitting with his head out the window. "I think you and I are going to sleep good tonight." The new floodlight that had been installed near the front steps of the cottage came on as she approached. "Well, this is nice," Winifred said as she pulled into the space under the house. After getting out and opening the rear door for Sam, she grabbed the pizza box.

He jumped down and began walking back down the driveway. "Here, boy! Let's get you upstairs and a bowl of food. I know that pizza crust was only an appetizer." He was slow to follow her up the steps. His attention was in the direction of the main house. "It's okay. You're staying with me now," Winifred assured him as she unlocked the door.

After filling Sam's bowl with kibble, Winifred put the pizza in the fridge and went up to the loft and changed from the dress into shorts and T-shirt. Back downstairs, she poured herself a glass of ice water and headed out to the porch to enjoy the cool breeze. The moon was still nearly full and drifted in and out between large patches of clouds—like a Halloween sky that sent eerie shadows across the landscape. It wasn't long before Sam joined her and stretched out on the floor. Winifred thought about all she had accomplished during the day with clearing the path and then her time with Anneliese. If she got an early start, she might be able to have her running trail finished by midafternoon and have time to think about the types of chairs and benches she would like to put out and perhaps order a hammock. With those happy thoughts, she dozed off while curled up on the couch.

Sam's low throaty growl woke her about forty-five minutes later. The temperature was dropping, and she decided it was no longer comfortable sitting outside. But before going inside, she walked over to the far side of the porch and looked in the direction of the house. Hector had planned on doing a test of the security lights and cameras after dark, but she saw nothing. She thought that perhaps he had done it while she and Sam were away. But Sam's radar picked up on something, and he ran to the front door.

She texted Hector: Are you at the house? He didn't respond. I'm letting Sam out. Meet you at the house. Then Winifred slipped on a hoodie and opened the door. She watched as the dog raced down the steps and waited for her at the bottom.

"Okay, boy. Go find Hector." She watched as he took off running down the driveway. She followed at a good clip, then lost him when she got to the fork that led to the gate and the house. She assumed he'd taken the branch to the house and continued. The house sat ahead—in darkness, the side door wide open. She thought about the many electrical devices that had been installed in the last few days. Perhaps a fuse had been blown.

Winifred reached the side door. "Hector, are you here? Is Sam with you?" Winifred shouted. She had a sick feeling in the pit of her stomach. Hector should have answered. She heard his footsteps coming toward her. "Hector, what's wrong? Why are the lights out? Is Sam with you?" she shouted.

Hector would have said something by now. Winifred's inner voice said to run. *Those footsteps aren't Hector's. I've got to get out of here. I need to reach a hiding place. Which one? The corner Ixora is closest.* She turned to run, when her hair was grabbed from behind. The force jerked her backward. "Help! Sam!" she screamed. An arm wrapped around her neck and tightened.

"Scream all you like. No one is going to hear you." It was a male voice, slightly out of breath. Like he'd been running.

"Sam!" she screamed.

"It's no use. I see the lights in the cottage. Your boyfriend is probably watching the tube with a cold one."

Boyfriend? He thinks Sam is my boyfriend. Winifred struggled to break free. But he only held her tighter. "What do you want?"

"You know damn well what we want. So, you just tell me where it is, and I let you go."

"I don't know what you're talking about," Winifred said as she kicked her leg back to try and knock him off balance. He snapped her head back. Pain shot down her neck.

"Where's Hector? What have you done to Sam?"

His arm tightened. Her head hurt. "Old Hector won't be coming to your rescue. Give us the box or bag and we're out of here."

"Drugs?" It was getting harder to breathe. "There's drugs stashed here?"

"Drugs? You stupid bitch!" He jerked her head to the side. Another sharp pain shot through her body. Her head felt ready to burst. "You know damn well what we're after. Hand it over and you live."

"I don't know what you're talking about. I've only been here a couple of weeks. The house is empty, and there's nothing in the safe room worth stealing." She took a breath. "Hector and I—"

"The old man says he's only the caretaker. Stupid old coot doesn't even know what he's been taking care of."

Winifred had a sick feeling that he had been tortured to get information on the location of whatever these guys were looking for. "Did you kill him?"

"Maybe; we didn't stick around to make sure. Now if you don't want to get the same treatment, then you can tell us where it is."

"I'm telling you that I don't know what you are after. All I know is that you've been breaking in here looking for something."

He shifted his weight, then reached into his pocket. The next thing she felt was a knife at her throat. "Time's up. We know you have the information and where it's hid. You've been searching too."

"What information do you think I have?"

"Bring her in here!" shouted another man.

"She thinks we're looking for drugs! Maybe she doesn't know!"

"Then kill her. She's been nothing but a thorn in my side. With the old man and her out of the way, we can take our time. We still have more than two weeks. Hell, I'm ready to blow the place and finish the job! But she's probably got the house booby-trapped."

Winifred could feel the blade against her skin. *He's going to kill me. I have to do something. Where's Sam?* With every ounce of strength in her body, Winifred filled her lungs and screamed,

"Sam!" She drew the name out as long as she could, then prayed that the dog was close enough to hear.

"Give it up. Your boyfriend isn't gonna come save you."

He really thinks Sam is my boyfriend. At that moment, she heard the terrifying growl and caught sight of Sam lunging at her captor from the side. At the same moment as the blade was pulled from her throat, the hilt of the knife hit her on the side of the head. She fell to the ground stunned. She could hear Sam barking and growling, the man screaming in pain. Winifred knew this was her only chance of escaping before the other man had time to get outside. She feared that he may also have a knife or maybe even a gun. She got to her knees and took a deep breath, then stood and ran to the far corner of the garage diving behind the large Ixora bush. Sam gave a loud yelp, then silence.

They've killed him. Winifred made herself as small as she could. Then she pulled her cell phone from her pocket and called 911. Her second call was to Lieutenant Connor. "It's Freddie," she whispered. "Two guys are here trying to kill me! I think they killed Hector at his house."

"I'm on my way!"

She then pulled her dark hoodie over her, muted her phone, and waited.

She heard their footsteps. "Where the fuck did she go?" It was the man from inside the house. "We have to find her. She couldn't have gotten far! The bitch can identify us!"

"No! She can't! It's too dark! She didn't see my face!" He stopped and was breathing heavily. "I'm bleeding! That monster nearly ripped my arm off! You can stay and search for the bitch, but I'm getting the hell out of here!"

Winifred heard the man shuffle off in the direction of the canal. It sounded like he was limping. The other one began hitting the bushes along the garage with something hard. He was getting closer when he yelled out in pain. "Fucking sword bush!

If you can hear me, bitch, you're as good as dead!" He threw something on the ground and then took off running toward the canal. She heard sirens off in the distance approaching fast. At the same moment, a boat motor started. The men were shouting at each other. Then the boat roared out of the canal.

CHAPTER THIRTY-NINE

A deathly silence hung in the air. More than anything, Winifred wanted to search for Sam. If it had been possible, he would have found her, huddled behind the Ixora. But he hadn't. There had been no sound from him since that horrifying yelp. Never in her life had she been as terrified as she was only a few minutes before when she heard Sam attacking that man, then his sudden silence. But listening to the other man beating the bushes with something heavy had been the worst. He'd been only a few feet away. His heavy breathing sent chills through her body as she curled into a ball and waited to die. The sound of police sirens had saved her. Now she needed to find Sam.

Her limbs were stiff and shaking as she braced against the garage wall and stood. Tires crunched on the driveway as the patrol car drew closer to the house. Winifred eased out from behind the Ixora. The moonlight did little more than cast shadows. Headlights were now close enough to illuminate the yard. Winifred ran around the corner of the garage. "Sam!" she shouted. She sensed the car behind her as it came to a stop. Its beams shone brightly on the backyard. Sam was lying on the ground near the patio. "Sam!" she screamed while running toward him. He tried to lift his head at the sound of her voice. "Sam!" Winifred reached him as his legs struggled to stand. "Easy, boy," she said in a soothing voice as she sat down beside him and began rubbing his side. He gave a soft yelp. She felt something wet and looked at her hand.

"Sam's bleeding!" she said as Lieutenant Connor reached her side. "They tried to kill him!"

Winifred scooted to the side to put the dog's head in her lap. He gave another soft yelp and tried again to stand.

Mike bent down to help Sam stand but quickly stepped back when he was faced with a deep growl.

"Easy, boy. Amigo." Winifred patted Mike's leg. "Amigo, Sam. He's here to help."

The dog relaxed back into Winifred's lap.

"What happened here? Who did this? You said someone was trying to kill you?"

"Hector! I think the men tried to get information out of him—it sounded like they killed him!"

"I've got paramedics on the way to his house."

"Sam and I got home around nine. He seemed agitated about something. Hector had said earlier that he would be coming back after dark to test the newly installed security lights. I figured Hector was probably at the house, so I let Sam out and followed. I was surprised that the lights had not come on when I pulled up to the gate and figured Hector was troubleshooting. The first guy attacked me from behind when I entered the garage. He had a knife at my throat when the second guy who was still inside told him to kill me."

"How did you get away?"

"Sam attacked the guy with the knife. He dropped the knife, and I ran to my hiding place. I think the second guy hit or kicked

Sam, because I heard a loud yelp and then silence. Then I called 911 and you."

Another Sheriff's car pulled up, followed by an ambulance. Sam struggled to stand and growled.

Winifred got up from the ground and held onto Sam's collar. "Amigos. Amigos."

"Freddie, your neck is bleeding." Mike Connor motioned for one of the paramedics to come over.

"I'll check inside the house. I assume the two got away in a boat."

"Yes. They left when we heard your siren. I think they cut the main power line here at the house, because none of the lights are working."

"Mrs. Forrester has a knife wound on her neck. And don't touch the dog!" Lieutenant Connor said to the paramedic. "And call the pet hospital on Marathon and tell them we have an emergency coming in," he said as his phone rang. Then he walked to the patio to take the call.

The paramedic looked at the wound on the side of Winifred's neck. "You're lucky. It's not deep. You won't need stitches." He was putting the last of the dressings to her neck, when the other paramedic came from behind the truck holding a short shovel in his hand.

"Ma'am, you really shouldn't leave gardening tools lying around. I nearly stepped on this."

"The landscape crew is finished working here. That should have been in the garage." Winifred looked at Lieutenant Connor as he walked back. "Maybe that's what the guy was using to poke into the bushes looking for me."

Sam growled, showing his teeth. "Let me see that," Mike said as he carefully took the shovel by the end of the handle and focused the beam of his flashlight onto the tool. He stepped away from the dog. "There's blood and hair." He looked down at Sam. "Is this what he hit you with?" Sam continued to growl. "His shoulder wound is still bleeding. One of you get a bandage on that. Freddie, you'll need to help with that." Mike popped the trunk of his patrol car and set the shovel inside. "I'm taking this and have it tested." He turned back to Winifred. "That call was from the officer who went to check on Hector. They beat him up. He was unconscious when they arrived. But he regained consciousness and was asking for you and Sam. The squad is taking him to the hospital in Key West."

The paramedic finished with Sam's dressing, then got a call while he was packing up his medical kit. "Mrs. Forrester, Mike. If we're done here, there's been an accident on Ramrod."

"I'm fine. Thank you for your help," Winifred said.

"Look, Freddie. They did a job on the safe room, but without power, there is nothing we can do tonight. Are you able to drive Sam to Marathon while I take a quick look around the canal? See if maybe they left something behind in their rush to leave."

"Sure. I'll go and get my car while you stay with Sam." Winifred bent down and put her arm around Sam. "Stay here with Mike. I'll be back in a minute. Good boy." She looked up. "Give Hector's sister, Sophia, a call and let her know what has happened."

Ten minutes later, Winifred helped Sam into the rear compartment of the Escalade that now was covered in a soft blanket. Then she turned to Mike. "I can't thank you enough for getting here so quickly. Another couple of feet and that guy might have found me."

"Any idea who they were? What about his voice? Did it sound familiar?"

"No. And I was too scared to think straight." She closed the rear door. "I need to get Sam to Marathon. Can we talk tomorrow?"

"Sure. I'll lock up here after I make a quick sweep of the area and the canal. I'll call you in the morning."

Winifred glanced in her rearview mirror as she headed toward the gates. The moonlight cast menacing shadows through the palm trees. Her piece of paradise had just turned deadly.

⚔

Winifred was turning left at the traffic light onto US-1, when the info center in the Escalade showed an incoming call from Shannon Mulaney. She pressed the ACCEPT button. "Hello, Shannon."

"Freddie, I've been so worried. Why haven't you answered any of my calls or text messages?"

"Sorry, I haven't checked my phone in the last few hours. I'm on my way to Marathon, so I can't talk long."

"It's after midnight. Why are you going to Marathon?"

"I'm on my way to a pet hospital. Sam got a knife wound that was meant for me. He was unconscious when I reached him. The bad guys got away, but not before Sam tried to take out the one who was trying to kill me." Winifred began crying as the emotions that she had managed to hold back had finally rushed to the surface. "Sam saved my life. Now I must save his."

"Freddie! Are you hurt?" Shannon asked in a tone that said she was struggling to maintain her calm therapist voice.

"Yeah. He just nicked me as Sam lunged at him."

"Where's Hector? Why wasn't he there to help you?"

"They got to him first at his house. He's on his way to a hospital in Key West."

"So, you are alone?" Shannon had now lost her calm voice.

"I've arrived on Marathon. I have to hang up and pay attention to the directions. I'll call you when I can," Winifred said as she pressed the END CALL button.

She knew her friend was going to worry and have a million more questions until she had the whole story, but right now her attention needed to be with Sam.

Ten minutes later, after a menacing growl from Sam, Winifred explained to the vet, Dr. Daniel Simpson, that it would be better if she was the one to lift Sam onto the gurney. She stayed at his side until he was given a sedative in order that the vet could begin the examination. The paramedic who had notified the vet had given him the details of what was known of the dog's injuries and how he had obtained them.

The doctor praised the paramedic on the pressure bandage that had been placed on Sam's shoulder, saying that it probably saved his life. Winifred stayed in the exam room during the procedure. The knife wound was deep but hadn't hit an artery. After the stitching was finished, Sam's head was examined. His left eye was swollen shut, and his mouth was bleeding. After cleaning the head wounds, the vet did full-body X-rays.

"Your dog is lucky. It could have been much worse. Since I was told that he had attacked the man, I swabbed his mouth for any DNA that could lead to whoever did this. Sam is going to be on an IV for a day or two. We'll need to monitor him and make sure there isn't anything else wrong before we can send him home."

"That can be a bit of a problem. Sam knows more Spanish than English, and his owner, Hector Morales, has trained him to be my bodyguard."

Doctor Simpson looked at Winifred with a raised eyebrow.

"I think I should be here when he wakes up. He's not a vicious dog. Just protective and lets strangers know he doesn't trust them."

"How about you come back around eight in the morning? And we'll see how it goes."

"I'll be here." Winifred stroked Sam's head with tear-filled eyes. "Doctor Simpson, Sam saved my life. I will do whatever it takes to save his."

CHAPTER FORTY

The clock on the dashboard read 2:30 a.m. when Winifred pulled up to the Windswept gates. She knew that with the electrical lines cut, the gates were operating on battery backup. She wondered how long it would be before they wouldn't work at all without the power being restored. She'd need to call Larry in the morning and let him know what had happened. Perhaps he could get there early and repair the line. Lieutenant Connor said he would be back in the morning to get the details from her, but she needed to be back on Marathon at eight to help with Sam. Troubling thoughts of how she was going to be in two places at once filled her mind as she drove the short distance between the entrance and the cottage. She was thankful when she approached, and the floodlights came on. She parked under the house but didn't turn the engine off. She somehow felt safer with the idea that if someone was hiding in the yard, waiting for her, she could back out and drive away. She was alone. Hector was in the hospital in Key West, and Sam was in the pet hospital in Marathon. There was no one to help her. The headlights reflected off the gentle waves washing ashore. *I can't sit here with the engine running until dawn. Maybe I should drive back to Marathon and check into a hotel. But that would mean getting out of the car and going upstairs and packing a bag. If it's safe enough to do that, then it's safe enough for me to stay here. I just need to keep the outside lights on and lock the door. Chances are that the bad guys are holed up somewhere and won't try anything—at least not tonight.* She turned off the engine and went upstairs.

Ten minutes later, Winifred was ready to get in the shower, when her cell phone rang. "Hello?"

"Hello, Freddie, it's Mike. I just received a call from the deputy I have sitting at your house that you've arrived back from Marathon. Someone will be there until we're sure the threat on your life is over."

"Thank you. I must tell you that I was seriously thinking about checking into a hotel. But now I can relax."

"How is Sam?"

"Besides the knife wound, he has a dislocated jaw, a swollen eye, and a bump on the top of his head. Doctor Simpson thinks he was kicked several times and hit with something rather heavy. I promised to be there at eight when he's fully awake. I'm afraid it will probably be late morning before I get back here."

"No problem. I may stop by and check the place out, since it was too dark to see anything. Electricity would be nice."

"I'll call Larry Reynolds first thing and let him know what happened."

"Sounds good. Keep in touch, Freddie," Mike said and ended the call.

Knowing that a deputy sheriff was on the property, Winifred was able to get a few hours' sleep. She woke at six feeling surprisingly refreshed and hungry. It was too early to call Larry and Hector's sister. Remembering that Eggs In Paradise opened for breakfast early, she decided to get dressed and get on with what was going to be an extremely busy day. She stopped by the main house to thank the deputy for being there and let him know that she would be gone most of the morning but could be reached on her cell phone.

Ten minutes later, Winifred walked into the restaurant. Captain Sally motioned for her to join her as Katie followed with a menu. "This is a surprise. We don't see you for days, then you show up at the crack of dawn," Katie said as she poured coffee into a cup.

"Yeah, I've been busy. I'll have the French toast and bacon," Winifred said while wondering how much of what had happened to tell them. But, she wondered, wasn't that why she had stopped there for breakfast—to talk to someone who knew her and her situation? She glanced at Sally, who was watching her over the rim of her coffee cup. A customer waved at Katie as she wrote down her order, then walked over to another table.

"You look like you're out in the middle of nowhere and you just ran out of gas. You gonna talk about it, or wait for me to pry it out?"

"Okay. I got home last night around nine, and the power was off at the gate and—" Sally put a hand up to stop Winifred from saying anything more and motioned for Katie to join them.

"You better hear this," Sally said as Katie sat down in the seat next to her.

Winifred filled them in on everything that happened after she and Sam returned home. "What were they looking for?" Katie asked.

"I'm telling you, I don't know! Hector doesn't know! All I *do* know is it isn't drugs! That question got the guy so mad he knocked me on the side of the head—I saw stars!"

"Maybe the Barilli family was into something else," Katie said. "Did he say anything about what it might be?"

"No. Only that it was in a box or bag. It sounded like the other guy was in the safe room. I could hear stuff being thrown around."

"How about Hector? Do you know how long he'll be in the hospital?" Katie asked.

"I talked to his sister, Sophia, last night while I was in Marathon. He's in the ICU. I'm going to stop by and see him later today."

"It doesn't sound like Sam is going to be much help for a while," Sally said as she finished the last of her omelet and sausage. "Sounds like you are going to be on your own for at least a week or so."

"I'll figure out something. There will be a deputy sitting at the house until other arrangements can be made. Right now, I have to call the electrician and get the power back on."

Sally thought for a moment. "I have an idea that might help. A few years ago, I bought a forty-five-foot Egg Harbor, sport fisherman with a tower. I'm doing deep-sea fishing trips out of Key West."

"Wow! The charter business must be booming if you can afford a yacht."

Sally laughed. "The feds were cleaning house on a guy in Miami—they took everything. I just happened to be in the right place at the right time. It's a 2002 model, and I got it for a song."

"Wonderful for you, but what's your idea?"

"I'll bring the boat up here and dock in your canal until you get your life together. That way you won't be alone."

"Absolutely not! I can't have you putting yourself out like that," Winifred pleaded.

"It wouldn't be an imposition. The boat is more comfortable than my tiny house, and having her docked there will certainly deter anyone from making late-night visits. I'll have my truck and come and go as usual. I'll still do my normal charters with the smaller boat."

Katie listened and had a more skeptical take on the plan but finally agreed that it could work.

Winifred looked at her watch. Seven thirty. "I've got to run. I need to be at the vet's office by eight."

"Then it's a deal; I'll bring *Lady Luck* by tomorrow. We'll work out the time later."

"*Lady Luck*?" Winifred asked with a grin.

"She came with the name! It's an amusing story—for another day," Sally explained, then paid the bill for both meals.

CHAPTER FORTY-ONE

The waiting room was beginning to fill when Winifred was ushered back to the area containing the various-sized kennels. She could hear a soft-spoken female voice speaking lovingly in Spanish. Sam was in a corner enclosure with a young woman sitting in a chair at his side. He was stretched out on a raised bed with an IV. She looked over her shoulder at Winifred. "Hello. You must be Mrs. Forrester. I'm Samantha, one of the vet techs. Doctor Simpson wants to keep Sam sedated for the rest of the morning. He did well overnight but began whimpering and making involuntary movements like he was having bad dreams. I don't know if he can hear me, but my voice seems to have relaxed him a bit."

Winifred walked into the space and stood next to the table.

She was torn between guilt feelings for leaving him and the need to get back to the house and meet with Mike Connor.

Samantha seemed to read Winifred's thoughts. "Don't worry about him, Mrs. Forrester. I'm here all day and will stay close. I'll take him for short walks. If I have any concerns, I'll call you."

Winifred bent down to Sam's level. "You stay here with these nice people, and be a good boy so you can come home tomorrow." She kissed the top of his head and stood. "Sam and Samantha. It sounds like a good team to me. Please take good care of him. I'll call this afternoon and check on him."

Winifred turned and walked across the room and out the door without looking back. She didn't want them to see the tears that she could no longer hold back.

⊨┼┼⊨

It was just after ten when Winifred pulled up to the main house and parked between the Monroe County Sheriff's car and Larry's truck. Mike Connor greeted her as she stepped out of the Escalade. "Good morning, Winifred. I assume you just came from the vet. How is Sam doing?"

Winifred looked over at the spot where she had seen Sam lying on the ground unconscious and bleeding. All the terrifying emotions of the night before came rushing to the surface. She choked back the tears. "He's in bad shape, but there are no broken bones. He's still under sedation and on an IV." She wiped a tear from her cheek. "I'll get an update this afternoon, but it looks like he will be there another day or two."

"That's one tough and determined dog. I'm sure he will pull through," Mike said as he began walking toward the door to the garage. "I'd like you to show me exactly what happened yesterday and then I want you to take a look in the safe room."

Larry was standing on a ladder connecting new wiring. "Morning. I'll have you up and running in a few minutes. Sorry to hear about Hector and Sam. Glad they're both going to be okay."

"Thank you for getting here so quickly. I'm going down to Key West later this afternoon and see Hector. I'll let him know you were asking about him."

260

Winifred then acted out how she had been attacked and then got loose when Sam jumped her attacker. "Instinct at first was to run and make it to one of the hiding places Hector had made for me away from the house, but it was a full moon, and the ground crew had finished clearing the property of the underbrush. I decided to duck behind the one closest and hope the second guy would assume I would run and start looking for me closer to the cottage." She demonstrated how she ran around the corner of the garage facing the front of the house and hid behind the tall Ixora bush. "I pulled my dark-colored hoodie up over my head and curled into a ball as close as I could to the ground and called 911 and you. I didn't look up. Then we heard the sirens, and he took off toward the canal."

"The man who attacked you. How tall was he? Could you tell his build? Was there anything about him that you remember?"

"He was about five feet eight, maybe a little taller, but not much. At one point, when I was struggling to get free, I threw my head back and he yelled out. I think I caught him in the neck under his chin. His arms were strong and muscular. He easily held me with his right arm while keeping the knife at my throat."

"Are you sure about that? He used his right arm. Show me."

"Yes." Winifred then demonstrated. "His arm wrapped around my chest pinning my right arm against my side. His left arm pressed against me holding the knife at my throat."

"So, he's left-handed," Mike Connor said as he spoke into a handheld recorder. "Can you remember anything else?"

"He was dressed in black with a mask. I only got a glimpse of his eyes when Sam attacked him. They were blue." She put herself back in the moment. "He was wearing a lightweight long-sleeved shirt that smelled of fish. He's white, light-skinned, and had a tattoo on the hand that held the knife."

"What did the tattoo look like?"

"I didn't see it clearly. His hand was turned." Winifred paused a beat. "It's weird because he thought I knew what they were looking for. He hit me on the side of my head when I mentioned drugs—like I was joking or something."

"Did he have an accent?"

"Not him, but the other guy did."

"What do you remember about the other one? The one who was looking for you?"

Chills sent a shiver through Winifred's body. "He was mean—real mean. He'd ordered the other guy to kill me, but Sam stopped him. This guy would have killed me in a heartbeat if he'd found me." She thought about the terrifying anger in his voice. "It's funny. It sounded like he hated me. He said I was a thorn in his side."

"You mentioned an accent."

"Yeah. I can't place it. Maybe Polish or Slovenian."

"Can you think of anyone who might want you dead?"

"No. I hired a private investigator, Harry Lincoln, in Detroit, to look into the Barilli family. Bianca, a grandniece of Lorenzo, is the last of them, and she runs the casinos in Vegas. She claims to have no interest in this property."

Winifred was still thinking of possible people whom she had angered that was connected to Windswept when Larry came around the corner. "You're all set. Power is back on, but as I told Hector yesterday, it isn't up to code. If you decide to restore the house, it will need all new wiring."

"Thank you for getting this done so quickly. How much do I owe you?"

"Nothing. Until the paperwork is filed with the county, the Barilli Family Trust is footing the bill."

"Huh. You would think Edwardo Gonzales, the attorney who handles the trust, would want to push the documents through before any more expenses are incurred."

"Yeah. They already have a whopper from me for all the security lights and cameras. Well, call me if you need anything, and give my regards to Hector when you see him."

"I will," Winifred said as she and Mike Connor followed him around to the garage door. "Okay, let's see what kind of damage was done to the safe room."

Winifred entered the room and flipped on the lights. "It looks like a tornado got trapped in here." She stepped over what looked like all the old movie film cans. The only ones untouched were the small 8mm ones that she had already viewed and were still sitting on the bar.

Mike had walked into the large closet. "Whew. They pulled the racks right off the walls."

Winifred could see that all the film cans had been tossed into the room. The empty racks were lying on the floor.

"They were looking for a wall safe or hidden cavity," Mike said as he pointed to several areas. "See these gouge marks? They were looking for hollow sections of wall."

"I remember how positive the guy inside was that I had the information on where *it* was hidden. He believed Hector and I had been searching for it."

"So why kill you?"

"Because—they would have two weeks to find it on their own—or blow the place!"

"You're sure about that?"

"Yes! That is exactly what the inside guy said. The one with the accent."

Mike stepped around the shelves and entered the room. "Okay, I don't see any point on wasting our time in here. You said Captain Sally will be docking her boat here. I suggest that the two of you try to put this place back together. No point in rushing. Whatever they were looking for isn't here."

"But they believe it is," Winifred pointed out. *And they'll be back.*

"Have you thought about going back to Chicago until this mess is over?" Mike asked as he walked out of the room.

"No! Hector and Sam nearly died because of me! I'm not running off and leaving them!"

"I didn't really think you would, but it couldn't hurt to ask."

They walked through the garage and out to the driveway. Winifred locked the door behind them.

Mike opened the door to his car. "What are your plans for the rest of the day?"

Winifred looked at her watch. "It's almost noon. Probably go up to the Egg and have lunch while I wait for news on how Sam is doing. If his exam went well, I'll drive up to Marathon and spend time with him. Later, I plan to drive down to Key West and visit with Hector. Maybe have dinner with Sophia and Maria."

"I'll have a deputy swing by this afternoon for a check and then tonight there will be someone here."

"And Sally will be bringing her boat by tomorrow," Winifred added. "I'll feel a lot safer just knowing that the power is back on, and the security lights will be working. It seems like nothing in this world works without electricity."

"I'm glad Captain Sally will be staying with you . . . real glad," Mike said in a serious tone. Then his whole demeanor changed, and his face lit up with a smile. "One good thing about Florida is our abundance of sun. We'll always have solar power."

Winifred slapped her forehead with the palm of her hand. "That's it! How could I have forgotten!" she said as she reached in her pocket for her cell phone. "The wildlife cams."

"What are you talking about?"

"Hector placed a few of those solar-powered cameras that activate when animals come into range. I have an app on my phone." She walked over to Mike as she scrolled through images of a raccoon and iguanas. Maybe there's the chance that one of the cameras caught something. She stopped scrolling. Her heart stopped, and her blood turned to ice. "Oh God. It's him!"

Mike Connor took the phone from her and studied the photo. "Who is this?"

"Aleksy Petrowski. The arsonist who tried to kill Shannon and me in Traverse City."

CHAPTER FORTY-TWO

Mike had a doubtful expression. "Are you sure? What would an arsonist in Northern Michigan be doing here?"

Winifred scrolled through the images taken by the security camera during the break-in of her garage at the cabin only three weeks before. She handed the phone to Mike. "Here. Does this look like the same guy to you?"

It only took him seconds to nod in agreement. "Yes. It's the same man."

"Harry Lincoln is going to want this information. He and the FBI and CIA are looking for him—but Petrowski's last sighting was in Belgrade, Serbia."

"Doesn't sound like he would be our man even though they could be twins."

"This guy is a kind of mercenary. He'll work for anyone and do anything for the right fee. So far, Harry has traced the money to Detroit and Miami."

"Well, this changes the dynamics of the situation. I think we should continue our conversation at the station."

An hour later, Winifred drove out of the Monroe County Sheriff's Office on Big Pine Key. She had provided Mike Connor with a copy of the dossier on Aleksy Petrowski and got Harry Lincoln up to date on the latest news. Mike alerted the FBI and CIA offices in Miami and put out a bulletin for the arrest of Petrowski. There was still nothing on the alert he had put out the night before to all the hospitals and urgent care centers in Monroe County for a man with severe dog-bite wounds. Winifred declined the offer of having a female deputy spend the day with her while she traveled back and forth from the vet's office in Marathon and the hospital in Key West. They both agreed that Petrowski was probably long gone or lying low until the heat died down. She would touch base throughout the day, and Mike would give her a call if any new information came in. She'd given an award-winning performance of strength and confidence during the meeting, but now as she approached the Seven Mile Bridge, she kept her eyes on the rearview mirror watching for any car that approached too fast. *Why did I say no to having a deputy for a day? A deputy with a gun.*

She didn't let her guard down until she walked through the front door of the pet hospital on Marathon.

Winifred was immediately shown to the room with the kennels. Sam was lying on the floor of his enclosure with his nose pressed against the door. He struggled to get to his feet as she approached. "Hello, boy. I mean hola." Sam's tail began thumping against the floor and then slowly stood. "Look at you standing already. And I see you've made a new friend—amigo," Winifred said as she rested her hand on Samantha's shoulder. Sam lifted his paw and whimpered his greeting.

"Good morning, Mrs. Forrester," the doctor said as he entered the room. "I see Sam is happy to see you. He had a restful night, and Samantha has coaxed him into eating. His eye is looking better, but I'll need to check his vision once it opens fully." Sam began pawing at the kennel door. "Let's bring him out and see how well he can walk."

Samantha stood and grabbed a leash from a hook on the wall. She opened the door and clipped it to Sam's collar. Winifred watched as they walked around the room several times.

"I don't see any damage to Sam's legs. He's just a little stiff, but he needs to be careful of the stitches in his shoulder."

Winifred bent down and put her arms around the dog. "When can I take him home?"

"Is your house on ground level?"

"No. It's on stilts, and he has the run of fifteen acres."

"His movements will have to be confined for a couple of weeks. He can take the steps, but slowly. Also, he'll need to be kept on a leash so that he doesn't open that shoulder wound."

"That won't be a problem," Winifred said as she rubbed Sam's head and neck. Sam whimpered when she got too close to the bandages on his shoulder.

"I'll need to keep him today and see how he does. That eye worries me. I'd like to give it another twenty-four hours and check it. If he continues eating without difficulty and doesn't show any signs of infection, then he can leave tomorrow afternoon."

It was three o'clock when Winifred was finally ready to leave Sam. Her stomach reminded her that she'd missed lunch, but she didn't want to spoil her appetite for dinner with Sophia and Maria at Chico's before heading over to the hospital on Stock Island to visit with Hector. The Egg would be closing for the day, so she called Katie and told her to keep the coffee on. More than food, right now, Winifred needed a friend.

Katie was standing at the door talking to the last customer when she pulled up to the restaurant. "Hello, Freddie. Come on in. The coffee is still fresh, and the last piece of key lime pie has your name on it."

Winifred followed her inside and waited while Katie locked the door. "Thank you. I need a friend who isn't going to tell me to pack my things and head back to Chicago."

"That sounds like something happened since you left this morning after breakfast. Something big."

Winifred walked over to the counter and sat on the stool closest to where Katie was working. "While I was meeting with Mike Connor at the house, I remembered the wildlife cams that Hector installed around the property. One of them caught the guy who was trying to kill me." Winifred pulled up the app on her phone and showed Katie the photo. "Have you ever seen this guy in here?"

Katie studied the rather grainy image. "No. He doesn't look familiar."

"His name is Aleksy Petrowski. He's the one who set fire to my cabin in Traverse City."

"What about the other guy? The one with the knife."

"The only photo of him is while he was running toward the canal. It's only of his back. But it does show him holding his arm and limping badly. Sam got him good. Mike is checking with all the hospitals and medical centers in the county. If he's still in the area, we'll find him."

"Wow! Good thing you had those cameras. I thought they had cut the power lines."

"These work off solar. They are used to track wildlife."

"Huh. I didn't know about those. Lucky for you." Katie set a mug of coffee and pie on the counter. "Maybe you shouldn't stay there tonight. You're welcome to spend the night with me."

"Thank you for the offer, but I'll be fine. Mike has scheduled a deputy to be on the property. In fact, deputies have been checking on the place throughout the day. Crazy thing is that I still don't know what is so important or valuable that they are willing to kill for it."

"Maybe you *should* go back home until this blows over. Let them, whoever *them* are, have whatever they are searching for and return in January when the property is legally yours."

"I heard Petrowski say that without me they could take their time and search for the next two weeks."

"There you have it! Leave while you can! Let the Sheriff's Department worry about these guys."

This was the second person whose advice was for her to head back to Chicago. Winifred was considering the possibility, when her phone rang. She picked it up off the counter and checked the screen. "That weird. It's Shannon. She always calls me at night." She swiped to answer. "Hey, Shannon. What's happening? Anything wrong?"

"What are you doing today at four fifty-five? Not a problem if you're busy. I can get a rental."

"Rental for what? I thought you were catching a flight for your vacation in Aspen."

"I decided to change my ticket to snow country for one in the sun."

"And that means what?" Winifred asked, feeling a bit worried about her answer.

"Can you pick me up at the Key West airport at four fifty-five?"

"Shannon! Where are you?"

"At the moment, Freddie, I'm sitting in the Miami airport waiting for the shuttle to Key West."

CHAPTER FORTY-THREE

Shannon Mulaney, Winifred's therapist and friend, was standing outside the Key West airport terminal when she pulled up. She looked like a Hollywood movie star waiting among common tourists. Her calf-length floral dress with cap sleeves and a handkerchief-pointed hem fluttered with the warm breeze around her long legs. Strappy gold sandals and a wide-brimmed hat completed the look of a woman who was somebody.

Winifred got out of the Escalade and popped the rear deck-lid, then gave her friend a welcoming hug. "Only one piece of luggage and a gym bag? You brought more clothes than this for four days in Traverse City!"

"I didn't have time to pack anything but the basics after changing my ticket." Shannon twirled around showing off the beautiful lines of the dress. "I bought this outfit in a darling little boutique in the Miami airport." She inhaled deeply. "Warm, humid air and all these palm trees. I love it!"

"Shannon, isn't this a bit last minute? We talked last night, and you were packing for Aspen."

"I changed my mind. And I almost didn't make it. The commuter jet from Miami to Key West had mechanical problems in Jacksonville. I could either rent a car and drive or wait until tomorrow. Well, that wouldn't work, so the attendant checked other flights. She found a puddle jumper that was scheduled to leave in half an hour from a gate on the other side of the terminal. I made it to the gate only to be told the flight was full—with ten passengers! I handed the woman my business card and pleaded my case saying that my patient was on a family vacation and they had been robbed at gunpoint. Your father had been shot and was unconscious in the Key West hospital and your dog had been beaten so badly that he was near death. You were inconsolable and needed me."

"Wow. That was some tale—but nearly true!"

"Well, the pilot happened to walk up to the gate and heard my story. He told the ticket attendant that I could sit with him."

"You sat next to the pilot? Where was the copilot?"

"I guess he didn't need one. It's a good thing I traveled light this time. My two pieces barely made it in that tiny compartment."

Winifred shook her head as she lowered the liftgate. "Only you could manage to get on a full flight and sit with the pilot."

"It was wonderful. You fly so low and can see everything. He pointed out dolphins, and coming in over Key West was amazing. We flew right over the roofs of houses and people walking. I felt like Katherine Hepburn in the movie *African Queen*. You know—flying into a tiny East African airport."

"And you look like *Audrey* Hepburn!" Winifred said as she turned in her seat to face Shannon. "Now enough of the small talk. Why are you here without any notice?"

"Because someone tried to kill you yesterday."

"Petrowski. Aleksy Petrowski tried to kill me *again*! Now, because of your impulsive behavior, *you* are a target as well!"

Winifred paused to collect her emotions. "Shannon, what were you thinking?"

"I was thinking about you being here all alone with Hector in the hospital and your bodyguard dog nearly dead."

Winifred pursed her lips as she turned back around in her seat. She remained silent as she pulled away from the terminal, then turned right onto South Roosevelt Boulevard and headed toward the historic district and Chico's.

"Wow! Look at this beach. I could spend a whole day here," Shannon remarked cheerfully.

Winifred decided it would be best all around if she left her frustration with Shannon behind and focused on enjoying their time together. "Maria was telling me that this string of public beaches is basically the largest in the Lower Keys until you get up to Bahia Honda, which is just before the Seven Mile Bridge." She turned right onto White Street, then followed her GPS to the other side of the island, where she made a left turn onto Eaton Street. "I know where I am now," she said as she turned off the GPS. She continued the two blocks to Margaret Street, then made the right-hand turn and headed to Caroline. A minute later, she was pulling into the driveway of Sophia's house. "We're here."

Shannon visibly relaxed. "Thank God. For a minute, I thought you were going to parallel park this thing. These narrow streets are barely wide enough for two cars to pass each other."

"Look who's complaining! The woman who has driven the streets of ancient cities all over Europe. Some of those you can reach out and touch the buildings as you drive by!"

"Yeah. But *I* wasn't driving a *truck*!"

"We're early. How about I show you Schooner Wharf? That is where the costume tent was when I became Captain Jack Sparrow."

Winifred and Shannon crossed the street and entered a courtyard next to the bar. Shannon immediately spied a shop called Designs on the Wharf. She ran over and looked in the window. "This looks like my kind of place. We have to go inside," Shannon exclaimed as Winifred followed.

"Good afternoon, ladies," said a stylishly dressed woman as she eyed Shannon's outfit. "You look lovely. May I help you find something?"

"Thank you. I picked this up in a shop at the Miami airport a couple of hours ago. I made a last-minute decision to fly down from Chicago and didn't have time to properly pack. I'm going to need clothes for this time of year."

"Well, you've come to the right place. We specialize in fabrics and designs for the tropics as well as a complete line of jewelry and accessories."

Winifred glanced around. "Shannon, we could spend hours in here; we don't have the time."

"All I brought are pants and shorts and a few tops—I need clothes. When can we come back?"

"How about tomorrow morning? I think we can come down here and shop and be back up to Marathon to pick Sam up in the afternoon."

Shannon reached out her hand. "I'm Shannon Mulaney. I'm visiting my friend here, Winifred Forrester. She lives on Big Pine Key."

"I'm Willa; it sounds like you'll be qualifying for our local discount."

"Thank you," Winifred said as she turned to leave. "We have just enough time to get over to Chico's. I told Sophia and Maria we'd see them around five thirty or so."

"Sophia is my closest friend," Willa exclaimed. "I've known her since I moved to Key West, and I'm Maria's godmother— looks like you get the *family* discount as well." She chuckled as she walked them to the door.

Once outside, Shannon focused on the tall masts and boats that she could see across the courtyard. "Tall ships? Can we take another minute to look?"

Winifred led the way to the wharf. "Okay, but not longer."

Shannon was admiring the two ships that were currently getting ready to cast off and leave for sunset cruises. Winifred moved on down the wharf toward the bar as she glanced at the line of yachts of varying sizes docked along the furthest pier. She suddenly stopped. "I don't believe it," she said out loud, giving Shannon a minute to catch up.

"You don't believe what?" Shannon asked.

Winifred pointed to the boat in the center. "*Gemini.*"

"*Gemini?* Is it the same boat that has been anchored by you?"

"It looks the same. But it can't be."

Shannon pointed to a man who was hosing down one of the boats. "Let's ask him if he knows the owner."

Winifred agreed and walked over to him. "Excuse me. It looks like you just came in from fishing."

"Yep. You lookin' to go out?"

"No. I was wondering if you happen to know who owns that boat over on there." She pointed. "Named *Gemini.*"

He didn't look up. "Yep. Hunter. He docks there when he's in town."

"Tall guy with long dark hair and beard?" Winifred asked.

"Yep. That's him."

"If he only uses it when he's in Key West, then whose dock is it?" Shannon asked.

"Chens'. They keep it for guests to use."

Winifred shivered. Her heart pounded. *The Chens and Hunter. The man who'd been anchored off Windswept?* "Any idea where I might find him?"

The guy stood, checked the two women out with his eyes, and seemed satisfied with what he saw. He nodded toward the Schooner Wharf Bar.

"Thank you," Winifred said as she and Shannon turned and walked the short distance to the entrance. Hunter was sitting on the far side of the bar where he had a full view of the marina. She was sure he had been watching her exchange with the man on the dock. He gave her a short nod of acknowledgment with a grin.

"That's Hunter. The guy with the black hair and beard. I need to find out what he's up to." Winifred was about to enter the bar and confront Hunter when the large group of tourists that had just disembarked from a party boat nudged their way past her. After a day of water sports and drinking, the rowdy group was hell-bent on more fun with a hippy-generation, guitar player singing a Jimmy Buffett song. By the time she and Shannon broke free, the man was gone. They exited through the far side of the room, but the elusive Hunter was nowhere to be seen.

CHAPTER FORTY-FOUR

Winifred and Shannon received a warm welcome when they arrived at Chico's a few minutes later and were taken to a small private room off to the side of the main dining room and bar. They were assured that there were no hard feelings; nor did Sophia and Maria blame Winifred for Hector having been beaten and hospitalized. Over drinks, Winifred got them up to date on the latest news, including the identity of Aleksy Petrowski.

"I don't understand. So, you believe what happened to you at your cabin is connected somehow to what is going on down here?" Sophia asked.

"Harry Lincoln, the private investigator I hired to dig into Petrowski, has followed the money to Detroit and Miami. He's a highly paid professional with international ties."

"Excuse the pun, but doesn't that seem like overkill?" Maria asked. "We're talking about a dispute over who will inherit one thousand acres on Big Pine."

Winifred glanced at both Sophia and her daughter. "I don't believe it has anything to do with the land—they are searching for whatever is buried or hidden there."

"Like what?" Sophia asked. "Something that Lorenzo Barilli hid?"

"I have no idea. But whoever is behind this believes Hector and I have been searching the safe room for it."

At that point, their waitress arrived with their food. Everyone ordered the daily special of ropa vieja, a dish of shredded beef cooked in a flavorful sauce with onions and bell peppers. It was served with rice and black beans and a side of plátanos maduro frito or fried ripe plantains. With everyone focused on their food and eating, Winifred was given a much-needed reprieve from discussing the events that were causing the churning in her stomach.

"This smells and looks wonderful. I detect a hint of cumin," Shannon said while placing her napkin in her lap.

"My mother was a fabulous cook. She could make the simplest meat taste fit for a king with her knowledge of spices, and you are correct about the cumin. This is her recipe. I hope you enjoy the meal."

"Speaking of family, we stopped in Designs on the Wharf and met Willa. We are going back tomorrow morning to do some major damage to my credit card," Shannon explained further. "Since coming here was a last-minute decision, I only had time to pack the basics. Willa assures me I will leave with a proper wardrobe for the tropics."

Sophia laughed. "Once she knows your size and style, she will put new arrivals aside and call you. But don't go crazy on this trip. Temperatures can drop during the winter months. You'll still need sweats and a hoodie, although the locals will tell you they are freezing."

"I wore sweats down on the plane. Then I bought the outfit I'm wearing at a shop in the Miami airport."

Maria held up her index finger while swallowing. "One of the most common questions from tourists is about our temperatures. The coldest on record is forty-one degrees, and the warmest is ninety-six. I bet you have hotter days than that in Chicago during the summer."

"Wow! You are right about that," Shannon added.

"Although our summer months rarely get above eighty-five or ninety degrees, the humidity levels can reach eighty percent."

"So, if the northern snowbirds come down for the winter, do the Keys locals fly north for the summer?" Shannon teased.

Maria laughed. "Those who can afford it do. Like the Chens."

Winifred glanced up at Shannon and gave her the slightest nod. The message was not to bring up what they had only an hour before learned about the Chens owning the dock that now held *Gemini*.

"Give me a call when you know what time you plan to arrive at the store, and I'll swing by if I can."

"We will, Maria. And maybe you can plan some touristy things for Shannon and me to do, since I haven't been back since my day as Captain Jack Sparrow."

"Christmas is our most festive season. The Conch Train will give you an overall history. The Hemingway House is a favorite. I can get you a private tour of Mel Fisher's Museum, and if we are going to talk pirates, then you need to check out the Wreckers' Museum. And no day is complete without our sunset celebration."

"Sounds like we'll be spending a lot of time here. I'm sure glad I won't be the one driving! Freddie's Escalade suddenly seems bigger on these streets. Not to mentions all the scooters zipping in and out of traffic."

"Many of the locals use scooters as their second vehicle. Although the ones you are describing are the tourists who have been doing the Duval Crawl."

Shannon laughed. "Everyone I know who has been to Key West talks about Duval Street and Sloppy Joe's. I'm okay if we skip those."

Winifred was thankful for Shannon's presence. She never failed to be the life of the party and kept the conversation light, while Winifred's thoughts remained with *Gemini* and Hunter and what role he may be playing in the current events happening at Windswept. As for tonight, she wouldn't be able to relax until she saw Hector and assured him that Sam was getting the best of care.

She thanked God for sending Shannon.

Winifred pulled into the parking lot of the Lower Keys Medical Center on Stock Island at seven thirty. She turned off the engine and sat staring at the front entrance without actually seeing it with her mind.

"Freddie? Are you okay?" Shannon asked softly.

Winifred took a moment to answer. "Yeah." She paused a beat. "I don't know what to expect. I don't know what to say to him. I feel like this is all my fault, yet I would have died if it weren't for Sam. It's all overwhelming."

"All three of you survived a horrible event. You move on together. Be there for each other."

"Thank you, Doctor Mulaney," Winifred said as she reached for the handle and opened the driver's side door.

Winifred stood outside room 210 and took a deep breath. She forced a smile before she and Shannon entered. Hector, heavily bandaged with varying-sized hoses and tubes protruding from his body, looked like he'd survived a terrorist attack. Jeopardy was blaring from the TV on the opposite wall. "Hello, Hector." Winifred tried to sound chipper, but her voice immediately turned somber. "I'm so sorry this has happened to you."

"Not your fault. They wanted information I don't have. They didn't believe me." Hector glanced at the woman standing behind Winifred.

"Hector, this is my friend from Chicago, Shannon Mulaney. She surprised me by flying in this afternoon. She traded in a ticket for a skiing vacation in Aspen to babysit me."

"Not at all!" Shannon exclaimed. "I swapped a ticket from cold, snowy Chicago to cold, snowy Aspen for two weeks in the warm, sunny Keys. And I'm loving how you turn palm trees and boats into a holiday celebration."

Hector grinned. "I have heard all about you—and your time at the cabin." He breathed heavily, then continued. "I'm glad you are here. Winifred needs a friend with her."

Shannon took his hand and gently squeezed. She looked deeply into his eyes and smiled.

"I've made friends here," Winifred admonished.

"Have you?" Hector sounded worried. "I'm not so sure."

Winifred was considering his words, when a nurse walked in the room and turned the sound on the television down.

"It's good to see Mr. Morales with friends. He spends too much time talking and worrying about his dog, Sam. He needs to focus on eating and gaining his strength so he can leave here."

Winifred looked directly at Hector. "Sam saved my life. The guy holding me had a knife to my throat. Sam leaped like Superman into the air and knocked the guy away from me. He got him good—did some major damage to the guy. Unfortunately, the knife got Sam in the shoulder. He is in a hospital on Marathon. However, I spent time with him today, and he is up and walking—and *eating*. I may be able to bring him home tomorrow afternoon."

"Hector told me how he trained his dog to be your bodyguard. Considering the circumstances, I'll talk to the doctor about allowing Sam to visit once he's able."

"Can you do this?" Hector asked in an amazed voice. "Sam and I are a team. We are never apart."

"For you, Hector, I will make it happen, even if I have to smuggle him in myself," the nurse said as she walked over to the machine at the head of his bed. "Now if you ladies can leave us, I need to spend some private time here with Mr. Morales."

Forty minutes later, the headlights of the Escalade illuminated the large ornate gates of Windswept. A tall narrow box was propped against the wall next to the door, with three smaller boxes sitting beside it. "That's strange," Winifred said as she put the vehicle in park and opened her door. "I didn't order anything."

"I did!" Shannon exclaimed. "I thought you needed a bit of Christmas cheer, so I ordered a prelit tree and tons of ornaments and decorations."

Winifred popped the liftgate as both ladies jumped out and went over to the boxes. Shannon rapped her knuckles on the metal door. "Sounds like steel and a huge lock. No one is going to just walk through this, at least not without a stick of dynamite."

They quickly got the boxes into the back of the SUV. Floodlights came on as Winifred pulled up to the gates and entered the code. "I'm happy to see that the security lights are working," she said as the large, heavy gates slowly opened with a groan.

Shannon studied the thick panels as they drove through. "Those look like solid steel. They must weigh a ton."

"Yep. Bulletproof."

"This place is beautiful," Shannon remarked as they drove along the driveway to the fork and additional security lights came on. "I remember your description when you first arrived. You said it was like driving through a jungle. You were sure you were going to need a new paintjob when you got back home. Now it looks like a high-class resort."

Winifred turned right and followed the driveway to the main house. She pulled up next to the Monroe County Sheriff's vehicle. "Hello. I'm Winifred Forrester. I really appreciate you being here."

"Ted Nickles. I've walked the property several times. Beautiful place you have here. I'll be leaving at eleven when someone else arrives. Everything's been quiet so far. I have your number if I need you."

"This is my friend, Shannon Mulaney. She just flew in from Chicago and will be staying here for the next couple of weeks."

"I grew up in Green Bay. If you left behind Chicago's cold wind this morning, then you'll appreciate a stroll along the water this evening."

"Thanks, Ted. I'll do that," Shannon said with a smile.

Winifred pulled away and headed for the cottage.

"Is everyone this friendly down here?" Shannon asked. "At home, you're lucky to get a response from 'good morning.'"

"Not *everyone*. But as a whole, I would say yes."

The floodlight came on as Winifred pulled up to the cottage and parked under the house. The headlights glistened off the water beyond. "Welcome home."

Shannon got out and walked to the edge of the concrete floor. "Wow! Can I walk out there?"

"Sure, but you might want to change your shoes first. Those heels won't last ten feet."

"Right." Shannon then opened the rear passenger door and rummaged through the gym bag she'd used as carry-on. She pulled out a pair of running shoes.

Winifred removed the luggage and boxes from the vehicle and set them on the pavement while she watched her friend half jog, half skip toward the water's edge. She looked like a teenager after her first prom—with her dress fluttering behind. A few minutes later, she joined her.

"This is incredible. Can you believe all the stars? How can they be so close? It's like you can reach out and touch them."

Winifred scanned the horizon. *And not a boat in sight. Not even Gemini.*

"Freddie? Anything wrong?"

"No. And you are right. The stars are amazing. And it's the perfect night for a walk, but I'm beat."

"You need chairs. So every night you can sit out here with a glass of wine and unwind under a blanket of stars." Shannon looked over at her patient. "It would be your therapy. The time when you can let your troubles, your fatigue, and your pain be carried out to sea."

"The Gulf—and chairs are on the list."

CHAPTER FORTY-FIVE

Thursday morning, Winifred woke to the welcome aroma of freshly brewed coffee. "Shannon?" She waited for a response. She threw back the sheet and got out of bed. "Shannon?" She leaned over the railing. There was no sound below. She slipped her feet into a pair of flip-flops and headed downstairs. After grabbing a mug of coffee, she wandered out onto the porch. Thankfully, *Gemini* was nowhere to be seen, but she saw Shannon leisurely walking back from the direction of the main house. "Good morning," she yelled out.

Shannon waved, then ran toward the cottage. "I'll be right up."

Winifred sat in one of the chairs facing the small table.

It was only a minute or so before Shannon appeared with a fresh travel mug of coffee. "I awoke at my usual five thirty. I couldn't get back to sleep, so I decided to go for a run. I remembered that there would be a deputy at the house, so I made a pot of coffee and took an extra mug in case he or she was still there. Tim and I sat on the low wall around the patio and talked until the sun began to rise. He's thirty-two, married with two children, five and three, with one on the way. They moved here four years ago from Buffalo, where he was with the police force. After seeing one too many kids die from senseless crime violence, he moved his family down here. His wife teaches at the local school. It's a charter school with approximately one hundred students. They love living here, although his wife complains about the heat during the summer."

"You learned all this over a cup of coffee *before* the sun came up?"

"Yes. And I would have prepared breakfast; except I'm limited to cereal and toast." Shannon paused for a long sip of coffee. "Freddie, we have to find time for a grocery run today."

"Clothing *and* groceries." Winifred laughed. "Remember how I complained about the shopping down here and how long it takes to get anywhere?"

"Yes. But I saw Winn Dixie near the traffic light."

"It took us forty minutes to get home from the hospital on Stock Island last night. Which is *before* Key West. Add another fifteen minutes to get to Schooner Wharf and Designs on the Wharf. So, you need to allow for an hour's travel time, providing traffic is light on US-1 just to arrive for clothing shopping. The store opens at ten, and my guess is we'll be shopping for at least an hour."

"So that blows the whole morning when you consider close to an hour back here," Shannon added.

"You got it. Then in the afternoon, we need to drive up to Marathon and check on Sam. That's a half-hour providing we don't hit a problem on the Seven Mile Bridge. And Captain Sally is bringing her boat."

"I'm beginning to understand that time management plays an important role in your daily life."

"Maybe we can squeeze in Winn Dixie on our way back from Marathon."

"Sounds good to me. I'm going to take a quick shower and change. Freddie, if it's okay with you, I'll make a shopping list while you shower."

"Perfect. I need one more cup of caffeine to jump-start my brain. How about a quick breakfast at Eggs In Paradise before we head down to Key West?"

"Sounds like a plan. I'm hungry," Shannon said as she stood and walked into the living room.

≒⊩⊪≒

"Good morning, ladies," Willa said cheerfully as Winifred and Shannon entered Designs on the Wharf at ten fifteen Thursday morning. "I've guessed your sizes and put a couple of things in the dressing rooms, but please take a look around first." It didn't take long for them to choose colorful combinations of pants, both long and short, and tops of various types.

After putting together three outfits for everyday wear, Shannon headed to the dressing room. She was pleased to see that Willa had indeed correctly guessed her size and flare for the dramatic. After deciding on the three outfits, she exited wearing a pair of black-and-white wide-legged pants in a geometric pattern. The matching top was sleeveless, with a low square neckline and short midriff length. Willa draped a long black scarf around her shoulders and tied it to the side. She added a wide-brimmed hat with a black band. "I love it!" Shannon exclaimed.

Winifred appeared in a similar outfit in sage green. "Wow! You look like you just stepped off a Paris runway." She studied herself in the long mirror. "I look like Gumby."

Just then Maria entered the shop. "Good morning, everyone." She walked over to Willa and gave her a hug. "I hope you're taking good care of my friends."

"Of course, I am," Willa said as she nodded toward the dressing rooms.

"Wow! Shannon, I love the look. That is the perfect outfit for the Chens' party Saturday night." Maria studied Winifred. "Yeah. Gumby isn't going to work. I didn't notice yesterday, when I saw the two of you together, how different you are—size-wise—I mean." She glanced back and forth at the two. "Shannon's taller, with the body of a model. Freddie, you're built more like me—short and curvy."

"Thanks, Maria. I don't know quite how to take that." Winifred glanced again at herself in the mirror. "What's this about the Chens? I didn't think they were due back until next week."

"They decided to fly back and watch the lighted boat parade Saturday. It will be the same crowd as the pirate party—you are both invited." Maria studied Winifred as if she were looking at her for the first time. "I have an idea." She looked over at Willa. "Do you still have those African print dresses?"

"Yes. Over in the corner."

"Freddie, I'll be right back," Maria said as she headed to the other side of the store. While Maria was gone, Winifred thought about the Chens. Why cut their trip short just to watch a boat parade? Or did it have something to do with Hunter and *Gemini* being in their dock? What was their connection? And if he were that good of a friend, why hadn't he been at the pirate party? Those thoughts were interrupted when Maria returned holding a long dress. "Here, try this. I fell in love with everything in the line the last time I was here, but the colors are all wrong for me."

Winifred looked skeptically. "I don't know. This is definitely not my style."

"It won't hurt to try it on. It can't be worse than the Gumby look."

Winifred took one more glance at herself in the mirror and cringed before heading into the dressing room. "You're right. It can't be worse."

Willa and Maria filled Shannon in on the various holiday festivities for the remaining weeks of the season while Winifred was changing.

"Wow!" everyone exclaimed as Winifred stepped out of the dressing room. The long dress hung from a wide gold chain, creating the high halter neckline exposing a generous amount of shoulders and an open back. A rich tangerine provided the exotic background for a chorus of African tigers, elephants, zebras, and giraffes. Side slits provided a flowing movement to the soft fabric.

"Now, *that* makes a statement," Shannon excitedly declared.

"But I want to blend in, not be the focal point of the room!"

"This screams that you feel good in your skin and don't mess with you."

"I'm a woman with a target on her back—this dress is the bull's-eye!"

"If you don't buy it, I will!" Shannon said as she walked into her dressing room to change back into her street clothes.

Winifred took one last look in the mirror. "Okay. I'll take it."

A few minutes later, both ladies walked up to the counter loaded down with their selections.

Maria handed Winifred a pair of large wooden hoop earrings. "These are the only accessories you need for that fabulous dress."

Shannon picked up a flyer from a stack sitting on the counter for the Holiday Celebration and Harbor Walk of Lights. "This is what you were telling me about. Key West has Christmas festivities from the day after Thanksgiving until New Year's Eve? There's a dozen or more events listed."

"We kicked off the holidays with the lighting of the Lobster Trap and the Fishing Buoy Christmas Trees and the Harbor Walk of Lights," Maria explained. "We do a couple of train and trolley tours at night to showcase our fabulously decorated homes and inns. I think you should plan on one of them."

"How come I didn't see any of this when I was down here during pirate week?"

"Because you spent your time as Captain Jack Sparrow evading the mysterious man who was following you."

"Yeah. You're right. I wasn't paying attention or looking for Christmas lights at the time."

The glaring sun greeted the three as they left the store at eleven thirty. Winifred juggled her bags into one hand and pulled sunglasses from her tote bag. "How about an early lunch and then Shannon and I head back to Big Pine?"

"First, I want to show you the cute little shops along Lazy Way Lane. It's right behind us and then we can walk over to the bar for lunch," Maria said as she guided Winifred and Shannon the short distance.

The row of festively decorated cottages looked familiar to Winifred. "I remember walking along here with the group of tourists after leaving the costume tent. I thought at the time that it was a place I wanted to explore in the future."

"Now you have the chance. It's all part of the twenty-acre historic seaport, including the Key West Bight Marina and everything along the boardwalk. We generally refer to it as Schooner Wharf."

"How about we do Lazy Way one evening when the lights are on? I'm about shopped out and would like to get back to Big Pine. We also may need to drive to Marathon if Sam is ready to come home."

"I agree," Shannon added. "Which way to the food?"

"There are several places here along the boardwalk, but I think the Wharf Bar will be the fastest." Maria led the way back the way they had come.

Winifred glanced over at the row of boats as they passed Bight Marina. The slip where *Gemini* had been docked the day before was now empty. *Where have you gone?*

Maria kept the conversation going over shared orders of conch fritters, coconut shrimp, calamari rings, and cheese sticks. By the time she had finished with stories of Key West's love of Christmas and every other holiday and event, Shannon was ready to end her life in Chicago and move to the city that ends each day celebrating the setting sun.

The waitress presented Winifred with the check, when her phone rang. After fishing it out of her tote bag, she looked at the screen with a frown. "Hello, Mike."

"Winifred, I have some important news. Can you swing by the station?"

"My friend Shannon and I are in Key West. We just finished lunch. Why?"

"The man who attacked you has been found."

CHAPTER FORTY-SIX

Winifred sat, with Shannon, across the desk from Lieutenant Mike Connor at the Monroe County Sheriff's Office on Big Pine Key. He opened a manila folder. Her stomach had twisted into tight knots the moment the deputy had given her the news over the phone. The masked man who had held a knife to her throat had been found. But where had he been located? By whom? What about Petrowski? Having Shannon at her side for the forty-five-minute drive to Big Pine didn't help relieve her anxiety. At any other time, driving along the thin thread of land that divided the Atlantic Ocean and the Gulf of Mexico would have calmed frayed nerves, especially on a picture-perfect day. But today's heavier traffic only slowed her progress, adding to her frustration on not knowing what Mike had refused to tell her. The news had to be bad, or Mike would have given it to her over the phone. Had he brought her back for her protection? She'd wondered on the long drive back if *Gemini* and its owner, Hunter, was somehow connected. Was Hunter her attacker? She hoped not.

"A man fitting the description of your attacker was fished out of the everglades two hours ago."

Winifred looked at Shannon and gave a sigh of relief but said nothing. She waited for the details.

"A young man and his buddy were taking his newly purchased airboat out for a run when they spotted what looked like the roof of a car under water off a little-used road outside of Homestead. He called 911 and stayed next to the vehicle to keep the gators away until the authorities arrived. A body was found sitting in the passenger seat—he'd been shot in the forehead execution style."

Winifred remembered passing through the everglades on her way down from Chicago that seemed to encompass most of the southern tip of the mainland west of Miami. "That's at least a two-hour drive from here. What makes you think he's our guy?"

"He has a tattoo on his left hand. But what got the attention of the Miami-Dade authorities is the severe dog bites. We assume they were bad enough that he needed to be treated at a hospital."

"A tattoo and dog bites on a man near Miami seems a little far-fetched. You really think this is the guy who attacked me?"

"The brown, older model station wagon is registered to a Stewart Johnson of Liberty City. It's one of the most crime-ridden neighborhoods in Miami. He's been in and out of jails and prison since he turned eighteen and juvie before that. But never for murder or attempted murder. That's what doesn't fit if he was the one holding a knife against your throat. He's worked construction jobs all his adult life and was known as Jackhammer Johnson. I think he was hired to help find whatever may be hidden *under* the safe room."

Winifred thought back to those moments. "I don't think his initial intent was to kill me. He wanted to scare me into telling him where whatever they were looking for was hidden. I got the impression that time was running out. They only had two weeks left and might have to *blow* the place. It was Petrowski who gave the orders to kill me."

"The back of the station wagon contained sledgehammers, pry bars, a jackhammer—and dynamite. Do you remember seeing a brown station wagon parked anywhere on the property?"

"No. But except for Hector's tour, I've only been inside the walls."

"Do they know how long the vehicle was in the water?" Shannon asked.

"We won't know for sure until the autopsy is completed, but initial guess is Monday night, probably sometime after midnight."

"If Johnson is our guy, then he and Petrowski take off in a boat and go to where they have parked the wagon. Jump in the car and head north to a Miami hospital. I learned at the Miami airport that Big Pine Key is a three-hour drive. Freddie had said at the time that Johnson was screaming all the way to the boat that Sam had nearly ripped his arm off." Shannon paused for agreement from Mike Connor.

"That is correct. We found quite a bit of blood on the dock and ladder. We are still waiting for a match."

"So Petrowski listens to his partner's pain and agony for over two hours before he pulls off in a remote area of the everglades and shoots him in the forehead. Why? Why not pop him somewhere closer to Big Pine? There must be dozens of places along that narrow strip of US-1 where he could have just killed him and tossed his body in the Atlantic, then driven on to Miami in peace."

"Good point."

"And how did Petrowski get away without a vehicle?" Shannon asked. She considered the possibilities. "Unless he called for someone to pick him up. If he were that close to Miami, then it wouldn't have taken another person long to drive to the isolated spot. Petrowski could have used that time to position Johnson in the seat and push the wagon into the water. I assume he figured the gators would take care of the body."

Mike checked the report. "All four windows were down. The seat belt was not latched. So, your theory is a good one."

"So, where's the boat?" Shannon asked.

Mike looked confused. "I don't understand."

"The getaway boat. It was either rented from a local boat rental, stolen, or someone loaned it to them. The timing from when they left Windswept to the estimated time of death is such that they didn't go far before ditching the boat."

"Good point. Nothing comes to mind, but I'll check the reported boat thefts. I'll call the local rental locations. It could be that they left the wagon at the marina, used the boat, then returned late at night, left it tied to the dock, and drove off after closing hours. In that case, a theft wouldn't have occurred."

"My exact thoughts," Shannon added.

"Doctor Mulaney, I like the way your mind works."

Shannon laughed. "It's what I do for a living. I ask a lot of questions, then analyze the answers I get."

Winifred reached over and took Shannon's hand and squeezed. "And, I feel so much better having her here with me." Freddie glanced over at the folder. "Do you have any photos of the scene?"

"I do. But the guy had been in that brackish water long enough to make a definite identification difficult." Mike removed several photos and slid them across the desk. "Does he look familiar?"

Winifred studied the photo of a Caucasian male very bloated with mottled skin. Deep lines furrowed her brow. "I can't be a hundred percent, but this looks like the guy who was sitting at the bar while I was at Chico's and then was following me in Key West during the pirate festival." She tapped the other photo showing the brown station wagon dripping water and plant material— looking like it had literally been dragged from a swamp. "I'm remembering back to the time when Maria and I were at the costume tent. I looked out and saw the man from Chico's standing against the hood of a car smoking a cigarette. Now that I think about it, I associated him with jobs in construction or a handyman, because of the older station wagon. It was dark brown with dents and rust—yes, this is the same man who was following me."

Mike scanned the last page of the report. "This is interesting. Two months ago, Valetti Construction in Fort Myers reported the theft of this jackhammer and box of dynamite. Both items contained the company's logo." He continued to read. "The firm's attorney, Edwardo Gonzales, handled the police reports."

"I don't believe in coincidences, Lieutenant Connor. I'm sure you don't either—and this is a big one."

"You're right, Doctor Mulaney. I need to make a few *personal* phone calls. One of them is to my buddy in the county clerk's office. I want the *unofficial* scoop on Freddie's attorney."

"After the whole mess-up with my filing, I asked Harry Lincoln to do a deep dive on Gonzales. I'll check in with him this afternoon." Winifred looked at her watch. "But right now, Shannon and I need to be on our way to Marathon. Sam may be ready to come home."

Mike Connor returned the photos to the file folder and stood. "I'm glad you're here, Doctor. Freddie needs a friend whom she can depend on. And we all can use the mind of a psychiatrist to help sort out the pieces of this nightmare of a puzzle."

The two ladies stood and moved to leave. "Please call me Shannon. I'm sure we will be spending enough time together to do away with formalities."

"And remember, Captain Sally will be arriving later today," Winifred added.

Mike chuckled. "Freddie, Shannon, Sally, *and* Sam living together within the high walls of Windswept. I should post a warning: Enter At Your Own Risk."

All three laughed as they walked to the door.

Winifred turned to Mike. "So, Stewart Johnson, my attacker is dead—but Aleksy Petrowski, who wants to kill me, is back in the wind."

Lieutenant Michael Connor gave an affirmative nod.

CHAPTER FORTY-SEVEN

Winifred punched in Harry Lincoln's cell phone number as she and Shannon waited at the traffic light at the intersection of Key Deer Boulevard and US-1. The call was going to voicemail when Harry picked up. He sounded rushed. "Harry, it's Winifred Forrester. Is everything okay? You sound out of breath and flustered."

"I'm only now getting to my office. It's been a day and a half, and at this point, I'm only accepting good news—which you never give me." Harry paused, during what sounded like him crashing into his squeaky desk chair. "What's up? Or should I be asking who do you want me to track down now? And before you ask, I don't have anything new to report."

"Well, sit back and take a breath. I have news for you. And Shannon is here with me now—you're on speaker. We only moments ago left the Monroe County Sheriff's Office on Big Pine. We're on our way to Marathon to check on Sam."

"Hello, Harry," Shannon said.

"Doctor Mulaney. Glad to hear you're down there. Winifred needs all the help she can get. And while you're there, enjoy what

Florida does best—we've had fog, rain, sleet, and four inches of the white stuff—all in one day!"

By the time Winifred had crossed the Seven Mile Bridge, she and Shannon had filled Harry in on what they had learned about Stewart Johnson.

"Huh. Very interesting. I'm wondering what, if any, connection he had with Gonzales or the Barillis."

"And why kill him? Petrowski obviously needed his demolition skills to search and possibly blow up the house," Shannon asked.

"If I'd been trapped in a car for over two hours with a man who was moaning with severe injuries and bleeding all over the front seat—I'd probably kill him too." Harry paused. His chair squeaked. "But seriously. The man was in bad shape and needed a hospital, not just some in-their-pocket sawbones. He would cause questions to be asked on multiple levels; a report would need to be filed with the county on the dog bites. Stewart Johnson had become a huge liability."

"Harry, I'd love to continue our chat, but we've arrived at the animal hospital. I'll give you a call once we get the coroner's report."

"And I will see what pops up on Jackhammer Johnson."

<hr>

"Mrs. Forrester, I'm so glad you're here," said the young lady at the front desk of the Marathon Animal Hospital. "You can go right back. Sam will be happy to see you."

Winifred and Shannon walked down the long hallway and entered the room where the dogs were kept. Samantha was sitting on a chair in front of Sam's enclosure. "Mrs. Forrester, I'm so glad you're here. Sam is feeling better and anxious to leave. He's been pacing and whimpering for the last three hours. I moved him to one of our large crates, but he began pawing at the door and barking. That upset all the other dogs, so I moved him back here." Sam immediately stopped pacing and sat with his tail wagging.

Samantha got up from the chair and motioned for Winifred to sit. Shannon, not knowing how Sam would react to a new face, remained by the door.

"Sam, my brave boy. It's good to see you up and walking," Winifred said in a soothing voice. She glanced up as an interior door opened and the doctor walked in.

"Mrs. Forrester, I'm so glad to see you. And I see that Sam is happy too." Doctor Simpson walked over and let Sam out. "Sam has informed us, quite forcibly, that he's ready to go home."

Winifred stood. "Are you sure? He doesn't look any better."

"I gave him a thorough exam this morning and took new X-rays. Right now, he needs time for his wounds to heal. I'm still concerned about his eye, but that can be treated at home, and I'll check it again in a week."

Winifred felt a moment of panic. She had very little experience taking care of an injured dog, much less one that looked like he just left the ring after a Muhammad Ali fight. "I don't know. I've never done anything like this before."

"I can help," Shannon said from the doorway. "I have an aunt and uncle who own a ranch in Wyoming. I spent many summers there. Between the cattle, horses, pigs, goats, dogs, cats, and chickens, there was always something with an injury or sick. I can even birth a calf. Sam will be a piece of cake."

Winifred introduced her friend and explained their relationship.

"Perfect," Doctor Simpson said. "And if Sam is feeling depressed or having a bad day, then Doctor Mulaney can handle that as well. I'll provide you with an antibiotic for infection, pain meds, and eye drops that you will administer three times a day. We will also give you a couple cases of canned food to use until his jaw is stronger."

"Maybe you should come over and meet your new patient," Winifred said with a chuckle. She walked over and put her arm around Shannon. "Amigo, Sam. Amigo." The two of them slowly moved toward Sam. His tail began wagging, then buried his nose in Shannon's outstretched hand. "I do believe this is going to work."

"I'll have you bring your car around to the side of the building, and we'll get Sam loaded and ready to go home," Doctor Simpson said, then gave orders to Samantha to put together the food and meds.

Five minutes later, Winifred had the Escalade parked next to the side door and Sam's blanket folded and positioned across the rear, driver's side seat. The hospital's door opened, and Shannon and the vet walked out, with Sam limping at her side. The German shepherd raised his front legs to jump onto the seat, then yelped in pain and sat down.

"Well, that's not going to work," Winifred said as she removed the blanket and moved to the rear of the vehicle. After opening the liftgate, she spread the blanket across that large space. "Okay, Shannon, how about you and I pick Sam up and place him in the back so he doesn't have to jump?"

"Got it," Shannon said as she moved to Sam's rear end.

Winifred tucked his head under her arm and began to lift. Sam tensed and gave a soft growl. "Okay, how about we each take a side and see if that works?" They repositioned themselves and tried lifting again. Sam yelled in pain.

"Trying to lift him is putting too much pressure on his wounds. This vehicle is too high. Do you have a smaller car, a sedan, that he can step into?" Doctor Simpson asked.

"No. This is the only vehicle I have, and Hector has a pickup truck."

The vet looked sorrowfully down at Sam. "Then I guess he stays here for a few more days."

"No, I can't do that to him." Winifred thought about her options as a plane took off overhead. "I have an idea. Shannon, you come with me." She glanced at the vet. "Hang tight. We'll be back in less than half an hour."

They had only driven a couple of blocks when Shannon pointed out a line of colorful Adirondack-style chairs placed along the road in front of a furniture store. "Those are exactly what we need down by the water! And look! They have matching footrests and side tables. Freddie, it's a rainbow of colors!"

"You are correct. Those would be perfect for lounging in the evenings with a glass of wine—but we don't have time now. Maybe we'll check them out when we come back next week for Sam's checkup."

It only took another minute to drive the short distance to the Marathon International Airport. Winifred parked near the main entrance. "Wait here. I hope this works. I won't be long," Winifred told Shannon as she left the engine running and hopped down.

Fifteen minutes later, Winifred ran up to the passenger door of the SUV dangling a set of keys. "We have a Toyota Camry for two weeks!"

Shannon lowered the window. "Why didn't I think of that?"

"You drive the Escalade back to the house. I'll pick up Sam and his supplies." Winifred wrote down the code for the front gates and reached into her tote bag for Hector's set of keys. "Use these to get into the house. I have an extra key hanging inside the supply room. Now I need to grab Sam's blanket and find a white Toyota."

⟞⊹⊹⟝

Sam was nearly dancing in his seat while they waited for Windswept's gates to open. A few minutes later, they pulled up to the cottage. "Huh. That's odd. Shannon should have beaten us home." Winifred got out of the car and glanced around. Nothing seemed out of place. All was quiet except for the sounds of boats out in the channel. Those bad feelings that were becoming so familiar began to creep in. *There is no way a woman who has found her way through small towns and large cities around the world could have gotten lost. There are only two roads between the airport and here.*

Sam gave one bark to get her attention and began pawing at the door. "Okay, boy. But you must stay on the leash." Winifred opened the rear door and stepped aside to let the large dog find his own way down the short distance to the ground. She and the good doctor had learned while trying several different methods to help Sam into the sedan that it worked best just to stand back and let Sam do it his way. With only one tiny yelp, Sam was out of the car and ready to take on the steps leading up to the cottage. "Okay, big boy. I'll hold the end of the leash, and you take as much time as you need on the steps." Winifred followed as he began to bound up the first three steps. He gave out a loud yelp and stopped. He looked back over his shoulder. "That hurt. Let's start out slow." Winifred moved to his side and rested her hand on his neck. "Okay. One step." She waited for him to take the next step. "Good boy." Winifred stepped to the next one while continuing holding onto his neck. Sam followed. "Good boy. Now you've got it." And they continued that way to the top step. He sprawled out on the porch floor while Winifred unlocked the door.

After opening the windows and slider, she got him settled in with a fresh bowl of water. Winifred then went back downstairs to get the paper bag containing the meds and cases of food. It took a while to complete, and still Shannon wasn't back. She reached into her tote bag for her cell phone when she heard the gates struggling to open. A moment later, the Escalade came into sight. Shannon maneuvered the large vehicle around the Camry and parked under the cottage. She then got out and walked to the rear and popped the liftgate.

"Where have you been? You should have gotten back before me. I was about to call you," Winifred said as she held up her cell phone to emphasize her point.

"I remembered that the shopping list was in my pocket, so I stopped at Winn Dixie for a few things." Shannon pointed to the contents in the cargo space.

"A few things! I see six bags!" Winifred said while she grabbed the first bag. "Did you count how many cupboards I have while you were making your list?"

"Not to worry. I'll make it work. Now help me carry these into the house before the frozen stuff begins to melt."

The last item was put in the fridge when Shannon's cell phone chirped. She glanced at the screen. "Freddie, can you please open the gates?"

"Why?"

"For the delivery truck. I asked them to text me when they turned onto Key Deer Boulevard. We'd better go downstairs and decide where to put everything before they get here."

"What truck? Everything? I didn't order anything."

"The truck that is delivering the chairs and tables I bought. I gave the guys a hundred bucks if they could get everything here today."

Shannon began walking toward the water. "Remember you said it would be great to have chairs to sit on in the evenings with a glass of wine?"

"I also remember saying next week—not today."

"Yes. But now we can enjoy the sunsets with friends."

"*Friends*? Shannon, did you just fall off the moon? I can't just invite *friends* over. People are trying to *kill* me—here—right here. Besides, *you* are my only friend."

Shannon gave Winifred a pleading look. "Then you and I will sit together and raise our glasses in a toast to our good fortune to be in the warm, sunny Keys and not in cold, snowy Chicago."

Winifred put her arm around Shannon. "Only you could make my life seem like a vacation."

"I hear the truck," Shannon said as she turned and walked toward the driveway.

⊨⊩ ⊪⊨

Half an hour later, Winifred and Shannon stood waving at the two delivery men as the truck drove toward the gates.

Winifred turned toward the water. Four chairs and footrests, each in a different color, sat in a semicircle facing the Gulf. Matching side tables waited between them for that first bottle and glasses of wine. "A rainbow of colors. Thank you, Shannon. Thank you for being my friend."

Shannon put her arm around Winifred's shoulder and squeezed. "I think it could use a firepit!"

"No!" Winifred teased and began walking toward the seating group. She had only gone a few steps when she noticed that Shannon wasn't following. She stopped and turned around to see Shannon pointing to something out in the water.

"Is that the boat, *Gemini*, anchored out there?"

Winifred didn't need to look. *Hunter.* "Yes. It was there when I got home."

"What about that one? It's changing course and coming this way."

Winifred turned back and surveyed the area she knew to be Big Spanish Channel, part of the Intercoastal Waterway. "That's a large deep-sea fishing boat. You can tell by the tall tower that sits above the upper helm station. It must be Captain Sally." Just then Winifred's phone dinged. She pulled it out of her pocket and glanced at the screen. "Yep. That's her. She wants us to meet her at the dock." She put the phone back in her pocket. "Let's head on over. We can watch as she approaches."

"What about Sam? Should we bring him?"

"This is his first few hours out of the hospital. Just the exertion of getting in and out of the car are making it up the steps wore him out. And I don't know how he will handle a strange boat and person arriving so close to the spot where he was injured."

"I didn't think about that. Maybe wait until later and take him for a short walk," Shannon said as they headed, at a leisurely pace, in the direction of the main house and canal. "Your first day here, you described the property as a thick unforgiving jungle. Now, only weeks later, it has the makings of a lush tropical resort."

"Hector and his amazing crew brought the land back to life. Many of the flowering plants and shrubs can once again breathe and enjoy the sun. Color is coming back to Windswept, especially in the bougainvillea, hibiscus, and Ixora." She pointed to several very large trees that hung with long, brown seed pods a foot or more in length. "Royal poinciana. Hector tells me that during the summer months, these will be covered in plate-size flower heads of a brilliant tangerine color."

"Yes. They call it the flame tree. I've seen them throughout South America and Mexico." Shannon paused to take in her surroundings. "Freddie, you can't let Windswept go. It is truly worth fighting for."

But is it worth dying for? Winifred mulled over that question as they approached the short wall surrounding the patio of the main house and sat down.

CHAPTER FORTY EIGHT

*L*ady *Luck* cut through the calm waters, now painted in shades from pink to crimson. The setting sun reflected off the tall tower, turning it into a vision of some abstract sculpture. Like the bones of a New York skyscraper breaking free from a burning horizon.

"She certainly knows how to make a grand entrance," Shannon said in a soft reverent voice.

"That she does. Quite the dichotomy."

Shannon glanced at Winifred with a questioning expression.

"You'll see. Now let's go over to the dock and turn some lights on to welcome our guest."

They watched as Sally threw the powerful engines into reverse and stopped at the entrance, then turned the boat around in order to back into the canal. Winifred and Shannon followed the boat along the dock until it stopped, and the captain tossed the bowline to Winifred. After tying it off, she joined Shannon at the stern and grabbed the line, giving it a couple of twists around the dock cleat.

"That was an impressive display of docking," Winifred said as she watched Sally place the fenders between the hull and the wall.

"Thanks. I've never fished in this area of Big Pine, so I wasn't sure how to approach your canal," Sally explained as she adjusted the last fender. "I used satellite imagery to get my bearings." Sally then jumped onto the dock and retied both the bowline and the stern line. "You know what's interesting is," she said while gesturing to the canal. "The shape and size of your private canal. From the satellite images, it looks as if this was dug for a new housing development. Just like the ones down a piece at Doctor's Arm and over in Eden Pines, across Key Deer Boulevard. There's the short piece to the right, behind the house where Hector keeps his boats, but the odd thing is this main stretch continues on for another thirty feet or more, then just stops." Captain Sally stepped back onto the boat and stretched out her arms to the side. "Welcome aboard *Lady Luck*." After helping the two ladies on board, Sally then reached into the cabin and flipped the switch that flooded the space with overhead lighting.

Somewhere deep in Winifred's subconscious, a bell rang, but as hard as she tried, she couldn't figure out why.

Shannon was the first to step in. "Wow! Floating luxury! This could be on the cover of *Yachting World*." She remembered Freddie using the word "dichotomy." On her first glance of Sally, Shannon had the image of a weathered Boston tugboat captain or perhaps a Portland, Maine, fisherman. What she saw now, in this luxurious main cabin, needed a polished captain for the yacht of the rich. Yes, a dichotomy. So, who was the *real* Captain Sally? Dr. Shannon Mulaney felt the challenge of every psychiatrist—to find the answer.

Darkness had set in by the time the three returned to the aft deck. Shannon leaned her shoulder against the rack containing fishing poles. "I don't know about either of you, but my stomach is telling me that it's time to fire up the grill. I picked up steaks, potatoes, and enough stuff to make a mean salad. And a key lime pie for dessert."

"A day on the water always makes me hungry. How about I finish up here, then meet you at the cottage?"

"Sounds perfect. I need to take Sam for a walk and introduce him to Sally," Winifred said as she climbed down off the boat and onto the dock.

"What kind of wine do you prefer?" Shannon asked as she was about to leave.

"Wine is for my guests. I'll be bringing a bottle of Jack to the party."

"Great. Freddie has Coke in the fridge."

"That will work. I won't be long," Sally said as she returned to the cabin.

Shortly after nine and with dinner finished, the three ladies wandered down to the row of new Adirondack chairs. "I see you're beginning to embrace our love of color," Sally said as she chose the seafoam chair and sat down.

"At least, I am. I saw these sitting in front of a furniture store on Marathon today. I paid the drivers a hundred bucks to get them here before you arrived. I also had a Christmas tree, and decorations shipped so Freddie would have a proper holiday."

"I admit, Shannon was right about being able to sit out here in the evenings. And adding the holiday magic to the cottage is on the schedule for tomorrow."

"I'm sorry I will miss the festivities, but I have a charter tomorrow. Good news is I'll be bringing dinner."

"I make a salmon dish that is to die for," Shannon boasted.

"Sorry, honey, but the only way you are going to get fresh salmon down here is to fly it in. And you can forget about perch, trout, and walleye," Sally teased.

"No worries. I picked up a Key West cookbook. You catch it, and I'll figure out how to cook it."

"And I'll make my famous tartar sauce," Winifred added.

"You are *not* putting that on my freshly caught fish! It kills the flavor," Sally scolded.

"Exactly!"

"So, you don't like fish?" Sally asked, as though the very thought was unfathomable.

"You told Katie and me that you spent your summers at your family's cabin in Traverse City—on the *lake*. And you don't like fish?"

Winifred gave Sally a sheepish look. "That's why I make excellent tartar sauce."

"Shannon, I'll have you creating fish recipes that our friend here will be eating without her mayo and relish sauce." Sally winked at Winifred. "And just for the record, I have my own spin on tartar sauce—for sandwiches only."

The three ladies toasted tomorrow's dinner, then settled into their chairs and watched the moon glisten across the calm water.

Winifred's gaze rested on the boat anchored off the larger Annette Key. "Sally, what do you know about Hunter? We saw his boat docked in Key West yesterday, but it was gone when Shannon and I were down there this morning."

"Yeah. That's him out there. I passed *Gemini* as I came in." She was silent for a few moments. "I know him well enough to say hello, but I don't know if anyone *really* knows him. Pretty much of a loner."

"Hector said he was a fisherman."

"Yes. But he doesn't do charters like most of us. From what I've heard, he goes after specific fish for his regular customers."

"How does that work?" Shannon asked.

"Restaurants, resorts, and small inns give him orders. Like they may be doing a special grouper dish or mahi-mahi. He fishes for the needs of his clients."

"I can't believe there's any good fishing out there," Winifred said.

"Oh. Quite the contrary. Locals find one of the best places is off the bridge to No Name Key. These waters are great for grouper, mahi-mahi, snapper, wahoo, and even tuna if you go out a bit."

"So why would he be spending the night out there?" Shannon asked. "Freddie, have you ever seen him anchored out like this before?"

"No. This is the first time. I usually see him during the day. Especially early mornings." *So why now, Hunter? Why is today different? What are you up too?*

Sally thought for a moment. "The only reason I can think of is that he has a large order that must be delivered by noon tomorrow. He's already on his spot or close to it. He'll get his lines ready and begin fishing at daybreak. You watch. He'll be out of the area by eleven." She checked the time on her phone. "It's after nine thirty. Can one of you drive me to the Egg? I left my truck there this morning and caught a ride with one of the guys who was heading into Key West."

"Sure. I can," Shannon offered.

"Thanks. I'll be out of here around five so I can get to the boat and get her ready for my eight o'clock group. We'll be fishing the Gulf off Marathon."

"I'll text you the code for the gates." Winifred finished the last sip of wine in her glass as she took a hard look at *Gemini*. The cabin lights were off. *Have you gone to bed, Hunter? Or are you watching?*

Winifred drew in a deep breath as she scooted out of the deep, slanted chair seat, and stood. She turned and took a few steps toward the cottage, then stopped. She turned back and waved.

CHAPTER FORTY-NINE

Winifred awoke to the sounds of Shannon moving around downstairs. She glanced at the clock on the bedside table—five o'clock. She got out of bed and leaned over the railing. "Shannon, what's wrong?"

"Nothing's wrong. I'm going for my morning run."

"Why so early?"

"I always get up at five and either run or hit the gym."

"But that's Chicago time, when you need to be at your office at nine. Life moves slower down here, and you're on vacation."

"So, what time have you been getting up? I know you've gotten in your morning runs since you've been here."

"Six, six thirty. I get in a quick jog and have coffee as the sun comes up around seven."

"Okay. That sounds good—for tomorrow. But I'm up and dressed now. So, I'll go for my run, see if Sally's left yet, and be back up here in time to make breakfast. We can eat on the porch as the sun comes up."

"Wonderful. Now I'm going back to bed."

At exactly six thirty, Winifred woke to the delicious aromas of bacon frying and fresh coffee. After crawling out of bed, she leaned over the railing to see Sam sitting at attention intently watching the activity going on in the kitchen. "Good morning, Shannon. Nothing gets my mornings off to a great start like your breakfasts. After I get dressed, I'll take Sam for a walk."

Sam looked up and gave a quick acknowledging bark.

"I've already taken him. He was a little stiff going down the steps. We got as far as the fork when he sat down for a rest. After a minute, he headed back and took the steps with a little more ease. He's very smart and is learning his limits."

"I think he's ready to eat, but I don't know how much to feed him. I'm leaving that for you."

"We'll figure this out together," Winifred said as she padded down to the kitchen counter.

Shannon handed her the instruction sheet that she had been given along with the food and medications.

"It only says to feed one can of food twice a day." Winifred looked at the size of the can, then at Sam's bowl. "This isn't going to be enough. Last night he gobbled this much up in a heartbeat. Do you think I should go ahead and give him two?"

"If it's only the volume of food that you are concerned about, then I would mix it."

"I don't understand. Mix with what?"

"We had issues like this all the time with sick animals on my uncle's ranch. Put a handful of Sam's regular kibble in his bowl." Shannon glanced at the can. "Is that beef or chicken?"

Winifred read the label on the can of food. "Beef." She then added a handful of dry food to his bowl. "Now what?"

"Mix in enough beef broth to get it soupy, then wait until it becomes mushy. At that point, add the can of moist food and stir the two together. Sam will love it."

"Except I don't have any beef broth," Winifred said sorrowfully.

"I bought cartons of beef and chicken yesterday. I always keep them on hand. I made up a pantry area in the utility room."

Ten minutes later, Sam was eagerly eating his breakfast as Winifred and Shannon took theirs out to the porch.

Winifred automatically looked out to where *Gemini* had been anchored. "I see Hunter is gone."

"Yeah. When I first left for my run, I saw the headlights of Sally's truck going in the direction of the gates, and while I was on my way toward the canal, I heard *Gemini*'s engine start. As I rounded the house, he was heading out." She pointed to a lone boat far out into the deeper waters of Big Spanish Channel. The rising sun reflected golden off its hull. "I think that is him."

"So, it is just like Sally said. Hunter's a fisherman going after a specific fish for an early-morning order for a customer."

Shannon swallowed a forkful of scrambled eggs. "You doubted that? What did you think he was doing—spying on you?"

"Of course not! Hector mentioned right from the get-go that Hunter was a local fisherman who had been mainly fishing these waters for at least the last two years. Although he mostly saw him around No Name Key." *What are you really fishing for, Hunter? Grouper or Windswept?*

"After I dropped off Sally last night, I drove up and down the streets in Eden Pines, on the other side of Key Deer Boulevard. Seeing all those decorated houses—most of them are not much bigger than this one and up on stilts—got me thinking about what we can do here."

"Shannon, it's only me and you, and we live behind high walls—no one will see our lights."

"They will from the water. And who cares? We'll do it for us. Can you believe how beautiful palm trees are decorated with white and green lights! Freddie, we must do it. I'll order the lights on Amazon; they will be here Monday."

"Maybe in Chicago. Down here we'll be lucky to get them by Christmas!" Winifred finished the last of her eggs and reach for a strip of bacon. "Remember, I don't own Windswept yet. We may never come here again."

"Okay, how about we start with the tree?" Shannon said as she stood and cleared her dishes, then stepped into the cottage.

Winifred took a deep breath. *Sure, let's fill this place with festive holiday cheer while we wonder if Petrowski is out there waiting for his next opportunity to kill me.*

"Freddie, do you have a box cutter or a pair of scissors handy?"

"Yeah. In the top drawer of the buffet." Winifred gave up any idea of relaxing with another cup of coffee on the porch. Instead, she stood and cleared her dishes and headed inside. Shannon was already slicing open the tall box containing the tree. "We'll need an extension cord."

"On it," Winifred said as she set her dishes in the sink and headed for the utility room.

Half an hour later, the tree stood in the center of the room. Shannon stood with a remote in her hand. "We can pick the colors for the lights." She pressed buttons producing clear, multi-colored, all green, all red, and flickering.

"How about just leave the clear lights and non-flickering? This tree takes up half the room as it is without adding multicolored bulbs flashing!"

"Freddie, you exaggerate! It's not half the room, and I have a plan once it's decorated."

An hour later, the tree was decked out in clear lights, silver garland, and ornaments the colors of the sea and sand. A large silver star shined from the top.

"Now we need to find a store that sells artificial flowers, like bougainvillea and hibiscus, to tuck in among the branches," Shannon said as she moved the mountain of empty boxes to the foot of the stairs. "Maybe we can store these cartons under the bed."

"The bed isn't high enough. The small ornament boxes will fit, but not the tall tree box." Winifred thought about her options. "Hey, we can take all of them over to the main house. The rooms are all empty. It's time I give you a tour."

"I'm dying to see the infamous safe room." Shannon looked up at her friend. "Sorry. Poor choice of words."

"Not a problem. We need to put the place back together anyway—maybe this afternoon."

"Perfect. Now, for this room. I admit to overestimating both the size of the space and the size of the tree. It's rather like me trying to get my size ten foot into your size seven shoe." Shannon took a quick glance around the room. "Let's start with taking down the card table. We can stand it up against the wall on the porch. It will be handy if we need it. I love this reproduction Heywood-Wakefield furniture. It should be highlighted, not hidden under blankets and sheets."

"I don't know what style you call it; to me, it's ugly and would be big bucks to have it reupholstered. And just for the record, I'm not into decorating with sheets. The cushions are so dirty I couldn't even sit on them—it all must go—if I become the official owner, that is."

"Fine. For now, I can move this end table to the opposite side and free up the corner by the slider. Then you can help me slide this sofa down a couple of feet next to the table."

Shannon picked up the two-tiered table with bamboo legs and sidepieces. "I think one of these legs is loose. It's probably just a loose screw; I might be able to tighten it." She flipped the piece over and checked the leg. "Freddie, you're not going to believe this."

"Is the leg broken? Maybe we can wrap it with duct tape or something. It will be fine."

"Nooooo. It's an *original* Heywood-Wakefield. Their logo is stamped on the bottom."

Winifred walked over and looked at the mark. "Are you sure?"

"One hundred percent." Shannon pointed to the logo stamped on the underside of the table. "An eagle with outstretched wings and the name through the center. The year 1826 is under the name."

"So, this is good?"

"Freddie, this is an amazing find. My desk in my office is a Heywood-Wakefield. I spent a fortune on it. During the 1930s and 1940s, the company started sleek new designs based on the French art deco. Their wicker and bamboo pieces, which this is, was more from a Japanese influence. And I can place this table after 1949 because that is the year they began using Phillips head screws." Shannon put the table down and moved over to the sofa. "Help me pull this away from the wall. I want to look for the mark."

Winifred took one end and Shannon the other. After tilting it forward, Shannon bent down and searched the backside of the frame. "It's here!" They set it back down. Winifred followed Shannon to the long buffet. Shannon pulled out the top drawer and found the mark on the left side. "Let's check the dresser and nightstand upstairs."

Fifteen minutes later, they were back in the living room. "Freddie, I can't believe this! All this old ugly furniture that you hate is worth a fortune!" Shannon paused a few moments. "I bet you've got twenty thousand dollars here. Maybe more."

"I still don't like it. You say after 1949? The main house was built in 1962. I saw home movies that Lorenzo Barilli made while it was being built and even with the interior decorator. Perhaps she chose this furniture. It looks like something from that period."

"Can I see those movies?"

"Sure. They are over in the safe room."

"Perfect. Now let's get this sofa moved so we can place the tree in the corner."

After tweaking the furniture along the wall opposite the kitchen, Winifred stood back for an overall look at the room. "You were right. The tree is perfect."

"Not yet. We have the colors of the sand and sea; now we need to find the brilliant colors of the tropical flora."

"It's funny. All my life I've had traditional Christmas trees with lots of red and green and maybe a splash of gold." She cocked her head to the right and studied the pastel ornaments. "I like this. I like it a lot."

Shannon headed to the kitchen. "I'm glad. Now, how about we take a break with coffee on the porch?"

A few minutes later, the two ladies were settled on the porch with Sam at their feet. Shannon checked her cell phone for any messages. "Ten thirty and we've put up a Christmas tree and found treasures sitting out in plain sight."

Winifred laughed. "I'm still not convinced about the furniture. But we are looking a lot more festive."

"I am curious. You said that you had looked through a lot of photos during Lacy Lorin's time here. Do you remember anything about the furnishings in the house?"

"No. But I only fanned through most of them. I wasn't looking for anything specific. I remember beautiful people, dressed in beautiful clothes, in beautiful settings."

"Could it be possible that this furniture was moved here from the main house?"

"Maybe. I remember reading in Lorenzo Barilli's journal that Hurricane Betsy in 1965 flooded the house. Perhaps, knowing its value, these pieces were moved here to protect them from any future hurricanes." Winifred paused a moment. "I know this cottage was built as a guest house during Lacy's time. Lorenzo never married Lacy, and after his death in 1979, the main house was closed up—never used again. Hector began working for Tony in

1993. It's possible that the younger Barilli came to Windswept and stayed in the guest cottage until his death in 2000."

"Windswept's history gets even more interesting. Perhaps Tony Barilli hid something in the safe room. It would make sense. The house is boarded up so no one would ever think to look there, and he hires Hector to watch over the place."

"Shannon, you have an amazing mind that sifts through unlikely possibilities."

"That is why I'm a psychiatrist. Since we're finished here, how about we take Sam and walk over to the house? That will give us a head start on the safe room. We can bring the photos back here to look at. Maybe run some of the home movies."

"Sure. But don't get your hopes up on the projector still working. Those guys really trashed the place."

Sam perked up at the sound of his name and the word "walk."

Winifred reached down and petted his head. *I wish we were going back to the house with more protection than you this time. Maybe I should call Mike.*

CHAPTER FIFTY

Winifred pulled open the large, heavy door to the safe room, then stepped back for Shannon to enter. "I probably shouldn't bother closing the door; the damage has already been done," she said as she flipped the switch for the lights and ceiling fans. Sam gave a low growl as he stood at Winifred's side.

"Wow! When you said those guys trashed the place, you really meant *trashed*! What a shame. It's like a mini theater." Shannon walked up to the stage. "They ripped down these lovely pink velvet drapes and tore up the flooring. Did they think whatever they are looking for was hidden underneath?"

"Yeah. They even yanked down the movie screen and tried to break into the wall behind it. What a waste. This room is constructed of poured concrete—walls, floor, and ceiling."

"Hence the need for the jackhammer," Shannon added while stepping over and around old movie reel tins, photos, miscellaneous supplies that Hector kept in case he needed to hold up during tropical storms or hurricanes. "It would be a shame to destroy this lovely, stamped floor. I bet the terra-cotta color would have been beautiful back in the day."

"What do you mean?"

"They added a terra-cotta colorant to the concrete; after leveling and smoothing, it was stamped in this pattern of squares to look like a tile floor."

"Huh. I didn't notice that before."

"Where do we start?"

"First, I want to show you the periscope I told you about."

Winifred raised what looked like the periscope on a submarine.

Shannon walked over to the device and rested her chin against the tube and looked into what could only be compared to binoculars. "I can see outside."

"Now turn," Winifred said.

"This is incredible. I can see in a complete circle around the property, and out into the Gulf." Shannon continued viewing. "I think I see Hunter. At least, it looks like *Gemini*. If that *is* him—then he is still fishing." Shannon stepped back. "I can see why Barilli had this device added to the room. He could be perfectly safe behind concrete walls yet keep an eye on what his adversaries were doing."

"Let's start by putting all these large movie cans back on the racks in the closet," Winifred said as she picked up the one containing *West Side Story*.

The first can Shannon grabbed was *To Russia with Love*. "More treasurers. Do you have the projector to run these larger reels?"

"Yes. Hopefully it hasn't been destroyed."

"Freddie, why don't I replace these movie cans while you pick up the photos? Perhaps you'll remember how you had them sorted. Or maybe toss them in a box and we can go through them at the cottage." Shannon stacked several cans in the crook of her left arm and headed to the closet. "Put aside any photos that show the furniture in the house. I'd like to figure out when the Heywood-Wakefield pieces were purchased."

Both ladies looked toward a commotion near the stage. Sam was working hard at bunching up one of the panels of drapery into a bed. He then plopped down with a contented sigh.

For the next half-hour, Winifred and Shannon worked in silence. Then Shannon stood in the closet doorway holding one can. "This is odd. All the movies were made in the late 1950s and early to mid-1960s. But here is one older Errol Flynn movie, made in 1935, *Captain Blood*. It's a favorite of mine but seems out of place with the others. It's a black-and-white movie about a doctor who is sent to prison for a crime he didn't commit, then escapes and becomes a pirate."

"Set it aside, and maybe if we can put the screen back up, we can make a movie night with Sally."

Shannon tried to open the large metal can. "That's funny. I can't open it. It seems to be sealed."

"Hector has some tools in the garage. You'll probably find a knife or a box cutter."

Shannon ran her index finger along the edge. "I don't think a utility knife will work—it appears to have been sealed with cement."

"Then set it aside to take back with us," Winifred said as she continued to scoop up the photos that were scattered around the room and placed them in a box.

Shannon set the round movie can on top of the bar and began picking up the small boxes containing the 8mm home movies that the burglars had knocked over. "The more we clear off the floor, the more confused I get about where something could be hidden and when. Except for water stains and naturally occurring discoloration of the surfaces, it appears that the floor and walls have not been altered since the room was built."

"Tony would have been thirty-three when this house was built back in 1962. It was literally constructed around this room. I would assume by that age, Lorenzo's son would have been well involved in the family business and quite possibly oversaw at least part of the project."

"Freddie, what if Tony had something valuable to hide? Maybe something hot that had to remain hidden for decades, like money from a bank robbery, or a jewelry heist."

"Huh. I hadn't considered that angle." Winifred paused to consider the idea. "You could be on to something."

"Jewelry, especially loose diamonds, wouldn't take up much space. Tony could even have tucked a bag in the walls during the pouring of concrete. Millions in cash, on the other hand, would. Suitcases could have been stashed under the stage, but that wouldn't be safe long term."

"I need to continue reading Lorenzo's journal. So much has been happening since I moved here that I've completely forgotten about it."

"Where is it?"

"On the top shelf in my closet. It's the wooden box that Edwardo Gonzales gave me. It had been in his safe since the death of Lorenzo in 1979."

"Looks like we have a new project. Instead of just fanning through these photos, we need to carefully look at each one—like we did at your cabin in Traverse City."

"Right. And speaking of my great-great-grandmother's photos, I still haven't found anything that directly connects her with Lorenzo—not a picture or even a mention in his journal."

"Since Hector worked for Tony, I wonder if he might have anything that might have been left behind that would give us an idea of what he might have hidden."

"I would like to stop by the hospital tomorrow morning on our way to Key West. We can ask Hector then."

"Perfect."

"And speaking of the good man, it looks like we are down to his things to put away. And since we don't know where they go, let's put the larger stuff in the closet and the smaller items on the bar."

"And I'm hungry. How about I take Sam and a few of these things and head back to the cottage and make sandwiches for lunch?"

Winifred grabbed her cell phone from the bar and checked the time. "It's one thirty! How about you take Sam to the cottage and bring the Escalade back? We'll load up these boxes and stuff and head over to the No Name for lunch. I saw a mouthwatering burger the last time I was there. I'd like you to meet Anneliese if she's working."

"Sounds like a plan to me." Shannon picked up the leash. "Come on, boy. Time for a walk."

Left alone in the safe room, memories of her attacker's knife against her throat came rushing back. She wondered if she would ever feel safe again. Winifred made a sweeping glance around the room. *What are you looking for? And, most importantly, who are you, and why do you want me dead?*

CHAPTER FIFTY-ONE

Shannon's mouth dropped as she followed Winifred to the bar at the No Name Grill. "Freddie, I actually think you under-stated the amount of money stapled to the ceilings, walls, and support posts in this room."

"Good afternoon, Freddie. And this must be Dr. Shannon Mulaney," Anneliese said in a welcoming voice as they approached the bar.

"I was hoping you would be working. I wanted you to meet Shannon, and we're starving. We lost track of time while clean-ing up the mess in the safe room."

"And you are in luck. I get off in ten minutes and can join you. How about the two of you head out to the patio in back and I'll send your waitress?"

"I don't see Hunter. Are you disappointed?" Shannon asked as they turned in the direction of the patio.

"Of course not. Knowing you, you'd jump at him and accuse the poor man of spying on me."

"And that would be bad?" Shannon teased.

"We are having a delightful lunch with a new friend."

"I'm glad I bought four chairs for the beach—if you can call it a beach. Now we can invite Anneliese for our evening wine time."

Winifred walked through the rear entrance and into the immense space. A thatched roof rose at least two stories above a paved floor. Large ceiling fans hung from the timbered framework along with a couple of life-size sharks. A family with a baby in a stroller occupied a table on the far side of the room. Winifred and Shannon sat down on either side of the picnic table painted in shades of turquoise and yellow.

A young lady in her early twenties approached. "Hello, ladies! My name is Jennifer," she said while handing out menus. "What can I get you to drink?"

Winifred ordered a sangria and Shannon a Yuengling on tap. It wasn't long before she returned with their beverages and took their food orders. Winifred ordered the Bourbon burger, which she had seen on her last visit, and Shannon the grilled yellowfin tuna sandwich.

Winifred studied the decor. The tropical space was confined by a high turquoise-painted fence.

"This reminds me of places I've been to throughout the Caribbean islands," Shannon remarked. "And the best part is it's only five minutes from home."

At that moment, Winifred glanced up at the door and gasped. "Where did he come from?"

Shannon turned to see Hunter following Anneliese to their table.

"Hunter, I'd like you to meet my friends, Winifred Forrester and Dr. Shannon Mulaney. Winifred has recently moved here from Chicago." The three shook hands.

"Pleased to meet you," he said with little emotion.

"Hunter is a regular, and since you often see his boat anchored off Windswept, I thought this was the perfect opportunity for you to meet," Anneliese said as she sat down next to Shannon.

Hunter remained standing at the open end of the table facing them. "Hello, ladies. I understand my fishing off the upper east side of Big Pine might have become questionable for you. I'm truly sorry if that has caused you any concern, but please understand that I mean you no harm."

"Thank you," Winifred said with a smile. His deep voice sent sensual vibrations through parts of her body that she tried hard to ignore.

"I've been fishing these waters for over two years now, and up until the last couple of weeks, there has been no activity anywhere near that walled property. I enjoy the peace and quiet away from the heavy boat traffic off Doctor's Arm and down toward the other housing estates that empty into Bogie Channel. And the west side of Big Pine is even worse with all the canals of Eden Pines Colony, Port Pine Heights, and all the streets off Ships Way, plus the boat traffic from the Middle Torch Key canals all emptying into Pine Channel. The best part is that the fish I primarily go after can be found off Porpoise and Annette and down around No Name Key."

"Thank you for explaining. We saw you in Key West. *Gemini* was docked in the Chens' slip," Shannon added. She watched for his reaction to her challenge.

"Yes. The Chens' chef is a customer. I was fishing swordfish for him, and tuna for one of the inns."

"Since you're a regular, I take it you live close by?" Winifred asked.

"Yes, it's the main reason I came down from my home port of Miami. Close friends of my parents built a home on No Name Key about fifty-five years ago. There were few residents back then, and their house is rather isolated but has a long dock and easy access to Big Spanish Channel. The couple are in their late eighties now but don't want to give up their dream house. I agreed to move down here and stay at the house to watch over the property."

"And fishing alone provides you with a good living?" Shannon asked.

"Good enough." Hunter glanced over his shoulder to see the waitress approaching. "I see your food has arrived. Mrs. Forrester, Doctor Mulaney, it's been a pleasure," Hunter said, in a tone that put an end to the conversation. Winifred watched as he walked back into the restaurant.

Jennifer placed their meals on the table and set a plate of fries in front of Anneliese. "Enjoy, ladies. I'll check back with you in a few minutes." She then walked over to the family on the other side of the room.

"Well, that was interesting," Anneliese said. "I've learned more about Hunter while sitting with the two of you than I have in the last two years."

Winifred studied Shannon's expression. "What are you thinking?"

"He is one handsome man."

"No. You are wearing your psychiatrist face."

"Why do you say that?" Shannon asked.

"Because I have looked at that face for two years now. Tell us, Doctor."

"Okay. What have we really learned about Hunter?" Shannon glanced at Anneliese. "He's a fisherman who prefers the eastern side of Big Pine Key. We knew that. And he is house-sitting, on No Name Key, for an elderly couple."

"You're right. The only new thing I learned was the house-sitting part," Anneliese added. "But it sounded like a lot."

"Hunter delivered a canned speech. We don't even know his last name," Shannon said with a puzzled expression.

Anneliese carried the conversation over lunch with accounts of her property management business. "I'd love for you to give me a tour of Windswept. Especially the house. It's part of Big Pine's history."

Winifred swallowed her last bite and wiped the juice off her chin. "This is, by far, the best burger I have ever had—and the messiest. Why don't you stop by later and join us and Captain Sally for a sunset and wine?"

"I'd love to, but I have a dinner date with Mike over on Ramrod."

"Then bring Mike. He knows his way around the property and even has the gate code."

"Thanks, Freddie. Maybe we will."

Just then Winifred's phone rang. She pulled it out of her tote bag and checked the screen. "I need to take this," she said with concern in her voice. She got up and took several steps away from the table. "Hello, Rosa. Is anything wrong?"

"No. I have great news! The filing has been made. You are now the official owner of one thousand acres on Big Pine Key. Windswept is yours!"

"Thank you so much for all you have done to push this through."

"I wasn't the only one pushing. Apparently, an officer from the Sheriff's Office on Big Pine was pushing too."

Winifred began walking back to the table. "Thank you; I know who that is, and I'm having lunch with his girlfriend as we speak. I'll talk to you soon." She ended the call with a smile that lit up her whole face.

"Good news, for a change?" Shannon asked.

Winifred stretched out her arms in joy. "It's mine! Windswept is officially mine!" She walked around the table hugging Shannon and Anneliese. "I'm ordering Wi-Fi and cable!"

"Well, I guess we will be having champagne tonight with friends," Shannon cheered.

Jennifer chose that moment to bring the check.

"I think this calls for key lime pie—on the house," Anneliese said as she nodded to the waitress.

Shannon chuckled. "I should have bought more chairs!"

CHAPTER FIFTY-TWO

It was late afternoon when Winifred and Shannon returned to the cottage. "How about I take Sam for a quick walk and then we can unload the boxes and take them upstairs?" Winifred said as she shut down the engine and opened her door.

Five minutes later, Winifred and Sam began their slow walk toward the main house. "You made it down the steps with little trouble. Now let's see if you can make it to the house for a second time today." Her back was a little straighter, and a new bounce in her step. Warm feelings of happiness and pride filled her for the first time since she had arrived at Windswept. The knowledge that she was now, in the eyes of Monroe County, the legal owner shouldn't have made such a difference—but it had. She smiled at the geckos that scampered across her path. The sounds of sudden rustling in the underbrush or trees no longer startled her. She was providing a habitat for the critters that also resided on her land. "It's ours, Sam. Windswept and all of its beauty and secrets belongs to me now." *Secrets. I need to find the answers.* "Come on, Sam. Time to head back and attack those boxes. We have a mystery to solve, and the clues must be in one of them."

By the time the two of them reached the cottage, Shannon was carrying the last carton up the steps. "That was a short walk. Sam's not up for it, or are you itching to dig into the box of photos?"

"Sam's doing great. I'm the one who gave up—there are clues in one of these to what's hidden, and I'm ready to start digging."

Shannon set the can containing the Errol Flynn movie on top of the fridge. "Okay. But first we need to move these out of the way. Between the Christmas tree and the boxes, we barely have room to walk. How about we push the buffet down to the corner and stack the cartons next to the slider? We can prioritize them by putting the home movies on the bottom since we don't have a screen to watch them on and the photos on top."

They had just gotten the heavy piece of furniture in place, when Winifred's phone chirped. She walked over to the kitchen counter and picked up the device. She read the message. "Sally is on her way. She has enough fish for dinner and the freezer. I guess photo searching is out for today."

"Sounds like we'll have plenty of food. How about calling Anneliese and inviting her and Mike for dinner? We can celebrate with champagne down by the water after."

⚜

"Sally, this fish is amazing," Winifred said as she scooped the last piece of grouper onto her fork. "I'm changing my mind about not liking fish."

"Knowing your need for tartar sauce, I decided on a specialty of mine. It's actually a take on the popular spicy coconut sauce made with coconut milk, curry paste, and aromatic spices. I first marinated the grouper fillets in fresh lime juice and a few of my own secret spices before searing them in coconut oil."

"And serving it with jasmine rice and asparagus is the perfect complement," Shannon said. "I hope you will give me the recipe so I can impress my Chicago friends."

"Me too. I can smother bass and walleye in this sauce back at the cabin in Traverse City during the summer," Winifred added.

"You can change it up by using ginger instead of curry or add soy sauce and give it an Asian twist," Sally said. "I also stopped by a friend's bakery on my way and picked up a dozen key lime tarts. Those will be perfect with the champagne that has been chilling."

"As long as everyone has finished, how about I help clear the table and take the dishes upstairs?" Anneliese said as she got up from the picnic table. "I'm ready for champagne and tarts down by the water in those tropical-looking chairs."

"Those were my idea. I had them delivered yesterday in anticipation of Freddie making new friends," Shannon teased. "I guess I will have to call the store and order a few more."

Mike stood and glanced around the space under the cottage. "As for tonight, how about I grab that folding lawn chair and Sam's bed and take them down?" At the sound of his name, the battered-looking dog got up and moved to Mike's side.

"I guess that is a 'yes' from our fearless guard-dog," Winifred said with a chuckle.

Twenty minutes later, the group stood in a circle in front of the colorful chairs. Mike raised his plastic tumbler. "I would like to offer the first toast." He paused a beat. "Freddie, you are an amazing and brave woman. Congratulations on becoming the new owner of Windswept. I look forward to watching you bring our infamous estate into a new era."

"I'm so happy that I was with you when you got the news," Anneliese said. "I will gladly give you as much assistance as I can."

"And I will always be at your side to advise, protect, and keep you supplied in fresh fish," Sally added, and everyone laughed.

"And lastly, I want to give this toast to the most strong, courageous, and generous woman I know. You started out two years ago as my patient and have become my dearest friend." Shannon blinked away tears. "I love you, Freddie."

Winifred gave her a hug, while the others looked on with quizzical expressions.

"Thank you. I'm not sure what I've gotten myself into or even what my future holds, but I know I've got the four of you at my side."

Winifred wiped tears from her cheek as everyone chose a seat. Mike took the old aluminum lawn chair.

"I want to add a firepit out here, but Freddie says no."

"That is a great idea, Shannon. You can toss on pellets to help keep the mosquitoes at bay," Anneliese added.

"I don't know which is worse down here, the no-see-ums or the mosquitoes," Winifred said, while swatting at the buzzing sound around her neck.

"It's a major problem. Monroe County has trucks that go up and down the streets and spray to help keep the insect population down. More so during the summer months when it's hot and more humid."

"Well, that is going to be a challenge. My skin is already burning, and my hair frizzing. And it will only get *more* humid!"

Anneliese laughed. "You learn to live with it. Air-conditioning becomes your best friend."

Up until then, Mike had remained silent. "Shannon, you said Freddie was a patient first. But you're a psychiatrist."

Shannon didn't answer. She looked over at Winifred and shrugged. As if to say the answer was not hers to give.

Winifred took a deep breath. "Two years ago, I suffered terrible losses. I couldn't sleep, wasn't eating, pretty much abandoned my employees. My mother-in-law, who lived next door, convinced me to seek help. I wasn't to the point of being suicidal but close. Doctor Mulaney came highly recommended, so I gave her a call."

"Freddie made amazing progress, showing great strength in dealing with the tragedies. We quickly became friends, which is something I never do with my patients."

"May I ask what happened?" Mike asked.

"It all began with my parents. They finally decided to retire two years ago in January. They sold their house and bought a motor home. One of those big ones built on a bus chassis. They were doing a West Coast trip. It started with a month in Alaska, where they met up with some friends who were also travelers. Then they headed down to Seattle. I flew out and joined them. We had three fabulous weeks visiting all the popular sites until I was called back to the office, and they pulled up stakes and headed south to California's wine country. That's about the time Dad's paranoia began. He called me from one of the winery tours and said he felt someone was watching them." Winifred hesitated before continuing. "I told him that they were part of tours. People probably were watching each other at times. Then while on the Pacific Coast Highway on their way to San Francisco, Mom called to say that Dad was driving her crazy with notions of them being followed by someone in a blue sedan."

"And this was abnormal behavior for your father?" Mike asked.

"Yes. He'd spent his life working in the store. He had this uncanny ability to know when a customer needed help finding something as opposed to just browsing. Or he'd look over at the door just as someone opened it and walked in. He always knew his surroundings, even in restaurants."

"I'm assuming it didn't stop there?" Mike asked.

"After a few days of Dad complaining about being watched, Mom suggested they head on down to LA and enjoy the sun. According to Mom, Dad kept looking in his side mirror for a silver Ford SUV with a cracked left-rear taillight. He thought it looked like a spider every time the driver hit the brakes. Mom said it was some kind of weird paranoia, and she didn't see anything odd about the traffic."

"Why didn't she take him seriously?" Sally asked.

"Because each time he pointed out the silver SUV with the spider cracks, the vehicle was from a different state. Mom mentioned plates from Pennsylvania, Wyoming, Texas, and Nebraska."

"Huh," Mike uttered.

"I guess the mysterious vehicle disappeared just north of LA, and Dad finally relaxed. So did Mom. They ended up in an RV park south of the city." Winifred stopped talking and wiped tears from her cheek.

"Freddie, you don't have to go on," Shannon said and took Winifred's hand.

"I'm okay." She took a deep breath. "Two days later, Mom packed a cooler for a day at Huntington Beach. Dad wanted to watch the surfers. They walked to a quieter part of the beach and set out chairs, an umbrella, and the coolers. After lunch, they decided to take a walk along the water's edge. They'd gone much further than they'd planned and were both exhausted when they returned to their spot. Mom pulled a half-full Gatorade from the cooler and handed it to Dad, while she opened a fresh bottle of water for herself. They both fell asleep. When Mom woke, she reached over to hold Dad's hand, which had fallen to his side. He was dead."

"Oh, Freddie. I'm so sorry," Anneliese offered in sympathy.

"There's more," Winifred said with a sigh.

"It wasn't long after we buried Dad when my daughter, Bridget, who was sixteen at the time, asked if she could go with her best friend and her mother to a dance club in downtown Chicago for one of their monthly teen nights. The kids had had to deal with so much tragedy that it sounded like a good idea. My son, Sean, who was only two years younger, asked to go as well. It sounded like good, clean fun, so I agreed. That morning, Bridget asked that I join them. She convinced me that I too needed a night out. Problem was, I had a conflict. A meeting had been scheduled for five o'clock at the office with a perspective new client. It was an appointment that I couldn't cancel. My offices are only a couple of miles away, so I agreed to meet up at the club as soon as I could." Winifred paused for several seconds. "It was after six thirty when I got a couple blocks from the club and was stopped by a sea of flashing red-and-blue lights. My gut shouted that something horrible happened, so I pulled over and left the car on the side of the road. I don't remember running those two blocks; I only remember being stopped by an officer when I approached the building. It looked like one of those scenes you see on the news with people running and screaming in all directions. I frantically tried to make him understand that my children were in there. I begged to know what happened." Winifred began sobbing and nodded to Shannon.

"Bridget, her friend Emily, and her mother, along with Sean, had just entered the club when a masked shooter opened fire. They died instantly. The man was never identified or found," Shannon explained. "For months after, Winifred and her husband Daniel put all their efforts into working with the police and FBI. There were no solid leads. The man just vanished."

"I can't finish the story." Winifred sobbed.

"Two months later, Freddie received a call from someone identifying himself as a special agent with the FBI. They had followed up on a lead in a small town outside of Gary, Indiana. The agent explained that information and photos of her family had been discovered during a raid on a cabin in a remote area. He asked that she come as soon as possible. Danny insisted they take his Mercedes, since she had been having brake issues with her SUV. In a rush to leave, Danny accidentally shut the car door on his hand, breaking two fingers. They decided that Freddie would drive the hour to the cabin and Danny would take her SUV the short distance to the hospital in Palos Heights, a suburb of Chicago where they lived. Before getting to the Indiana state line, Freddie received a call from Danny saying that the brakes weren't acting right on the highway and he would need to pull over. While on the phone, she heard a loud crash, and the line went dead. Instead of continuing on to the cabin, Freddie turned around and found her way to the highway that Danny would have taken to the hospital." Shannon paused. "She arrived at the scene as they were putting her husband's body into the ambulance. He had been rear-ended by a tractor trailer going full speed."

"What happened with the FBI agent? Did he contact you about missing the meeting?" Mike asked.

"No. It turned out to be a crank call. The FBI office didn't know anything about a raid on a cabin."

Mike and Sally looked at each other for a long time without a word. Finally, Mike spoke. "Freddie, I'm so sorry. I can't believe you have had to live through such tragedies." He paused as if he was searching his mind on how to continue. "Did you tell this story to the private investigator you hired?"

Winifred wiped her eyes with the hem of her tank top. "No, I didn't tell Harry Lincoln. It doesn't have anything to do with the Barilli Trust."

"Yet he was hired by the trust to find a direct descendant two years ago. Maybe someone else already knew about your father's connection."

"Are you implying that someone in the Barilli family planned to eliminate my father and me?"

"And her children and husband were in the wrong place at the wrong time?" Shannon asked in disbelief.

"I believe Freddie stands in the way of someone in the Barilli family finding whatever it is they are looking for," Mike stated the obvious.

Winifred took a long, deep breath. "And now I own it."

Shannon inched forward in her chair and looked at Mike. "Let me put your words into perspective. Someone in the Barilli family has been trying to keep the rightful heir away from Windswept so they had easy access to the safe room in order to find whatever it is that Tony Barilli probably hid there." Shannon paused a beat. "As of today, Freddie is the owner, so legally the loot belongs to her."

"And she owns the house that will cost a fortune to renovate and be tied up in permits for the next couple of years unless she decides to demolish it in the next few months. At which time, she may find said loot," Anneliese added.

Mike looked at Sally. "How long do you plan to stay on the property?"

"As long as I'm needed—or Freddie kicks me out."

"Are you and *Lady Luck* still equipped for those Caribbean charters?"

"Yes, we are," Sally said with assurance.

Mike then looked at Winifred. "Do you own a gun?"

"No, I don't, but Danny had one."

"Do you know how to shoot?"

"No. I don't like guns."

"I do," Shannon added. "Back in my college days, I dated a local police officer. He was two years older than me and thought taking me to a gun range was cool. I got pretty good."

"Captain, can you take Freddie and Shannon out somewhere for a lesson and refresher?"

"Sure can. I believe we can find some time early next week for some deep-sea fishing."

"How about tomorrow?" Mike asked.

"We were planning on spending the day in Key West tomorrow. Hector's niece, Maria, is planning to give us her private tour of the city and then watch the lighted boat parade with the Chens—in their condo," Winifred explained.

"Sally, are you going?" She glanced at Winifred and Shannon and back at Mike. "Yes. We're taking Sam along too. The Chens have their own security."

"I know of the Chens." Mike studied the faces of both Winifred and Shannon. "You should be fine. Enjoy the festivities, but be aware of your surroundings." He glanced back at Sally. "You'll be taking precautions?"

"Absolutely."

Half an hour later, Winifred and Shannon sat alone on the porch of the cottage. Mike and Anneliese had left directly after he'd been satisfied that everything would be under control during the visit to Key West. Sally walked off in the direction of *Lady Luck,* and Sam was now snuggled in his bed that Shannon had carried back with her.

Shannon was the first to break the silence. "Well, this has turned into an emotional evening."

"Did you notice the meaningful looks between Mike and Sally?" Winifred asked.

"There was definitely unspoken dialogue going on. And besides the fact that she has a gun on board and Mike knows that she knows how to use it, there was more—much more."

"Like he was practically ordering her to be with us for the day, which included Sam." Winifred thought about how Mike had reacted after hearing her story. "Shannon, do you believe someone in the Barilli family hired Petrowski to kill me—and my father? That there has been a target on my back for two years?"

"I never connected the dots. Freddie, I'm sorry, but until tonight, I didn't put the two together. Not until I looked at your story through Mike's eyes."

"He's right. This nightmare won't end until we find whatever is so valuable or important that they are willing to kill over it."

"Freddie, we thought the issue was over the inheritance of Windswept. That the person orchestrating this wanted to prevent you from owning it. But it's actually about timing. With you out of the way, the Key Deer Refuge would inherit. It could take years before their plans for the property would go through any necessary committees. Then apply for permits to make changes to the main house, or even demolishing it could take a year before bids are reviewed, and a contractor decided upon, and work begins. With ownership going to you—their timing runs out."

"We need to start going through those photos, continue reading Lorenzo's journal, and watch the home movies again. I might have missed something the first time."

"I think it's too late to begin now. Maybe start first thing in the morning before breakfast."

"Agree. I think we should cancel the tours with Maria and meet up with her later in the afternoon after a quick visit with Hector in the hospital."

Shannon stood and walked to the slider. "Sounds like a plan. Now I'm heading to the bathroom and then upstairs to bed."

"I think I'll sit here for a while. I'm glad we didn't see *Gemini* off on the horizon this evening."

Shannon smiled. "Yeah. He would have been a distraction—for you."

"I was talking about the boat."

"Right." Shannon walked into the room, then stopped and looked over her shoulder. "I wonder what he looks like under all that facial hair. He does have one gorgeous head of hair."

"I didn't notice."

Shannon's smile grew wider as she headed to the bathroom.

CHAPTER FIFTY-THREE

Winifred awoke at seven. She immediately became concerned at the lack of sounds downstairs or the aromas of breakfast being prepared. She got out of bed and leaned over the railing. There was no sign of Shannon, and Sam's bed was empty. *Huh. They must have gone out for a walk. Time for me to hit the bathroom and get dressed.*

Once down in the living room, Winifred heard movement out on the porch and went to investigate. There she found Shannon bent over the card table arranging piles of photos. Sam was stretched out on the floor.

Sam's tail began wagging as he looked in her direction. Shannon glanced over her shoulder. "Good morning. As you can see, I got an early jump on organizing the photos."

Winifred walked over to the table. "I guess you have. How long have you been at this?"

"I woke up at five and couldn't get back to sleep. I decided to start work on sorting. I set the table up for a work surface and the chairs for categorizing by topic or items of interest—like the Heywood-Wakefield furniture." She handed Winifred a stack of photos. "These were taken inside the house during the years 1963, '64, and '65. The pieces are in place."

Winifred looked at each one. "You were right. Everything must have been chosen by that interior decorator I saw in the home movie. I wonder why they were moved to the guest cottage?" she said, after setting the pictures back on the table.

Shannon handed her a few more. "These are all marked on the back. After Hurricane Betsy, 9-8-65. As you can see, the furniture is now up off the floor. And the lower part of the walls is water stained."

"I never noticed this when I first went through the photos. I didn't even make the connection between the furniture that I'd been using here in the cottage and the fact the same pieces were in these pictures."

"You weren't looking specifically at the decor. You were probably looking at Lacy Lorin and all the beautiful people surrounding her. There are quite a few with Lorenzo Barilli." Shannon glanced around the porch. "I've covered nearly every horizontal surface with photos. I think we'll eat downstairs on the picnic table—I'm sure Sally will be joining us."

"I'll text her. I also must call Maria and let her know we won't be down until this afternoon—maybe around three. That will give us enough time to stop and see Hector."

"Why don't you get dressed and take Sam for a walk while I start breakfast? I should be finished by the time you and Sally get back here."

An hour later, with breakfast finished and the timing to leave for Key West moved to one o'clock, Sally decided to head over to *Lady Luck* and wash the salt spray off from her trip two days before. Winifred went up to the loft and grabbed the metal tube containing the blueprints and the wooden box she had gotten from the attorney. After removing the contents of the tube, she laid them out flat on top of the buffet. She set the box on the floor.

Shannon entered from the porch. "The last of the photos have been sorted. I think we should leave them where they are in case we need to refer to them later. You were right about Barilli's yacht. It was a beaut."

"There was a boat registration in the wooden box for a sixty-two-foot yacht. That must be the one you saw. And I saw a photo for a 1955-nineteen-foot Chris-Craft Capri runabout. Did you see any angles other than the front and side views of the yacht?"

"Now that you mention it—no. But I'm sure it was like all the other boats of that size. There are plenty of photos of Lacy and her friends on the Chris. It must have been a favorite toy."

"Yeah. I remember seeing those as I flipped through one of the stacks." Winifred studied the first page of the layout for the main house. "The last time I looked at these prints was a full week ago. It was the first time Hector took me to see the safe room."

"The floor plan was certainly designed for entertaining. The fireplace is an architectural detail dividing the living, dining, and kitchen areas. Very open-space for that era—very Southern California."

"Looks like a house designed for a Hollywood starlet with lots of guests," Winifred said as she quickly flipped through the remaining detail sheets. "I think we can skip the rest of these."

Shannon removed the set of prints and put them on the sofa. "Looks like the next page is landscaping on parchment paper."

"The patio at the back of the house and heart-shaped pool are shown. The walls and gates are in place, with palm trees grouped at the entrance. But the guest cottage isn't here. I knew it was built a few years later, but it wasn't even considered in 1962." Winifred laughed and pointed to the corner. "Look, there is a beach down past the pool. I wonder how long that lasted!"

Shannon didn't respond. She continued to be focused on the diagram of the landscape.

"Do you see something?" Winifred asked.

"You are seeing details—where things are placed. I'm looking at the whole fifteen acres inside the walls," Shannon paused and pointed to the upper right corner. "There is that notation about the canal already in place."

"Yes. I saw that. Why?"

"Lorenzo Barilli wants to build a seven-foot-high concrete-block wall around all those acres, yet look at where he places a three-thousand-square-foot house—close to the canal. Why? He's got all this open space. If I were placing a house designed for entertaining house guests, I would put it closer to the center of the property with larger patios and walkways. Not all bunched up on one-third of the space."

"I see what you mean. This plan has plenty of room to the left of the house for a tennis court, gazebo, or tiki hut. And there is no mention of a future guest cottage."

"Look at the scale of the canal. It's already too large for the property and then you place a beautiful house close by." Shannon shook her head. "It doesn't make sense."

Something about the size and shape of the canal pricked at the back of Winifred's brain. Something she had seen—but where? "Shannon? Did you find any photos of the canal when it was being dug?"

"No. And I would have noticed. Something like digging a canal out of solid limestone would have interested me."

Winifred moved on to the next sheet. "Looks like a topographical map of the island."

"Interesting. And it looks like someone has penciled in the boundary lines for the one thousand acres, including the walls." Shannon bent over for a closer look. "What are all these dark circle-like areas. They seem to be all sizes, with one big one over by the hammock."

"The freshwater ponds. The big one is the Blue Hole."

"Notice how many are on your land. And there are several larger ones not far outside your walls."

Winifred took the parchment, landscape sheet and laid it on top. "Now, this is *very* interesting. It's not to the same scale, but close enough. Notice how the thousand acres covers many of the freshwater ponds. I wonder why!"

"Are they, or were they ever used for anything other than water for the deer and other wildlife?" Shannon asked.

"Not that I am aware of, but it would be a good question for Hector or Sally." Winifred glanced at the few remaining blueprints, when another loose sheet caught her eye. She pulled out the well-worn document and laid it on top. "Now I remember what has been bothering me since the size of the canal was mentioned after Sally docked her boat. She remarked that our canal was about the same size as other ones that lead into housing developments. I saw a hand-drawn map of two housing developments. One of them was named Casa Santiago. At the time I asked Hector if he knew where it was located, and he'd never heard the name."

"And the map you found matches this one?"

"I think so, except this one was professionally created." Winifred read the description on the lower right-hand corner. "It looks like the larger development, which is basically on this side of Key Deer Boulevard, is named Casa Santiago. The smaller one on the opposite side of the island, approximately where Hector's house is located, is called Pirates Cove."

"Is there any way we can find out if permits were ever obtained?"

"I'll call Rosa on Monday. Maybe she can check into it. It's dated December 21, 1960."

"Perhaps you should call Harry Lincoln as well. See if Tony Barilli was ever connected to a bank heist or jewelry store robbery. If we're going to continue with the idea that it might have been him that hid something."

Winifred's cell phone chirped. She read the message. "It's Sally. She's finished with the boat and heading over."

"Should we roll these up and put them back in the tube?" Shannon asked.

Winifred thought about showing the documents to Sally. She trusted Sally. Mike Connor and Anneliese trusted her. But what did they really know about the salty boat captain who owned a yacht named *Lady Luck*? "Yes. Let's put them away before she gets here."

Captain Sally knocked on the door a few minutes later. Shannon let her in while Winifred took the metal tube upstairs and placed it on the shelf in the closet.

"I've got *Lady Luck* sparkling clean. I hope Hector won't mind—I used his hose and brushes."

"No problem. I'm sure he would have offered if he were here."

"By the way, I see Hunter has been fishing off Mayo Key," Sally commented as she headed to the porch.

"Really? I don't think either of us even looked outside," Winifred said as she descended the stairs from the loft.

"Sally, how about you help Freddie clear the table and chairs on the porch while I make us something for lunch?"

Winifred walked over to the railing and looked out toward Mayo. *Gemini* glistened in the noon sun. *What are you up to today, Hunter? You are anything but a common fisherman.*

CHAPTER FIFTY-FOUR

"I'm sorry, but dogs are not allowed inside unless they are service animals," said the woman sitting behind the information desk in the waiting room of the Key West hospital. She stood and leaned over the desk. She looked at the dog that appeared to have survived a mob attack. "I'm pretty sure he or she doesn't qualify."

"Can you please check a list that might have the names of those expected today? I called ahead this morning. The names are Winifred Forrester, Dr. Shannon Mulaney, Captain Sally, and this is Sam."

The woman checked her computer screen, then looked up at Winifred. "*That* is Sam?"

"Sam is a hero. He belongs to your patient Hector Morales. Sam got his wounds saving my life. Hector has been asking for his dog."

"Yes. Yes, I see the note. You are welcome to go up."

After the elevator ride to the third floor and the long walk to the corner room, the four of them all piled into Hector's room at once. Sam was so excited he would have jumped on top of his master if he could have. Instead, he settled for standing next to the bed with his front paws on Hector's chest.

"Hello, Hector. You look so much better. I brought the whole crew with me."

"It is nice to see you again, Shannon. I hope you are enjoying your visit and our weather."

"I am, Hector. I love Windswept, and Sam and I have developed quite the friendship."

He glanced over at Sally with a frown. "You are part of Freddie's *crew?*"

"I am. *Lady Luck* and I are camped out at Windswept for a while. I hope you don't mind if I use your dock supplies. I'm very impressed with the tiki hut you have for fish cleaning."

Hector smiled. "Of course, Captain. You are welcome to use anything I have—including anything at the house—Freddie has the keys."

Winifred's brow creased at Hector's words. *Why are you offering Sally the use of stuff at your house? What do you have that she knows about? And why would she want it?*

"Hector, do you know what the freshwater ponds were used for in the early days?" Winifred asked. "Shannon and I were thinking of the obvious like watering livestock and crops."

Hector glanced over at Sally with a questioning look. "Not really. I know they are important for our deer population."

"My father and uncles liked telling the story about how a human skeleton rolled out of a pond when one of the early canals was being dug," Sally said with a chuckle.

"Right. I remember seeing the picture on the front page of the newspaper. The construction crew had just set off dynamite next to one of the ponds and the bones fell out with the rubble." Hector paused. "I was just a little kid, so it must have been in the mid-fifties."

"Did they ever figure out who it was or how long they had been down in the pond?" Winifred asked.

Hector looked at Sally and shrugged. "I'm sure there would have been some type of investigation done at the time. But that's all I know."

"Why the interest in the ponds?" Sally asked.

"During my first time in the safe room, Hector gave me a metal tube that had been stored on the top shelf in the closet. This morning Shannon and I were looking at the blueprints of the house, landscaping designs, and a topographical study of Big Pine. We noticed how many ponds of varying sizes were located throughout the island."

"Hector, does the name Casa Santiago mean anything to you?" Shannon asked.

"No." Hector coughed and cleared his throat. "It means House of Santiago or House of Diego."

"What about Pirates Cove?"

"No. Nothing."

"Did Tony Barilli ever mention that his father intended to build one or two housing developments on the land?" Winifred asked.

Hector took a few moments before he answered. "Not that I recall. Either he didn't know about those early days or didn't care. He didn't come down much."

At that moment, a nurse entered the room pushing a stand containing a computer screen and all kinds of electronics. "Mr. Morales was up and walking the halls this morning. If he keeps up the good work, he may be going home by the end of the week. But at the moment, I need to spend some alone time with him. Can you wait out in the hall for a few minutes?"

Winifred walked over to the bed and took Sam's leash. "Hector, we should probably leave now. We're meeting your niece Maria at the Custom House and later all of us, including Sam, are watching the lighted boat parade with the Chens."

"From their penthouse?"

"Yes."

Hector gave a rumbling laugh. "Sam at the Chens'! I'd love to see that." His laugh ended with a coughing spasm. "Have fun," he said as they walked out into the hallway.

Winifred was almost to the door when she turned back. "Hector, do you by any chance have a movie projector screen? We took the home movies to the cottage to watch again, but we need a screen."

"Yes. In the coat closet by the front door. I thought you looked at all of them."

"I'm beginning to think I missed something important. Something about the size and placement of the canal—and Casa Santiago."

⟞⧓⟝

"Great news about Hector going home," Winifred said as she opened the rear door of the Camry for Sam to climb in.

Shannon opened the other rear door and slid in next to Sam. "I found the story about the skeleton interesting. I wonder if Tony Barilli could have hidden something like diamonds in one of the ponds on Windswept land!"

"I don't think he would have done that unless the pond was inside the walls and in an area that was hidden from the house and cottage," Sally said as she opened the front passenger door. "Unless the pond was under the safe room."

Winifred started the engine while everyone buckled up. "We'll take a closer look at the blueprints tomorrow morning."

An alarm sounded on Winifred's cell phone.

"What's that?" Sally asked.

"I don't know. I've never heard it before." Winifred checked the screen. "It's the security camera that Larry installed next to the canal."

Sally leaned to the side to get a better look. Shannon scooted to the center, between the front seats.

"A boat is approaching the canal! There are two men with masks." Sally took the phone from Winifred and studied the image. "They are looking out toward Spanish Channel." She turned the screen so all three of them could watch.

"Something scared them off. They are heading back out—fast," Shannon added.

Winifred took a deep breath. "We need to get back to Windswept. I'll call Maria and cancel."

"Freddie, not so fast. Let's think about this," Sally advised. "The guys are gone—for now. If we go back, it only puts you in danger, should they decide to return. We don't know what they saw that made them leave quickly. You need to call Mike Connor."

Winifred pulled Mike's contact information up and hit call. He answered almost immediately. "What's up, Freddie? Is everything okay in Key West?"

"Mike, you're on speaker. We just left Hector. I received an alert from the security camera that faces the canal. Two guys showed up wearing black masks. They were in a boat approaching the dock when something out in the water spooked them. They turned around and headed down Bogie Channel."

"How long ago did this happen?"

"A few minutes. Should we come back?"

"Is Sally with you?"

"Yes. Mike, I'm here. We're fine. I suggest we continue with our plans."

"I agree. Freddie is safer with you and the Chens. I'll send a deputy to the property in case they come back."

"I suggest that the car be parked next to the garage and out of sight from the canal. But he or she will have a clear view of the channel leading to the canal. I would suggest using *Lady Luck*, but I have her tied up at Hector's wash station on the back leg of the canal."

"Not a problem. Keep to your planned schedule—and, Freddie, act normal. Don't mention this to *anyone*. I will call you *only* if there is a problem. Do not call me. You don't know who may be listening."

"I understand," Winifred replied.

"Captain?"

"Understand, Mike."

Winifred's heart raced. She glanced at Sally and Shannon. "What do we do now?"

"We do what Mike ordered. For now, we forget anything happened and head into Key West," Sally emphasized.

Easier said than done. I wonder if Aleksy Petrowski's face is behind one of the masks!

A few minutes later, as Winifred turned right onto North Roosevelt Boulevard, she turned to Sally. "The vet mentioned that there is a large pet store somewhere along here. I'd like to get one of those harnesses for Sam. He seems uncomfortable with that large chain around his neck."

"I know the one," Sally said. "It will be on your left before you get to the light at First Street and Palm Avenue."

"And I just saw the cutest yellow convertible in that dealership we passed. It looked like a Mini Cooper, the perfect little car for driving on these narrow streets."

"*I* don't have a problem driving the Escalade down here. *You* are the one who has a problem."

"I think you should at least consider a little car. You could keep it at the house when you're back in Chicago. And just fly in and out. You'd never have to worry about not having a vehicle."

Winifred pulled into the parking lot of the pet store. "Something to think about, Shannon. Now let's take care of Sam's needs."

The store clerk helped fit Sam with a style of harness that was commonly used for service dogs that had a handle and wouldn't put pressure on his shoulder wound. While Winifred worked with the salesperson, Shannon and Sally loaded up a basket with treats and toys. Half an hour later, they were back in the car heading for the indoor parking garage next to the historic Custom House where they were to meet Maria.

⟫⟨+⟩⟪

Winifred pulled into the building. "There she is standing by that cute golf cart."

Maria waved and pointed to the open space next to where she was standing.

"You can't get better than this," Sally said as she unbuckled her seat belt. "It certainly pays to have friends in high places."

Winifred chuckled. "Or the keys to the city."

Shannon slid out of the back seat, then waited as Sam hopped down.

Maria crouched down and threw her arms out wide. "Sammy!" she yelled with excitement.

Everyone watched as the big dog gave his best attempt at a run and crashed into her. They both fell over.

Winifred looked at Shannon and Sally. "*Sammy?*"

"I guess we know who his favorite person is," Shannon remarked.

Maria got up and brushed herself off. "It has been a while since he's seen me. I would say he looks worse than he feels."

"It's wonderful to see him this excited. Although he would have jumped up onto Hector's bed if he could."

"We have a little over an hour before the Chens' watch party begins." Maria pointed to the pink, six-passenger golf cart with fringe hanging from the roof. "How about an abbreviated tour?

Key West has a colorful history dating from 1821. By the 1830s, we were the wealthiest city in the United States, due mainly to the wrecking industry. I plan to give you a private tour of the museum at a later date—it's much too crowded today."

"What about the earlier history? We've heard that Big Pine Key had its own pirate," Winifred asked.

"The first documented discovery of the islands was by Ponce de León, the Spanish explorer in 1513. Spain then claimed ownership until 1763 when the British took possession. Then Spain got it back until its secession of Florida to the United States in 1819." Maria paused a beat. "Is that what you are looking for?"

"Do you know anything about the old story about a human skeleton falling out of one of the freshwater ponds back in the 1950s when the canals were dug?" Sally asked.

"No. I sure don't." Maria was quiet for a moment. "There is a local historian, Stanton Knox, who knows everything about the Keys. We carry autographed copies of his books in the gift shop. I think you should talk to him."

"Could we pass on the tour today and check out the gift shop instead?" Shannon asked.

"I remember that you had a lot of pirate information when I was here last," Winifred added.

"We also carry the same books and literature that they have at the Wreckers' Museum. You might be interested in those as well."

⟫⟪⟫

Winifred had a death grip on Sam's harness as she pressed the button in the elevator for the penthouse.

"Relax, Freddie. Everything will be fine. We're here for a party—look happy," Shannon said in her doctor voice.

"I am relaxed."

"No. You look like your grandmother has been kidnapped. And you are carrying a suitcase full of ransom money. Hold Sam by his leash and put on your public smile."

Winifred inhaled deeply and smiled as the elevator doors opened.

The reception lobby was empty except for the security guard sitting behind the desk. He smiled at Maria. "Good evening, Miss Morales." He glanced at his computer screen. "I'll check you and your guests in." He looked down at Sam. "This must be the hero we've heard about." What sounded like a small dog could be heard barking on the other side of the door leading into the apartment. "This is going to be interesting. The little princess isn't used to having competition for center stage." He stood and walked over to the door and opened it. "Enjoy the evening."

Mrs. Chen greeted them holding a white Maltese Terrier with what looked like a diamond clip holding its topknot. Long, silky hair draped over her arm. "I am so happy that you were able to come. Please forgive Luna. She is letting Sam know that this is her world."

Sam gave Luna a soft, throaty growl. Winifred petted his head. "Amigo, Sam. Amigo." He looked up at her as if to say, "Really? Do I have to be nice?" Winifred nodded. "Yes, Sam. Be nice to the little dog."

"I will hold her for now, but later they will work it out. Maria has told us of the attack on you and Sam's bravery in saving your life. Please be assured that you are safe here. Our home is always open to you."

"Thank you, Mrs. Chen. The county clerk has filed the documents. Windswept is officially mine—I just have to stay alive to enjoy it." Winifred stepped aside. "I want you to meet my friend from Chicago, Dr. Shannon Mulaney. She will be staying with me for the next couple of weeks."

Mrs. Chen took Shannon's hand. "Please call me Mira. I am so happy to meet you. I know of your excellent reputation. Several of our friends are patients of yours. Key West needs someone of your caliber. I hope you enjoy your stay."

"Thank you for your kind words. I love what I have seen so far. Maria will be taking us on a tour of the city."

"I'm glad to hear that. Key West is unusual in many ways." She looked deep into Shannon's eyes as if she were struggling with thoughts. "We have time before the parade begins. May I steal you away to my study for a few minutes?"

"Of course." Shannon left with Mrs. Chen as Maria reached for Winifred's hand.

"Freddie, you're not going to believe this, but Stanton Knox is here."

Sally took ahold of Sam's leash and followed them to the far corner of the room. A distinguished-looking man sat in a high wing-back chair. His dark tan set off a full head of gray hair and closely cropped beard and mustache. He reminded Winifred of the actor in the Dos Equis beer commercials. After introductions were made, Stanton invited the ladies to join him at the grouping of chairs where he would remain until everyone moved out to the balcony to watch the parade of brilliantly lit boats. Stanton lifted a silver-handled cane that rested next to his chair. "I'm afraid walking and standing for long periods of time is something I try to avoid." He paused while everyone took a seat. Sam curled up at their feet but kept a watchful eye on Luna. "Mrs. Forrester, Maria here tells me that you are the new owner of the infamous Windswept."

"Yes. The paperwork has been filed with the county. It hasn't even been a month since I was told about the inheritance. It came as a complete surprise, and I'm trying to find as much as I can as to its history and the history of Big Pine. But with every piece of information comes even more questions. Maria believes you may be able to help me. We stopped by the Historical Society's gift shop. I bought copies of your books as well as everything relating to the early pirating in the area."

"So, you have heard about the pirate, Captain Diego Alverez, who favored the waters around Big Pine and No Name Key."

"Yes. Is it true?" Winifred asked.

"Who knows for sure. I mention what I've read and the legends in my books. But local history dating back to the 1500s is sketchy at best."

"I told Winifred about the skeleton that was found on Big Pine back in the late fifties," Sally added.

"Ah yes, that I do know about and devote a whole chapter to skeletal remains that have been found throughout the Keys." Stanton paused to rub his left leg. "The bones were old and believed to have been those of an early homesteader."

"Do you know what happened to them?" Sally asked.

"They were finally sent to the Smithsonian to be further tested. I contacted them at the time my book was going to print for an update. The closest they could come was 1590 to 1700. But you must consider that the first recorded settler wasn't until 1870."

"From the documents I was given. We know that King Philip II of Spain deeded the island to a high-ranking member of the Spanish aristocracy in 1560. So, there could have been people there during that time."

"Possibly. With today's new technology and DNA testing, they could probably get closer, even what nationality he might have been."

"So, he could have been alive during the time of Captain Alverez?" Winifred stated.

"Yes, it is possible," Stanton admitted.

Luna chose that moment to approach with her long, silky white hair sweeping the floor around her. She gave Sam a sharp, high-pitched bark. He gave her a soft growl. She sat down at a safe distance and gave him another bark. He gave her another growl.

"As Mrs. Chen predicted, they will work it out," Maria said.

Stanton shifted in his chair and stretched his leg out in front of him. "I do believe we may be in for some rain tonight."

Winifred stood followed by the others. "Thank you so much for talking with us. You have been a great help. I look forward to reading your books."

Stanton eased out of his chair. "Good luck to you. Please don't hesitate to call me should you have questions. Maria has my contact information."

Winifred was surprised at Stanton's tall, slim physique, and excellent posture for a man who depended on a cane.

"We should probably head to the dining room. Mrs. Chen always puts out an amazing spread for these events," Maria said as she led the way.

Luna also stood, providing Sam with her most aristocratic show stance, her diamond clip sparkling in the setting sun that streamed in through the floor-to-ceiling windows that overlooked the harbor. Sam gave a soft growl. "I agree, Sam. She is quite full of herself," Sally said as they followed Winifred and Maria across the room.

"The Chens certainly know how to put on a watch party. There is every type of food one can eat while standing from sliders to sushi." At that moment, Shannon walked over to the table and joined the group. "That must have been some conversation you had with Mrs. Chen,"

"Life-altering," Shannon said while adding mini shish kebabs to her plate.

"What does that mean?"

"I can't talk about it here."

Winifred gave her a questioning look with one raised eyebrow.

"I'll explain on the way home."

A member of the staff entered the room through a swinging door and approached Sally. "Excuse me. I set a bowl of water on the floor in the kitchen for your dog."

"Thank you. I'm sure Sam will appreciate that," Sally said as she set her plate on a side table and followed the woman into the kitchen.

Ten minutes later, Sally and Sam left the kitchen and met up with the others who were on the balcony watching the first decorated boat pass by.

Winifred smiled as she made room for Sally along the railing, then immediately her expression turned to one of concern. "What's wrong?"

"Nothing," she said while juggling her plate and the end of Sam's leash.

"Something is very wrong. Did Sam bite Luna in the kitchen?"

"I overheard the staff talking. The yacht is returning in the morning. Something about needing drugs."

CHAPTER FIFTY-FIVE

As soon as the boat parade ended, Winifred, Shannon, and Sally said their goodbyes and waited for the elevator doors to open in the Chens' lobby. Maria remained inside talking with friends. After stepping on, Shannon pressed the button for the ground level, while Winifred checked her phone for any new messages. "Have you heard anything from Mike?" Shannon asked.

"No, and I've been checking every half-hour. I haven't been able to enjoy the party knowing that those guys came back. We should have left earlier."

"Mike said he would call only if there was news—so there's nothing happening—relax," Shannon said as she shifted her tote bag onto her shoulder.

"Sally, what's this about the Chens and Dr—"

Sally cut Winifred off. "And their cute little dog, Luna. Did you notice how she followed Sam wherever he went? And then they did that butt sniffing and tail wagging as we were getting ready to leave. I do believe Luna may be in love,"

"Like *Beauty and the Beast*," Shannon added.

"Sally, what has this got to do with—"

"It's about Sam making a friend. And he handled himself so well with that very expensive floor mop," Sally said as the doors opened at the ground-level entrance to the building.

After everyone exited and began walking toward the parking garage, Winifred turned to Sally. "What is wrong with you? I was trying to ask about what you overheard in the kitchen about the Chens getting more drugs. And all you wanted to talk about was their *dog*! I can't believe they are dealing or smuggling drugs."

"Freddie, the elevator had cameras and listening devices. Did you really want the Chens' security team listening to what you were about to accuse them of?"

Winifred stopped suddenly. "No, of course not. I wasn't thinking."

"What are you both talking about?" Shannon asked in a concerned voice.

"I was in the kitchen with Sam when I overheard the staff talking about the yacht arriving in the morning. One of them mentioned that they needed to find more drugs."

"*Medical* drugs!" Shannon shook her head. "Freddie, I can't believe you were going to blurt out something like that when you didn't have the facts."

"So how do *you* know what they are doing?"

"I'll tell you about my conversation with Mira Chen on the ride home. Sally, do you mind driving? I want Freddie's full attention."

Ten minutes later, Sally turned left onto Truman Avenue from Whitehead Street. "Okay, Shannon, time to talk. I heard something about a life-altering conversation."

"The Chens have a foundation. A very large, well-funded foundation. One branch provides medical care to impoverish areas or in times of disaster. That big, beautiful yacht is more than a toy for the rich—it has a large storeroom on the lowest level that can be turned into a surgical suite if needed. Along with any friends who may be on board for a luxury cruise, there are two medical doctors and nurses. This evening, they got word of a situation in Haiti that they need to prepare for. The medical staff will fly out tomorrow to assess the situation and put in the orders for supplies."

"That's amazing. I knew about the foundation, but not exactly what it does."

"I'm sure, Sally, that you are aware of the large homeless population in Key West. And those of all ages and background, who are not homeless but have mental issues of one kind or another."

"You're right. Many of them live under the bridges," Sally said as she continued on North Roosevelt past the dealership with the little yellow convertible sitting out front.

"Mira Chen gave me examples of why the city's population, ranging from the homeless to the multimillionaires need a psychiatrist with my experience and ethics."

"She offered you a job?" Winifred asked as if that was an insult.

"Not a job. But to help me start up my own practice, here in Key West."

"Sounds like a lot of pro bono work. You can't support a lifestyle down here on free services," Sally added as she waited at the light for the bridge to Stock Island.

"There is another branch of the Chens' foundation that helps finance all kinds of programs here in Key West. From food trucks that park at designated locations where the homeless are to medical clinics and clothing centers. The foundation would subsidize the work I do for them."

"Sounds like you would need to live here. What about your practice in Chicago?"

"At this point, Mrs. Chen is only asking that I think about it. Should I want to pursue the idea further, then we will meet at a later date at which time she presents her proposal."

"Wow! You are certainly right about it being life-altering. What do you think?" Winifred asked.

"I have no idea. She took me completely by surprise." Shannon was feeling overwhelmed; she needed to change the subject. "How did your conversation go with Stanton Knox? What good fortune that he happened to be at the party."

"Everything he mentioned was interesting, but as usual, we walked away with more questions. Sally asked him about the skeleton story. The bones eventually found their way to the Smithsonian, where they were dated somewhere between 1590 and 1700. That puts us back to the original Spanish deed, and the pirate, Captain Diego Alverez."

"Sounds like tomorrow we examine everything in that wooden box you were given."

And figure out what scared off our masked intruders—or who. Hunter?

CHAPTER FIFTY-SIX

S tanton was correct about rain moving in overnight. At the first clap of thunder, Winifred and Shannon awoke and ran downstairs to the porch. They removed all the photos that had been left on the card table and chairs. They restacked them inside by subject on the couch, closed the sliders, and went back to bed. Within minutes, the rain arrived with a vengeance, pounding the metal roof a mere seven feet above their heads.

"Do you have earplugs?" Shannon asked.

"No. It never occurred to me that we would need them."

"This is like trying to sleep in a tin can during a hailstorm. I think I'll get up. Maybe look at those blueprints more carefully," Shannon said as she swung her legs to the side of the bed, stood, and walked over to the closet. After retrieving the tube of prints, she went down the steps and spread the sheets out across the buffet.

A minute later, Winifred came down the steps with the wooden box tucked under her arm. She glanced around the small space, which had gotten smaller with the addition of the Christmas tree. There was one unoccupied Heywood-Wakefield chair. "I think I'll sit here while I go through the contents of the box." She moved the coffee table closer to the chair. "Is there something in particular that you are looking for in those blueprints?"

"I want to study the elevation page for the safe room. If the concrete for the floor was poured over a cavity, then the substructure might have required special reinforcement."

"So, you are thinking that whoever hired Petrowski knew about the area, thus needing someone to operate a jackhammer."

"Yes. And speaking of our burglars, it was nice of Mike Connor to have a deputy sitting here until we got home."

Winifred pulled the stack of photos from the box. "The officer said he walked the property several times during his shift and didn't see any signs of trouble. He liked your chairs but thought we needed a firepit."

"See. Isn't that what I've been saying all along? I'll look for one the next time we go to Marathon and . . . here it is. There *is* a void under the safe room. It's roughly five feet wide and fifteen feet deep."

Winifred set the photos on the coffee table, got up, and walked over to the buffet. "Show me."

"The shadowed spot on the blueprint." Shannon pointed. "Someone darkened the area with a pencil and added the coordinates."

"And look at the closet wall next to where the periscope is located—it's hollow." Winifred pointed to the spot. "Hector commented on the reasoning behind why the burglars had been using a sledgehammer on the walls when they were made of cement block."

"Someone had access to these blueprints and made the penciled notations. But was it before or after the box was given to the attorney for safekeeping until the end of the Barilli Trust?" Shannon continued reading the information at the bottom of the page. "Whoever it was didn't bother to read or perhaps didn't understand the details and instructions."

"I don't understand."

"The empty hole was to be filled in with a particular type of cement and let to cure for a month before the flooring was poured."

"So, our theory about Tony Barilli hiding something under the room doesn't fly." Winifred sounded disappointed and walked back to the couch.

"I wouldn't discount the idea that Tony hid something on the property; it just isn't under the safe room—unless he knew about a second, smaller hole that might have been found after these official prints were made."

"*Official* is the operative word here. I don't believe any crime lord has made a practice of following official rules. At this point, I'm not believing anything I see or read unless I can touch it."

For the next hour, the only sounds were those made by the storm raging outside.

At three o'clock, Shannon checked the weather app on her phone. "It doesn't look like this heavy rain is going to let up until six or so. How about I make a pot of coffee and we keep going?"

"Sounds good to me. So far, I'm not seeing anything new in these photos, but I'm setting aside the ones of Lorenzo and— and the one—the one photo that proves the bloodline."

Shannon glanced over at Winifred, who was studying one picture. "Freddie, what is it?"

"A photo of Lorenzo's yacht."

"I've got a whole stack of yacht photos."

"Not looking at the stern." Winifred held it up for Shannon to see.

"*Chivonne.* He named the boat *Chivonne.*"

"He loved her." Winifred sounded surprised.

"Freddie, it could just be a coincidence."

"An *Italian* giving his precious yacht an uncommon *Irish* name?"

"Is there anything else in the box that ties Lorenzo to your family?"

"No. I would have found it when I went through the contents while I was staying at the resort on Marathon." Winifred considered what this new information meant. "So, Lorenzo knew that he and Chivonne had a son."

"Not necessarily. Perhaps he named the boat after his first love—the young woman he never forgot."

"I guess it's possible. But if Edwardo Gonzales went through everything in this box, then he would have questioned the name of the boat and its significance in Lorenzo's life. He has a painting of his own boat on the wall above his desk and a large model of it on a table. He would have searched until he found out who Chivonne was."

"Freddie, are you suggesting that the attorney is behind this? That *he* hired Petrowski?"

"Not really. But Gonzales did hire Harry Lincoln to find any other possible heirs. First thing in the morning, I need to call Rosa and Harry."

Shannon stopped halfway to the kitchen to make the coffee. "Listen."

"Listen to what?" Winifred asked.

"The rain is stopping. How about we forget about the coffee and try to get at least a couple hours' sleep? We can pick this up later, after breakfast."

Winifred yawned. "Sounds good to me."

Winifred was jarred out of a sound sleep by a sharp bark from Sam. "What is it, boy?" He gave another bark as she rolled out of bed and reached for the railing. He sat at the foot of the stairs looking up. His tail began wagging when he saw her. At that moment, Winifred became aware that the room was filled with the first rays of morning sunlight.

Shannon began to stir. "Was that Sam? What time is it?"

"I think he needs to go outside. I have no idea of the time, but it's light out." Winifred was nearly knocked over by the excited canine when she reached the bottom step. "Okay, boy. Let me grab your leash and we'll go for a walk." Winifred was still half asleep when she slipped into a pair of flip-flops that were sitting by the front door. "I'll be so glad when I can just open the door and let you run."

Sally was relaxing in a deck chair in the aft end of her boat when Winifred and Sam reached the canal. The aroma of coffee drew her closer.

"Well, aren't you a sight in your pajamas and flip-flops? By the looks of your hair, I would say you literally *just* rolled out of bed."

Winifred focused on the large mug of coffee in Sally's hand. "Permission to come aboard, Captain."

Sally got up and walked over to the side and reached up to help her friend step onto the boat. Sam followed. "Have a seat. I bet you could use a strong dose of caffeine," Sally said as she went into the cabin.

"Thank you. Shannon and I had a rough night. As she so accurately described, it was like trying to sleep in a tin can in a hailstorm."

Sally returned with a large mug. "Ah, yes. Your metal roof. And as I recall, your bed is merely a few feet below. But we needed the rain. December begins our dry season, which will run through March or April. It's nearly perfect weather with the average temperatures between seventy and eighty, low humidity, and an almost constant breeze from the trade winds. It's our plant life that suffers."

Winifred settled into the deck chair and shook her head. "My hair begs to differ with you on the low humidity part." She took a sip of the hot liquid. "Shannon and I ended up spending hours going through the blueprints and the contents of the wooden box I received from the attorney. We didn't go back to bed until the rain let up."

"That must have been around four," Sally guessed.

"Sam woke me out of a sound sleep when he needed to go out. So here we are."

Sally reached down and stroked Sam's head. "I must say you are looking much better, big boy. And your eye is nearly back to normal. The vet is going to be happy with your progress."

"That reminds me, I need to call him tomorrow and schedule Sam's next appointment. I'm very proud of how well he handled himself yesterday with that crowd of people—and Luna."

"I hope you found new information, since you were up most of the night."

Winifred brightened and turned to face Sally. "Shannon noticed on the one sheet of blueprints that there was a void under the safe room. Someone had shaded the spot with a pencil and added its coordinates."

"Fantastic! So, something *is* buried there!"

"No. In the detail at the bottom of the page are the instructions on what kind of cement to use to fill the hole."

"It's possible then, that whoever is behind these burglaries has seen this page but never bothered to read the detail."

"That is what Shannon and I believe. Maybe we should make a large sign and post it at the garage, saying: No treasure. Hole was filled in before the house was built."

Sally looked pensively out over the water. "What this means is that someone other than Lorenzo Barilli has been in possession of that metal tube."

"Not really. Hector pulled the tube down from the top shelf in the closet of the safe room. Anyone with the combination to the lock could have entered the room and found the tube."

"Right. Blueprints probably weren't considered important. What besides the wooden box did you get from the attorney?"

"Nothing. But that led me to my find of the night." Winifred paused to finish the last sip of coffee. "Barilli named his yacht *Chivonne*. That connects the dots to me."

Sally got up and took the empty cup. "How?"

"My great-great-grandmother Chivonne Harrigan O'Reilly was Lorenzo Barilli's first love—when he came to America from Italy. They were both eighteen."

Sam got up suddenly and went to the side of the boat. He began whining. "He must hear Shannon or smells bacon frying. She probably has breakfast started. We should head back," Winifred said as she grabbed the leash and helped Sam onto the dock. Sally closed and locked the cabin door before going ashore.

⇒≪┼ ┼≫⇐

"Wow! Looks like the two of you trashed the place last night," Sally teased. "There isn't a horizontal surface that isn't covered with photos or blueprints." She walked over to the slider and opened it. "We could eat out here if we wiped everything down."

Shannon stood at the entrance to the tiny kitchen. "I vote to go out for breakfast."

Winifred eyed her friend. "Looks like you've put the time to good use while Sam and I were out. You've showered and look fabulous in one of your new outfits." She unhooked the leash and hung it next to the door. "I look the same as when I crawled out of bed."

"How about you shower and get dressed while I show Sally the blueprints?"

"And then we get breakfast at the Egg. I'll drive separate, since I need to get ready for an early-morning charter tomorrow."

An hour later, Winifred, Shannon, and Sally were seated at her usual table, with Sam curled up in the corner.

"Good morning, ladies," Katie said as she set mugs on the table and filled them with coffee. "It's nice to see you again, Doctor Mulaney. I hope you are enjoying your time in paradise."

"Please call me Shannon. I've spent the holiday season in places all over the world, and none of them can live up to what I've seen so far in Key West."

"Sounds like you may be in danger of catching the Key fever."

"What's that?" Shannon asked.

"You come down to the Keys on vacation and never leave." Katie laughed. "I know. It happened to us after Irma."

"It's how us locals measure time," Sally explained. "The years have a way of running together down here, but you never forget the hurricane years. Irma came ashore on Cudjoe Key on September tenth of 2017. Big Pine took the brunt of the dirty side of the storm. We sustained major damage. Many businesses never reopened."

"I'll be back in a minute for your orders."

Shannon thought about what Sally had said as she perused the menu. There would be a great number of residents before and after hurricanes and tropical storms who would need psychiatric help. Those who lose everything or just can't cope. She was beginning to understand the unique needs of these people.

"Know what you want?" Winifred asked.

"Yes. I'm beginning to think I do," Shannon responded.

Winifred felt that Shannon's answer wasn't about her choice of food, but she didn't press her further.

Katie returned to the table. "Know what you want?" Sally ordered her usual, Winifred her favorite French toast, and Shannon ordered French toast, bacon, and fresh fruit. "I'll give this to the cook and be right back. I want to hear about what you're finding."

A few minutes later, Katie returned. "So, what's the latest?" she asked as she sat in the chair next to Shannon.

"The guys came back while we were visiting Hector. But something scared them off," Winifred explained.

"How would you know that if you were in Key West?" Katie sounded confused.

"Larry, the electrician, hooked up a security camera. I got an alert on my phone and saw the two masked guys approaching the canal. I couldn't see what frightened them off."

"Wow! That's amazing. Have you figured out what the burglars were after?"

"No. But Shannon noticed on one of the blueprints a void or hole under the safe room. She also was able to determine from the notes at the bottom of the page that—"

Katie cut Winifred off. "Hold that thought. A customer is at the register. I'll be right back. This is so interesting."

While she was gone, Winifred's phone chirped. She glanced at the screen. "It's Mike. He wants to meet at the house." She texted back that they were at the Egg having breakfast. "Maybe I should just call him." Mike texted back. "He says we should stop by the station after we leave here."

Katie returned to the table. "Sorry, that took longer than I expected. I had four tables all leave at once."

"Not a problem. Mike Connor contacted me and wants us to stop by the station. We need to eat and run."

"Your food should be ready. I'll check on it."

A few minutes later, Katie returned with their orders and fresh coffee. "Sally, a couple came in earlier; they are staying for the month on Ramrod and wanted a recommendation for a charter. I gave them one of your cards."

"Thank you. I appreciate it," Sally said as she dug into her steak and eggs.

Shannon poured maple syrup over her French toast. "Katie seems very nice."

"Yeah. She and her husband bought this place, dirt cheap, after it was nearly destroyed by Irma. They cater to the locals."

There were no further comments or discussions while the three ate in silence. Sally ran through all the scenarios of what Mike might have found out and what might be needed of her in the coming days. Shannon's thoughts revolved around her meeting with Mira Chen and what it might be like to live full time in Key West. Winifred's mind was a jumble of thoughts between everything she needed to accomplish that day and the need to reread Lorenzo Barilli's journal. And where was Hunter? *Gemini* was nowhere in sight that morning—and she had been looking.

CHAPTER FIFTY-SEVEN

"I'm glad you're here, too, Sally," Mike Connor said as he ushered the three ladies and Sam into the office and closed the door. "I'm glad to see that Sam is looking much better. His eye is almost back to normal, and he is showing no signs of limping."

"It was all I could do this morning to keep up with him, and he's taking the stairs well. I had Shannon drive on the way over here so I could call the vet. He's squeezing Sam in tomorrow as the last appointment at six."

"We are all going to be happy when Sam has free run of the property again," Sally added.

Mike gave her a quick nod. "I asked you in because I have more information—and more questions."

"I was expecting you to call me yesterday," Winifred said as she took the far-end seat in front of the desk. Sam sat at attention next to her. Shannon took the middle seat, and Sally the one on the far left.

"I said I would contact you only if needed. Now is that time. Can you pull up that security cam footage? I'd like to look at it in detail."

Winifred dug in her tote bag for her phone and retrieved the images. She handed Mike the phone and watched as he studied the frames. "See what I mean about something scaring them off?"

"Yes. But there is nothing to indicate what that might be." Mike continued to study the images. "One guy is definitely looking back over his shoulder as they approach your canal, but the other one is looking up. They both duck their heads and turn the boat and speed back in the direction they came from—Bogie Channel."

"Yeah, I noticed that. The boat is a common deep-vee hull with a center console and outboard motor. You see them everywhere down here."

"But notice that it's larger than the fast little skiffs they have used in the past. In the first frame, the camera picks up the motion before they make the approach to the canal. They are moving at a slow speed and haven't yet put on their masks. They would appear to be two local fishermen. Now as they make the turn, they slip on the masks and continue in a straight line for the dock."

"What does that mean to you?" Winifred asked.

"It means that they chose a boat that won't attract attention. They weren't looking for speed or maneuverability, only a common fishing boat."

"Who knew that you would be in Key West for the day?" Mike asked.

"I don't understand," Winifred said as she looked from Mike to Sally.

"It means that those guys weren't trying to conceal themselves until the last minute when they approached the canal. They expected to have Windswept to themselves."

"Sally's right. And although you can't tell in these images, I would suspect that there is a jackhammer and the necessary tools to break through concrete on board."

"Back to my question. Who knew your plans for the day?"

Winifred searched her mind. "We told you and Anneliese the other night. Hector, Sophia knew, and, of course, Maria, who arranged our schedule."

"No one else?"

"Maria might have told the Chens since we were invited to their lighted boat parade watch party," Winifred added.

"I might have told Katie, but I'm not sure about that," Sally confessed.

"Okay. So, people knew our plans. But what scared them off?" Shannon asked. "They both look up, then duck and speed away. Maybe a drone? Maybe a tourist is checking out what the boarded-up estate owned by a mob boss looks like. Or just someone wanting to know what's beyond the high walls."

Mike pushed a photo across the desk for them to see. "A boat fitting that description was found abandoned on the far side of No Name Key. We found this lodged in the motor." He set a bullet next to the photo.

Sally picked it up, studied the shape, then looked at Mike. "A rifle? This came from a long-range, high-powered rifle."

Winifred glanced at Sally and back to Mike. *How does she know that? Why did Mike give the bullet to her?*

"That is what I believe, Captain." Mike looked at Winifred. "I'm sending this to ballistics in Miami today. I should have a report by the end of the week."

"This tosses out my drone theory," Shannon added. "Then who shot at them and why, if they looked like local fishermen?"

"Did any of you notice boats in the area?"

"Hunter was fishing out in the channel during the early-morning hours, but he was gone before we left," Sally answered. "There was the usual boat traffic, but nothing registered with me as suspicious."

Mike stood and picked up the photo and bullet. "That's all I have. I'll let you know if anything new turns up." He then walked everyone to the door.

"If you and Anneliese aren't busy tonight, I would like to invite you to join us on board *Lady Luck*. I have some fine wines and liquor for guests and a bunch of appetizers in the freezer that I would like to use." Sally looked at Winifred and Shannon for confirmation. They both eagerly nodded their acceptance. "Would sevenish work for you?"

"I believe Anneliese is free, but if not, then I will certainly be there," Mike said as he opened the door, then walked everyone out to the parking lot.

Sally headed for her truck, while Winifred unlocked the Toyota and opened the rear door for Sam.

"Well, that put a new spin on everything," Shannon said as she opened the passenger door and slid in.

It sure does. And I'm afraid the only people I can trust 100 percent are you and me.

⟞⟝⟞⟝

Once back at the cottage, Winifred glanced around the room. "Sally is right; we did trash the place. How about if you put all the photos of Lacy Lorin and her friends back in the box? Leave out any with Lorenzo and good shots of the yard—and any of the safe room. I'm going to call Rosa."

A minute later, Edwardo Gonzales's secretary answered the call. "Rosa, it's Winifred. Is this a good time to talk?"

"Yes, I'm happy to talk with you. How is everything going?"

"The answer to that would take longer than either one of us has. But I do have a couple of questions."

"Sure, I'm happy to help."

"I wonder if you can contact your friend at the Monroe County Clerk's Office and find out if Lorenzo Barilli had filed a permit to build two housing developments named Casa Santiago and Pirates Cove. Both were located on the same thousand acres of land that he won in the Vegas poker game back in 1960. I have the original blueprints showing the canals and lots—also the permit numbers."

"Wow! You do realize that is a long shot—forgive the pun. But I'll try."

"The other question is more recent but may be confidential. Do you know if Lorenzo Barilli's grandniece Bianca has been in touch with your boss recently?"

"I know who that is, but I don't believe she has anything to do with the Barilli Family Trust."

"And no one from the family has contacted Edwardo? Has he met with anyone in the last month or so who has an interest in Windswept or asked questions about the trust?"

"I don't think so. Only Hector, because he managed the property. But I can look at his calendar for the last few months if that will help you."

"Thank you. That would be a big help—and it's important."

"Wait. Mr. Gonzales has had a couple of meetings with the financial adviser who manages the trust. Does that count?"

"It certainly does. Do you know the details of why they met?"

"I know the last meeting was to give the finance officer at the bank a copy of your paperwork. You should be hearing from someone at the bank soon to sign the necessary documents to transfer the funds into your name."

"I have a local financial adviser? Are you saying that the money in the trust goes to me as well?"

"Yes. You didn't know that?"

"No. I guess I've been so busy trying to stay alive and figure out what is so valuable here that someone is willing to kill, that I've forgotten to ask for the fine print of my inheritance."

"Freddie, what are you talking about? Someone tried to kill you?"

"I guess it's a good thing that you haven't heard about what has been going on down here. Maybe my suspicions are all wrong."

"Suspicions about what?" Rosa sounded totally confused.

"Forget it for now and *don't* mention it to Edwardo."

"Okay, I won't. Anything else?"

"Yes, is there any way that you can access the trust bank statements?"

"Maybe. I have the bank login because I make the deposits and pay the bills online. Although Mr. Gonzales paid the trust bills himself. Give me a day or two and I'll get back to you."

"Thank you for all your help, Rosa," Winifred said, then ended the call.

Shannon put the last of the photos in the box, then set the box on the floor next to the Christmas tree. "I'm glad you had your phone on speaker. Are you really thinking that Gonzales is behind this?"

"I don't know what to believe anymore. But he hasn't exactly helped things along."

"Why didn't you ask her to check the attorney's calendar for the name Petrowski? That would have answered everything."

"Because I don't want her to slip up and mention the name to her boss. That would tip him off that we are looking at him as a suspect in this whole mess."

"That was smart. And since we are talking about your attorney, how about taking another look at the wooden box he gave you?"

"We can ignore the photos this time. I've already pulled the most important one. The one that proves Lorenzo never forgot Chivonne. But let's keep these separated from the others just in case we need to refer back to them."

"What's left?"

"A ring of keys and this journal. But it didn't look important."

"Did you actually begin reading or just flipped through the pages?" Shannon asked.

"I skipped around and read a page here and there."

"Freddie, if we are going to figure out what these guys are after, we need to look at everything that happened back in 1960."

"You're right—as usual. How about you look through the books we got at the gift shop and see if you can find any mention of what happened here on Big Pine? One of Stanton's books deals with the pirate years. Maybe our pirate, Captain Diego Alverez, is referenced somewhere. And I'll start reading the journal."

Half an hour later, Winifred set the journal aside and rubbed her eyes. "One thing I've learned so far is that Lorenzo had atrocious handwriting skills. I've read doctors' notes that are more legible that his."

"Let me know if you get stuck. I'm pretty good at reading illegible."

"Barilli is showing no signs of having a heart or any compassion for the family who treasured their Spanish heritage for over four hundred years. On January first, he wins the thousand acres, which is all the family has left out of the original Spanish land grant from 1560. Three weeks later, he flew down to Key West and meets with the mob boss they called Havana and gets a tour of Big Pine Key. Barilli is disappointed that there are no structures on the property. But he *is* impressed with the new housing developments with homes that butt up against canal systems. Being the businessman that he was, he began formulating the idea of selling off the land, a quarter of an acre at a time. Over the next few months, he contacts the contractors who are building the canals, those building the homes, and a local attorney. By December, he has the necessary plans drawn and submitted to the county for the permits." Winifred stood and stretched. "I need a break. What have you found?"

Shannon turned the book she was holding around so Winifred could see the back cover. "Is Stanton really this handsome?"

Winifred walked over and looked at the photo of the historian. "He's younger there, but yes. He may be more distinguished looking now. I think he's one of those men who become more handsome as they get older."

"How come I didn't meet him?"

"You were talking with Mrs. Chen. Stanton has a bad leg and uses a cane. He spent a lot of his time in a corner of the main room in a comfortable chair."

"Anyway, I'm reading about the wreckers during the 1800s. Can you believe Key West built a whole, well-organized industry on watching out for ships that wrecked offshore? They saved the passengers and crew that were still alive, removed the contents that were auctioned off and then used the salvageable timber and fittings from the ship to build their houses. I like these people—very industrious!"

"What about the pirates?"

"That was earlier, during the 1500s into the 1700s. Key West at that time was occupied by a few Native American tribes. Although Spain claimed ownership of the Keys, there were no other recorded settlements."

"Interesting. So how did anyone know about Big Pine's Captain Alverez?"

"We keep reading—but after I prepare a quick lunch."

"Sounds good to me," Winifred said as she walked toward the front door. "Come on, Sam; I think we both could use a walk."

Sam made it down the flight of steps with no difficulty and then set the pace of their walk to the main house and back. Winifred noted along the way that Gemini was nowhere to be seen. Shannon had lunch set out on the porch when they returned. They dined on chicken salad made with sliced grapes, celery, and chopped walnuts served on croissants with lettuce. Fresh fruit and iced tea finished off the refreshing meal.

"Thank you, Shannon, for another wonderful lunch. Sitting here, overlooking the calm waters of the Gulf with a bright blue sky and a gentle breeze—well, I can imagine how life here could be."

"Without all the drama? I'm beginning to think I could too."

"Sounds like we are both feeling the beginning stages of Key fever. The disease seems to be quite common down here." Winifred stood and collected their dirty plates. "We should get back to reading if we are going to figure out the cause of this drama."

Winifred skipped over Lorenzo's financial calculations and notes regarding the various contractors to his thoughts about the running of the extensive project. "This is interesting. He's brought Tony down. They have rooms in a local motel. Lorenzo is impressed with his son's ideas for the layout of the two subdivisions by adding open spaces for parks. He is debating whether to turn over the construction project to Tony and return to Detroit to handle family problems up there or stay and send his son back to Detroit."

"Does Lorenzo mention what the family problems are about?"

"Not yet." Winifred looked over at Shannon. "Can you check the prints of the subdivisions and see if there is any green space noted?"

It took Shannon a few minutes to find the plans for the two subdivisions. "Yes, there are several parks. Pirates Cove has a total of fifty, quarter-acre lots and one large park. Casa Santiago has a total of one hundred fifty lots of the same size and three parks or open spaces."

"What I am reading matches with the original plans."

"The big question is: What drastic event caused this massive project to cease?" Shannon asked.

"I'll keep reading."

"What we now know is that Lorenzo Barilli, along with his son Tony, was only interested in developing the land and selling off the lots, not building homes," Shannon surmised. "At this point, there is no mention of holding back acreage or building a house for themselves. The name Windswept isn't shown anywhere on these subdivision plans." She then laid the Windswept landscape sheet over the one with the canals. "Look at this."

Winifred stood and went over to the buffet. Shannon pointed to the current canal. "See how your canal overlays perfectly with this one? There are lots that butt up against the canal and the leg that goes off to the right where Hector keeps his boats."

"However, on the original plan, both canals keep going and multiple canals run off the main one." Winifred bent down to get a closer look. "The main one, my canal, keeps going almost to Key Deer Boulevard. The lots on the left side would back up to the property next door. All the other canals branch to the right and fall in line with Hector's leg."

"How many acres are within the current walls of Windswept?"

"Fifteen. And they don't match up with anything in the original plan," Winifred added. "Not a lot line or park area. It looks like something happened while they were putting in the main canal, which is wider than Hector's leg, and everything was scrapped. Nothing more was done until six months later when the blueprints for Windswept were produced."

Winifred stepped back. "This is getting complicated. How am I going to keep track of the many details and timelines?"

"I know," Shannon said as she walked over to where she had left her briefcase. She pulled out a fresh legal pad and pencil. "Here, let me show you how I keep track of my patient visits." She drew a circle in the middle of the page and wrote in Lorenzo Barilli's name. Then, in the corners, she wrote the names of Tony, Bianca, Edwardo, and Hector. "As you find information, you list it under their names. That way you can begin connect-ing the relationships." Shannon then flipped to the next page and at the top wrote, "Timeline." She then wrote the dates of all the important dates from 1560 to the present. "You do the same with timeline. Under 1560, you add 'Spanish Deed'; under 1960, you list 'poker game,' 'Barilli wins Windswept,' and still under that, you're going to put 'subdivision plans'; and under 1961, 'Windswept constructed.' See what I mean?"

"Yes. Like the crime and murder boards you see on TV."

"Exactly. It's at least one way to connect the dots."

"I know it is a rhetorical question, but how do we find our inciting incident? The one monumental event that sent Lorenzo Barilli off in a totally different direction." Winifred glanced at the wall clock. "It's after three. I need to get ready for Sam's vet appointment on Marathon."

"Do you want me to come with you or keep reading?"

"Keep reading. There isn't anything you can do except keep me company, and I have Sam."

"What about returning the Camry?"

"Sam's making amazing progress, but I don't think he is ready for the Escalade yet."

"Okay. I'll keep reading. Do you want me to continue where you left off? I'll take notes and fill you in when you return."

"Perfect. I'll pick up Chinese on my way back. There's a place in the Winn Dixie Plaza."

"And we've got cocktails on *Lady Luck* at seven," Shannon added.

CHAPTER FIFTY-EIGHT

"Welcome aboard," Sally said as she greeted Mike and Anneliese, then helped them into the cockpit. "Please come inside where we won't have to worry about the vicious mosquitoes. Freddie and Shannon are already here."

"Wow! Sally, this is so unlike you," Mike said, without thinking about how his words sounded. "Sorry. No offense. But the Captain Sally I know is a no-nonsense, extremely capable woman in every sense—this boat is all glamor."

"He's right about that," Anneliese added. "It belongs on the cover of some yachting magazine. How did you choose to spend big bucks on something so unlike you?"

"*Lady Luck*'s story is a long but interesting one. I'll tell you all later. Right now, help yourselves to drinks and food. Shannon's helping me to understand the importance of presentation."

"Well, I must say you've nailed the whole package. I was mesmerized by the many lights as Sam and I walked over. The image of *Lady Luck* dressed in tiny white lights from the top of her tower to the outline of her cabin. The soft deck lighting and illumination from every port and window created something magical against the evening sky." Winifred accepted a glass of Pinot Noir from Shannon. "It has me thinking about lining the driveways with solar lights. I believe it would add a welcoming look to the property."

"I can help you with some ideas. Tomorrow, I'm getting two of my clients' homes ready for the season. One of them lives in Boston and owns several car dealerships. His wife writes a column for a newspaper. They both work from the house from December to April. Their place has a rather Nantucket feel. The other couple are gay and live in Manhattan. They also have careers that make it easy to work while they are here. The style of that house is very sleek and modern, with lots of marble and glass. The floor plan was designed for entertaining."

"I'm still debating about what I should do. Do I remodel Lorenzo's sixties' ground-level house that so depicts 'old Florida' or demolish and build something totally different?"

"Why don't you and Shannon come with me? That way you can get a firsthand look at what your options could be. Both houses are open water lots, like yours. I think you'll be surprised."

"How much time are we talking?" Winifred asked.

"Not more than an hour or two."

Winifred and Shannon looked at each other and nodded. "What time do we meet?" Shannon asked.

"How about nine?" Anneliese suggested.

"Perfect. Now I want to try a little of everything. Especially these cute shrimp kebabs." After piling her plate high with the varied array of hors d'oeuvres, Winifred took a seat at one end of the curved white-leather banquette.

Shannon sat down next to Winifred, while Mike and Anneliese chose the similar banquette on the opposite side of the room. Sally stood behind the galley counter.

"Okay, Sally. Don't keep us waiting. What's the story behind this gorgeous boat?" Mike asked.

"Back in 2002 Miami, a rather unsavory man they called Jimmy the Greek had this forty-five-foot Egg Harbor custom-built to his specifications. Only the hull and mechanics are factory; he had the interior installed at a separate location. The story was that he was opening a new luxury charter business, where he would take select couples on three- or four-day cruises to various Caribbean islands resorts. The boat's interior was to be fitting his clientele. The bar was designed to hold and protect its contents during rough weather. The finishes on the wooden walls and cabinetry are a highly polished lacquer." Sally leaned against the counter, resting her elbows on the surface. "During this time, a young member of the DEA out of Miami, named Troy Cameron, took notice of this flashy yacht, especially since it was known to be owned by Jimmy the Greek. During the next two years, Troy noted that after each Caribbean trip, there would be an influx of drugs on the streets—his gut said it was being smuggled in *Lady Luck*. He became so sure that he scheduled searches of the boat when she docked. But neither the officers nor the dogs could find anything. Now you must understand that young Officer Camreon had a gut that was never wrong. He routinely appeared in press conferences, courtrooms, and the front page of the Miami newspapers. I guess you could say he'd become a DEA celebrity, and it didn't hurt that he looked like he'd just stepped off the cover of *GQ*. If I had been twenty years younger, I'd have become a groupie."

Everyone laughed and kept their full attention on Sally.

"As you can imagine, his gut—and his pride—wouldn't let *Lady Luck* go. Years later, Jimmy's luck ran out, and he was picked up on a totally unrelated charge. Officer Cameron had the boat impounded with the orders to tear it apart. That is when they found out what a custom interior could mean." Sally spread her arms wide to draw attention to the galley. "This cabinetry is a whole unit that releases into the room—so does the bar. The high gloss on the wood isn't for show. It's a substance that was developed by our military to mask scents—it literally confuses a dog's scent glands, sending mixed messages to the brain."

"I've never heard of that. So, every time the DEA sent dogs onboard, they came up with zilch." Mike stood and walked over to the bar and studied the walls. "It's as smooth as glass."

"From what I've been told, it's applied like lacquer or thick varnish covering every crack and gap, then hardens."

"Amazing. So how did you come by it?" Mike asked.

"Years later, I was visiting a friend, who was the secretary to the commanding officer at the time. It just happened that the agency was holding an auction the next day. I was in the right place at the right time. The interior was torn apart, so they practically gave it away."

"So, what ever happened to Troy Cameron?" Shannon asked.

"I think the notoriety made his job too difficult to stay in Miami. At the time I bought *Lady Luck*, I looked him up on the internet. He was living in Bar Harbor, Maine."

At that point, everyone got up and refilled their plates, while Sally refreshed their drinks.

Mike leaned against the galley counter. "Speaking of law enforcement, I've got news on our would-be burglars."

"Was it Petrowski?" Winifred asked.

"The two men haven't been identified yet, but one of them left some blood behind in the boat. Which had been stollen from a campground." He walked over and sat back down. "The dispatcher had several calls that afternoon of seeing a fishing boat driving erratically at a dangerous speed in shallow water. One caller said he observed a boat that looked to be in trouble heading for the far side of No Name Key. I sent deputies over, and they found the boat sitting in two feet of water in an isolated area. They searched the island and found nothing."

"What about the residents? Did they see who was in the boat?" Winifred asked.

"No. But the interesting thing is that the boat was empty. Not even a pair of sunglasses."

"So, what does that mean?" Shannon asked.

"It means they had help. They were able to call someone who was close enough to find them on No Name Key and help remove the equipment that would have been used—probably at least a jackhammer."

"You got it, Captain. The big question still remains—who? Who knows Winifred's plans and activities? Those guys were taking their good old time."

"Because they didn't expect anyone to be on the property until late at night—after the lighted boat parade and the forty-five minutes or so that it would take to drive back. How are we going to stop this?" Winifred said in an angry voice.

"Figure out what they are after and eliminate it. Sorry, Freddie. I can't help you with that," Mike said as he looked over at Sam.

"The vet was very impressed with Sam's progress. His eye shows no damage and should be fine—I just need to continue the drops for a few more days. He doesn't need to wear the shoulder strapping to protect the sutures, which should dissolve in another week. As long as he doesn't go running around like a crazy dog, he can be let loose."

"That is wonderful news." Mike turned to Sam. "Are you ready to go back to work, boy?"

Sam reared up on his hind legs and gave one sharp bark. Everyone laughed.

Winifred glanced at Mike in time to witness a strange look he gave Sally. She gave him a slight nod in return.

What is going on between the two of you? Are you working behind my back? Doing what?

CHAPTER FIFTY-NINE

The next morning, Winifred awoke at seven to the aroma of fresh coffee. She headed downstairs to find Shannon and Sam sitting on the porch.

"Good morning. There's a fresh pot," Shannon said as she raised her empty mug for Winifred to take and refill. "Sam and I had an early-morning run. He did great, kept pace with me, and didn't try to take off. Sally has left for her charter."

"Have you noticed anything strange between Mike and Sally?" Winifred asked as she headed to the kitchen.

"No. Like what?"

"Like sly looks, nodding or shaking heads without speaking, the way he sometimes uses her name and other times only refers to her as 'Captain.' Like at his office yesterday, when he gave her the bullet fragment to look at before he showed it to us."

"Now that you point them out as questionable, I guess I have noticed. But, honestly, I didn't put any importance on the actions. Friends sometimes do things like that—you and I do them."

"I guess you're right. Perhaps I'm being overly sensitive. Everything seems to send up red flags with me lately." Winifred handed Shannon her mug and then sat down at the table. "You seemed deep in thought when I walked out earlier. Anything bothering you?"

"I was thinking about Mira Chen's offer. And my life."

"I think you have a great life. You have a successful practice. You get to travel. You have an active social life."

"All that is true. Except it doesn't mean anything. I'm not making a difference."

"You are making a huge difference in the lives of your patients. Look how you have helped me. I was ready to give up."

"That's helping a handful of people. Down here I could possibly help a hundred or more."

"You're seriously considering this?"

"I am."

"Did you learn anything interesting while reading the journal?"

"Most of what I read had to do with Lorenzo's excitement over the beginning of construction of the canal. He wants to start taking movies to preserve the experience. Tony wants to hire one of the large construction companies in mainland Florida to come down and build the canal system, thereby completing the project in half the time. I get the impression that Tony hates the environment and just wants to get back to his old life."

"And Lorenzo has other ideas?"

"He's making references to 'the book' and has made several phone calls to Havana with questions about the early years when his family owned the whole island."

"I wonder what book he's talking about?"

"I'm sure it can wait till later in the day. How about you shower and get ready for our tagalong with Anneliese while I make breakfast?"

Winifred gulped down the last bit of coffee, then stood and went inside. "Works for me."

—≈‡ ‡≈—

Shortly before nine, Anneliese texted Winifred that she was at Winn Dixie picking up some groceries and that they should meet her at the house. She texted the address.

Fifteen minutes later, Winifred parked on the street in front of a large house of gray cedar siding, with white trim and a flamingo-pink front door. Matching colored pink pots were strategically placed containing pink bougainvillea and other colorful plants. "This does have a Nantucket vibe—except for the palm trees."

A minute later, Anneliese pulled behind her and got out of her vehicle. "I see you found it okay."

"Yes. The house is charming. A combination of north and south," Winifred remarked.

"That's it exactly. Now help me with these groceries and I'll give you a tour. The Parkers are taking three days to drive down. As I mentioned, they arrive tomorrow. The last thing she wants to do is grocery shopping before they are even unpacked. I maintain a file on every client's preferences from the food they like to the laundry soap. I have the house cleaned and stocked with food before they arrive. Each client is different."

Winifred unpacked the plastic bags, while Anneliese put everything away. "How does that work?"

"Each family maintains a household account at my bank, which they feed money into. From that account, I pay the various service companies such as lawn care, pool maintenance, monthly bug spraying, and a cleaning crew. I have a personal monthly fee depending on the services that I provide."

Shannon glanced around the large open space with a ceiling that had to be a story and a half high. A series of sliding glass doors opened onto a porch that ran the length of the house and gave access to the beautifully landscaped yard below. A round formal dining room faced the front yard. "You said a couple live here? The house looks huge."

"The Parkers have a large family that trickle down throughout the season. Their two grown children and their families will be here for Christmas and stay until the first. Other family members will trickle down during the coming months."

For the next half an hour, Anneliese gave a tour, pointing out the wine tasting room off the kitchen and across from the library complete with spiral stairs leading up to a turreted children's playroom. "The Parkers love their family, but they also love their privacy. So, the house has two first-floor primary suites, one at each end of the house. Above the primary on the left are three smaller guest rooms, with multiple beds for the kids. It also contains its own laundry room. The larger primary suite on the right is used by the Parkers and has one bedroom on the second floor above that Mrs. Parker uses as her office. Mr. Parker has an office next to the front door with its own entrance onto the front porch."

On their way out, Anneliese gave them a tour of the yard containing a large, irregular-shaped swimming pool that took up much of the space with a hot tub and waterfall. An island sat in the middle, with a single small palm in the center. Down near the pier that jutted out into the Gulf stood a tiki hut for fish cleaning. The entire backyard was done in pavers, giving it a resort feel. A complete outdoor kitchen, bathroom, changing rooms, and garage sat beneath the house.

"What an amazing home, and it all sits eight feet above ground. The landscaping is beautiful, and I love the way they tucked it among the pavers. The high white fencing provides privacy from the neighbors. Do they have a boat?" Winifred asked.

"Yes. The boat and two jet skis are stored at a facility up off Route One. They will be brought around after the Parkers arrive. And this whole property is less than one acre."

After locking up, Winifred and Shannon followed Anneliese to the next home. It, too, was oceanfront property. The house was the total opposite in appearance. The stucco exterior with its double-curved staircase leading up to a two-story entrance was more Mediterranean in style. The interior rooms flowed together with white marble floors. A grand piano sat opposite the oversize door in the foyer. There was a white marble gourmet kitchen with a separate prep room for caterers. Behind the kitchen was a full gym. A dramatic curved staircase led upstairs to a generous-sized seating area. An apartment-size master suite with its own rooftop terrace facing the Gulf, two en suite guest rooms, and two offices completed the second floor. All the rooms facing the Gulf had floor-to-ceiling windows. The yard contained a semiraised swimming pool and hot tub completely surrounded by a wide deck with about a dozen lounge chairs. Off to one side was what looked like a Grecian temple that housed a bar. Palm trees dotted the grounds, but little else in the way of landscape. A long pier jutted out into deeper water. This was a house built more for dramatic impact than functionality.

"And you manage this as well?" Winifred said at the end of the tour. "It's so different."

"It may not look it, but the services needed are very much the same on a monthly basis."

"Are you trying to convince me to demolish and build a—a—a huge statement house on stilts?" Winifred asked.

"No. You have the most beautiful piece of property on Big Pine. I'm only showing you what newer construction looks like. Windswept is yours now—live it to the fullest."

"It's a lot to think about. Right now, I'm only thinking about being safe. My world is *very* small, and I'm always looking over my shoulder, so to speak."

"When you are once again safe, and ready to expand that world, I'll be here to help you."

CHAPTER SIXTY

Winifred clicked her seat belt into place, turned over the engine of the Escalade, and cranked up the air. She took one long look at the house, then pulled onto the street.

"So, what are your thoughts about new construction?" Shannon asked.

"Both of those, although beautiful and well-designed floor plans, are way too much house for one person."

Shannon took a deep breath, then let it out slowly, as if she wasn't happy with Winifred's answer but not sure how to respond. "You're not alone. You're making friends. Have you enjoyed the evenings with Sally and Mike and Anneliese?"

"Of course. But I don't need a big house to entertain a few friends outdoors. I liked the yard in the first house. A big pool, separate kitchen under the house, the space covered in pavers make it easy to walk on with lots of soft lighting. I can easily create that by raising the house I have eight feet above ground. I liked the walls of high windows overlooking the open water in the second house. I can also do that with the house I have, since I would need to replace all the windows with new hurricane-proof ones."

"How do you see yourself in this life?"

"I have a successful business to run in Chicago. I can spend a few months during the winter here. I love how they celebrate Christmas. Perhaps, I could come down for December and January. Those are typically my slowest months."

"Has the business suffered any while you have been in Florida?"

"No. I conduct my weekly Monday-morning meetings via Zoom. My assistant, Caroline, can practically run the company on her own. She hasn't called me once with a problem."

"How do you feel about that?"

"I know the everyday operations are running smoothly. I'm more or less the creative side of the firm. The person who takes a new client's wishes or needs and develops the plan for my tech staff to implement. I just feel like I should be there for them. You know—brainstorm. Be there."

"What I'm hearing from you is a loss of control. And perhaps a sense of guilt for being here in warm weather and sun and your employees are trudging through the snow."

"Maybe. A little." Winifred chuckled as they waited for the gates to open. "I know what you are doing, Doctor Mulaney. I don't need a therapy session."

"Leaving Sam out in the yard while we were gone seems to have worked out well," Shannon said as she settled into a chair on the porch, then set the books written by Stanton Knox on a side table.

"I figured we wouldn't be gone much more than an hour, and it would be a good test for him. Having him greet us at the gate felt warm and welcoming." Winifred set the wooden box on the table, then sat down with Lorenzo's journal. "I checked Sam's sutures, and they're fine. I like having him here with us."

Shannon looked over at her friend and smiled. She then chose the book on pirates.

Winifred opened the journal. "I see you put a paper clip on the pages that mention the book. I'll read those first before I pick up where you left off." A few minutes later, she looked up. "I sure wish we had that book. I'm puzzled about his sporadic mention of not being able to find evidence of the Spaniards. It's looking like the key to what happened back then."

"I'm not finding any mention of a pirate by the name of Captain Diego Alverez."

"Yeah. Stanton didn't remember the name when I asked him."

"I think I'll google it and see what pops up," Shannon said as she set the pirate book aside and picked up her cell phone.

Winifred was making notes that Lorenzo had hired a cousin of Havana's to begin digging the main canal. "Wow! Here it is. The beginning of the rift between father and son."

Shannon looked over. "I'm getting nothing about our pirate. I have learned that the names Diego and Alverez are very popular. I think I have a hundred listed all over the country, but no pirate. What have you found?"

"Our Tony is a hothead. Even though Lorenzo told him no on hiring a contractor from the mainland, he went ahead behind his father's back and hired a large outfit to start on Pirates Cove with the promise to finish Casa Santiago. Their construction trailers would be arriving in a week. Apparently, Tony is viewing this as a family business since Lorenzo, as head of the family, won it in a poker game. Lorenzo, on the other hand, sees this as his personal property. He's having a battle with his conscience about building the subdivisions after Havana begged him not to destroy the land. He wants Lorenzo to read the book first—to find its history."

"If Gonzales didn't give you 'the book,' then perhaps Lorenzo hid it somewhere in the safe room."

"Oh boy! I hope not. If Hector hasn't found it in the forty years that he's been managing Windswept and it didn't turn up in any of the stuff we've put back in place after the robbery, then I don't know how we would ever find it."

"Keep reading."

Winifred read a few more pages. "This is interesting. Lorenzo mentions that Katerina doesn't like the names. That they are too old fashioned. She wants to name Casa Santiago Gulfside Estates and Pirates Cove should be called Sunset Acres."

"Who's Katerina?" Shannon asks.

"I don't know, but I've heard the name before. Maybe from Harry Lincoln." Winifred continued reading. "Lorenzo is upset with Tony for agreeing with Katerina and angry that Tony has discussed the plans for Big Pine Key with her. Lorenzo reminds Tony that Katerina is not blood—not his blood—and therefore should not be privy to Lorenzo's business. Tony argues that Katerina does have Barilli blood and should be included."

"That must have been some blowup," Shannon remarked.

"And it isn't over yet. Tony tells his dad that maybe he should buy a house in the Hollywood Hills and spend more time with his movie star girlfriend and leave the Big Pine subdivisions to him to manage."

Shannon whistled. "I don't think you talk that way to a mob boss, even if he is your father."

"Yep. Lorenzo sends Tony back home to Detroit and tells him not to return—ever."

Shannon sets the book on pirates on the side table and stood. "Words said in a heated rage. I wonder if he ever regrets them?"

"I'm going to call Harry and get the lowdown on Katerina."

"And I'm going to the kitchen and see what I can put together for lunch."

A minute later, Winifred had Harry Lincoln on the phone. "Winifred, what kind of trouble have you gotten yourself into this time?"

"Hello, Harry, you're on speaker; Shannon is with me. I'm reading Lorenzo Barilli's journal that I received from Edwardo Gonzales. He mentions a woman named Katerina. She seems to be connected to Tony."

"I've pulled the Barilli file up on my computer." He paused to do a name search. "Yes, Katerina was a cousin of Tony. She was five years older. He seems to have looked up to her. At one point, during the middle 1960s, Lorenzo sent Tony to Reno to buy and reopen an old casino that had been closed for a number of years. It looks like he took Katerina with him."

"If I remember correctly, Bianca Barilli Morano runs the Vegas operations. Is Katerina still in Reno?"

"No, she passed away in 1980 from a brain aneurism. She had a one-year-old daughter at the time. Tony was her godfather and named her Katrina, after her mother, Katerina. He and his wife raised the baby as their own."

"Where is Katrina now?"

"She continued to live in Reno until her death five years ago. She was on a white-water rafting trip with friends on the Colorado River. She fell overboard during a dangerous set of rapids. Her body was found four days later about three miles downriver. I have a copy of several newspaper articles written at the time."

"Who identified the body?"

"The medical examiner's report lists her aunt, Bianca."

"Interesting. What about Tony?"

"He stayed in Reno and expanded the Barilli operations until his father died in 1979. Then he returned to Detroit and became head of the family until his death in 2000."

"Thank you. This helps. Now on another note—have you found anything more on Petrowski and a possible connection to Gonzales?"

"No, not yet. Lorenzo doesn't hire Gonzales until 1970 after his engagement to Lacy Lorin ends, at which time he draws up the Barilli Family Trust. Tony keeps the attorney on after his father's death."

"And you still don't believe Bianca is behind this?"

"That woman has more business sense than all the Barilli men put together. She owns Nevada. She doesn't care about a measly thousand acres in Florida—period."

"I understand. But keep digging on Gonzales. He seems to be our weak link."

"Will do. Keep me in the loop," Harry said, then ended the call.

"Well, that was interesting," Shannon commented as she set chicken salad sandwiches and fruit on the table. "But it does fall in line with what you are reading."

"That is the operative word—'reading.' Which I will continue after lunch."

Twenty minutes later, Winifred carried her plate to the kitchen, made a bathroom break, then returned to the porch. She settled into a chair and picked up the journal.

Shannon stood. "I need to move around." She looked over at the dog asleep in the shade. "Sam, how about a walk?" After hearing the work "walk," Sam jumped up and ran for the front door. "I guess that would be a yes. I'll check out the yard around the house and canal."

"Great idea. I'll be right here when you get back." For the next hour, Winifred kept reading and frantically making notes on what she was learning. *How could I have missed this? Captain Diego Alverez was here, and he left a chest of silver coins behind.*

Winifred looked up when the front door opened and Sam rushed in with his tail wagging.

"Freddie, it's beautiful out there. We had a great walk and . . . what's wrong? You look like something happened."

"Shannon! It's true! The pirate was here, and he left a treasure! Lorenzo found it."

Shannon walked across the room and entered the porch. "Freddie, slow down and start at the beginning."

"Okay—the beginning. Lorenzo sent his son packing and decides to stay on the property after what he's been reading in the book. So, he goes down to Key West to see his buddy. At that time, he buys a Cadillac off the lot of a dealership, then a carload of supplies, including a movie camera, projector, and screen, then heads back to Big Pine, where he buys a mobile home and generator and has them delivered to a spot about where this cottage sits. About a week later, the canal is progressing. The crew has completed Hector's leg and is moving forward toward the next leg. During this period, Lorenzo is happily filming the operation. He particularly likes the dynamiting parts. The steam shovel operator and crew leave for the day after blowing up the next section, which is in line with one of the small freshwater pools. Lorenzo talks about how he wants to film the pile of rubble after he had filmed the explosion. He begins filming the mound of debris, when a section of wall begins to crack. Water began to pour out from the pool, leaving the void open to the canal. A small wooden chest tumbles out. Lorenzo mentions how difficult it was to climb down to the box. It was intact but too heavy to carry up the pile of stone. Having hung out at construction sites as a teenager, he knew how to operate the steam shovel. He praises himself for being able to use the machine to lift the chest out and set it down without damaging the chest. He mentions how beautiful the carvings are on the lid. He gets a large screwdriver from the work trailer and pries open the chest. I can tell Lorenzo is excited because his handwriting gets worse—like he's shaking. The chest is filled with silver coins."

"Wow! This must be what our bad guys are after. Does Lorenzo say what he does with the coins?"

Winifred read a few more pages. "The box is too heavy for him to carry all the way to his trailer, so he gets his car and manages to lift the box into the trunk."

"What does he do with the coins?" Shannon asks eagerly.

"I don't know. He doesn't mention the silver anymore. His handwriting is still shaky and says that he must continue reading the book in case it mentions where more treasure is hidden."

"So, if his assumption is correct and there was more treasure hidden in the ponds and pools, then it should have been mentioned somewhere in Big Pine's history, since Captain Alverez had access to the whole island."

"You're right. And the only person who might know the history is Stanton Knox. I'll give him a call," Winifred said as she grabbed her phone.

"Can you trust him with what you have read?"

"I think we have to. What does it matter? The bad guys know it's here and are willing to kill for it."

CHAPTER SIXTY-ONE

"I'm so glad you called me when you did. I was just leaving a meeting with the director of the Florida Keys History and Discovery Center on Marathon. I'm working on a new book about the Keys during the 1960s. I intended to call you and beg for a tour of Windswept and any photos you might have of Lorenzo Barilli and Lacy Lorin."

"Stanton, I would like you to meet my dear friend, Shannon Mulaney. She lives in Chicago and will be staying with me until the first of the year."

He took Shannon's hand in a warm greeting. "I can't tell you how happy I am to meet you, Doctor. Mira Chen has told me about you and the offer she hopes to extend to you. I'm sorry we didn't meet at the watch party."

Shannon's face was glowing at his words. "Mira Chen invited me to spend a day with her. I've decided to take her up on her offer."

"Wonderful. Once you see, firsthand, what she has done for this city and specifically its veterans and the homeless, you will be eager to join our team."

"*You* are part of her team?" Shannon asked in an amazed voice.

Stanton lifted his left leg a tad. "Like many of our veterans, I, too, carry mementos of war. I help where I can. Sometimes one just needs a person who's been there to talk to. The proceeds from my books go to the Chens' foundation."

"I see the signs for the Naval Air Station when I pass the exit on Route One at Boca Chica Key. We have a friend who is a patient at the Key West hospital nearby. I was surprised the first time a fighter jet flew overhead. Are they part of the group that you help?" Winifred asked.

"No. Key West is a big training center for military operations. It's a state-of-the-art operation for naval combat fighter training. There are several locations across the city for housing and offices." He glanced from Winifred to Shannon. "These young kids are down here for their training, then leave for their assignments. But they do add another interesting dimension to the city. I hope you seriously consider Mira's proposal."

"I am. And Key West intrigues me more every time I'm there.

"Now, Stanton, how about we give you a tour of a 1960s estate? Except for the furniture that was removed after one of the hurricanes, the house is exactly as it was the day Lorenzo Barilli had it boarded up."

He took a few steps to take in front of the house. "I love the architecture, and so perfectly preserved. May I take photos?" Stanton asked. "I love the gates."

"You may—and the gates are bulletproof." Winifred chuckled.

An hour later, Winifred, Shannon, and Stanton Knox walked out of the main house as Sally pulled up in her truck. They all went over to greet her.

"Sally, do you remember Stanton Knox? He stopped by for a tour of the house and safe room for an upcoming book he is working on about the Keys during the 1960s."

Sally got out of her truck and shook Stanton's hand. "Of course, I remember. It's a pleasure to see you again."

Stanton nodded in the direction of the canal. "I couldn't help but notice *Lady Luck.* Any chance I'd be lucky enough to get photos?" He laughed as he raised the large professional camera that hung around his neck.

"I did promise you, once upon a time, a tour and pictures," Sally said as she glanced at her watch. "You've got just about enough time before it starts getting dark." She glanced at Winifred. "Would that be a problem? I've got mahi-mahi for dinner, and all I need is your kitchen and grill."

"What you do with fish is magic. The reason I asked Stanton to stop by can wait." She looked over at him. "Can you stay for dinner?"

"Yes." He took a quick glance at Shannon and back at Winifred. "I'd love to. I'm free all evening."

Well, isn't that interesting? "Sally, why don't you and Stanton do your thing and Shannon and I will get the grill going?"

"The photos are all stacked on the counter by content. You will find all the ones with Lacy Lorin and Lorenzo together. Take any that will help with your research."

"I wish I had better information for you regarding the early settlers here on Big Pine, but there isn't much more than you already know. Except for the bones of a few large animals that the government surveyors claimed to have found back in 1873," Stanton explained. "Unfortunately, they didn't consider them important enough to even take photos of. They described them as the size of cows and were primarily in the area of the Rockland hammock."

Winifred walked out onto the porch. "I'd like to show you Lorenzo Barilli's journal."

Standon followed her. He glanced through a few of the pages that were paper-clipped as important. "Unfortunately, Winifred, from everything you told me over dinner and from the look of this journal"—Stanton handed it back to her—"it doesn't mean anything without proof. I'm sorry. If only you had the home movie that Barilli mentions and can see the chest falling out of the void, or the actual chest, or the book that he refers to. Or best of all—a coin."

Winifred took the journal from his hand and set it down on the table next to the box.

"Is that the box the attorney gave you?" Stanton asked. "May I take a look?"

"Sure, but it's just a worthless decorative reproduction."

Stanton picked it up, seeming to gauge its weight. He ran his fingers over the carvings, and then to everyone's surprise, he smelled it. "I'm not so sure it's worthless. It's heavy for its size, meaning that the wood is a very strong and dense oak. It's nearly black with age." He handed the box to Winifred. "Run your fingers across the carvings. See how rough the edges are, and if you look closely, the chisel marks are clear. Also, these are hand-forged square nails."

"Yes, now that you point them out"—Winifred handed the box back to Stanton—"Why did you smell it?"

"Have you traveled to Europe and visited old castles and cathedrals?"

"Yes," everyone said in unison.

"Think back to how the rooms smelled, especially the ones with wood-paneled walls. They would have had a musty, almost moldy, odor."

"You're right. I do remember," Shannon remarked.

"Now, each of you, close your eyes and smell the box."

Winifred felt like she was back in chemistry class. And was the last to take a whiff. "I can pick a faint mustiness."

Stanton then shook the box and set it back on the table and opened the lid. "Do you have a tape measure?"

"Yes, inside the buffet," Winifred said.

"I'll get it." Shannon then walked inside.

"What are you looking for?" Sally asked.

"Just a hunch. I've examined a lot of old artifacts and furniture on my travels. This small chest intrigues me."

Shannon returned with the tape measure and handed it to Stanton. He then measured the inside depth and then the outside. "As I suspected," he murmured.

"Suspected what?" Winifred asked.

"There is a two-inch difference between the measurements." He closed the lid and picked up the box. He began pressing the nailheads in different sequences around the lower sides. After a few minutes, everyone heard a slight sound inside the box. Stanton opened the lid to find that the bottom had opened to reveal a secret compartment. A leather-bound book sat nestled in the center, along with a small velvet bag with a drawstring.

Winifred removed the small book and bag. "How did you know?"

"Once I was sure of the age, due to the patina of the oak, the nailheads, and the musty odor, I was sure what the chest had been used for," Stanton stated as he passed the box around. "This was most likely a lady's traveling chest. She would put small items of clothing like gloves and hair coverings in the top portion, perhaps a brush, comb, and such articles. Jewelry and perhaps coins in the secret compartment below. Chests like these were popular during the 1500s all the way into the 1700s. However, this one looks more Spanish than English or French."

Winifred opened the bag and dropped a silver coin in her hand. "Wow, could this by our evidence?" She studied both sides, then handed it to Stanton. "What do you think?"

"I'd be able to give you a definitive answer if I had my computer and reference books. But it looks Spanish." He removed his cell phone from his pocket and began entering information. After a few minutes, he held the screen to the Winifred. "It looks a lot like this one. Spanish and dates somewhere around the mid to late 1500s. That looks like the profile of King Philip II."

"We have our proof. Captain Diego Alverez was here!" Winifred shouted.

"Or someone was," Stanton added under his breath.

CHAPTER SIXTY-TWO

At proximately nine o'clock, Stanton and Sally left. Stanton promised to call the next day after contacting a friend at the Smithsonian with information on the coin. Sally wanted to walk the property with Sam before turning in for the night. She had another charter scheduled and would be leaving before sunup.

Shannon picked up Lorenzo's journal. "I guess you and I are going to spend the rest of the evening reading."

Winifred grabbed her cell phone off the table. "I need to call Mike Connor first." She pressed his number and waited.

"Hello, Freddie. Is everything okay? Did something happen?" Mike asked in a concerned voice.

"We're fine, but I guess you could say that something important did happen." She took a deep breath to calm her nerves. "We found the book Lorenzo Barilli referred to in his journal, along with a silver coin. Stanton Knox was here and believes it is Spanish and—"

Mike cut her off. "Freddie, I'll be right over." The line went dead.

"That was short. I assume he's on his way."

"Yeah. He didn't sound joyful."

"Neither do we," Shannon added.

Winifred picked up the silver coin. "It does look old. But in beautiful condition. If I didn't know better, I would think the box and coin were souvenirs from the Wreckers' Museum."

"I'm glad Stanton was here. It could have been days or weeks before we would have found the false bottom. He seems to be highly intelligent, but modest, has many different interests, and gives his time willingly. He's like an onion—with many layers to peel." Shannon paused a beat. "I like him."

"And it doesn't hurt that he is extremely handsome," Winifred added.

"Hmmmm," Shannon murmured as she began to read.

Winifred opened the cover of the leather-bound book. "Leticia Albornoz 1918, Madrid, Spain." She turned the page and began reading. "This is interesting. Leticia writes about an American soldier, by the name of Salvatore Giordano, who is there in a local hospital recovering from the terrible influenza outbreak. With Spain remaining a neutral country during the great war, many soldiers are being sent there to recuperate."

"Isn't that the name of the Key West crime lord Lorenzo called Havana?" Shannon asked.

"Yes. I believe so, Giordano the second." Winifred continued to read. "He was interested in history, so Leticia began reading the book written by her ancestor, Don Santiago Albornoz, on his life and travels back in the late 1500s. After she finishes the story, Salvatore convinces her that she should translate the book into English for future generations. She states that because her knowledge of the English language is so limited, she asks the young soldier to write for her." Winifred flips through the pages. "The handwriting does change to what I guess could be male."

Shannon got up from her chair on the porch and looked out toward the gates. "I hear Sam barking and see headlights coming this way. Mike Connor must have arrived." She walked into the cottage and opened the front door, then waited to greet him.

He parked the patrol car at the bottom of the steps. Sam and Sally jogged up as he got out. They all went up the stairs together. Sam was in the lead.

Winifred stood in the middle of the room. "You didn't need to rush over, Mike. This could have waited until tomorrow."

"I don't think so, Freddie. Now, show me what you've got." Mike followed her out to the porch. He examined the box, noting the false bottom. Then he looked at the coin under the bright light on his cell phone. "Wow! This looks almost new. It must not have been in circulation for long. And you say the historian, Stanton Knox, is helping you?"

"Yes, we met him at Mira Chen's watch party. I had questions about the pirate, Captain Diego Alverez, and the earliest history of Big Pine. And I'm helping him with a new book he's working on about the Keys during the 1960s."

"He believes this coin is real? And more of these are buried here?"

"Stanton is sure the coin is real and believes it to be Spanish. He's going to have a friend confirm the exact date."

"So, now we know what these guys are after, and they seem to think it's buried under the safe room. Does Lorenzo say where he buried it?"

"We haven't gotten that far. Only that the chest tumbled out of the freshwater hole while he was filming the site after the workers left for the day."

Mike picked up the box. "Does Knox think this was the box that fell out of the hole?"

"He didn't say. Only that it could be from the 1500 or 1600s because of the square hand-forged nails, the rough carvings, and the smell."

"The smell?" Mike asked as he lifted the chest to his nose.

"The musty odor. I think it smells more like burnt wood," Shannon added.

"Do you think whoever is behind this has found the coin and the leather-bound book?"

"I don't think so," Winifred answered. "Once Stanton determined its possible age, then he examined the box for a hidden compartment and then knew to look for a trigger that would open the bottom. We never looked that closely at its construction. I don't think Gonzales did either, and from what I know, this chest has been in his safe since Lorenzo gave it to him."

Mike glanced at Sally, then back at Winifred. "We've suspected him as the mastermind. But why now? He's had the box for over forty years—and who's his accomplice?"

"I'll call Rosa first thing in the morning. Tonight, Shannon and I keep reading."

"I'll call the office in Key Largo and have him picked up for questioning. As for tonight, stay inside and keep your door locked. If you see or hear anything, call the station and let Sally know. But don't leave!" Mike said emphatically, then walked across the room to the door.

Winifred and Shannon stood at the top of the stairs and watched as Mike opened the door to his patrol car. He turned to Sally. "Captain, you know what to do."

Sally only nodded, then began walking toward the canal and *Lady Luck.*

CHAPTER SIXTY-THREE

It was close to midnight when Shannon stopped reading and set Lorenzo's journal in her lap. "I've got at least part of our mystery solved." She paused a beat. "After realizing that the treasure was hidden at the bottom of a freshwater pool and thinking that there could be more, he stops the building of the canals. He studies the topography map, shades and marks all the locations, then realizes that many of the pools and ponds are on his thousand acres. He comes to the conclusion that if he goes ahead with the building of the subdivisions and more treasure is found, then word would get out. He'd have every treasure hunter in the country descending on his property."

"You look like you're questioning something."

"Yeah. I have the same thoughts as Lorenzo did. If after the US takes control of Florida and the Albornoz family gets to keep a thousand acres out of their original six thousand, why did they choose land in the middle of nowhere?"

"Perhaps Leticia will clarify that later in her story."

"What has she said so far?"

"The family originated in Toledo, Spain. Part of the old Castile region. Then when the king moved the capital from Toledo to Madrid in 1560, Don Carrillo Albornoz moved the family as well. At that time, King Philip II awarded Don Carrillo the deed to an island not far from the island called Isla Juana, which is now Cuba. Apparently, according to Leticia, Havana was founded by the Spanish to act as a stopping point for their galleons returning to Spain. Albornoz was so excited about the gift that he asked the king's permission for his youngest son, Don Santiago, to travel to Florida on one of the next ships heading down to the Americas. Philip II arranged for the son to travel with the most successful captain on Spain's newest galleon. The two men apparently hit it off and became the best of friends. During that long trip, Don Santiago learned enough of the art of commanding a fleet of galleons, that on the return trip when one of the ships captains was killed in a bar fight in Havana, he was given the post. Santiago then set sail for his family's island thinking he would find another suitable port to host Spanish ships. What he found was land surrounded by shallow water and occupied by only a large herd of small deer, pools of fresh water, and tall trees."

"Wow! Albornoz couldn't have been too happy with his king and his *generous* gift. What happens next?"

"I don't know. But I bet he doesn't take this snub lightly."

An hour later, Shannon puts down the journal. "I don't know about you, but I could use some coffee. I know what you mean about Lorenzo's penmanship. My eyes need a break."

"Me too, although it is getting even more interesting."

Later, Winifred and Shannon stood at the porch rail with their mugs of muchly needed caffeine and looked out over the Gulf with the blanket of stars overhead. Winifred took a long sip. "I wonder if it looked the same back in the 1500s. Were the tiny islands of grasses and mangroves there or only open water between the larger bodies of land?"

"I know that between reading Leticia's story and living in the mobile home, Lorenzo is beginning to soften. Although he did drive into Key West and buy a pump to drain the larger pool that sat where the safe room is."

"Did he find anything?"

"I have to keep reading. But I'm thinking maybe he did, or why build his house on that spot?"

Winifred went back to her chair and picked up Leticia's book and began reading where she'd left off. A few minutes later, she looked up at Shannon. "Santiago returns to Spain with a galleon filled with a ton of treasure from the Americas. He's given a hero's welcome from the king for bringing the ship back safely and is given a portion of the money. He then buys a house near the palace for his young wife, Catalina, who is part of Queen Anna's court."

"I love his wife's name," Shannon interjected.

"Now with the official title of Captain, Santiago approaches the king asking for two smaller ships in order to return to Florida and explore the lands sitting in the shallower water that runs between the two long reefs that have taken so many of Spain's galleons. He also asked for skilled divers to search any sunken ships they might find and bring the lost treasure back. Young Albornoz gets his two ships and sets sail for the family island."

"And I've found out that Lorenzo has been thinking about Tony's suggestion to buy a house in the Hollywood Hills. He thinks, 'Why not here?' and flies to California and proposes to Lacy Lorin, promising to build her a fabulous estate in the Florida Keys. She accepts, and he abandons the subdivision idea."

"Where does he put the coins while he's gone?" Winifred asked.

"He decides to wrap the chest full of silver in long ropes and lowers it down into the freshwater pool that he had drained and filled in with rubble from the canal dig. He hires someone to live in the mobile home and watch over the property while he's gone." Shannon pauses a beat. "He returns a month later with the plans, drawn up by a Hollywood architect, for a home that looks very much like the new modern houses in the Hollywood Hills."

"We know that the most current plan for the house includes the safe room that would sit over that drained freshwater pool. Hector mentioned that the room was designed by an engineer at the naval station." Winifred considered the various possibilities and came back to just one. "What if Gonzales got tired of reading Lorenzo's handwriting like both of us have and stopped there? He would come to the conclusion that the treasure was still in the hole—and it might be."

"Speaking of eye fatigue, I'm about finished for the night. We know why and how Windswept came to be. The rest of the coins probably are under the safe room. I can pick up reading tomorrow."

"Me too. We know that Santiago Albornoz has outfitted his two ships and gotten his crew together. I'm at a good place to stop for the night." It was after one thirty when Winifred turned the last light out and crawled into bed. Before closing the porch for the night, she'd looked out toward Annette and Porpoise Keys. *Gemini* was nowhere to be seen.

CHAPTER SIXTY-FOUR

S am woke them the next morning at five thirty. His low-level growling alerted them that something was happening outside but not the angry growl of trouble. Winifred looked over at the clock on the bedside table. "It must be Sally leaving. She has a charter today." She got out of bed and leaned over the railing. Sam was sitting at attention at the foot of the stairs. "Good boy. Thank you for alerting us, but it's okay. Only Sally leaving. It's okay. Good boy." Sam then trotted back to his bed, and Winifred returned to hers.

Two hours later, Sam barked once, then waited. He barked again and waited. "He needs to go out," Shannon said in a groggy voice. "I'll let him out and put a pot on."

Winifred waited until Shannon called up to her that the coffee was ready. She swung her legs over the side and, for a moment, considered lying back down.

"Come on, sleepyhead; we have work to do."

Winifred got up and looked over the railing. Shannon stood below holding a second mug of coffee. "I'm coming. I'm getting too old for these all-nighters."

"We weren't up all night. I think we both have a major case of brain fatigue," Shannon said as Winifred reached the bottom step and handed her the steaming cup.

Winifred immediately walked over to the porch railing. "I see Hunter is out beyond Annette. Funny how I never hear him coming or going."

Shannon joined her. "I'm guessing he's close to two miles out. Unless he revs those engines, we wouldn't hear him. Not like the smaller boats that zip around the closer, Bogie Channel inside the grassy bank."

"I don't know whether I feel threatened that he is out there or relieved," Winifred murmured as she settled into a chair.

"How about a quick breakfast of cereal and toast?" Shannon asked. "Unless you want to run up to the Egg for your favorite French toast."

"French toast sounds good, but I think I'd rather stay here. I need to call Rosa around nine."

"Okay with me. I should call Mira Chen and let her know I'm ready to meet."

"And then we read," Winifred added.

Shannon sat down in the other chair. "And then we read."

At nine fifteen, Winifred's phone rang. She glanced at the screen. "That's weird; I was about to call her." She accepted the call. "Hello, Rosa. I take it, you've found something."

"Yes. It doesn't make any sense to me. I'm worried that Mr. Gonzales may be in some kind of trouble."

"Rosa, Shannon is with me. I'm putting you on speaker. Tell me what you have. It might be what we are looking for."

"Well, you asked about the bank records and any meetings with the Barilli family. Mr. Gonzales is very old school and prefers paper statements, which I don't think he ever destroys. So, I made a spreadsheet in my computer and entered the dates from his calendars with the bank transactions. Three years ago, he paid Harry Lincoln Investigations twenty thousand dollars to find any legitimate heirs. Two years ago, he made three cash withdrawals, each in the amount of twenty thousand. Last October, he withdrew another twenty thousand in cash. And this is the scary part. The day before you arrived to sign the papers, Mr. Gonzales withdrew a hundred thousand in cash."

"This is beginning to make sense to me. What do you find scary?"

"I checked the safe. I found fifty thousand dollars."

"Wow! That makes fifty thousand in cash was spent in less than one month. Did any of those withdrawals match with meetings?"

"No, but they were in line with trips to Miami."

"Are there any notes in his calendar about who he was meeting in Miami?"

"Not the office one, but he keeps a personal pocket calendar."

"Thank you, Rosa. This is a huge help. But I must tell you that a deputy from the Monroe County Sheriff's Office will probably be stopping by to talk to your boss."

"Oh, he's canceled his appointments for the week. I think he and his wife are taking the boat on a trip."

"Interesting. Let me know if you find anything else."

"Oh, one more thing," Rosa said before hanging up. "I called Mr. Russel Reinhart, the financial adviser who handles the trust's account, to ask if he'd met with you yet." Rosa paused a beat. "He was told, by Mr. Gonzales, that you were out of the country until after the first of January."

"Thank you, Rosa. Send me Mr. Reinhart's contact information." A chill rushed through Winifred's body as she ended the call.

"Well, if there was any doubt in my mind that Gonzales was the mastermind, it's gone now." Shannon finished washing the last of the breakfast dishes. "I'm going to take a quick shower and call Mira Chen to set our meeting date."

"While you're in the shower, I'm going to call Russel Reinhart."

Twenty minutes later, Shannon exited the bathroom wrapped in a towel, with her short curly hair still damp. She headed for the stairs to the loft, then stopped short after seeing Winifred huddled on the bottom step. "What's wrong? Something bad happened while I was in the bathroom. What is it?"

"To say that Reinhart was surprised to hear from me is putting it mildly. You would think I had risen from the dead."

"Okay, so what did he say?"

"Due to the fact that Christmas is only a few days away and the end of the year so close, he needs to see me today. Something about needing to get tax filings in for this year. There are documents that I must sign first."

"Okay. I don't see a problem with that. Why are you upset?"

"His office is in Miami."

"Oh. I still don't see a problem. How long does it take to drive to Miami?"

"Three hours, on a good day."

"In that case, you need to jump in the shower and get dressed. While you are doing that, I will call Mrs. Chen and schedule our meeting for later in the week." Shannon glanced at her watch. "We can be at his office a little after one."

Shannon then raced up the stairs to the loft, while Winifred headed to the bathroom.

Half an hour later, Winifred entered the living room to see Shannon dressed in black slacks, a white tank top, and a black men's-style shirt.

"You look nice. I thought you might have worn something dressier. As long as we are in Miami, we might as well take advantage of the opportunity and do some shopping and have a nice dinner."

"Today is the only time Mira can spend the day with me. She and her husband are flying home to Chicago to spend Christmas with their children and grandchildren tomorrow. They return on the twenty-ninth in time to prepare for their big New Year's Eve gala."

"Shannon, you can't miss this. You go to Key West, and I'm perfectly fine with driving to Miami by myself. After all, I had no problem driving down alone in a snowstorm. I'll take the Escalade; you can take the Camry. Or maybe we should switch, since I'll need to take Sam with me."

"Okay, you get dressed, and I'll call Mira back."

"And I'll call Mike and let him know our change in plans."

Twenty minutes later, Winifred and Shannon were in their vehicles waiting for the gates to open, when Sally drove through and stopped. "What are you doing back? I thought you had a charter," Winifred asked.

"It's canceled. Where are you two off to?"

"Shannon is spending the day with Mira Chen in Key West, and Sam and I are on our way to Miami to sign papers with my financial adviser."

"Well, this is perfect timing. Since I now have the day free, I'll go with you to Miami, and that way, Sam can stay here and watch over the property. Maybe we should take the Escalade and let Shannon have the Camry."

"Wow! Okay. That will work," Winifred said as she exited the Toyota and opened the rear door for Sam.

"Do you mind if I drive?" Sally asked. "I know all the back roads in case we get stuck in traffic, which often happens the closer we get to Miami."

"Sure. Why not? I can use the break and just sit back and relax." Winifred bent down and petted Sam. "You are staying home today and patrol." She looked over at Sally. "I should go back to the cottage and put his bed and bowls of fresh water out while you park your truck. It could be tonight before we get back."

Fifteen minutes later, Sally and Winifred were driving through the gates. "*Gemini* is out there off Annette," Winifred mentioned.

"Yes. I saw" was all Sally said.

During the three-hour drive, Winifred filled Sally in on everything that had transpired that morning and what she and Shannon had read in the journal and Leticia's book. She and Sally reviewed everything they knew about Aleksy Petrowski and where he might be hiding, but more about who his accomplice might be. They tried to remember each time when and where he had someone close by to pick him up when their boat broke down. But during the entire trip, Winifred couldn't get the uneasy feelings churning in her gut as to how Sally's charter suddenly canceled in time for her to return to Windswept and make the trip to Miami.

Between the GPS and Sally's knowledge of the city, she had no problem finding the office building in downtown Miami. They arrived in Russel Reinhart's office at one thirty. Based on his voice over the phone, Winifred wasn't sure what to expect, but it surely wasn't the man who welcomed her and Sally. Although of average height and weight and perhaps in his early sixties, it was his long, chiseled face and eyes of an indiscriminate color behind round Harry Potter glasses that threw her off. Well, that and the light-blue seersucker suit and bow tie.

Winifred stood and shook his hand. "I'm Winifred Forrester. This is my friend Sally Rogers."

Russel looked over at Sally. "We will be about an hour. You may stay here, or there is a nice coffee shop down in the lobby."

"Thank you. It was a long trip. I think I'll stretch my legs and head downstairs for a while."

Winifred followed him into a very bland beige-and-brown office in complete contrast to his flashy attire.

"I must say I was shocked to hear from you this morning. I hope nothing unfortunate happened to cut your trip short."

"No. There must have been some miscommunication. I wasn't out of the country, and the only trip I have been on was to Big Pine Key to take possession of my inheritance."

Russel shuffled papers on his desk around. His frown deepened to the point that Winifred thought for sure his glasses would pop right off his nose.

"I don't know how this happened. I never make these kinds of errors." He then had his assistant come into the office and notarize Winifred's signature on a handful of documents.

"Mr. Reinhart, since we are both short on time, can we begin with how money is transferred out of the account?"

"Only Mr. Edwardo Gonzales had the authority to transfer funds. The account was originally set up by Mr. Lorenzo Barilli in the name of the Barilli Family Trust."

"When did Mr. Gonzales begin withdrawing large amounts?"

Russel appeared flustered. "Well now, I guess it would have begun back in 1998. There was a transfer of funds in the amount of two million dollars from the trust to the Barilli U.S. & International Properties, LLC."

"Do you remember that transaction?"

"Yes. I was new to the firm. Mr. Anthony Barilli moved the funds to make it easier to pay for the repairs and rebuilding needed for Windswept and other properties that he and his daughter owned that were damaged by Hurricane Georges on September twenty-fifth."

"Daughter?" *Had Tony legally adopted Katerina's baby?* Winifred wondered. *And what repairs?* As far as she could tell, no improvements had been made since Lorenzo passed in 1979. The two million was taken out nineteen years after

Lorenzo's death and two years before Tony's death. So, what was the money used for?

Russel Reinhart flipped through several documents. "Yes, I have the signed and notarized signatures dated October 15, 1998, of Anthony Barilli and Katrina Barilli."

"You're sure?"

He passed the document across the desk for Winifred to read. "What about more recent ones?"

Russel read off the same ones that Rosa had given her.

"That sounds like a lot of money to have been withdrawn over the years. What is the total amount in the account now?"

Russel flipped to the last page. "Ninety-nine million, eight hundred forty thousand and—just under a hundred million."

"Wow! Do you know how much Lorenzo initially put in?"

Russel scanned the document. "The Barilli Trust was started with one hundred thousand in cash."

And a box full of five-hundred-year-old Spanish coins buried under the house.

"I don't understand. I've had investment accounts for many years, and they don't grow like this would have."

"Mr. Barilli was very interested in the new business technology. He believed it was going to revolutionize the way his Nevada casinos operated in the future. He gave orders to invest heavily in IBM and computer software companies, the new semiconductors, telecommunications, and even the beginnings of aerospace technology. We bought a ton of Apple when it went public. Well, you'll see. I think it's safe to say that the Barilli Family Trust will grow faster than you can spend it."

"Can you give me a printout of the portfolios and the transactions made through the trust?"

"All of them?" Reinhart asked, as if she had wanted him to produce the moon.

Winifred put on her sweetest smile and a dumb-blonde pose. "I'm so sorry to cause you so much trouble. And I just know how busy you must be. But this is all new to me and so confusing. High finances just terrify me. I don't want to do anything stupid."

"Of course. You must be completely aware of the portfolio. If you have a few minutes, I'll have my assistant print out a copy for you."

While they waited, Winifred gave Russel her banking information for her new checking and saving accounts at the bank on Big Pine Key. He explained the process needed for her to transfer funds. A few minutes turned into twenty before she was finally able to leave the office, with a manuscript amount of paper. She met up with Sally in the coffee shop.

"Everything go okay?" Sally asked.

"Russel answered a lot of my questions, confirmed our suspicions, and brought up new questions."

"Want to share?"

"I'd rather not go over everything twice. We need to get Mike over again. Hopefully this evening. Maybe by then I can get my head around what I've learned."

"What's in the box?"

"My investment portfolio."

CHAPTER SIXTY-FIVE

On the way home, Winifred called Shannon to say that she and Sally would arrive around five thirty. Shannon stated that she would be home around four and have steaks ready for dinner. Winifred then called Mike and let him know that she had new information and invited him to join them. After passing through the gates, Winifred and Sally noticed the patrol car parked by the main house, and Shannon and Sam were standing with Mike over by the canal. "Something's up," Sally said and drove over to the site and parked next to the other vehicle.

Sam trotted up to the Escalade, with Mike and Shannon following. "What's going on?" Winifred asked.

"Around noon today, we received an anonymous tip that a suspicious boat had entered the Windswept canal. We immediately sent a patrol car. Unfortunately, the deputy used the siren and lights. The boat was already making the turn into Bogie Channel when the deputy made it out to the end of the dock. But he did get a good look at the two men. He identified the one as Petrowski."

Winifred's heart sank. "What about Sam? Didn't he scare them off?"

"Petrowski must have somehow drugged him. Sam was out cold when the deputy arrived."

"What happened to the security camera? I didn't get an alert on my phone."

Mike walked over to the camera and pointed. "Looks like they shot it out." The unit was hanging by the wires.

"Were you able to pick up Gonzales?" Sally asked.

"He wasn't at his office. His office manager said he and his wife were on a boating trip. The deputy stopped by their house anyway and found his wife there. She said her husband was on a business trip. He may have taken the boat, but she wasn't sure. She tried calling him on his cell, and when he didn't answer, she tried the number for the boat. No answer. She was very cooperative and said she will contact us when she hears from him."

"It doesn't look like we can do anything else out here, and the mosquitoes are eating me alive. We at least have tons of citronella and incense sticks around the picnic table."

Everyone headed to the cottage, where Shannon already had the charcoal going, which was hot enough to begin grilling. She pulled the baked potatoes out of the oven and the salad from the fridge. Within a few minutes, everyone was at the picnic table with drinks in hand just waiting for Shannon to pull the steaks off the grill. Over dinner, Winifred caught everyone up on what she had learned from Russel Reinhart and how it matched what Rosa had said. She omitted the extent of the Barilli Trust's bottom line. Saying it was a sizable amount.

"What worries me," Mike said, "is that Petrowski and friend pulls up to the dock in the middle of the day like he'd received a formal invitation."

"We now have confirmation that Gonzales has been running the show. He hired Harry Lincoln, and I'm betting that those twenty thousand dollar amounts that correspond to the deaths of my father, son and daughter, my husband, and lastly me were paid to Petrowski. But there has been a lot of cash going somewhere else." Winifred paused a beat. "I wish Rosa could find Edwardo's personal calendar."

"We need to find our local connection," Mike said. "Gonzales is too far away to be making daily decisions. My theory is that he's simply the paymaster in this well-organized operation. Someone local with a connection to all of us is the real mastermind."

They each looked at one another. "From now on, we don't talk about our plans with anyone—period. I don't care if it's your mother," Mike stated emphatically.

"Did you try to trace the anonymous caller's location?" Sally asked.

"It was a burner phone," Mike replied.

"Did your officer notice if *Gemini* was out there?" Winifred asked.

"The deputy looked for any boats in the area who might have seen something, and there were none."

You weren't watching Hunter. I kinda wish it had been you making the call.

"I don't know about any of you, but I feel like we're going in circles. Freddie and I are operating on very little sleep, and we've both had an exhausting day. I suggest we call it a night and pick up in the morning."

"I don't have a charter tomorrow, so I will be here all day."

"Speaking of charters," Winifred said, "how come today's charter canceled and you suddenly show up here just at the right time?"

Sally glanced at Mike. "I called her right after you called me about your plans changing. I didn't want you driving to Miami alone."

"I then asked a buddy of mine to take the group out on my boat."

Winifred looked at Mike. "So, you decided I'd be safer with a fisherman riding shotgun?"

"A well-armed fisherman—woman," Sally said as she reached under her shirt with her right arm and pulled out a handgun.

"You were carrying a gun? All day?" Winifred nearly shouted.

"Yes. And you should be thankful, not angry," Sally said as she set the Glock on the picnic table.

"Why? Why would you take it upon yourself to carry a gun?"

Mike raised his hand. "Because I told her to. Remember all the times I told Sally to be prepared?"

Winifred thought for a moment. "Yes. I guess I do."

"I was telling her to carry a gun—a big gun, which she is licensed to use."

"Did you have that cannon on you during the Chens' party?" Winifred asked.

"Not in their home. I left it with the guard when we first entered."

"Does Hector have guns?"

"Yes," Sally and Mike said in unison.

Winifred dried the last dinner plate and put it in the cabinet. "Shall we read for a while? I probably have an hour or two in me before I crash."

Shannon wiped out the sink. "Yeah, I would like to know what happens next."

They both headed to the porch and settled into chairs and began reading where they had left off.

An hour went by, when Winifred looked up. "Santiago and his two surveyors determine where the highest places on the island are, while members of his crew begin felling trees. They have plenty of food between the deer, fish and iguana, and, of course, the fresh water. Santiago keeps someone up in the ship's crow's nest at all times. During one bad storm, a ship was blown off course and crashed on a nearby reef. The call went out, and the crew jumped into the dinghies and rowed out to the site. There were no survivors, so the crew spent the next hours removing the valuables and cargo from the wrecked ship and loaded them onto Santiago's two ships. The next day, they continued bringing ashore everything that they could use on the island. Every lantern, piece of furniture, tools, decking, and sections of the hull are taken ashore. They then began building structures for shelter and housing. A year later, the crew is living in barrack-type buildings. They have watchtowers to look for wrecks at each end of the island closest to the barrier reefs that take so many ships to their graves. Santiago has made short trips to Havana and the various closer Caribbean islands for supplies, including cows, chickens, and goats. When Santiago returns to Spain, he brings jewels and expensive fabrics and gowns for his wife and the family, along with a chest of Spanish coins. For the king, he brings large trunks of treasure. Catalina has a gift for him—a son. When Santiago leaves again, he takes more supplies for his growing community on Big Pine. Leticia writes that Santiago builds a fine home for himself at the edge of the forest. That must be the hammock. He hopes that he can one day bring Catalina and his children to his island for a visit. Apparently, this goes on for ten years or more."

"Sounds like your Captain Santiago Albornoz has become the Keys' first inhabitant to live off the wrecked ships."

"Definitely. Now, what have you learned about Lorenzo?"

"He designs Windswept's walls around the topography map and the location of the ponds, as well as the sketches in Leticia's book. He worries a lot about the possibility of the locals finding coins in the bottom of a pool or pond. So, he creates the pirate legend using the name Diego, which is short for Santiago, and changes Albornoz to the easier pronounceable name of Alverez."

"Which is why Stanton can't find any written record of Big Pine's pirate. I haven't found any drawings yet. I'll flip through the pages further on." Winifred set the book aside. "I know I'm changing the subject, but why didn't you tell us about your visit with Mira Chen?"

"I wasn't ready yet to share it with anyone but you. And, quite frankly, I'm not so sure I want to even now. Other than to say the Chens' foundation is amazing, and I can see myself helping so many people who otherwise wouldn't have access to my knowledge."

"Where would you live?"

"That's another reason to stay. The Chens own three houses in various locations in the historic district. They are used by out-of-town relatives and friends, primarily families, who don't want to stay in a hotel. One of the homes is larger than the other two shotgun styles, with three bedrooms. At some time in the past, a smaller, single-story house was moved to the lot and attached to the main house, forming a courtyard with a small swimming pool and fountain. Both houses have porches facing the yard. Mira showed me how I could live in the larger two-story house and use the smaller one bedroom for my office and consulting room. The yard is completely fenced in and would be suitable for outdoor therapy sessions and mini workshops. I couldn't believe how tranquil and peaceful the space is with the splashing fountain and all the palms and exotic bushes and plants. There is an old garage at the back corner to store pool and garden supplies, along with lawn furniture when not in use. And it has enough off-street parking for three cars. Mira would rent me the house on a month-to-month basis for a year, and then if I want to stay, she will extend a long-term lease, or I could find a place of my own."

"Have you made up your mind?"

"Not enough to commit. But I did tell her I would let her know in the morning."

"I know you haven't asked me, but I'm facing a major life-altering change as well." Winifred smiled. "And except for the bad guys, I'm liking the new me. I've decided to raise Lorenzo's house eight feet and bring it into the twenty-first century—make it mine."

CHAPTER SIXTY-SIX

The next morning, Winifred woke up to the wonderful aroma of bacon frying and fresh coffee. She got out of bed and headed down to the bathroom and then her much-needed first cup of the day. She sat at one of the two barstools sitting at the kitchen counter and took a long sip of coffee. "You look like you've been out for a run already."

"Sam and I decided we couldn't wait for the sunrise, so we went early, and I collected the data chips from the wildlife cams."

"Oh good. Maybe we'll catch something of our unwanted guests yesterday." Winifred located her laptop and brought it to the counter. She inserted the first chip. "This one shows Sam doing his vicious barking routine at the edge of the canal. Petrowski tosses Sam a large piece of meat. A minute later, Sam wobbles off drunk-like, then collapses. They pull up to the dock and tie off. Petrowski tosses a large canvas bag onto the dock and gets out of the boat. His buddy struggles with lifting a jackhammer, when Petrowski suddenly stops. He then tosses the bag back into the boat and jumps in. The other guy is untying the lines, while Petrowski takes the wheel—and they're off."

"Can you see any other boats in the area?"

"No. Not on this one. I'll check the rest." After testing three more, Winifred finally inserted the cam that points out into the water. "This picture clearly shows no other boats around, not even *Gemini*."

Shannon had breakfast on the porch table by the time Winifred took the last chip out of her laptop. "What's on for today?"

"The only thing I know about is that Hector is being released from the hospital. One of his sisters and her husband is picking him up and bringing him home. They are going to stay with him until he can handle everything on his own."

"We should take Sam over for a visit," Shannon said before taking a bite of omelet. "Sally's truck is here, but I didn't see her. There were no lights on in the cabin."

"Huh. That's odd. She is usually up early. If her truck is here, then she didn't go to the Egg for breakfast."

"I guess it will be a stay-at-home day for us," Shannon said between sips of coffee.

"Speaking of home, I think I'll spend some time in the main house with a tape measure and notepad. After touring those two houses with Anneliese, I have some ideas. I'm actually getting excited about the project."

"What about the heart-shaped pool?"

"Oh. It's definitely gotta go. I'm thinking about the large, irregular-shaped one with the island in the middle. It would be more natural-looking, especially on this property."

"Maybe a bridge over one part with a hot tub and waterfall," Shannon suggested.

"Oh yeah! And a thatched-roof tiki hut for fish cleaning and an outdoor bar."

"I get the bar part, but are you planning on cleaning fish?"

"Hell, no! I'll build that for Hector and Sally."

"I'm coming along to help you plan. Do you have enough money for a tennis court, gourmet kitchen with a high-end gas range, whole-house generator, and temperature-controlled wine tasting room with cooler?"

"Yes" was all Winifred said with a smile.

An hour later, both women had showered and dressed in slacks and tank tops and were ready to head over to the house with Sam, when Winifred's phone rang. She looked at the screen and frowned. "Hello, Mike. What's up?"

"Is Shannon with you?"

"Yes. We were on our way to the house with a list of ideas. I've decided to keep it and have it raised the required eight feet."

"Can you hold off on that and come here to the station instead? And bring your laptop."

"Sure. We'll leave right now."

"Once again, our plans change. Jump in the Escalade. We are meeting with Mike." Winifred petted Sam. "Sam, patrol, good boy. Patrol." She watched as Sam trotted toward the main house.

"What about Sally?" Shannon asked as Winifred climbed onto the driver's seat.

"Mike didn't mention her."

A few minutes later, they pulled into the parking lot of the Sheriff's station on Key Deer Boulevard. After entering, they went into Mike's office and were surprised to see Sally.

"I picked Sally up earlier. I want her truck to remain visible from the water so if anyone decides to visit, they will think she is there—on her boat."

"Good idea. Our unwanted visitors seem to arrive when nobody is home." Winifred paused a beat. "So, what's happened?"

"The Coast Guard got a call from a shrimp boat captain about a yacht drifting off the coast of Alabama. They found the boat and boarded. It belongs to Gonzales. He was found dead at the helm. The initial report is a massive heart attack."

"Was anyone else on board?" Winifred asked.

"No. And due to the heat, they don't know how long ago he died. The medical examiner in Mobile will have a full report in a few days. Which brings us to the Christmas holiday."

"I wonder how many people knew we suspected him!" Sally said.

Winifred pulled her phone out. "Mike, do you mind if I call Rosa? She may have some new information."

"Of course. Anything will help at this point."

Winifred punched in Rosa's number from her contact list. She took a few rings to answer.

"Hello, it's Winifred. I'm at the Sheriff's Office here on Big Pine, and we have news. I'm putting you on speaker."

"That's good. I came in early this morning to go through the office again looking for the personal calendar. I finally found it in the safe and have been doing a search of names that are not on my calendar."

"Rosa, this is Lieutenant Mike Connor. I hate to stop you, but I received news about your boss. The Coast Guard found his boat adrift off the coast of Alabama. If appears he died of a heart attack. He was alone."

"Oh, poor Mrs. Gonzales. She is such a good woman. Very religious."

"Rosa, what have you found?" Winifred asked.

"Now, mind you. This personal calendar is only for this year. But there are a lot of meetings and phone calls to someone with the initials KB. I've cross-referenced them with our client list. I found six matches, but they are either too old, live out of state, or deceased."

"When was the latest notation?" Mike asked.

"Four days ago. Some of the dates have other notes. Like, done or missed or added dates like tomorrow, next Thursday.

Almost all of them are close to his visits to Miami. And three of them match dates after cash withdrawals from the trust." Rosa paused. "I hope this helps. I'll continue to search."

"Rosa, I'm sending an officer to your office within the hour. Give the calendar to him or her, and if anyone in the future, *anyone*, asks for it, play dumb. You don't know anything about it. Understand?"

"Yes. I will put it in an envelope and mark it, 'Petty Cash.'"

"Good thinking, Rosa. I'll be in touch," Winifred said.

"Thank you, Rosa. Don't hesitate to call me if you find anything else or need help," Mike said.

"I will. I suppose this place is going to get really busy, real soon. Lieutenant Connor, what should I do with the cash? It shouldn't be in the safe. It belongs to Winifred now. It's money Mr. Gonzales pulled from the trust. It isn't marked for anyone."

Mike looked at Winifred. "How much are we talking? A few hundreds?"

"Fifty thousand."

"Oh crap!" Mike ran his fingers through his hair—several times. "Rosa, we will call you right back."

Mike thought about the various possible scenarios. "The money could be held as evidence for who knows what. But, on the other hand, it belongs to Winifred. Rosa could say that it was given to her at the time she signed the documents as the heir to the trust."

"What if we use the money as a carrot?" Sally offered. "We know the money wasn't intended for Freddie. I bet it was payoff funds for whatever is happening now or going to happen. It just might draw out our local mastermind."

"Great idea. Winifred, I want you to ride along with a deputy to Key Largo and pick up the money and personal calendar. As the official owner of the trust, you can sign for it. And make sure your name is all over those documents."

CHAPTER SIXTY-SEVEN

"I'm going along," Sally stated.

"No. This needs to look like a routine Monroe County Sheriff's officer assisted job."

"No offense, Mike, but who are you going to send who is better than me? Are you willing to put Freddie's life on the line when Petrowski shows up? If he isn't already there. The person who killed Gonzales is going after the money—payment for a job well done."

"No one said he was murdered. It could have been a heart attack."

"Are you willing to put money on that? Petrowski is a killer—a cold-blooded killer. A life to him is worth nothing. He's already tried to kill Freddie twice—that we know of. She'll be a sitting duck from here to Key Largo. At least, put a vest on her."

Mike thought about what Sally had said. "Freddie will be with an officer in a patrol car."

"How about I follow in an unmarked car?"

"I can't get one here in time."

Sally stood and rested both hands on the edge of Mike's desk. "How about a badass Harley?"

Mike rolled his eyes. "You win. But expect trouble." Mike turned to Shannon. "You'll need to drive Sally over to her place."

"Can I go back to Windswept after I drop her off?" Shannon asked.

"Sure, Sally's right; Petrowski won't be there. But Sam is. You'll be fine."

"What about Rosa? Will she be safe when we leave her office?" Winifred asked.

"Good point," Mike said. "There may be files or evidence in the safe that would link the mastermind to Gonzales."

"Thinking as a psychiatrist, I believe Gonzales has at least one insurance policy that he can hold against Petrowski and the mastermind. Edwardo knows he's had a mob boss as a client for many years and been in cahoots with killers," Shannon stated. "The bad guys don't want that left behind for someone like the FBI to find."

"I'm calling Rosa back and tell her the plan. She'll have an hour and a half before you arrive to clean out the safe and any important files. I'll suggest she put them in her car and then leave after you."

"Mike, may I suggest that she doesn't go home but to a family member or friend's house until this is over?"

"You're right as usual, Captain."

Winifred eyed Mike. *There you go with the Captain thing again.*

Deputy Cheryl Cruz nodded toward the entrance to the Bahia Honda state park. "There she is, as planned."

Winifred looked out the side window from the back seat of the cruiser. A large black motorcycle waited to pull out. The rider wore khaki-colored cargo pants, a Hawaiian shirt, and a black helmet with full visor.

"Are you sure? It looks like a tourist after a few hours at the beach. I think it was a man."

"It was Sally—I'd know her bike anywhere."

"If you say so." Winifred set her leather oversize tote bag on the seat. "I feel like a prisoner back here. Why can't I sit up front?"

"Only other officers sit up here—you're not. Mike wants you in the back. You stay in the back."

Cheryl kept the conversation on neutral topics and her eyes on the road and the motorcycle. At times, the bike would be in front, at times behind, and several times pulled off into parking lots and gas stations. Never once did the rider glance into the patrol car.

"Sally is making me nervous. It's hard to figure out what she's doing."

"I must say, I'm impressed. I'm getting a crash course on how to follow a vehicle without looking like one is being followed. Every time she speeds ahead, she's changing the traffic pattern and checking out the leading vehicles. When she pulls off, she's watching for anything unusual and if someone might be following us."

At exactly noon, Deputy Cheryl Cruz pulled into the parking lot of the attorney's office in Key Lago. She remained seated while looking in the rearview mirror. "The vehicle is driving past now. It isn't slowing down, nor did the driver look this way—a male with a baseball cap turned backward."

"Who are you talking to?" Winifred asked.

"Sally." Cheryl removed an earbud. "She's been watching a suspicious silver Chevy, Malibu, belonging to someone on Marathon." Deputy Cruz got out of the car and walked around to Winifred's side and opened the door. "It's okay for us to go in."

A minute later, Winifred entered the office to find Rosa in tears.

"I'm so glad you made it okay. I've been so worried. Lieutenant Connor has been on the phone helping me stay focused. I have boxes of folders in my car. I left some unimportant files and personal stuff in the safe so it wouldn't be empty, plus the petty cashbox. After you sign the letter stating that you were given fifty thousand dollars in cash as owner of the Barilli Family Trust, I will make a copy and put it in the safe as well."

Winifred took Rosa's hand. "You've done a great job." She glanced around the office. "The rooms look normal. Everything in place. If anyone breaks in it will look like you just stepped out for lunch."

"I will put the sign in the window saying I will be back at one o'clock."

"Good. Now let's see how much money we can stuff in this tote bag. I left the contents on the back seat, so we'd have more room." Fifty thousand dollars in hundreds took up more space than the bag would allow. The rest Deputy Cruz stuffed in her shirt. "If Petrowski is out there watching, I hope he doesn't notice that I've gained fifty pounds since I walked in."

Twenty minutes later, Winifred and Cheryl left the building and quickly entered the patrol car that had been sitting with the engine idling. "So far so good," Deputy Cruz said as she backed out of the parking spot and pulled up to the Overseas Highway. "Wow! That was close!"

"What happened?" Winifred asked as she scooted forward to look out the windshield.

"Someone almost rear-ended that big motor home. It happens all the time. With only one road in and out of the Keys. You get long backups, and someone will be kind enough to let another motorist in. Then the person behind isn't paying attention and slams into the good Samaritan. It makes it more difficult to see traffic ahead if you are behind a motor home or large truck."

"I'm glad there wasn't an accident. I wouldn't want to be sitting here, stuck in traffic with all this money."

The deputy crossed onto the southbound lane and glanced in the rearview mirror. "I see Sally just now pulled in behind us." She inserted an earbud. A few seconds later, she turned to Winifred and smiled. "Sally says we have clear sailing all the way home. You can relax now."

Sally then pulled out and around them and weaved in and out of the line of traffic ahead. They didn't see the black Harley again until they were well past Islamorada.

———

Winifred and Cheryl Cruz joined Mike Connor and Shannon in the driveway at the main house. Sally pulled up behind the patrol car and climbed off the Harley.

"Sally, you're wearing black pants and shirt. We saw you in khakis looking like you just got off the Conch Train in Key West."

"You are so observant, Freddie. I needed a different look for the ride home."

"Well, I'm happy our adventure went off without any trouble. Petrowski wasn't there after all," Winifred said with a sigh of relief.

"Oh, he was there all right. Parked across the street two doors down."

"I didn't see him." Cruz sounded dumbfounded.

"You weren't supposed to," Sally added. "He won't be using his left hand any time soon."

"What happened?" Mike asked.

"Petrowski was driving the silver Chevy Malibu. He caught my attention because he kept about a quarter of a mile back regardless of the flow of traffic. After you pulled into Edwardo's parking lot, I kept going, then turned around in time to see the silver car pull off the road several buildings down from where you were. I ducked into a vacant lot and parked in front of a tall hedge and changed into black clothes so I would blend in with the bike." Sally paused a beat. "Expecting trouble, I got into position and waited. He was waiting as well. When the two of you approached the car, he raised his arms and aimed, and then when Cruz opened the rear door, he locked his arms and was ready to fire. I fired first. He won't be using his left hand for a while, and the right one will hurt like hell."

"Why didn't you kill him? Did you miss?" Winifred asked.

Sally looked at Mike. "If I thought Mike wanted him dead—he would be dead."

"She's right. We still need to find our mastermind. And Petrowski is the only one who can point us in the right direction. We know who owns the car he was driving. I have someone picking the owner up now."

"So, Petrowski was the guy who almost rear-ended that motor home while he was trying to leave the scene," Cheryl added.

"Right. I did see that," Sally added. "Although I was able to keep track of him at first, I lost him in Islamorada. He could have jumped over to the Old Highway 1 and waited it out until he was sure we were long gone."

"I think it's safe to say he won't be coming around tonight. Sally, can you take care of the money?"

"Of course; I have just the place. I keep large tote bags on board for my guests for when they go shopping. I'll go and grab a few."

Not long after, everyone sat on the luxurious white leather banquettes in *Lady Luck*'s main salon and watched Sally safely store the bags of money in the secret compartment behind the liquor cabinet and slide it back into place. "All safe and sound."

"The money is. I'm not so sure about Shannon and me."

CHAPTER SIXTY-EIGHT

Anneliese greeted Winifred and Shannon with a joyful smile as they walked into the No Name Grill. They had left Sam at home to watch over Windswept with Sally, although Mike had felt certain it would be a quiet night. Having missed lunch, Winifred began thinking about the Bourbon burger she'd had at No Name. Shannon agreed to an early dinner, but Sally wanted to stretch out and relax on the boat. At four thirty, they climbed onto the high stools as Anneliese placed coasters. Shannon ordered a Yuengling on tap and Winifred a Merlot. Shannon took a long sip of the ice-cold brew, while Winifred fingered the stem of her glass. Hunter sat in his usual seat. He acknowledged them with a quick nod and a smile.

"How's it been going? Mike hasn't said much."

"We've just been busy reading the journal and looking at Lorenzo's old pictures," Winifred answered as she perused the menu. "I drove here wanting that delicious but horribly messy burger that I had the other day."

"But?"

"But I think I'll order a pizza instead."

"What about you, Shannon?" Anneliese asked.

"I'll split a pizza. How about one with everything but anchovies?"

"You got it. I'll put the order in and be right back."

"What's with you? You've talked about that burger for the last hour. That's why we came here." Shannon glanced over at Hunter. "Ah, I get it. You don't want him watching you eat with sauce running down your chin." Shannon paused a beat. "I wouldn't either."

Anneliese returned. "How was your day?"

"Okay. I've decided to keep the house and have it raised. With the added square feet where the garage and safe room are, I can make some changes to the floor plan. Maybe put in a large master suite and office. Expand the kitchen and create a great room and keep the fireplace. I really liked the outdoor space of the first house you showed us. I can see something similar at Windswept."

"I had a feeling you might go that route. I have an architect friend who can help you." Anneliese left to take care of other customers.

Winifred leaned closer to Shannon and whispered, "He's making me nervous."

"Why, because every time you glance his way, he's looking at you?" Shannon took another sip. "I think it's cute. He's not wearing a ring. Although many married men don't."

"I don't care. He's not my type. I don't even know what he looks like under all that hair."

"But you do wonder."

Half an hour later, Anneliese arrived with their pizza. "Enjoy, ladies. Let me know if you need anything." She went to walk away, then turned back and leaned in. "It's interesting that he comes in the same night as you."

Winifred slipped a slice onto her plate. "I wonder what she meant by that!"

Shannon glanced over. Hunter was getting ready to pay his tab.

Winifred took a bite as Shannon nudged her. "I think he's coming this way."

Sure enough, he walked over and stood between them. Winifred's heart raced; she felt the electricity between them.

"Mrs. Forrester. Doctor Mulaney. Nice to see you again. I hope you're enjoying this fine stretch of weather we are having."

His voice sent tingles up her spine. She could barely chew the bite of pizza.

"Yes, we are, and especially all of the Christmas festivities," Shannon said while giving Winifred time to swallow.

"I hope fishing has been good. I see *Gemini* quite often," Winifred managed to choke out.

"Yes, it has. And I see that Captain Sally is docking *Lady Luck* at your canal. Beautiful boat. Sally is an excellent charter captain. I hope she is keeping you well supplied with fish."

"We had mahi-mahi the other night. It was delicious, and she is also an excellent cook."

"The captain has many talents. Well, ladies, I must run. Enjoy your pizza—stay safe."

"Good night," Winifred and Shannon said in unison.

Stay safe? What was that about? Winifred wondered.

Annelies returned with a grin as wide as the Joker's. "Well, that was interesting. And—he bought you both a drink."

"Why did you make the comment earlier about us being here at the same time?" Winifred asked.

"Oh, I haven't seen him since the last time you were here. When you sat on the patio and I introduced him." She paused a moment. "Although I am part-time. He has probably stopped in when I wasn't working."

⊫╬⊨

Winifred hadn't yet pulled out of the parking lot, when her cell phone rang. The incoming call appeared on the Escalade's info center screen. "It's Mike." She pressed Accept. "Hello, Mike."

"Freddie, I got a call from Rosa."

Winifred pulled off to the side and parked. "Go ahead. Shannon is with me."

"About two hours after Rosa left the office, the alarm company notified her of a break-in. The dispatcher told her that he had already called the Sheriff's Office. While Rosa was on the phone, they got a signal of a fire on the premises. The dispatcher called the fire department, who already had a truck on the way."

"Is Rosa okay?"

"She arrived safely at her sister's place in Fort Myers. The condo where she lives is in a secure building."

"That is wonderful news. Anything on the fire?"

"I'm waiting for a return call, but the fire marshal believes it was arson. There is a strong smell of an accelerant."

"Do you think Petrowski doubled back and broke into the office?"

"I called Sally and asked her. She doesn't think he would have been able to with his hand messed up. Which means he had help."

"Should Shannon and I be worried?"

"No. At least, not tonight. Are you at home?"

"On our way. We sat at the bar. Anneliese was working. Hunter was there."

"Was he? I'm sure I'll hear about it. I'll call in the morning."

⚓

Sally joined them shortly after they arrived at the cottage. Within a few minutes, the three were on the porch. For the next hour, Shannon listened as Winifred and Sally each gave the details of their role in securing the fifty thousand dollars—and preventing Petrowski from killing Freddie.

"What about you, Shannon? How was your time alone here?" Winifred asked.

"I spent my day reading. I finished both Lorenzo's journal and Leticia's book. Although my day wasn't as exciting as the two of you, it was just as productive."

"Do you know where the treasure is?" Sally asked.

"Not exactly. But let me start at the beginning with Leticia.

"Captain Santiago names the island Tierra de Riqueza, which translates to 'Land of Wealth.' He returns many times laden with much-needed supplies. Each time, he finds that the population has increased with shipwreck survivors, many of them crew members. Several of his original crew have married and have a family. The new buildings that replace the ones taken out by storm surges are being constructed above ground. Santiago has a fine house on the edge of the hammock that survives the tropical storms. He has a system of lowering the chests of treasure taken from the wrecks into designated freshwater pools for safekeeping. Those he has indicated on the map with an *S.* In 1575, at the age of thirty-five, his father dies, and Santiago is called home. He is now the head of the family and must take his rightful position in Philip II's court. Knowing he will not be able to make many more trips to the island, he returns with a man who will be his agent or a form of mayor. He installs the man in his house. When Santiago leaves, he takes all the chests with him, except a small chest of Spanish coins, which he leaves behind."

451

"Is that the one Lorenzo finds?" Winifred asks.

"It isn't clear, but I assume so. Because two years later, his crew and their families return to Madrid. The agent had been told, while in Havana, of a severe storm that had nearly destroyed the island of Puerto Rico and was moving across San Domingo toward Cuba. Ships were leaving the harbor and heading north into the Atlantic. The agent returns and packs everyone and their personal possession onto the two ships, along with the small livestock that might not survive like chickens and goats. They head out into the Gulf, away from the dangerous reefs toward Mexico instead of the Atlantic. The hurricane follows the northern coastline of Cuba and directly crosses the middle islands of the Keys, then turns and heads up the western side of Florida. Once the storm passes, they return to their island to find it desecrated by the storm. The buildings had all been leveled—blown out to sea. The few treasure chests that had been safely lowered into the designated freshwater pools were raised and carried onto the ships. They then set sail for Madrid."

"But Deigo's chest was still there," Sally deducted.

"Santiago's salvage operation has made him a powerful member of Spain's aristocracy and the Albornoz family rich. His plan is to return in five years with a fleet of new and better ships, and the materials to rebuild. However, in 1579, six months before his planned departure, he is bedridden by an influenza pandemic that began in Asia, then spread to Africa and then Europe. His last thoughts—the last line in his journal was that Tierra de Riqueza remain in the family."

"Havana, Salvatore Giordano II, was right about Big Pine having history." Winifred shook her head in frustration. "I can't believe he risked losing it in a poker game when the family had protected it for over four hundred years. I certainly look at the property with more compassion."

"I want to hear the rest of Lorenzo's journal," Sally stated.

Shannon set Leticia's book aside and picked up Lorenzo's. "I'll continue. Barilli made numerous mathematical notations when describing where the drained pool was located under the safe room floor. If Gonzales didn't finish reading the journal, then he wouldn't have known about the grid. If he did, then he got the calculations wrong. The hole is definitely there, and I can find it. I can also tell you with certainty that Lorenzo is going soft after reading Leticia's book—Santiago's story. He often mentions the love in his heart for the house and where it sits on Santiago's land. The warmth he feels in his heart while standing in the living room looking out over the Gulf. I have the impression that although it has always been thought that Lorenzo built Windswept for Lacy Lorin, I'm not so sure anymore. I think he built it as a monument to Santiago and the Albornoz family."

"Boy, that's a stretch from what we know," Sally said with doubt in her voice.

"At the end, when Lorenzo knew he had only months to live, he came back. He opened the house and lived alone, keeping his heart safe and true to Diego." Shannon fought back tears. "I'm even developing a love for the land and would hate to see it change."

"Wow! Now I want to finish reading them myself," Winifred said.

Sally stood. "It's getting late. I'm going to turn in for the night. Any Christmas Eve plans for the day?"

"Christmas Eve? It can't be! I'm not ready! I haven't even thought about my family up north. I should have had the cabin in Traverse City prepared for my cousins and their families. They would have arrived today."

"Freddie, they are adults and do this every year. Besides, you have your property manager. He knows you're down here, and I'm sure he has taken care of everything, as he does every year."

Shannon gave her friend a hug. "Let it go. Tomorrow, we do what we want to do with our *new* family."

"After listening to both books, I think I would like to see the house again. Maybe tomorrow we can work with Barilli's calculations and determine where in the safe room floor Diego's treasurer is hidden."

Winifred and Shannon looked at each other and nodded. "Works for us. I'll text you when we are ready to head over. I think I should send Sam out to patrol while you walk to the canal."

"Good idea. Maybe call Lenny and let him know that the security camera needs replacing."

Winifred walked Sally to the door. "Thanks; I will. Have a good night."

CHAPTER SIXTY-NINE

The next morning, Winifred and Shannon met up with Sally, who was sitting on the wall that edged the patio of the main house. Winifred looked out over the calm waters of the Gulf. "What a beautiful day. The weather report calls for sunny and a high of seventy-five. I called my aunt Celise. Everyone arrived at the cabin yesterday. The men are taking the kids out this morning to cut down a tree. It will be decorated and ready for Santa by the time the kids are sent off to bed. I'm kinda sorry I'm missing the festivities. Christmas is a magical time for children."

"Perhaps next year you can bring your family down here. Santa arrives by boat instead of a sleigh, and you do have a chimney," Sally added. "Your family can help me decorate *Lady Luck*, and we'll participate in the Key West Lighted Boat Parade."

Winifred thought about all the many ways she could bring happiness to her family now that money was no longer an issue. "I could charter a jet and bring the entire family down for the whole month of December. They could become a family of pirates during Pirate Week." She glanced around the open acres between the house and the cottage. "There would be the large winding pool and waterfall, lots of lounge chairs, water sports, and a tennis court." Winifred looked at Shannon and Sally with a huge smile. "It will be wonderful!"

"I'll be living in Key West where everyone can crash after fireworks," Shannon said excitedly. "I'll be gaining a family!"

"Me too!" Sally added.

All three hugged before going inside.

Winifred searched the horizon. *Gemini* was nowhere to be seen.

⇒⊢⊣⇐

Lorenzo's journal was not going to give up its secrets easily. Using the numbers as feet and inserting them into the calculations, the treasure would be in the center of the room. And looking logically at where someone would place a secure room over a hole full of Spanish coins, it probably would be the center. But when Shannon placed the parchment landscape sheet over the blueprint page showing the floor plan, it didn't match.

"We know based on the freshwater pools within Windswept's walls that the notations that are shaded in pencil are correct. If that were true, then the treasure hole isn't under the safe room. But we know it is."

"This is so frustrating! The only thing I really like about this room is the floor," Winifred blurted out.

Shannon studied the floor. "I remember commenting on the floor on my first visit and how lovely the terra-cotta-colored cement was. And how it had been stamped to look like tile." She glanced over at Winifred. "Maybe the floor itself is the answer." Shannon looked again at the notations. "It's not feet. It's tiles! How did I miss this? The whole floor is a grid—like a chessboard!"

Winifred and Sally looked at each other and shrugged.

"Okay, Freddie, you are the length. Sally, you are going to move from side to side. Freddie, how many squares make up the length of the room?"

"Seven."

"Sally, the width?"

"Eight."

"Freddie, I'm missing three squares. Look in the closet."

"Yep. You've got ten in total."

"Okay, Freddie, you move down five tiles. Sally, move toward the center by four." Shannon waited. "Freddie, move back two. Sally, move back three."

Winifred and Sally were standing on the same tile—next to the periscope.

"I think Lorenzo had the large steel plate mounted over the spot."

"But he wouldn't have access to the treasure," Winifred pointed out.

"Yes. Just like when the chest originally fell out of the fresh-water pool. He cuts out the square we're standing on and digs down. He had filled the hole with the thin, porous cement, so as he chiseled out the limestone, the concrete would give way—brilliant."

"So, how do we get it out?" Shannon asks.

"Hector comes home this afternoon. We borrow the necessary tools and have Mike help us in a few days—after Christmas."

Sally moved away from the square. "Sounds like the perfect plan. For now, how about we get out of this stuffy room and go outside?"

Once out in the fresh air and sunshine, Winifred looked out over the horizon. "That's odd; it looks like *Gemini* is anchored in a different spot—inside the grassy bank."

Sally shaded her eyes and looked to where Freddie was pointing. "He must have just gotten there and not yet dropped anchor."

"Why don't we take a look at the yard while we're out here and get some ideas of where things should go?" Shannon said as she skirted the patio.

Winifred and Sally followed. They were approaching the old heart-shaped pool, when they heard a blast from *Gemini*'s horn. Then long and short blasts.

"Down! Get down!" shouted Sally as she ran for the canal. Within seconds, they heard the sound of a speedboat moving fast toward them.

Winifred looked to the side and saw one of the Ixora bushes that Hector had pruned. "Follow me," she said to Shannon as she bent as low as she could and dashed for the bush. The boat slowed momentarily and turned as a barrage of bullets sprayed across the yard. Shannon and Freddie flattened themselves against the ground. Winifred held Sam down between them. A moment later, all was quiet, except for the boat motor that was idling and the sound of a larger boat moving in.

"It's okay now. You can come out," Sally shouted.

Winifred and Shannon stood and brushed the small stones from their arms and legs. Sam took off running toward the canal. They inched their way around the Ixora and looked at the scene before them. *Gemini* was now close to the mouth of the canal, with Hunter on the bow holding a gun pointed at the occupants of the speedboat. One of them was draped against the side.

Winifred took in the scene. Hunter was still holding the driver of the speedboat at gunpoint but was now looking over in the direction of *Lady Luck*. She followed his gaze to the top of the boat's tower. Sally stood holding a rifle. "What the hell?"

Winifred and Shannon ran to the entrance of the canal. Petrowski's body hung partially over the side of the boat, his left hand bandaged—a hole in the center of his forehead. A minute later, Sally joined them carrying a high-powered rifle with a large military-looking scope. Everyone then looked toward Bogie Channel and the approach of the Coast Guard.

Winifred wasn't sure what to do or say next when she heard sirens out on Key Deer Boulevard.

By the time Mike Connor arrived along with another patrol car and deputy, two of the Coast Guard officers had boarded the speedboat. One took control of the driver, while the other one, who appeared to be in charge, moved Petrowski's body to the seat. He looked up at Sally. "This your work, Captain?"

"Yes, sir."

The officer held up an AK-47. "This guy wasn't taking any chances. Mike, can you keep our friend here until the medical examiner arrives? It could take a while." He then looked over at Hunter. "Thank you. Without your call, we wouldn't have been in the area."

"It was a boat I didn't recognize hanging around close by but not doing anything. Stupid, he should have at least been holding a fishing rod and looked like he belonged."

Winifred finally found her voice. "Mike, you can move the boat around to the far end of the canal where Hector keeps his boat. There is plenty of parking for the medical examiner."

The Coast Guard officer steered the speedboat behind *Lady Luck*. Mike gave orders to take the driver into custody, while the officer got back on their boat, which had pulled up alongside.

Meanwhile, Hunter had returned to the helm and idled, while the Coast Guard left the area.

Winifred's attention returned to *Gemini*. "Hunter!" she shouted. "Do you want to stay and talk to Lieutenant Connor?" She pointed to the now-empty space behind *Lady Luck*. "There is plenty of room."

Sally stood at the dock ready to grab the bowline as Hunter approached. Mike then arrived and positioned himself to grab the stern line. "I have a deputy with the body watching for the medical examiner." He looked over at Sally. "Nice work, Captain." After putting two fenders out and tying off, Hunter stepped onto the dock.

"It was Hunter here who gave me the warning SOS with *Gemini*'s horns. I had just enough time to get into position. It was close."

"How did you get the rifle and climb the ladder and load and all that stuff?" Winifred asked.

"The gun was already up there and ready to go. The tricky part was getting to it in time."

"That sounds like you knew this was going to happen."

"Not really, Shannon. More like anticipated," Mike clarified. "That's why I suggested that Sally dock *Lady Luck* here. She has a great line of vision from the tower."

Winifred focused her attention on Sally. "Now that I think about it, why wasn't the Coast Guard officer surprised that you'd taken out Petrowski with a shot to the head? And Mike doesn't care that you carry a gun. And people call you Captain instead of Sally, not only because you are a fishing boat captain."

Sally gave Mike a questioning look. He nodded. "Because I'm Captain Sally Rogers, a captain in the army reserves. I'm a retired army sharpshooter."

Winifred couldn't have been more surprised. "And after all this time, you didn't tell Shannon and me?"

"There are only a few people who know. Those who might need my services or others in the reserves like the Chens' security guards."

Shannon gave a knowing grin. "That explains the times when, as a psychiatrist, you didn't fit the mold as a local fisherman. Freddie and I would have felt a whole lot safer if you'd told us before now."

Sally gave Mike the "I told you so" look.

"That was my call," Mike said. "I didn't want to take any chances that you might accidentally slip up during conversations when outside the group of us."

"Does Anneliese know? Or Katie? Or Hector?"

"No, none of them," Sally said. "But the Chens know."

Mike turned to Hunter. "Now, you know. What's your story? I've seen you around, and Anneliese has mentioned you as a regular at the No Name."

"I fish for specific customers like restaurants, resorts, and inns—and the Chens' chef. I've found some favorite spots in this area, and it's not overly fished. I'd heard that someone had taken over Windswept, and I recently met Winifred and Shannon at the No Name. They seemed like nice ladies, and knowing the history of the place, I've made a point of keeping an eye out when I'm working offshore." Hunter glanced at Sally. "That's why that speedboat caught my attention today."

"I'm glad you were here." Mike pulled out his card and handed it to Hunter. "Feel free to call me if you see any other suspicious activity around here."

"I will. Now, unless you need me for anything else, I have some grouper to deliver."

"No. Thanks again for your help."

Hunter boarded *Gemini* and started the engines. Sally and Mike untied the bowline and the stern line and tossed them on board. Hunter looked at Sally and nodded toward *Lady Luck*. "You've got a beautiful boat. I've seen her off Key West and the islands." He then looked at Winifred and Shannon. "Nice seeing the two of you again—stay safe."

A deep frown creased Winifred's brow. *There he goes again with the 'stay safe.' What else does he know?*

⚔

The first thing Winifred did after watching Mike drive off with his prisoner was to call Harry Lincoln. After giving him a blow-by-blow account of the day's events, she took a deep breath. "Harry, there must be a link that goes directly to a Barilli."

"I would agree, except Bianca is the only Barilli left. I believe today's event was about the fifty thousand. Petrowski knew you had taken possession of the cash. After you left Key Largo, he returns and raids the office and safe, then sets fire to eliminate any possible connection to him. And today was personal. Hence the need for the AK-47."

"Eliminate me and take his time looking for the money?"

"You got it." Harry paused a beat. "I think the gig was up for him. The so-called treasure was just another side-job. You had become a huge thorn in his side—the hit he hadn't been able to complete. He was after only two things now—you and his last payment."

"I agree, but keep on the Barilli angle. That family and Edwardo Gonzales are the only ones who know about the treasure. And he's out of the picture."

Winifred turned to Shannon. "Two days in a row that we've lost control before noon. I can't wait to see what tomorrow brings!"

CHAPTER SEVENTY

The adrenaline that was still pumping through Winifred's veins had her up at six. Shannon met up with Sally on her morning run with Sam. The three then caught up with Winifred as she left the bathroom after her shower. "Merry Christmas, Freddie!"

"Merry Christmas, Shannon. Merry Christmas, Sally." She bent down to give Sam a hug. "And to you too, boy. I bet there are some presents for you under the tree."

"How about we start off with mimosas on the porch after we give Freddie a chance to get dressed?"

Fifteen minutes later, the three were standing at the porch railing looking out over a beautiful sunrise and toasting to their first Christmas together.

"Hunter must be taking the day off. I don't see him anywhere," Winifred said, feeling disappointed.

"How about I make another round of drinks while you watch me cook?"

Winifred turned to Sally. "You're going to love this." A few minutes later, they sat on stools at the kitchen counter and watched as Shannon whipped eggs and cream with spices for the French toast, while bacon sizzled in a pan. Then she chopped green onions and red peppers for the giant cheese omelet.

"Do you two always eat like this?" Sally asked.

"This is nothing. Wait till you see what she can do in a *real* kitchen."

"I'm already designing Freddie's new kitchen, with a professional gas stove. Of course, she will need a giant propane tank, since there isn't natural gas in the Keys."

"While we were at the cabin in Traverse City, Shannon was cooking for everyone who walked through the door."

"I look forward to the new dishes we can create together, because if I remember correctly, the only fish you do is salmon."

Shannon laughed as she began dishing up the plates. "You are correct. But I have a dozen ways to deliver mouthwatering salmon."

"Between the two of you, I'd better add a gym and exercise room to the plans."

An hour later, Winifred and Sally were in the middle of washing the dishes, while Shannon relaxed on the porch with another mimosa, when Freddie's phone rang.

"Merry Christmas," Winifred answered cheerfully.

"Hello, Mrs. Forrester?"

"Yes, this is she."

"This is Bianca Barilli Morano."

Winifred's heart stopped.

"Hello! This is a surprise."

"I'm sure it is. After the lengthy and rather heated discussion I had yesterday with Harry Lincoln, I decided to fly down and put this whole mess to rest."

"Wonderful. Where and when would you like to meet?" Winifred asked.

"Windswept in an hour."

"Wow! You do work fast. We can meet at the main house. It's to the right after you pull in and—"

"I know the way. Have the gates open," Bianca said and ended the call.

Winifred looked up at Shannon and Sally. Our day is now planned. "Bianca Barilli Morano will be here in an hour."

Exactly one hour later, a black limousine pulled up to the main house. The driver got out and opened the rear door. The woman gracefully eased her way out of the vehicle and stood. She was taller than Winifred would have expected, with chin-length silver-gray hair that was sleek and shiny. She wore wide-legged black cotton slacks with a matching sleeveless, rather boxy-looking boat-necked top that just covered her waist. Large turquoise earrings fell to just above her shoulders. The overall look was runway chic and just as expensive. Black strappy sandals peeked out from beneath her slacks as she walked toward them.

Winifred held out her hand in greeting. "Hello, I'm Winifred Forrester. Welcome." She then introduced Shannon and Sally.

Bianca glanced around, taking in the house and grounds. "The last time I was here, Lacy Lorin was still in the picture."

"Much time and many hurricanes have changed both the house and the property. Would you like to go in now?"

"Yes, of course," Bianca said in a strong, confident voice.

Shannon and Sally opened the sliders that spanned the rear patio, giving a more pleasant entry than through the garage.

Bianca hesitated at the patio and looked out over the yard. "I see that horrid pink heart-shaped pool is still there—very tacky.

Nearly everything was shades of pink, even the poor house. I see it has weathered well with time to a soft salmon."

After a quick walk-through, the tour ended at the safe room. Bianca walked in first and laughed. "I think it looks better now after your burglars trashed the place!" The others followed her and fanned out. "This was supposed to be Lorenzo's room. His safe space away from the Hollywood crowd that always seemed to be here. He would stand at that periscope and watch the boat traffic out in the Intercoastal Waterway, the colors of the setting sun through the clouds and the constellations at night." Bianca moved to the center of the room. "Lacy had that stage built and turned Lorenzo's room into a movie theater." Biance waved her arms toward the sidewalls. "She had pink velvet drapes covering the walls and above the stage. Even the chairs were covered in pink. It was enough to make you gag."

"I take it, you didn't approve of Lorenzo's fiancée?" Shannon asked.

"I loved my uncle. He taught me a great deal growing up. And I was determined to make him proud when he put me in charge of the new Vegas operation.

"Winning this land in that poker game back in 1960 was no win, in my mind. He began to change, lost interest in the empire he had built in Detroit—he was the don no longer. He spent his time here." Bianca's voice turned bitter. She glanced at the floor. "And now you believe a member of my family is looking for treasure. I don't believe it." She waved her hand as to dismiss the thought. "Maybe Tony would. He and my younger sister, Katerina, were thick as thieves. Tony tried to convince Lorenzo to return to Detroit and let him and Kat build the subdivisions. Instead, he built this monument to a Hollywood wannabe star, who ended up leaving him. Lorenzo was heartbroken. He boarded up Windswept and never returned—not until he knew he was dying."

"We believe, after reading your uncle's journal, that he did find a chest of silver Spanish coins. We found one that he had hidden in a box, which he had given his attorney for safekeeping."

"If our calculations are correct, we know where it is. Tomorrow, a friend of ours is going to help us retrieve the chest," Shannon explained.

"Is it possible for me to see this coin?"

"Of course; it's at the guest cottage, along with everything of your uncle that we've found."

"Excellent. But, first, I'd like to see the dock where he kept his boat."

"I have quite a few photos of the boat that you might like to see. Right now, Sally has her boat docked there. She's been staying here to help watch over the place."

Ten minutes later, they arrived at the canal. On the way, Winifred noticed that *Gemini* was anchored off the grassy bank as he had been the day before.

"Sally, this is your *yacht—Lady Luck?*"

"Yes, it is," Sally answered with pride.

"I love the name. Could you give me a quick tour?"

Winifred and Shannon stayed in the salon, while Sally showed her around.

"This is so luxurious. With that name, I would use it for floating, high stakes poker games. Out to Cuba and back." Bianca laughed. "Think about it. You could make a fortune!"

⋘⧾⧾⋙

Everyone except Sally piled into the limo for the drive to the cottage. Sally drove her truck and parked next to the Camry.

While Winifred showed Bianca the Spanish coin and the many piles of photos, Shannon and Sally prepared a delicious lunch of grilled mahi-mahi with a mango salsa and white rice, followed by key lime pie. They dined at the picnic table, with the calm waters of the Gulf in the background. With Sam curled up at Winifred's feet. The limo driver, whom Bianca had hired for the day, said he wished all his riders treated him so well.

After lunch was finished and the limo driver went back to sit in his vehicle, Bianca talked about what it was like growing up Barilli. At one point, Winifred was distracted by the sound of a boat motor approaching, then stopped. Sam growled. She looked out to see if *Gemini* had moved—it hadn't. She decided that Hunter must not have seen the boat as a threat. There were, after all, other residents close by, and being Christmas, they probably had family over, and boating was always on the agenda. Winifred bent down and petted Sam. "It's okay. Stay."

For the next hour, Winifred, Shannon, and Sally filled Bianca in on everything that had happened to her since hearing of her inheritance. And what she and Shannon had learned about her great-grandmother Chivonne and the young man who had just arrived in America from Sicily.

"I'm so sorry to have dragged you into my troubles like this, but really all roads kept leading back to your family. And as Harry Lincoln kept telling me, you are the last Barilli."

"All this over a possible sixteenth-century treasure that doesn't even belong to the Barilli family—how like Tony."

"You still think Tony is somehow behind this—from the grave?" Winifrid sounded incredulous.

"I realize he can't be. But after Lorenzo passed, Tony considered Windswept to belong to him. Of course, there were limitations on what he could do until the trust legally passed to him on December thirty-first of this year. His passing in 2000 changed that. Maybe he had an arrangement with the attorney—Gonzales certainly was involved."

"Maybe with Petrowski out of the way, this will all end," Winifred said with a sigh.

Just then, there was a huge explosion that shook the cottage and vibrated the ground beneath their feet. "Everyone down!" Sally shouted. She pulled her gun from her waistband as debris began falling. Alarms began going off throughout the neighborhood.

"What happened?" Winifred shouted. She looked for Hunter; he was coming in fast.

"An explosion!" Sally shouted through a cloud of dust. "Freddie, call 911!"

Winifred scanned the horizon for Hunter. He was still a ways out. She called 911.

Although under the protection of the cottage, it seemed like an eternity before the dust settled, and Sally walked out into the yard. "I think it was the house!" Sally shouted. "Stay here. I'm going to check it out." Sally then began running.

"No way! I'm going too!" Winifred shouted, then followed Sally.

Shannon and Bianca followed, along with the limo driver.

Winifred's lungs were burning as she approached the fork in the driveway. A person in a hoodie was running toward the house from the direction of Hector's boat and tiki hut.

Winifred, Shannon, Bianca, and the driver stopped suddenly when the house came into view. The outer walls and roof of the garage were gone. "No! No! No!" Winifred shouted and began running.

Sally reached the hooded person standing on what had been the steel inner wall of the safe room, now lying on the garage floor. Chunks of concrete, cinder block, and the roof littered the ground. A gaping hole was all that was left of the once-impenetrable space. "I've got a gun! Turn around!" Sally shouted.

"It's not here. The treasure isn't here. It wasn't true?" The familiar female voice sounded more heartbroken than angry. She turned slowly and looked at Sally.

"Katie?" Sally held her position with the gun.

Getting closer, Winifred noticed that *Gemini* had entered the mouth of the canal. She and Shannon reached Sally first. She was holding a gun on the hooded person whom Winifred had seen running toward the house. Sam was sitting at his side—tail wagging. The guy turned his head and looked over his shoulder.

"Katie?" they said in unison.

The sound of sirens were approaching fast.

Bianca and the driver, breathing heavily, stopped next to Shannon.

Katie pushed back the hood and slowly turned around to face the group. Her eyes nearly popped out of her head when she looked at Bianca.

"Katrina?" Bianca took a few steps closer. "It *is* you . . . I don't understand. I identified your *body*."

A Monroe County Sheriff's vehicle came to a screeching halt. Mike Connor got out and ran over to the group. He looked at Sally like she had lost her mind. "Why are you holding a gun on Katie?" He glanced at the hole that was all that was left of the safe room. "What the hell happened here?"

"Mike, first, I'd like you to meet Bianca Barilli Morano— Katie's aunt." Winifred watched his astonished look.

Hunter ran up to the group. "Katie, what's wrong? Why are you dressed in a hoodie now?" He glanced at Sally. "Why are you holding a gun on Katie? I thought you all were having some kind of Christmas get-together."

Mike ran his hand through his hair. "Sally, you can put the gun down; she isn't going anywhere." He turned to Hunter. "What's your role in this?"

"About an hour ago, I recognized Katie's boat as she approached from Bogie Channel. She was wearing that goofy pink hat she always wears when on the boat. All of you had left in the limo, except for Sally who drove her truck, and went over to the cottage. I figured she was joining you. I watched as she docked behind *Lady Luck* and carried a duffel bag into the house. I thought she was setting out Christmas presents or something. I got suspicious when she came out of the house wearing that dark hoodie and ran toward where Hector keeps his boat. My gut was telling me that something was very wrong. I was raising the anchor when I heard the explosion. I still didn't associate Katie with setting it."

They all turned to see another patrol car and fire truck pull up.

Katie turned back and faced the crater. "I can't believe it isn't there. Tony was so sure. Even Gonzales said it was there—under the floor."

"Katrina—why?" Bianca pleaded. "My God, how could you do this? Petrowski? All this killing?"

"I learned from the best—Auntie. I never went soft like you." Katie spit on Bianca. "I'm the only *true* Barilli! The treasure is *mine!*"

Mike motioned to a deputy to come over. "Katie. What name is on your driver's license?"

"Katherine Richards."

"Katherine Richards, you are under arrest for arson, attempted grand theft, conspiring to commit murder, aiding and abetting a known criminal . . . that's just for starters." The deputy pulled out his handcuffs. "No need for those; just get her out of here," Mike said.

Everyone followed Mike out of what had been the garage and over to a safe distance away from the fire truck. "Okay, we need to clear out and let the fire department have the scene."

"Mike, I need to check on my boat!"

"Sally, I took a quick glance when I docked," Hunter said in a reassuring voice. "It looks like *Lady Luck*'s luck held. Except she looks more like the Grey Lady. Mike, if you don't need me for anything, I'll go with Sally and help check out her boat. Then I'll head out."

"Excuse me, Lieutenant Connor, I'd like to go to the station. Katrina is going to need a new lawyer—she may have killed her last one. And I need answers." Bianca turned to Winifred. "I booked a suite at the Hilton in Key West for the night. I'll extend my stay as long as needed. I'd like to get together again, if it's okay with you."

"Yes, I'd like that. You have my number."

Winifred patted Sam's neck. "Come on, boy. Time to go home."

CHAPTER SEVENTY-ONE

The power lines to the house had been taken out in the blast, and it was already dark when the fire department left the scene. Winifred, Shannon, and Sally's first look at what was left of her house needed to wait until morning.

Sometime after dinner, the three realized they had completely forgotten about Christmas when Sam began sniffing around the packages under the tree.

"Yeah. Most of those are probably yours," Winifred said to Sam.

For the rest of the evening, they drank wine, opened gifts, and played with Sam and his new toys—just like Christmas at the cabin with the kids. Well, almost.

⊫⊨

At nine the next morning, Winifred, Shannon, and Sally met Mike Connor at the house. Due to safety concerns expressed by the fire marshal, they were told not to go in until Mike arrived.

After looking at the major cracks in the outside walls, the three decided that it probably would be a good idea to wait. Instead, they walked around the yard.

"Hector's crew can clean a lot of this debris up." Winifred looked at the rear side of the house. The windows were blown out, and the wall leaned toward the patio. "I wonder how the canal side looks?" She then began walking to the side and scanned the walls. "Huh. This side fared better. Except for the missing windows, the wall looks good." She turned to look over at the canal, which was approximately two hundred feet from where she was standing. "Not much debris, just a lot of gray dust. How did *Lady Luck* make out?"

"No damage that Hunter and I could find."

Winifred's heart did a flip-flop at the sound of his name. "Wonderful news," she said as she glanced out at the horizon— *Gemini* wasn't there.

Sam was the first to hear a vehicle on the property. He took off running around the front of the house toward the driveway.

They caught up to Mike at what was left of the garage.

"I talked to the fire marshal this morning. They found evidence of C-4. Enough explosive to take down an apartment building. Petrowski must have had a stash ready to use on the floor; then Katie decided to finish the job herself, except she wasn't familiar with the stuff and used all of it."

"I wonder why it didn't take out the whole house," Winifred asked.

"She and Petrowski wouldn't have known that the walls were lined with thick steel plates. The force would have been contained, and the extreme pressure blew out the weakest welds—those on the garage and outside walls," Sally explained. "This side of the house took the biggest hit."

"I can't believe Katie was the mastermind all this time—right under our noses—a trusted friend."

"I began to wonder about her after our last meeting in Mike's office. I remembered talking to her about our plans when I was having breakfast that morning. Then I thought about all the times she quizzed me about Freddie and what you were doing and how long did you plan to stay." Sally paused a beat. "So, the morning of Christmas Eve, I got to the Egg at my usual five thirty. I mentioned, loudly enough for those regulars around me to hear, that we were all leaving the next day, yesterday, around noon and going into Key West for the day. That Hector had been released from the hospital and was staying for a few days with his sister. We were celebrating the holiday together. My plan was to watch, from the boat. If Katie, or any of the regulars arrived, I'd nab her and call Mike—mystery of the mastermind solved."

"But then Bianca called," Winifred added.

"Yep. Case closed. You can now get on with your life, Freddie. I hope it's here," Mike said while giving her a pat on the back.

"Yes, I will be staying. I guess I'll give that architect friend of Anneliese a call. Instead of the Barilli 1960s, I'll look at sixteenth-century Spanish architecture in honor of Captain Santiago Albornoz and his love of this island."

"I'm sorry Diego's treasure isn't here. But at least you have one coin," Sally added.

"I was so sure of the calculations," Shannon stated. "And look, there *is* a void where the periscope sat. Lorenzo just changed his mind at the last minute."

So, where did he put the chest?

⇥⊢⊣⇤

Two days later after grocery shopping, Shannon set a bag of tortilla chips on top of the fridge and noticed the old movie reel can. She had placed it up there to get it out of the way when they had brought all the stuff from the safe room. "Hey, Freddie, I found

475

that old, sealed movie can. The Errol Flynn movie, *Doctor Blood*. What about having a movie night? I'd love to see those old home movies."

"Great idea. We can stop by and check on Hector and pick up the screen. I'm sure he would love to spend time with Sam. We'll take the can; maybe Hector can figure out a way to open it."

Hector was able to show Winifred how to break up the cement seal with a hammer and screwdriver. Inside, they found one 8mm home movie wrapped in a pillowcase. That evening, while Winifred set up the projector and screen, Shannon put together a tray of salsa and chips, along with a bowl of popcorn. They began with the mystery movie that wasn't marked with a date or content like all the others.

The old cellulose film was brittle and difficult for Winifred to wind onto the sprockets. It finely grabbed, and the scene appeared on the screen. The first minute showed the dynamite blasting the limestone into a pile of rubble. Then the steam shovel operator waved at Lorenzo as he began removing the fragments of stone. After watching a couple of minutes of shoveling, the operator climbed down from the machine and waved goodbye. The movie stopped. Then picked up again at a later time in the day closer to dusk. Lorenzo is filming the construction site and the back wall of the newly dug canal when the undisturbed wall begins to crack. He zooms in as a section breaks apart and begins to crumble. A rounded-top box tumbles out onto the floor of the canal. Lorenzo stops the camera. When the picture starts again, it shows the chest sitting on the ground next to the steam shovel. It looks like what you expect a pirate chest to look like, with a round top and metal strapping. Lorenzo pries open the lid. The last frame is a close-up of the chest full of coins.

"This is the proof!" Winifred shouted excitedly. "Shannon, we found it! Lorenzo found Diego's chest of money just like Leticia had written. He left it behind at the bottom of a freshwater pool for his return trip—the trip he never got to make."

"Freddie, I don't want to be a downer on your high, but all we have is a movie. The hole that Lorenzo put the toolbox in was empty."

Winifred ran the film through to the end and removed the spool. "You were right about the treasure being under the periscope, except it wasn't there." She stood and unplugged the cord. "If you don't mind, I think I'm done with all this stuff. There is no treasure. We have one four-hundred-year-old coin in perfect condition. That's enough for me."

A week later, Winifred and Shannon had an appointment with the architect, and the following day, the demo would begin to clear the land. That afternoon, Sally stopped by to see what ideas the architect had in mind.

At two o'clock, they all met in the living room of what was left of the main house.

Winifred began the review of their meeting. "The architect was sorry that the house can't be salvaged. He thought it was the perfect example of Florida midcentury modern and would have had great potential with an upgrade. He was amazed at the well-built fireplace, which hadn't sustained even a crack from the blast." She laughed. "He isn't so sure about going back four hundred years to the 1500s for the new house. He doesn't think a monastery-like design would fit the landscape. He does like the thought about something along the lines of the old Spanish villas in the Caribbean. He's excited about the challenge."

Sally stood back and studied the fireplace. "I see what he means. Why did Lorenzo build a chimney that could withstand earthquakes in a climate where a fire would seldom be needed?"

"We know from his journal how much he loved this house. And Bianca told us how his body had been found by the groundskeeper. He apparently had died alone in this room while sitting on the hearth."

"That's it!" Winifred said as she glanced around the space. "We need to clear some of this debris." She realized that any supplies from the garage would have been blown across the yard. "Shannon, run back to the house and get his journal and earmark all those references about his heart. His penmanship was horrible. I think he was writing 'hearth' instead of 'heart.' Also, there is a push broom and dustpan in the shed under the cottage. Sally, take me to Hector's place. We need to find tools to break up this mortar."

Half an hour later, the three were back in the house.

After sweeping the floor clear around all four sides of the fireplace, Shannon read the passages. "I agree about the words. 'Hearth' works in the sentences even better than the word 'heart.'"

"Where do we start?" Winifred asked. "I've never demolished anything larger than sandcastles." She looked at the pile of tools Hector had sent them with. "There were three sizes of sledgehammers, from a small one not much bigger than a hammer to one that would take two hands to lift and swing; three types of pry bars; several types of chisels and a shovel. I know what each of those is but not how to use them to break apart the mortar as Hector suggested. Maybe we should see if Mike can come over and help."

Sally picked up a long-handled sledgehammer. "We're three intelligent women. We don't need a man."

"Okay. So, we use our brains first before we begin to wail on a wall of stone," Shannon suggested. "We don't know how big the toolbox is that Lorenzo transferred the coins to after the chest broke apart. But, regardless, that amount would be heavy—very heavy."

"After watching the home movie of the time when the chest rolled out of the hole, we know that he brought it to the surface with the steam shovel. Then the chest broke open. He found the old wooden toolbox in the contractor's trailer and filled it with the coins." Winifred paused a beat. "I remember when I was a kid, Harrigan's sold tool chests like the one in the movie. They were well made to hold up under a lot of weight and had handles on the side."

"Based on that, he would need a solid base, and he mentioned the hearth specifically," Sally added. "And we know he died while sitting on this one, in the living room. I say it's behind. The hearth is protecting the treasure. But which side of the firebox? Right or left?"

"He was right-handed. If he thought he was dying and wanted to reach the place where he had hidden the treasure"—Shannon placed her hand over her heart and stumbled toward the fireplace. She ended up on the right side. "I say we start here." She pointed to a line of mortar just above the hearth.

Sally lifted the sledgehammer and took a swing at the stone. A good-size chip fell on the floor. She swung again—a larger chunk of stone came loose. "At this rate, it will take us a week."

"Okay, Hector was specific about breaking out the mortar. That makes sense." Winifred picked up a chisel and the smallest sledgehammer. She went over and placed the steel blade against the line of mortar and hit it with the sledgehammer. They watched as more of the cement broke apart. "That's it. We can do this!"

Sally picked up a heavy metal chisel and placed it in one of the cracks and hit it with the larger sledgehammer. Shannon then took a crowbar and began pulling out the lose stones. The three women, acting as a team, each with her own job, began breaking up the wall. Half an hour later, they had a large enough hole in the stone and cement block behind to see inside.

Winifred pulled her cell phone from her pocket and turned on the flashlight. While kneeling on the hearth, she looked inside the hole. "It's here! I can see the top of the box!"

After immediately going into fits of laughing, cheering, high-fiving, and hugging, the three women stepped back and faced the opening in the stone facade of the fireplace.

"So, how do we get it out?" Winifred stretched. She was hot and sweaty with a sore back. "That was a lot of hard work to make one hole. How do we get a heavy box out?"

"The hearth is twenty-four inches high and about sixteen inches deep. If we try to lift it out over the hearth, then we will need to take enough stone and cement block out above for two of us to reach in and pull it out." Sally paused to calculate the space. "We're talking about four feet square."

"No way!" Shannon exclaimed. "We'll be here all night. My body won't last that long. Between the hot afternoon sun and no breeze, this place is heating up like an oven."

Sally pulled her shirt up to wipe the sweat off her face. "Or we take out enough of the hearth to pull the box straight out. We don't know how that is constructed. It could be solid cement block."

"I say we try that first," Winifred suggested. "At least, it will be easier on our bodies."

Two hours later, and after a lot of brute force with sledgehammers and pry bars, they pulled the heavy box out onto the living room floor.

Shannon began laughing. "You gotta love the guy. After leaving all those false clues and knowing he would be betrayed by someone, he hid it in plain sight!"

CHAPTER SEVENTY-TWO

The following afternoon, Mike, Winifred, Shannon, and Sally sat on deck chairs in the cockpit of *Lady Luck*. She was now washed and her brightwork polished. Sally had provided everyone with their preferred beverages as they looked out over Windswept's now-barren landscape. Even the chimney was gone.

"Are you sorry it's gone?" Mike asked Winifred.

"Not really. The house was Lorenzo's world. I'm looking forward to building my own. And I have his legacy to protect."

"That was quite the sight to see. And we all got to play in a pirate's treasure. Well, maybe not a real pirate—but treasure nonetheless." Mike glanced over at Sally. "I assume the loot is well protected."

"Absolutely. At the moment, it is keeping company with a stash of cash."

Mike laughed. "I wouldn't expect anything less."

"I suggest that we check every freshwater pool and pond on the thousand acres with metal detectors," Sally suggested. "We know from Leticia's book that treasure was stored in the ponds.

It is possible that coins or items could have fallen out and been left behind. I can bring the equipment tomorrow, and we can get started. Hector can help us set up a grid of where they are located. It could take us a week or more to complete."

Winifred scooted forward in her chair. "That is an excellent idea! I've already let my assistant know that I won't be back for another few weeks or so."

"I can rearrange my schedule in Chicago so I can stay and help," Shannon added.

"When I'm not on duty, I can help as well. I'm sure Anneliese would be available."

Winifred sat back and crossed her legs. She then turned to Mike. "What else do you know about Katie—or Katrina?"

"Growing up as Anthony's adopted daughter, Katrina Barilli knew about her mother's business operations with Tony. Once the DEA began watching and raiding the structures on the property, Tony and Katrina began using the many ponds located across the thousand acres to hide the drugs that were wrapped in watertight packaging. Tony had always referred to Katrina as his daughter, and with the Barilli name, she thought that Windswept would be passed down to her. So, once she was old enough, Katrina took over much of the Florida operation. Katrina came down here after Irma to see what damage had been done to the property. Seeing the devastation all around the island, she figured it might be the perfect time to take advantage of the chaos in the storm's aftermath and resurrect Tony's smuggling operation. Using Windswept as a layover until drugs could be sent up north to Detroit. But she needed to be local, so she faked her death using someone she had befriended who looked enough like her to be her twin. She even convinced her look-alike to get the same tattoo. Then killed her in a manner that would appear to be drowning and battered by the rapids on the Colorado River. Katrina created a new identity, and Katherine Richards was born. She set up business in a building heavily damaged by Irma. A restaurant catering to local fisherman was perfect for keeping a finger on the pulse of the island and putting out false information when needed."

"Where did she get the funds to finance her new life?" Shannon asked.

"I believe that two-million-dollar withdrawal from the trust back in 1998 was a nest egg for Katrina," Winifred suggested.

Shannon whistled. "You can't get more cold-blooded than that."

"Katrina always considered Tony as her father, and he treated her as the child he never had." Mike paused a beat. "Her operation changed two years ago when Gonzales clued her in about the trust and how the private investigator he hired had found your great-grandmother. The fact that her name and the name of his yacht were the same clinched it for Katie. She then went from smuggling to killing off Chivonne's descendants."

"So, during all those years, why didn't she go after the treasure?" Shannon asked.

"I don't believe Gonzales put much importance on the box he was holding in his safe until Petrowski was unsuccessful at eliminating you in Chicago and then in Traverse City. At that point, Gonzales decided to open the chest and check for any other secrets Lorenzo might have had before he must turn it over to you. He then informs Katrina, Katie, about what he has read in Lorenzo's journal—then the race to find the treasure begins."

"We were correct in our assumption that the mastermind was known to us, and Gonzales was the paymaster." Shannon raised her glass in a salute. "To having all our loose ends tied up nicely."

"Not quite." Mike nodded toward the open water.

Winifred's radar had picked up on *Gemini* minutes before when he was still out in Big Spanish Channel and made the turn between Porpoise Key and the grassy bank. Her heart began beating double-time. She wanted to hear his voice, to smell the salty air on his skin.

"Hunter and I had a meeting earlier. I asked him to stop by."

They all watched as he entered the canal. Sally got up and jumped onto the dock. She then walked over and watched as he pulled the throttles down and reversed the engines. *Gemini* glided toward the dock as Hunter tossed her the bowline. Sally looked into his eyes with a question. His long beard and mustache had been trimmed short. His black hair professionally styled. "I'll explain." A minute later, they were boarding *Lady Luck*.

Winifred's heart sank at the sight of this new person. If Mike had asked him to come, then something bad was going to happen, and it included a man she didn't recognize.

"Hello." Hunter gestured toward the cleared yard. "Winifred, you don't waste much time on getting things done. Mike tells me you plan to stay and rebuild. I'm very happy to hear that."

Sally brought Hunter a chair. A deep frown creased her brow, as if she were fighting with a mental problem or memory.

"I know you're shocked at the change in my appearance. The DEA began watching this property when Anthony Barilli started using it for smuggling drugs and other contraband after his father died. It was part of his pipeline to Detroit. I guess you could say that the operation was a sideline for him. It wasn't consistent enough for the agents to nab them. After he died in 2000, it dried up. Then after Hurricane Irma, we began seeing more activity in the area yet couldn't find the source. The connection and all leads went cold. Then two years ago, word on the street was unusual activity on Windswept land, on both sides of the island. The DEA couldn't find anything but knew that someone was using this property for something illegal. I know Florida and the Keys, so I was sent here two years ago to try and make a connection. After six months, I came up with nothing and was pulled off the job. But I just couldn't let it go. After a few months, I put in for a leave of absence and came back down. I've been living the life of a local fisherman ever since while keeping an eye on the property. Then you arrived, and suddenly the place was alive with activity."

"Was the story you told us when we first met at No Name true? Are you really house-sitting?" Winifred asked.

"Yes, I am . . . or was. My gut is telling me that the Windswept mystery is solved and now has a new life—with you. I'll be putting in for a new assignment."

"So, you're with the DEA?" Sally asked. "You remind me of someone, but I can't quite place it. Have you ever worked in Miami?"

"Yes, back in my younger days. I'm too old for that scene now." Hunter stood. "I should be leaving. I just wanted to stop by and say goodbye."

Mike stood and shook his hand. "Thank you again for your help. I'm glad you were out there watching. But I must say I had my doubts at times."

Shannon stood. "Thank you; I wish I had known earlier that you were on our side."

Hunter smiled. "Key West needs a doctor of your caliber and reputation. I hope you take the Chens' offer and stay."

Winifred stood. "I'd rather give you a hug," she said as she wrapped her arms around him. "Thank you for everything. Thank you for watching over us. If you ever find yourself in the Keys, I hope you stop by and see our progress. I have big plans for this place. And a new family."

"Winifred, I'm sure that *Gemini* and I will be returning—the fishing's great!"

"Please call me Freddie."

"And please call me Troy. Troy Cameron."

Sally shook his hand with a smile that lit up her face. "I was one of your groupies back in the day. I've had this weird feeling about you. I just couldn't put my finger on it."

"And you wouldn't believe how happy I was the first day I saw *Lady Luck* docked here. You've taken beautiful care of her."

He stepped onto the dock with everyone following. They helped him shove off and waved as he entered Big Spanish Channel.

Winifred wiped a tear from her cheek.

Shannon put her arm around Freddie. "He'll be back."

EPILOGUE

One year later

Winifred moved the Chicago office of Forrester & Forrester to Traverse City with a satellite office on Big Pine. Her employees can now work from either office. She spends the months of June, July, August, and September at the cabin with her family, who are there for the summer when the kids are out of school.

The Spanish-style villa on stilts was constructed on higher ground, closer to the guest cottage, with the tennis court placed where Lorenzo's house had been. Topsoil was brought in to fill the heart-shaped pool and the crater left after the explosion of the safe room, providing the perfect planting beds for several palm and tropical trees and shrubs. The new house was designed for large-scale entertaining and plenty of guest rooms for her Michigan family when they come for visits. It was completed in time for her aunts, uncles, and all their children to arrive for the month of December. Winifred even had enough sand brought in to create a beach for the kids—knowing that the next hurricane would take it all out to sea. She has deeded over the adjacent twenty-five waterfront acres to the descendants of Santiago Albornoz.

The Heywood-Wakefield furniture will be sent to a professional for cleaning and reupholstering, while the guest cottage is undergoing a major facelift.

Hector continues as the estate manager, with a generous increase in pay, full benefits, and a new truck. He orchestrated the entire landscape project over the year to include the large winding pool with bridge and waterfall, tennis court, tiki hut, and plenty of outdoor lighting. Anneliese and her company have been hired to handle the day-to-day operation of the house and property along with Hector. Larry, with the help of Forrester & Forrester's tech team, has tweaked Danny's security system that he'd installed at the cabin, in Traverse City, for Windswept. Winifred and Hector can now monitor the property during and after tropical storms and hurricanes. He and Sam continue to live in the house in the hammock. Hector and Winifred made a visit to the Florida Keys SPCA in Key West and adopted two German shepherds to keep Sam company when he visits. Luna accompanies the Chens during visits to Windswept—she and Sam have become best friends.

Winifred has donated five hundred acres containing the largest number of freshwater pools and ponds to the National Key Deer Refuge.

Shannon bought the little yellow convertible and lives in the house provided by the Chens in Key West. She holds weekly therapy sessions in the tranquil courtyard next to the pool and fountain. She and Stanton Knox have become "an item" as they say. Together, they are creating ways to provide new services for the local veterans and help the homeless with temporary housing, especially during tropical storms and hurricanes.

Sally has become another "aunt" in Winifred's family and enjoys teaching the young Harrigans and O'Reillys all about boating, fishing, snorkeling, and all the adventures that living in the Keys has to offer. She is expanding her luxury charter business throughout the Caribbean. *Lady Luck* has moved to a new dock next to *Gemini*.

Troy Camreon moved back to the house on No Name Key and has been permanently assigned to the DEA's Key West office. He is giving Freddie all the time she needs to heal wounds and feel comfortable in her new life before making their relationship permanent.

The treasure is on temporary loan and display at the Key West Shipwreck Museum until it can be determined what laws, if any, it may fall under. Since it was found on private property, it doesn't fall under the Marine Protection, Research and Sanctuaries Act of 1972 or the Florida Historical Resources Act, which covers all navigable waterways. International laws could come into play, since the coins are known to have come from a Spanish ship, but not which ship. Regardless, Winifred plans that the treasure and its story be housed in a museum for all to enjoy. After using the metal detectors in the freshwater pools and ponds, nothing older than twentieth-century trash was found at the bottom.

AUTHOR BIO

Pamela Ann Cleverly grew up in Cleveland, Ohio with stories suddenly popping up in her head when needed to settle her three younger brothers' rowdy behavior, or her own boredom.

Years later with the adult responsibilities of being a wife, mother and moving to Toronto, Ontario the stories stopped.

Fast-forward twenty-three years and back in Cleveland, Pamela suddenly found another story in her head. So she began writing and hasn't stopped.

She writes her stories from the rolling hills of northeastern Ohio with her two tiny Yorkshire Terriers, Hemingway and Peluche, nestled on her lap.

www.ingramcontent.com/pod-product-compliance
Lightning Source LLC
Chambersburg PA
CBHW072332020726
47506CB00004B/860